I0730258

A TAPESTRY OF DEAD

D.S. QUINTON

ISBN: 978-1-7366590-3-8

Copy Editor: James Osborne

Cover design: Jeff Brown Graphics

Interior formatting: Mark Thomas / Coverness.com

PROLOGUE

The summer of 1963 was one of great change. The world felt the Vietnam War rage. The United States saw great unrest as the civil rights movement gained momentum. And somewhere in the city of New Orleans, a girl struck out on her own to save the people she loved. From herself.

Del's unwanted supernatural ability awoke that summer, just as someone read from a grimoire that called forth the Gris-gris man. The tricky ol' bastard of a spirit who bound the souls of those who crossed his path. Defeating him took a heroic effort and left Del gravely wounded.

Then when six-year-old Clara went missing, Del used her abilities again to find the girl. Only then, she began to attract the attention of things she'd never dreamed of. Even in her worst nightmares. Little did she know, every time she tranced—looking into someone's past— she was creating a *crease*. And the crease led the spirits directly to her and her family.

Barely surviving the spirit attack which left her mentor strangely incapacitated, Del left the comfort and protection of her benefactor, to live on her own. But this decision was not without peril. Although she was beginning to understand the nature of monsters in the spirit world, it was the human monsters she had yet to encounter.

And here the true evil unfolds.

CHAPTER 1

Del walked alone and felt the eyes upon her. She always felt the eyes.

In the light of day, the eyes of people she didn't know glanced at her, inspected her, leered. Sometimes they saw her beautiful face, sometimes her scars. At times they were repulsed, other times they lusted. But they always looked.

At night the eyes were different. Night eyes always came from shadows and dark places, regardless of the light. These eyes were dangerous.

Night eyes were hungry.

Having just finished her shift at The Hidden Note jazz club, she walked home via the best lighted street she could take. The lights meant safety for most people, but to her, it just made the shadows darker. And she knew what slept in the shadows.

Her ears still rang from the loud music at the bar. Despite the place being advertised as a jazz club, tonight—being a slow Tuesday—they'd had a young band of four guys whose only real talent was turning the volume knob up too far. They played "Louie, Louie" by The Kingsmen over and over at the screaming request of a few drunk groupies, and Del couldn't get the song to stop playing. Her head pounded from the thumping bass and she smelled like smoke, but she'd made almost fifteen dollars in tips. That wasn't bad, considering she had to pay for the tray of beers she'd dropped.

As the fresh air cleared her head, she thought of her eccentric family and wondered what they were doing. When she'd left, almost a month ago, she was full of nervous excitement, but hadn't realized how much she'd miss each one. Each night she fought the urge to trance-out and check on them. She wanted to see their faces—especially Jimmy's—but didn't want to draw anything else to the house, which was why she'd left in the first place. This was the only way to protect them, she reminded herself. She'd keep them safe this way until she could learn what had happened to Mama Dedé. Then her mentor could help her set the house—and spirits—back in order.

Jimmy, her oldest friend from the orphanage, was more like a younger brother to her, despite them being nearly the same age. His mental condition kept him trapped at a much younger age, so when they came to live together it was a relief to her. It was easier to protect him this way. Little did she know then that Jimmy would show a surprising ability to survive.

Del rubbed her eyes and yawned. The shadows slid past her as she walked. She hadn't realized her shifts would be so late when she took this job—her first *real* job. Happy to have found work so quickly, she accepted it without knowing exactly what was involved. She knew she'd be taking customers' orders, but didn't realize that *customer service* meant different things to different people. Some people were pleasant enough, but others had their own idea of what *service* she needed to provide.

She wasn't sure if she'd be any good at this job, but was determined to stick it out. For now, she only worked the slow nights; the girls with more experience worked the busier nights. They probably made a lot more in tips, she thought, because they knew how to move through the crowd and handle the drunks. Del didn't know that. She also thought they made more money because of the way they dressed. But Del didn't have any clothes like that either, so she'd have to make do.

Walking the dark streets hadn't bothered her when she used to sneak out of the orphanage. How much her life had changed since then—for good and bad. Those nights sneaking out of the orphanage and walking the alleys had seemed like magic to her. It was a hint of the freedom that was to come, without the worry of what could happen. Now, after a crash course in what life could really throw at you, she was more mindful of things. But the swell of pride she felt, knowing she'd found the job on her own, meant she'd work the hours she had to, even if it meant walking home late.

Turning her focus back to the street, she felt a new set of eyes following her—three pairs, in fact. They were from the three men who had just finished peeing in the alley across the street.

Here, away from Armand's house and her family, she wasn't afraid to trance. So what if she created a *crease* in a place where she wouldn't stay long? And her light trancing—*flashing*, was how she thought of it when it was done quickly—had become so second nature to her, she didn't think it did much harm. Flashing didn't produce deep insights, but it was useful to tell if someone was ready for another drink. It was sort of like reaching out and mentally touching them.

Del flashed to the three men across the street. Not only had they noticed her, but they had noted that she was alone. She felt this in their pulse somehow. They had decided to follow her.

Usually—from her limited experience—the guys would catcall her, whistle and shout, but not pursue her if she showed no interest. These men were different.

The three men following her now had said nothing when they turned in her direction. In fact, she felt they were trying to remain quiet.

She still had several blocks to go before she was home. Most nights she didn't think about it, but those few blocks were the darkest. She'd just left the lighted area where the clubs and their neon signs competed for patrons and had transitioned to an ill-lit residential area. The type that always surrounds seedy bar areas. Here, the live oaks stretched their gnarled limbs out over the street, casting long shadows and hiding alley entrances.

Del felt for the wrench she kept tucked inside her leather jacket. Why she'd picked it up that day from the street, she hadn't known. Lying there, discarded, covered in grease, the wrench had slipped past the view of its previous owner. Just a bit of the untarnished chrome had glinted at her, catching her attention. Taking it home and cleaning it, she found it felt good in her hand. It had weight, but not too much. It fit awkwardly in a large pocket inside her jacket.

She took the wrench out and held it in her right hand. She didn't brandish it like a weapon, but she didn't hide it either. It glinted a dim warning that was lost down the dark alleys.

Running footsteps!

While Del was fishing for the wrench, the men—having made silent signals to each other—split across the street and quickened their pace. By the time she heard them, they were nearly on her. She broke and ran. Quiet curses and pounding feet chased her. Even in pursuit they were careful to stay quiet.

Sprinting into the street, she opened a slight gap, but the men stayed close behind. She heard muffled commands—a pursuit strategy—but couldn't risk trancing, not even a flash, to learn their plan. If she lost her balance the pursuit would be over quickly.

They ran like young hunters.

Up ahead, her street was coming to an end. It ran into a cross street and ended there. She had to decide: left or right. Her mind ran through scenarios, scenes of potential outcomes. She moved right, then made a quick left. Her apartment was to the right. She didn't want to lead them that direction. Staggered breath echoed in the night air, both hers and the men, but she ran on. Someone gave orders behind her and one man broke off through an alley to her left. They seemed to know this part of town better than she did, and were anticipating her escape.

Dim shadows obscured the uneven cobblestones of the streets. She nearly fell twice. Old streetlamps, tall and stoic, observed the chase without emotion. They'd seen this play out before.

She was gasping for air now and felt panic tighten her throat. The long shift in a room full of smoke hadn't helped her. She was tired and slowing down. In a few minutes she'd have to stand and fight.

Following the dark street around a slow curve to the left, she saw the third man running up the street at her. He'd cut through a short alley or backyard, knowing the winding street would turn this way. She paused for a second, thinking to turn and fight the two men behind her, before the third caught up. She might be able to slip past, she thought.

She quickly dismissed the idea. She still had a bit of wind in her and thought she could outlast them if she could find her own shortcut.

With the third man bearing down on her she glimpsed a possible escape. A dark opening suddenly appeared up ahead. She raced towards him, beating him to the opening and turned right.

She instantly realized her mistake. This alley was a dead end.

She was trapped.

CHAPTER 2

The old woman felt a commotion coming and came out of the shadows to see it. She peered down the street. At her age the nights were long, and she no longer slept, but still, she didn't much care for commotion. She preferred the night because of the solitude, but now someone was about to disturb it.

Her clouded eyes scanned the twisted silhouettes, and she took inventory. She knew every tree, every odd angle from a streetlamp that had begun to lean over. She even knew where the trashcans typically sat and how they looked through each season. She'd been here a long time and was observant, so she *should* be able to recognize these things. And yes, the things were in their usual places. But something new was coming.

Of course, there were always transient things that passed her way—people, mostly, moving from one state of living to another—but she recognized them for what they were. She'd seen so many over the years, she no longer worried about cataloging them and let them slip from her memory. But she felt a permanence growing in the air now and thought to be ready.

She raised a crooked finger and swiped the air in front of her, like flicking off a light switch. By doing so, she marked a spot in the air with a shimmering smudge. The moon sat bloated in the sky, and to her eyes the swipe in the air glimmered with moonlight and glowed around the edges. Like a smudge on a windowpane, the mark in the air hung suspended, and waited. She added two more marks to the air and read the signs.

She knew the moon was typically silent on matters of the human race, but occasionally it had an opinion. She studied it for a moment, then nodded slightly. Tonight, the moon was in a place for mischief, so mischief was afoot.

Looking to the right, she peered down the empty street. The mischief would come from that direction, she thought. The air was different down there, and changing quickly. She adjusted her stance slightly as an old moonbeam tried to peak around the edge of a tree and see her. Tricky moonbeams, she thought. They were always playing silly games. Just like children they were. Children or old lovers actually, full of mischief.

She watched as a girl ran into the middle of the street. She'd made a left where the streets met. Had she made a right, the mischief would have gone away, and the woman would have gone back into the shadows. But now she was interested because the girl was bringing the mischief right past her.

As the girl approached, the woman raised her finger again and held it aloft. With a quick swipe, she marked right where the girl passed and studied this. She rubbed a whiskered chin and looked back at the moon for confirmation. Its opinion hadn't changed.

The woman saw that the girl was followed by two men, one

further behind than the other. Then she saw a third man coming from the other direction. He would get to her first. Someone was in trouble.

The old woman seemed to ripple in the night breeze, threads of wind, shadow and moonlight stitching her into the fabric of this place and time. She was elemental.

Across the street from her was an opening that looked like an alley but ran up against the back of an old structure: Claudine's Chicken Shack. Claudine had abandoned it years ago, but the neighbors said that sometimes it still smelled of grease in the hot summer. This neighborhood—just off the river—smelled like a lot of things. The cobblestone streets were bad to soak up everything and not let it wash away. Over the years, the smells of cooking grease, engine grease, mop water, urine and the sweet rotting smell of magnolia fruit had built itself up, layer upon layer, into a rich *street stew* aroma that was unmistakable. Some even said the dead could recognize their own street by its unique smell.

As the girl turned down the alley towards the back of the chicken shack, the woman shook her head and moved a little closer to the street. She couldn't help now. The first man had just arrived behind her and was blocking the exit from the alley. Another smell would be added to the streets soon.

The woman wondered…if she'd been younger, could she have helped? *Would* she have helped? Before she could answer herself, the screaming began, and she forgot the question. The moon was right again.

The trees and buildings seemed to lean together slightly, muffling the screams from the alley. Neighborhoods in the Crescent City were private places and liked to keep their secrets.

She'd heard plenty of screams before, but not like this. This wasn't just fear or pain. This was true terror. For the first time in many years, the old woman was hearing a scream of terror. And she was curious.

Something unexpected was happening in the alley across the street.

CHAPTER 3

The next morning Detective Marcel Valcour arrived at the corner of Desire Parkway and Abundance Street. The absurdity of the two names was not lost on him. He was in one of the worst parts of the city, simply called "Desire." It was a ward that, due to its unfortunate proximity to Lake Pontchartrain, the Mississippi River, and the train yards, had never been, nor ever would be, a *desirable* place to live. In fact, there was nothing to desire here, because there was no abundance.

He wondered briefly why people gave such absurd names to places like this. He understood the desire to project positive thinking—and perhaps that's what had occurred here—but he'd once heard of a place called Desperation, Nevada, and couldn't imagine why anyone would name their town such a thing. What exactly were they trying to project with that name?

He stepped out of the car, ran a hand across his clipped, black hair and instinctively straightened his tie. He wasn't naturally vain, but as a newly-minted homicide detective thought it important to look the part.

His slender frame stood tall—almost too tall for his pants—and he instinctively tugged the knees down. Having typically owned hand-me-down clothes from his older brothers, Marcel had always dealt with ill-fitting clothes. First, they were too long, and he tried to remember to roll up the ends so they wouldn't fray. For a while they'd be the right length, but soon, they'd be too short, and the tugging would begin.

Marcel walked into the alley and was struck by a strange realization. He smelled the sweet aroma of honeysuckle and the bitterness of chicory coffee—someone had their kitchen window open—but the smell was laced with the acrid tang of leaking body fluids.

The city had many layers.

"Mornin', officer. What do we have?"

Officer Babette Thibodeaux looked up and closed her notepad. "Another dead girl, unfortunately."

"Cause of death?"

"Not sure. The coroner hasn't been here yet. No blood. No puncture wounds."

"Rape?"

She lifted the cloth so he could see. "Most likely, given the condition of the body. Some bruising on her neck and wrists. Finger marks here." She pointed to the wrists. "But these are different." She indicated the bruises on the neck. Then she added, "Similar to the other two."

"Don't jump to conclusions."

"Yes, sir. Just reporting what I see."

Marcel knelt at the side of the body and held the sheet. "Damn. What a shame. Pretty girl." He looked closer at the neck, then at her wrists. After several seconds, he dropped the sheet.

"Finger style bruises on both wrists, but the neck bruises... are those bite marks?"

Babette tilted her head and shrugged. It was a possibility.

"Do men often bite like that during sex?"

She cleared her throat gently. "Why would I know?"

"I— oh… sorry," Marcel said. "I just thought… never mind."

He continued. "Kinda hard for one person to make all those in the heat of the moment."

She nodded again, then said, "You may want to have forensics test this brick." She indicated an area between the legs of the victim that ran far past her feet. "Lots of skid marks, don't you think? Like he was trying to get traction? Might have been wearing shorts. That could be skin and blood from his knees."

Marcel thought about the other two cases he was working: both young females, one black, one white, both from the same part of town, similar marks, but not exact. Similar enough to become a disturbing pattern.

"Observant. But you know the department isn't considering female detectives, right?" Marcel said.

"Like I need a reminder?" said Babette. "Doesn't mean I can't try. Gotta make the world a better place."

Marcel nodded absently. He had only been on the police force for a few years when he decided he wanted to be a detective. After seeing people he knew fall victim to violent crimes, his mind had been made up. His reasons for becoming a cop in the first place had more to do with his jailbird older brother who ultimately died from his profession, but he'd pushed those memories away long ago.

The arrival of the coroner brought him back to the dead girl in front of him. The marks, the MO, and his gut, all told him the same thing. By the end of the day the station would be talking about the serial rapists. At least two, he guessed. And it would be Marcel's job to find them.

"You're right," Marcel said. "It is similar to the other two."

CHAPTER 4

Armand Baptiste roamed the early morning hours and listened to the grand house. It was very quiet.

Although this had been his lifestyle for many years—quiet contemplation of the occult—the arrival of his extended family: Del, Mama Dedé and Jimmy, had brought him unexpected happiness. He found that despite his years of bachelorhood, he quite enjoyed the hustle and bustle of having guests, and thought they had quickly fallen into a comfortable rhythm, if rhythm was the word for it.

Who would have thought that this odd crew, each person with their own eccentricities, could fit together so completely? All pieces to the most unique puzzle. But the complexities of this puzzle were unfathomable. The possibilities were endless. So many pieces were still unknown and much of their own stories yet unwritten.

But now that Del was gone, and Mama Dedé fallen ill, the silence had returned, and the house had taken on a cold and distant feel.

He touched objects at random, hoping to find a forgotten bit of story or interesting fact. Anything he could latch his mind onto.

The book he was planning to write about legends and their origins flashed briefly in his thoughts—he really needed to finalize the outline—but the task seemed too passive. It was the sort of thing a recluse would do.

He had no idea what *active* task he desired, but his world was out of balance, and he needed to set it right. He feared if he didn't find something to occupy his mind soon, he would go quite mad.

He wished they were all sitting around the upstairs library, fire crackling, waiting for one of his grand stories. But alas, story time would remain silent for now.

"Hi, Ahman," said Jimmy.

Armand turned and saw a flat, sleepy face. The boy's hair stuck out in all directions, and he dug sleep out of one eye.

"Good morning, Master Jimmy," Armand said. "You're up rather early."

"Is Deh home?"

Armand sighed and shook his head. "No. I'm afraid Del's not home. Maybe we'll—"

"I deamed she was home."

"You did? Was it a good dream?"

"Yeah, it petty good I guess. We was pwayin."

"Indeed. And what was the game?"

Jimmy scrunched his face. "Mmmm, I fohgot."

Armand began making breakfast. He heard Mama Dedé moving about upstairs and wondered if today would be the day she would snap back to her old self. He was cautiously hopeful, but could see the stark reality on her face every day: she wasn't getting better.

"Whey'd she go?" Jimmy asked.

Armand thought about the morning he found the four letters

on the table and his heart sank a little. He understood why Del left, but was terribly worried for her. She was just coming into her own and had yet to experience all the tricks the world could play against her.

"Remind me what your letter said. She was taking a—"

"A twain!" A look of magic spread over Jimmy's face. His eyes sparkled with the dream of an incredible journey.

"That's right, a train." Armand nodded thoughtfully. "You must understand that each one of our lives are special. We each have a long and winding journey to take. And there are many wondrous things to discover along the way. Del is on her journey now, but we'll be waiting for her when she returns. But remember, we did just speak with her on Sunday."

Jimmy stared out the kitchen window as if seeing his own journey wind through the stone garden and beyond. Or perhaps he was just trying to remember the phone call. He tilted his head as if tracking something that had moved outside the windowpane.

"But enough philosophy," said Armand. "Perhaps we could continue our chess game today. I'll explain another opening gambit that—"

"I get you king again," Jimmy said, turning back from the window and cracking a wide smile. "Yust 'ike dis," and he jumped an invisible knight around the table, "cunch, cunch, cunch."

Armand twisted his moustache, remembering the game. "Yes, well... that *was* a rather unexpected ending for that style opening. Very well played on your part." His finger emphasizing the point. "But I'll be on the lookout next time."

He returned his attention to the frying bacon and flipped each piece carefully. Speaking over his shoulder he said, "Speaking of the game, I meant to ask you—" A metallic clink told him his audience was engaged otherwise.

Jimmy had lost interest in the conversation and began moving items around the table. The salt and pepper shakers looked to be positioned as pawns. Torn remnants of an old newspaper had become random other pieces. A candle stick was the queen—Armand knew this somehow. And then there was the fork. It was a special piece. Only instead of moving to the rules of chess, Jimmy had it slithering around the table. Slow and quiet, he slid the fork: around his plate, past the pieces of paper—which Armand now realized were surrounding the queen in a rough circle—and off the board in an effort to attack the queen from behind. Suddenly he stabbed the fork at the base of the candle stick and made little whimpering sounds as if the queen were dying. Then, one by one, the pieces of paper were piled onto the fork-snake, smothering it.

The smell of burning bacon pulled Armand back to his domestic duties.

Jimmy reset his macabre chessboard and started another game.

*

Mama Dedé laid in her bed but floated through layer upon layer of dreams. The smell of frying bacon tickled at something in the back of her mind, but it wasn't strong enough to pull her forward. She had a sense of where she was, in a house that she had once occupied. But which one? She couldn't pin it down.

She'd lived in many houses as a child, always moving. But the house in her dream felt like the St. Augustine Transitional Home for Girls house. Only it was larger, with many more rooms. Maybe it had always been this size and she'd simply forgotten. Perhaps it had hidden rooms she was just now discovering. Regardless of the reason, she felt utterly lost in it.

The feeling of being lost—or having lost something—pervaded her dreams and sent her hurrying from room to room. It wasn't panic yet, but her heart raced as if panic was near. Something was wrong. She'd misplaced an item. Or a person was gone. Or someone was dead. She felt all these things, then none of them. All she could do was search around the next corner and never look back. A cold wind had dominated those dreams, always behind her, but never pushing; it was a sucking wind, always trying to pull her backwards. She had to keep moving.

The rooms of the house were extraordinary, and she took each one in stride. She never realized she lived in such a fascinating place. She'd just found a giant hall that extended off the back of the building—it was extremely long—filled with wooden boxes of her dead husband's belongings. It didn't matter that she'd never been married. She had to keep these things and was glad to have found them again.

A circular staircase took her up to a room that was filled with smoke. It would soon be on fire, and she needed to find a hose to put it out.

One hallway had holes in the wallpaper. Apparently, worms had been eating the walls for years, and now their tiny heads had poked clean through the wallpaper. She could stick her finger into a hole if she wanted, but then the worms would crawl under her fingernails, and she'd never get them out. She was tempted to stick her big toe against the wall just to see how it felt, but always curled her toe away at the last second.

Now tiny people whispered to her from beneath her bed. She was tired of exploring the house and wanted to go to sleep, but the voices warned her not to. If she did, her bed would be covered with a wallpaper blanket and the worms would crawl in her ears.

Yes. That had already happened, she thought. She was hearing them now.

CHAPTER 5

Del sat in her one-room apartment, on the second floor of a leaning boarding house, and waited for the sun to fully come up. She'd been up most of the night, alternating between having bad dreams and staring at the door. She'd been waiting for someone to suddenly start pounding on it, demanding for her to come out and surrender. In her dreams—or maybe she'd been awake, and it was her imagination—she'd always hesitate a bit too long and they'd break the door down and take her away. She didn't know who the people were or why they wanted her, but the pit of her stomach told her that something bad had happened last night and that was the reason. She assumed that meant she was responsible. It was the same feeling she'd get in the orphanage when she was being sent to see Sister Eulalie.

Swallowing back the thought of the sister, Del tried again to remember what had happened last night. Thankfully she didn't have to work tonight. She didn't think she was up for it. All morning she'd try to remember the exact events, but came up blank. She'd tried trancing, but the scene was pretty much obliterated to her. Mama D had said in the past that was due to her hormones working overtime, but she was pretty sure it was something else last night.

Adrenaline.

Pure unadulterated adrenaline. The kind that shocks your body and mind into a state it's never experienced; squeezing you into a slightly different mold of yourself that you didn't know existed. Then, when it releases you, it seeps out of your pores like poison from a wound. And you stink with it.

Yes. That had destroyed the memory scene of last night's attack.

In a way she felt lucky to have escaped real harm, but at the same time, felt she had nearly discovered something about herself. Surprisingly, she hadn't been *overly* frightened by the men chasing her. She couldn't put her finger on why, but had thought that if things had gotten worse, she could have defended herself. It was probably foolish to believe, but it was there.

Deciding that the events would remain hidden for now, she stood up and faced the door. She had to go out at some point, and couldn't very well live in here as a recluse.

She risked a flash-trance to the other side of the door and down the hall. Nothing was there.

How stupid. Just go out.

She tightened her jaw against the unknown enemy that lurked in the back of her mind, opened the door, stepped out and closed it behind her.

Taking a deep breath, she lifted her chin. She had made the decision to leave the safety of Armand's house. She had chosen to begin her ten-thousand-hour journey to understand her gift. So, she needed to get on with it. She went down the hall of the boarding house, descended the sagging stairs and walked out into the light.

Outside she felt a little better. The wide-open space and fresh air helped to lift her mood. But the rock laying in her stomach, and the lack of sleep, prevented her from feeling anything close to happiness. She slowly retraced her steps from the night before.

There was really only one way she would have come home. The larger highways prevented easy walking, and there was one street that led straight into the bar section where she worked. It only made sense that she would have come this way.

Crossing the street at a T-intersection, she turned right and stopped dead in her tracks. Standing in the middle of the street, she suddenly realized she'd walked back to the street she'd run down last night. Less than twenty-four hours ago she'd sprinted down the street, now on her left, turned at this very intersection and ran into the darkness. Straight ahead of her was where the one man had split off from the group to get around the front of her. Up ahead was where the road made a sharp left and she'd been forced to make a right, into a dead-end alley. That's where her memory ended.

Del looked around suddenly, as if the men were bearing down on her again. A cold chill—her mind told her it was a wet, dead hand from a river—brushed the back of her neck and she slapped at it wildly, turning in all directions.

Nothing was there. But the goosebumps crawling over her skin told her something had been.

Continuing up the street, her dread grew as she got closer to the alley. She saw a police car, then a plain black car. Backed partially into the alley, with its front end sticking into the street, was a hurst.

Del unconsciously slowed as she approached the alley. A few kids with bikes had stopped in the street—which had surprisingly little traffic—and were getting an eye full. Keeping to the other side of the street, her intention was to walk straight past, but she couldn't keep from looking.

A body bag was laid out on a stretcher and a man was pushing it into the back of the hurst. A police officer was doing paperwork on a clipboard. Del thought if she could just get a glimpse of what the officer was writing, perhaps it would help her remember what had occurred last night. She flashed into the scene long enough to see:

Cause of death: Unknown

and

Responding officer: Thibodeaux

But before she could even find the person's name, the officer looked up, directly at her.

It was an unnerving experience. One moment she was viewing the officer's notes, the next she was looking at herself standing on the opposite sidewalk. She hadn't realized she had stopped.

Officer Babette Thibodeaux, having the feeling of being watched, looked up just in time to see Del staring across the street at her.

CHAPTER 6

Del stayed gone all day.

Despite having dozed sitting up on a park bench, she was exhausted. Her head hurt from trying to trance back into the alley scene and she'd finally decided to go home. Well, that wasn't completely true, she realized on the way. She'd decided to go back to her apartment, but she wasn't close to thinking of it as *home*.

She walked the streets of her new neighborhood with a wary eye. Working as a cocktail waitress, she'd quickly learned about men's intentions, and felt like a curtain had finally been pulled back for her. She was beginning to understand how protected she'd been at Armand's. But it had been stifling too, with Armand, Mama Dedé and sometimes Frank watching over her—debating about her like she wasn't even there. They would sit around the fireplace table talking late into the evening, while she sat on the loveseat; there she was within range to hear them talk about her, but just far enough away from being an adult that they rarely spoke *to* her. But… they all *had* saved her the first time something unnatural came for her, hadn't they?

That answer was a resounding 'yes.'

Had she repaid them sufficiently when the spirits came and swarmed the house?

That was debatable.

She'd basically called the things to the house without even knowing it, putting them all in danger. And hurting Mama Dedé the most.

She'd eventually make amends for it, but wasn't sure how. She had so many things to do already.

She told herself she'd call Armand tomorrow and ask about Mama D. She also needed to check in on Frank, to see how he was mending after his *mild* heart-attack. She needed to send Jimmy something; he was surely wondering how her adventure was going. Sending a letter to him probably wouldn't be that exciting, but she had to think of something. *When is rent due?* she wondered. Did she even have enough money to buy something for Jimmy? She didn't know that either.

This journey of hers may be more difficult than she'd thought.

*

Later that evening, walking home the way she'd run last night, she came to the same T-intersection and stopped. Looking up the street to her left, she could see the police cars were gone, most likely long ago. And so was the body.

Maybe it wasn't the guy from last night.

(Don't be stupid. You know it was.)

A wave of nausea washed over her, sending cold chills down her back. She pushed down a desire to be sick, then swallowed. A quick flash behind her proved there were no lurkers. There was nothing more than streetlamp shadows creeping the cobblestones, and she was getting used to creeping shadows.

She crossed the street and headed up the sidewalk. The tree limbs wove stick fingers in the air, causing twisted patterns of moonlight to lace the ground before her. She felt like she was walking into a hidden neighborhood—much different from today—seeing something that no one else could. And all of this without trancing.

She wondered if the memory of last night's events were hidden here, somewhere in the shadows. But, if they were, did she really want to find them?

She couldn't say one way or the other.

As she neared the end of the street, just before it took its sharp left turn, she stopped. The alley was right across the street. She tried to remem—

"Girl," someone whispered.

"Oh!" She spun, searching the shadows. "Who's there?" She stepped back into the street, ready to run.

A crooked finger came out of the darkness. It was attached to a gnarled hand which extended from a thin wrist. Before Del could speak another word, the finger swiped the air. The urge to run left Del instantly. She stood, somewhere between reality and a dream, and watched as a pair of eyes came out of the dark to study her.

The shape of an old woman slowly emerged, as if walking straight out from the fabric of night. She was shorter than Del, who at five-foot-six had to peer down at some women, but the shape had a large presence. There was strength there. The face—which was mostly hidden by a hooded cloak—was sharpened by age. What skin Del could see was the color of wind and wrinkles, falling somewhere on the spectrum of grayed leather. Loose-fitting layers of clothes rippled around her, giving the impression she was in constant motion.

Del imagined the woman's body, beneath all those layers, stooping forward in a perpetual, stumbling-forward sort of way, but she could tell her footing was sound. And the eyes were alarming.

As Del stood in her partial dream state, she imagined she'd seen those eyes before. Maybe not the exact set of eyes, or color, but *something* was familiar. So familiar in fact, it unsettled her. It was as if the eyes inspecting her were illuminated by a deep internal source, moonlight, bluish gray, from another world. And somewhere deep inside, they glittered like stars.

"Come," the woman said. Del stepped back onto the broken sidewalk.

"What path do you folla'?"

Del heard the sounds, not with her ears, but from far away, as if they'd traveled a long distance to reach her, suddenly arriving in her mind. She blinked at the question. Her mouth opened to form a response, but the words were slow to come. Her mind was stuck in a fog.

Seeing the trouble, the old woman grunted and waved her hand at Del as if shooing away a fly.

Del's mind cleared instantly. "Oh…," she muttered, blinking. "What happened?" She looked around, half expecting to see the veil that had been pulled from her mind, lying on the sidewalk. She inspected the woman again. "I'm sorry, what did you say?

Patiently, the woman said, "What path do you folla'?"

"I… I don't know what that means. Do you mean, where am I going?"

"In a sense."

"Like right now?"

"Perhaps." The woman cocked her head to stare at Del with the other eye.

Shaking her head, Del said, "I'm not… I'm just walking. Nowhere in particular."

The woman nodded. "Ahh…" Looking behind her, she whispered, "She ain't got a path." Then added, "Not yet anyways."

Looking past the woman, Del said, "Who are you ta—?"

"Arlo."

"What?

"You'ken call me, Arlo."

"Oh, OK. I'm Del, Miss Arlo. Who were you—?"

"No. No 'miss.' Jus' Arlo."

Del considered leaving Arlo to her mutterings, but was still trying to see to whom she had spoken. Just then the shadow of a cat caught her eye. It walked past the corner of the small house whose driveway they were standing in. The shadow moved from the darkened front yard, clinging tightly against the foundation corner, and slid along the wall headed toward the back. Only, Del never saw the actual cat, only its shadow.

"Doan mind him," Arlo said. "He knows his path."

Del turned her attention back to the strange woman. "He does?"

"Yah."

"Well, don't all cats?" Del thought Arlo's statement was too obvious to leave unanswered.

"Only if dey've chosen," Arlo said.

Deciphering cryptic speech was not what Del had planned for her evening. She turned to leave but hesitated. Before she knew it, a question tumbled forth.

"And what about my path?"

Arlo turned the direction Del had been walking and moved in slow deliberate steps. "Dat's a question fer sure… what path you on." The words slid away like midnight musings.

Del followed the woman instinctively.

"I'm not sure, I guess. I—"

"Well, I ken see dat. Your konseye didn't set'cha?"

"My what?"

"Your *konseye*. Your ment'r. You got da sight, don'tcha? I can feel it in you, you got so much."

Del nodded slightly, unsure how much to divulge. "I might have some sight."

"Yah, you might. And you got a ment'r?"

Del thought about Mama Dedé sitting at home in front of a cold fireplace. She didn't imagine it warm and crackling like before; she only thought of it as cold and drafty, sucking the life out of Armand's house and all who were there.

"Yes, but…"

"But they ain't he'ped you find yer path yet? Did you anger 'em?"

"No. Well… I mean, she's sick right now, but—"

"Sick? She dyin'?"

"No!" Del stopped and eyed the old woman. "At least… I don't think so," she said quietly. She scuffed the toe of her boot against a tree root that had grown up and over a cobblestone. "How did you know I had the sight?"

"It's easy enough to see," said Arlo. "I can still see a lot with dese old eyes. It's da commotion I'm wonderin' at."

"Commotion?"

"Mmm hmm. Quite da commotion last night, eh?"

Wide-eyed, Del stared at the woman.

"Mmm hmm," the woman continued, "quite da commotion."

Del followed Arlo's eyes. She was looking across the street at a dead-end alley. Her moonbeam eyes glowed even more than before. Having walked out from beneath the shadows of the trees, the moonlight bathed them both in ethereal blue light, and Arlo's eyes glittered like they were filled with faraway galaxies.

Across the street, halfway down the alley towards Claudine's abandoned chicken shack, Del saw the remnants of something flutter. At first, she thought it was a piece of police tape, but the longer she looked, the more she thought the fluttering thing was watching her.

Glancing sidelong at Arlo, Del asked, "What do you know about the… commotion?"

With a squinting eye, Arlo looked Del up and down, as if unsure about the quality of an item just before purchase. After a long moment she looked past the girl, into the night sky. Her finger stroked the air in quick little swipes, an ancient tally that could only be calculated by moonlight.

Arlo inspected the invisible runes, but came away even more perplexed, scratching her head. The answer wasn't what she expected.

"You see somethin' over dere?" Arlo nodded across the street.

"You mean the alley?"

Arlo grunted her annoyance. "Whadaya *see?*" Her finger tapped her cloaked head at her temple.

Del looked at the dark alley and thought. A memory of a dream formed in her mind, and she tried to peer into it. She was looking at the place she'd run in to hide, just last night, but the events eluded her. She rubbed her forehead above her left eye. A dull ache had started there.

"Just pierce it," Arlo said. "All you got to do is look."

Del stared on, barely hearing the woman's words. She saw a dark alley but nothing beyond it. Perhaps her mind wouldn't allow her to see, or was hiding something from her. Either way, she couldn't remember what happened there and couldn't get herself to trance back to see it. A dark scene lay hidden, and she was unsure what it said about her.

"…yer path, girl."

Del jumped. "What?"

"You got to find yer path," Arlo said. "'Dis city got enough lost souls a'ready without you *not* having a path to folla'. We cain't have sompin' like you wanderin' around as well."

"*Something* like me? What does that mean?" Del crossed her arms and stared at the old woman.

"You gotta learn, it don't matter *who* dey are, only *what* dey are. And dey'll always be dere."

"Who's 'they'?" Del asked. "What are you talking about?"

Arlo motioned Del close and clasped the inside of her arm. Facing down the street, Arlo held up her hand, but this time drew her finger slowly down like she was feeling a piece of fabric. It was deliberately slow. Then her hand made a shape as if grasping the air in front of her. Like a magic trick, the air parted, and the thin curtain of reality was pulled aside.

Slowly, within a small patch of air, the night scene dissolved and Del saw beyond the living world, and into the world of the dead. It was not like when she was trancing. In a trance, she simply replayed the events of the living. Now, she felt the warm wind of life flow away from her as the cold world of death beat its monotonous drums, marching its inhabitants ever forward.

It was terrifyingly close. In that world, barely a nightmare whisper away, the dead were many, and they looked at Del. Their decayed, eyeless faces were all turned to her. Their gaping mouths pleaded silent prayers and cursed foul omens. Hundreds of shapeless images, crowded together in the dark, walked toward a distant light; they walked toward the silver light of the Del-Orb that no one understood, but all the dead could see.

Del tried to pull away, but Arlo held her tight. Surprisingly strong, the woman held her at the edge of the abyss and let a sea of death look upon her.

Del wanted to cry. She wanted to scream, to breathe, anything that would tell her she hadn't slipped beyond the veil. She screamed for Arlo to stop, but her voice seemed far away. Tiny. She imagined it was trapped in a swirling void that had opened above a cemetery earlier in the year; a void that had tried to suck her down. There were faces in that void too.

"…stop, please…" Del whispered. "I don't… no more." She struggled to turn her face away.

With a swipe, Arlo closed the veil and left the dead to wander.

Waves of heat and cold rolled over Del. She pulled away from Arlo and stumbled out into the street. Tremors shook her body as she slapped away invisible molesters. She couldn't shake the feeling of cold dead river hands groping her body for warmth.

The inquisitive eye of Arlo inspected Del's face. "I'ken see dat's da firs' time da veil's been pulled fer ya. As I said, don't matter who dey are, only what dey are."

"And what are they?" Del asked weakly.

Something between surprise and suspicion flashed over Arlo's face, then disappeared. "Why, dey da los' dead, a'course."

Del looked up in surprise. "The lost dead?"

"You dint know?"

Del shook her head.

"You dint call 'em to you? Promise to help 'em over?"

"No."

"Ask 'em fer a favor as payment?"

"What? No!"

Arlo nodded. She believed Del was telling the truth. At least to some degree. "Some just need a guidin' hand to get over, but others… dey want more. Dey *need* more. And maybe dey're willin' to trade. For da help, you see. But dat's tricky business." Arlo rubbed her hands as if a sudden cold had set into them. "Yeah, dealin' wit' da dead is tricky. Hard to tell da good from da bad. Sometimes dey don't remember demselves. And right now, I cain't tell one from da udder. But dat don't befront me. I ain't who dey followin'."

Del's heart pounded. She swallowed hard and tried to shake the macabre scene from her mind.

Why hadn't Mama D warned me about this?

Then a twinge of guilt hit her. Maybe she *had* tried to warn her. Probably did, and Del just wasn't listening.

"How many you had to put down?" Arlo asked.

"Put down? Well…" Del thought about the two times she'd faced something *unnatural*. Both times she didn't actually *put* anything down, in fact, she'd barely survived the encounters. And, she'd had a lot of help, probably more than she knew. "Well…"

The woman had heard enough. "You cain't halfway folla' a path; you won't get anywhere. And you cain't folla' no path, 'cause you'll end up where you doan wanna be.

"No. First, you got to find yer path; den you got to take it!"

Despite the gentle breeze, Del felt sweaty and sick. Her head spun with questions. Who was this strange old woman? What did she really want? Was it a coincidence that one of the few people she'd met outside of work understood something about her that she didn't even know? And what if her path—once she actually found it—could help Mama D? Wasn't that what she was after anyway? Didn't she owe it to the woman who had cared for her, had tried to teach her? The answer was obvious, but warning bells sounded in her head. She didn't know who this woman was or if she could trust her. So, she decided to test the waters with Arlo.

"Can you help me?" Del asked. "You know, find my path?"

Arlo grumbled and stroked her chin. "I ain't a ment'r in da ways you're lookin' fer."

"Well… maybe there's something I can help you with. Maybe *we* can make a trade." Del felt a twinge of pride that she was negotiating with the woman. It was a very adult thing to do.

The old woman considered this and consulted the moon. It had tired of the conversation and had slipped out of sight, leaving her to decide on her own.

"Well, we doan want da likes of you out here with no path. Wouldn't be good for any of us."

"Us? Who are you talking about?"

"Mmm, don't worry about dem. Maybe you'll meet 'em someday. Got to set yer direction first."

Del flashed over the scene, trying to catch a glimpse of something nefarious in the woman, but saw nothing. At some point later, she would think back to this moment and wonder if she saw *anything* at all when trancing on Arlo, but the missing scenes of life didn't register with her now. She knew Arlo was *some* type of practitioner, but Del felt she was now on equal grounds with the negotiations.

Arlo decided. "You come back around tomorra' night. We'll see what needs to be done. Maybe dere is something you can help me with."

"Tomorrow night? I have to work tomorrow night and—"

"Bah! You come 'round when you're ready. I'll be here."

A small twist formed at the corner of Del's mouth. She wasn't quite sure she was ready to enter into this trade. "OK… but I kinda work odd hours. And they're pretty late."

"Don't matter," Arlo said. "I don't sleep nights anyways."

Del thanked Arlo and took her leave. She walked wide of the street, not wanting to plow straight through the group of spirits that had amassed there. She then wondered if she could see them if she tried. She flashed a quick look, but nothing was there. Part of her was relieved she saw nothing, but part of her was disappointed. Did she not have the ability to see as much as she thought? Or were there more places to look than she ever realized?

Arlo watched the girl leave. Somewhere behind her the shadow of a cat slid silently around the wall of the house, then across the front window. Yes, the cat knew its path well. She then turned her eyes back to the night sky. The moon had returned to give its final thoughts on the matter. Its red face stated its opinion of Arlo's decision.

"I know, I know…" Arlo waved it off. "It could be a danger to show her more. But we got to know. Den we can decide what to do."

CHAPTER 7

In a ramshackle shotgun house near the river, Terrance "T-bone" Hebert paced the dismal front room where he slept, stopping occasionally at the window. The heavy curtains which blocked the sun stunk of smoke and a general uncleanliness. They hadn't been washed for years. Now that the sun was setting, he pulled them back slightly, causing a cascade of dust to shake loose, and peered outside, squinting.

"Man, where is he?" Terrance said to the room.

He dropped back onto the sagging, sweaty couch, which was his bed, and cursed under his breath. He picked up the phone, which sat on an end-table, thought about dialing the number again—he'd already tried four or five times—then let it fall back into its cradle with a loud clatter.

From down the hall came a sharp warning. "You keep fuckin' with that phone, I'm beatin' your ass!" said Billy.

"Sorry, man," said Terrance. He squirmed on the couch, scratching his arms and legs. "But where the hell is he?"

Then, not wanting to anger Billy any further, his voice faded to nearly a whisper. "Ain't nobody seen him in a whole day. Maybe I should call his mama and—"

A door slammed opened from the back of the house. Heavy footsteps marched down the short hall. William Guidry, aka "Billy Bash," strode around the corner of the room and with surprising speed kicked the coffee table, sending it smashing into Terrance's shin. Beer cans scattered.

"Ow! Man…" He grabbed his throbbing leg. "Why'd you—?"

"Shut the fuck up, T!" Billy said, suddenly standing over him. He was naked except for a worn pair of boxer-shorts. Strong arms and legs were in perfect proportion. A thick neck and roughly chiseled head completed the profile of someone who could have been a boxer. But Billy had chosen a different path.

Billy's short blonde hair stuck out in all directions. His red eyes said he was nursing a hangover, which meant his temper was even shorter than usual.

Terrance was grateful to be able to flop on Billy's couch—it was the Taj Mahal compared to some places he'd slept—and didn't want to piss him off, so he said no more about his throbbing shin. When Billy had offered him the couch a few months back, he hadn't realized it came with *extra duties*, but would have taken it regardless. Billy was connected. He made things happen. And it got him off the street. Sort of.

At first, the requests were no big deal and he'd quickly agreed to being Billy's gopher. "Ass, Gas or Grass," Billy had said, "Nobody rides for free." And wasn't that the truth. Nobody rode free on Billy Bash. At least, not for long. You either got on the train, or you got rolled over by it. Left behind. Sometimes left for good.

Terrance looked up and for a reason he couldn't explain, noticed Billy's nipples were erect. But then again, everything on Bill Bash stood at attention at one time or another.

"I'm serious," Billy continued. "You keep bitchin' and you can take your ass back to the street."

"Come on man, T-bone's cool," Terrance said of himself. "I'm just lookin' out fer us, dat's all. I'm the guard dog, up in here. I'm the—"

Billy turned and strode back down the hall.

Terrance changed his tune quickly. "Hey, uh… Billy. When you gettin' up, man? I'm 'bout ready for some juice!"

From down the hall, Billy said, "Stay off the phone T, and earn your keep." Terrance heard the refrigerator door open, then Billy said, "Aren't you supposed to be making a pickup tonight anyway?"

Terrance cringed and scratched his arms. "Tonight was Harold's run, man. Dat's why I think somethin' happened to him last night. He shoulda checked in by now." He grimaced and rubbed his bruised shin, but said nothing. He wasn't sure how Billy would take this news and didn't want to give him any other reason to explode.

Billy came back into the living room, flopped down into a pink recliner, and opened a can of beer. He took a long drink, then belched. "He's your guy, T. You vouched for him. Did he skate?"

Terrance squirmed, avoiding Billy's stare. But he couldn't avoid looking at Billy's knees. Fresh scars.

"Billy, dat dude's cool, he wouldn't—"

"Then where the hell is he?"

"I'm tellin' you man, dat chick… you know, from last night… I think she was a witch." Terrance nodded knowingly. "Yeah man, my auntie, she like a hundred years old or somethin', and she can do some spooky shit. She says there's witches way more powerful than her. Can turn you into frogs or snakes, make you forget who you are. Even make you go crazy."

Billy snorted his drink of beer and it ran down his chest. "You're jonesin', T. You must need a fix. That shit ain't real."

With wide eyes, Terrance whispered, "But what about da light?"

Billy stopped in mid-swallow. "I thought it was the damn cops. A setup. So I split. You were ahead of me, what did you see?"

"Harold took da shortcut and got to da alley first. I stopped before I got dere, I couldn't see shit. My eyes were all flashin' from runnin' and—"

"Whatever!"

"Anyway, I got almost to da alley when I heard him scream just as da flash of light hit and—"

"Wait. You mean you heard *her* scream."

Terrance shook his head. "Naw, man. Harold's my cuz. I've been hearin' him scream like that since we was little, when his brothers used to beat him. They was just playin' but it was usually playin' at beatin' us up."

Billy suddenly wondered if Terrance was right. Being the larger and heavier of the crew, he always brought up the rear. Besides, Terrance and Howard worked for him; they did the chasing, he did the eating. But he hadn't even made it to the alley entrance before he saw the flash of light. And, thinking it was a setup, and that Harold got snagged, he'd veered off between the houses and went home the long way. He thought he remembered hearing a scream, but one sounded like another to him, and he couldn't be sure. But, if Harold *had* gotten snagged and was in jail, he should have heard from him by now. Unless of course, he was squealing to the cops.

Several scenarios opened in Billy's mind.

Harold shouldn't have had any dope on him. Billy never went hunting with dope. That would be stupid. He'd told T the same thing multiple times, and thought he understood the consequences if a guy he vouched for broke the rules. But then again, could you really trust a junkie?

So, either Harold got pinched, which he doubted due to no communication. Or, Harold was snitching, which he equally doubted. Or the chick had done something to him. And what if she was a witch? Wouldn't that be interesting?

"Watchoo thinkin'?" Terrance said.

A smile crept across Billy's face as he pulled a small piece of plastic wrap from the waistband of his boxers. A grayish lump lay within the plastic, wrapped tight. He dangled it in the air, like a hypnotist's watch.

"I'm thinkin' it's time for you to juice up and go figure out what happened to Harold. After that, we find that witch and show her what's what."

Terrance's eyes lit up. Not at the thought of finding the girl—he didn't participate in that sport anyway; that was Billy's hang up. In fact, most of the time Terrance was so high—which meant T-bone was in control for a few days at a time—that Terrance had little to no memory of the events that occurred. He had vague recollections of wild parties and crazy sex in alleys and bushes, but they quickly went the way of his buzz, out of sight, out of mind. No, his eyes lit up at the sight of the little baggy with his juice in it—or, soon-to-be juice. And, like a hypnotist's suggestion, he instantly became T-bone, a street junkie who was grateful to live in the Taj Mahal on a scratchy couch. And who'd do anything to stay there.

Billy sat the bag on the crotch of his boxers, which was already bulging.

T-bone's eye's dimmed slightly. The voice of Terrance, cracking, emerged with a whisper. "Come on, man…"

"Nobody rides for free, T."

Terrance scratched his arms, staring at the little baggy as Billy made it go up and down on his shorts. Up and down. Up and down. Another hypnotist's trick.

And like a light switch being flipped off, reluctance disappeared into the background of Terrance's mind. A little up and down wouldn't be that bad.

As T-bone paid Terrance's rent between Billy's legs, Billy closed his eyes and imagined what he'd do to the witch when he found her.

CHAPTER 8

The rat stuck its nose in the air and sniffed. Its whiskers twitched. It was feeding time.

The noise of the day had subsided, which caused the rat to awaken and respond to its empty stomach. Besides, it had young to feed.

It gently stepped over the three blind pups that lay helpless in its nest. At five days of age, they were blind and deaf, but felt the warmth of their mother leave. Their hairless pink bodies, like fat sausages, came to life and squirmed against the rush of cold air, but they couldn't move far. They lay still, waiting.

The nose of the rat stuck out from a hole in the ground, where the nest was built, and surveyed the area. It twitched several times, thinking it smelled something new, possibly food. With a quick jump she was out of the hole. Night was upon it.

It sat up on its haunches and washed its pink fingers. Soft, pink and hairless, the hands of the rat looked alarmingly like human baby hands. Its rat toes, longer, but just as pink and hairless, looked like deformed baby toes that had grown wild, gnarled and gangly. It bent its head and licked the oversized knuckles, cleaning away the mites that lingered between them. Then it turned its red eyes to the cemetery.

Swift and darting, its eyes scanned the landscape. It knew the area well. It scampered forward, picking up random debris and sampling it. A recent storm had blown foliage and trash into the cemetery—a gift from the rat gods—and it would eat its fill tonight. The supple pink fingers twitched in anticipation.

A shadow moved and froze the rat in its place. This was something new. The rat sniffed, almost ran back to the protection of its hole, but held its ground, poking its head higher. It still had pups to feed, after all. It would fight the intruder if needed. Or eat it.

Tiny drops of saliva filled the pouches of its mouth. Its stomached grumbled at the delay and urged the rat forward. Nose sniffing, whiskers twitching, it took two steps forward and stopped. The shadow moved again and the rat hunched. It twitched and looked. Where was the intruder that caused the shadow to move? It must be close.

Without warning, the shadow struck out and the rat jumped. The rat squealed in pain as it felt the cold bite of the shadow pierce its stomach. It hit the ground and flopped in fiery pain. Fluid leaked from its stomach and a squirt of urine released into the air. The shadow was already consuming the liquid.

The rat gnashed at the air and jumped again. But the shadow was too fast and had stretched out beneath it. The rat landed on the shadow and felt its baby fingers and gnarled toes burn with unnatural pain. It had never faced an enemy like this one. It tried to jump, run back to its nest and hide, but that time had passed. The shadow pierced its neck and stuck like a barb. The rat kicked its baby-toed paws at the shadow, but it was too late. As its eyes dimmed, it saw the shadow rise up over its head and seep into its nostrils. The shadow, once known as Scarmish, would feed from the inside out.

There was little essence to the rat, no soul, just a bit of life-energy. But Scarmish had been reduced to feeding on vermin. In its black-tattered state, the thing known as Scarmish had barely survived its journey back from the Desert of Dust. It had been nearly obliterated. And it had used much of the twins' energy, who were bound to it, just to remain in existence. But now it was feeding.

As the Scarmish-shadow fed from the rat body, it spread out like a faint cloud of poison gas. Black and deadly, it crept over the ground looking for something else to feed on. Finding a hole in the ground, just a few feet from the diminishing body of the rat, the shadow felt the tiniest wave of warmth in the air. Tiny morsels, but something was better than nothing.

The blind and deaf pups laying helpless in the nest tried to squirm away from the cold death. Each one gave a tiny squeak as the black shadow punctured their pink skin.

The Scarmish-shadow began to eat the tiny squirming sausages—also from the inside out.

CHAPTER 9

The next morning Del arose late. She'd struggled through another bad night of sleep. Remnants of old nightmares haunted her. Arlo intrigued her, but in general, she simply didn't know what to do with her time, and her mind spun constantly.

She'd imagined her new life much differently. For one thing, she saw it happening in a house. Certainly not as big as Armand's, but somehow as cozy. She'd imagined visitors and large meals. And friends.

But in her tiny apartment, with gray walls and a shared bathroom, there was no room for any of that. Even if she had friends, she wouldn't bring them here.

She walked to a small café, buying a paper on the way. It was the second print of the day, scooping up any straggling stories that didn't make it into last night's run. She'd learned that the first run had to be printed the night before to hit the streets at five a.m. But some papers, like the *Times-Picayune*, immediately started a second run for the lunchtime crowd. It was thinner and had some overlap in stories, but it gave the appearance of late-breaking news. So, in a strange way, she was now the early bird.

She ordered coffee and a blueberry muffin that was on sale. She hadn't realized that her apartment wouldn't come with a kitchen, and didn't want to pay the extra for breakfast service. So, she was learning to be frugal.

Sitting at an outdoor table, she sipped her coffee and looked around. She loved this aspect of being on her own. The café was across from a school, with a small park just down the street. This meant there was a constant stream of people walking past. She'd watch them come and go, like she used to do in the orphanage. Only now, she imagined she was one step closer to living a life like theirs.

Sometimes she'd pretend to read the paper, but listen to the snippets of conversation that floated by. Wondering what those families were like, she'd try to guess something about each person. In a way, it felt like practicing to be a reporter. There was a story there, somewhere. Granted, sometimes she found that what she thought she was guessing at was actually something she'd picked up from a quick trance of the person. But it was becoming harder to tell one from the other, and preventing herself from doing it was almost impossible. It happened so easily now, she often didn't detect it.

In the distance, a boat's steam whistle sounded. Del wondered who was on the boat and if they were going somewhere exciting. Most likely a working barge, she knew, but maybe not. The Mississippi was a large river and had carried untold numbers of people to other destinations, and destinies. Maybe it would carry her away some day on a *real* adventure. Some day.

She unfolded the newspaper, looked around to ensure no one was watching her, then gave it a quick sniff. The inky, woody smell of the paper meant that some interesting bit of information was just waiting to be discovered. She wondered what she'd learn about the world today.

Scanning the front page, she decided to skip the national politics. She flipped to the second page and the headline screamed out at her.

Serial Rape Gang Strikes Again!

A shadow passed over Del at that moment and a faint, sick feeling quickened her heartrate. She read the article with growing dread.

A young girl had been found dead yesterday morning. She was believed to be eighteen or nineteen, but she had no identification. The physical trauma was similar to two other cases the police were investigating. They now admitted it appeared to be the work of the same people. And for reasons they could not release, due to the ongoing investigation, they would not say what the similarities were. Only that if anyone had any tips to call the N.O.P.D.

Del closed the paper and slyly looked over each shoulder. She suddenly felt guilty for reading such a terrible thing right out in public. It was silly, she knew. Terrible things occurred every day, and people needed to know what was happening in their world. But wasn't it the same as people who rubbernecked to look at an automobile accident? Looking for the gory details just to be able to cringe and say, *What a tragedy*, while the whole time thinking, *Glad it wasn't me*. Was she participating in a form of socially acceptable voyeurism?

When she'd decided to be a newspaper reporter, she dreamed about breaking a big story, but didn't consider it may be about serial rapists.

She shuddered.

And what about the poor girl?

No… *Girls!*

She wondered. Had there been any follow up from the paper to tell their stories? How many others would there be?

Suddenly her stomach dropped. This article could have been talking about her. She could have been the third victim.

The half-eaten muffin suddenly sat like a rock in her stomach.

She thought about her walk (run) home just two nights ago. She willed the muffin to stay down, but it was a troublesome thing. The sweat breaking on her forehead confirmed it.

The men that had chased her, was it possible they were the same men the police were looking for? Was the other girl dead because Del had somehow escaped?

Another body count for me.

She felt the self-pity start to creep in, but tried to shake it away. Maybe it wasn't really her fault.

(But what about Jo?)

OK. I know.

(And Mama D.)

I know! Stop it!

She looked around quickly, afraid that she had spoken out loud to herself. She was tired of feeling like this. She didn't know how to break the cycle of feeling cursed, but had to, soon. This wasn't the life she wanted.

Wiping the sweat from her forehead, she straightened up and took a deep breath. She'd been clenching her stomach so tight while reading the article, she hadn't realized how shallow she'd been breathing. With the rush of air, a new emotion washed over her.

Her jaw locked and her mouth set in a tight line. Grabbing the paper, she left the remnants of her breakfast and marched down the sidewalk. The nearby park was sunny and filled with lounging people.

No one would think it strange to see a girl sitting there, lost in her thoughts. Little would they know she'd be hunting for answers.

*

Deep in her trance, Del floated. Since the day she left Armand's, she'd tried to limit these sessions, especially toward anyone in the house. She didn't know how long a *crease* lasted. Forever maybe? Hopefully not. But knew that she had created the ones that drew the spirits to the house. And for that reason, she avoided looking in on her extended family. But today she couldn't help it.

She'd never had an addiction, nor knew anyone who did, but imagined that it must be very much like this. As soon as she slipped into her trance, a warm feeling of *normalcy* enveloped her. She was safe in her trance. She had power here. And in a strange way, things made more sense to her here. She never thought she'd consider trancing normal, but over the months that's exactly what had happened. And now that she was back in—fully in—she didn't want to leave. Her mind ran wild.

Like a movie reel on high speed, people's history unfolded before her. She was watching their lives in reverse. In her mind she floated over the park and saw the people who had just been here. They left trails everywhere. Normal people couldn't see these trails; they weren't like footprints in the mud, more like dust trails in the air. The trails wound around randomly, coming and going in all directions. It was amazing to see how many people occupied the same space in the world, only at different times. There were definite patterns to it all. She realized those cosmic patterns were dictated to a degree by the physical layout of the world people traversed; roads and buildings, for instance, meant that people passed along certain paths more frequently than others. But in wider spaces, like the park, it was more than just random. There seemed to be some areas that people always went to, and some they never did, or rarely. It was almost as if there were many doors to many other worlds hidden at these locations, and she just hadn't learned how to see them yet. It struck her as quite curious, and she wondered if one day she'd learn their secrets.

Before she knew it, she was at Armand's house, looking up at it from the sidewalk. She must have followed her own path back without realizing it. In fact, she was pretty sure this was the route she'd walked the morning she'd left. She remembered looking over her shoulder and thinking a wayward shadow had slithered down the outside wall, but she didn't see it this morning. It was probably waiting by her apartment now, although she hadn't seen any… visitors there either. But that was the point of her leaving anyway, to lead the spirits away from the house. But had it been enough to help Mama D recover?

Although she'd called Armand and Frank every week—sometimes speaking with Mama D—that was the only type of communication she risked. It had been a struggle not to look, but now, hoping the *airways* had been cleared of her influence, she looked in.

*

In her trance, Del spent several minutes hovering above each room. She started in the kitchen, where Armand was searching the air trying to remember how to make something or find a lost ingredient. She smiled to herself when he said, "Oh yes, the chamomile is in the cupboard," but heard none of his usual excitement upon arriving at the answer. Shifting her view, she gazed closely at him and saw a deep weariness in his face. It was in the eyes, and it alarmed her.

She then moved, as if walking, through the foyer and saw the study she had locked Jimmy in during that terrible, long night of the spirit invasion. It still pained her to think about it, and she said a quick prayer that he didn't remember any of it.

Floating up the stairs, she heard muffled talking and recognized the voice immediately. Her vision snapped to high above the library and she looked down upon Jimmy sitting at a chess table, opposite the fireplace wall.

A warm feeling filled her as she watched her friend in her favorite room. Images of late nights, roaring fires, and witty banter from the three elders flashed through her mind. Her favorite loveseat—which secretly she thought of as her personal space—sat by the railing awaiting her return. Viewing the room from this vantage point, an odd thought occurred to her. On those late nights, the three elders would always sit by the fireplace. The equivalent of the 'adult' table. Jimmy was usually playing somewhere else, but occasionally sat at the very table he was at now, playing another game or drawing. She always sat between the two, too old for the kids' area, but not quite able to break into the adult section. Oh, she was invited into many adult conversations, but an equal number of them were *about* her, or *at* her, instead of *with* her. Despite everything, she felt she was still outside the circle.

Focusing back on Jimmy, she saw that he was not just playing at anything, but appeared to be actually playing chess. Had Armand taught him the rules since she'd left?

She didn't know exactly how the pieces moved, but knew each one had special abilities. The king and queen were obviously important, but the others had their own unique strengths. The strengths weren't supposed to be magical, she thought, but the way Jimmy was moving them, he'd obviously granted them more power than normal.

As a parting gift to her friend, Del imagined a butterfly composed of colors from the stained-glass window that sat high in the wall. It shimmered briefly in a ray of light that spread across the chessboard.

"Hey," Jimmy said, reaching for the phantom light, "how'd you get in h—?"

Del killed the image. Her fear of drawing the spirits back to the house was too great. She left her friend sitting in a room quickly fading to gray.

*

Before moving down the hall, Del flashed back to her body—still sitting on the park bench—and confirmed she was safe. She could tell the day had aged a bit by the shadows, but knew she had plenty of time. Now it was on to her mentor.

Entering her room through the ceiling, Del was shocked at the sight of Mama D.

Oh my God! She's fading away. How much weight has she lost?

Del hovered close and was struck with another strange sensation. Somehow, the air felt thick around the woman, almost wet. And Del wasn't even in the room. She flashed back to the park to see if it had suddenly started raining—it hadn't—then back to Mama D's room.

The woman appeared to be sleeping, but Del feared it was something more. She was breathing lightly, but nothing else. She looked for Mama D in her trance, hoping that the woman was trancing as well. She searched the vision of the room for the telltale yellow wisps the woman left behind, but saw none. She searched for dreams, but her mind was empty.

I need to go back, she thought. *She needs me. How can I help her from here?*

(You can't go back. You know that.)

I have to do something!

(You've already done enough. The results are lying right there on the bed.)

A flash of lightning went off in her mind.

Shut up!

Her mind was a storm, heaving, cresting with anger, then sliding into a trough of black guilt.

The shell of Mama Dedé was lying there, but everything else (her mind? her spirit? her soul?) seemed to be utterly gone.

Del pulled back from the trance as tears spilled over her eyelids. She had to speak with Arlo. She had to find her path so she could help the woman who'd helped her so many times.

She got up weakly from the park bench. She'd been in the same position for several hours. As she staggered home, coaxing life back into her sleepy legs, her mind became fixed. Like a beacon in a storm, she saw a tiny glimmer of hope rise before her; a north star showing her the way. She'd finally find her path.

She never even considered where the path would ultimately lead her.

CHAPTER 10

Marcel ducked under the police tape and walked halfway down the alley. It was short, only about forty feet in length, and ended with a degraded wooden fence. The fence leaned backwards against a cinderblock wall of an abandoned building that was only accessible from the other side of the block.

An overflowing dumpster sat at the back of the alley and an assortment of discarded tires had been stacked around for makeshift seats. The dead man's body was arched over one of these stacks—three tires high—in a spread-eagle *Holy Jesus* stare. The arms were flung back over his head and the mouth gaped so wide Marcel thought the jaw might be broken. The man's feet touched the ground on one side of the stack, as the backs of his hands dragged the other. The fingers were clenched in twisted, spasmodic shapes.

He tilted his head and looked at the face. "What the hell happened to him?"

The officer shook his head. "Shit himself to death, the way he smells."

Marcel ignored the comment and looked back toward the street. From the mid-point of the alley—standing against the wooden fence—the alley was cloaked in shade from a large tree on the neighboring lot, and a myriad of vines that had escaped their yards. The vines had grown over the hard corners, causing the alley entrance to fade into shadow. You couldn't see it until you were almost upon it.

This was mostly a residential neighborhood—despite the abandoned cook shack standing behind him—and not an affluent one. The alley had been slowly consumed by the decay of an aging neighborhood and essentially forgotten.

The officer continued, "No noticeable wounds, puncture or blunt force. Other than the smell… and the look… beats me, maybe an overdose? But he doesn't look like a junkie."

Marcel walked back to the front of the alley and surveyed the street. It was oddly quiet.

He looked left down the shaded street. A couple hundred feet down, another road dead-ended into this one, but from the opposite side of where he stood. To his right, the street continued, then curved sharply to the left. Over time, this neighborhood—just a remnant of one now—had been bisected and chopped up, leaving this odd fragment of a street, which didn't see much traffic. In fact, because of the way the major highways were laid out, this little bundle of a dozen houses—six to a side—had nearly been forgotten. He hadn't known this part of town existed until this morning.

"Anything else?"

"Well, there's that." The officer pointed to a chrome wrench laying off to one side. "Looks too clean to have been layin' there for long. And then there's this." He leaned over and pointed to a small red lump on the man's forehead.

"Barely a bruise," said Marcel.

"True. Didn't bleed."

"No."

"But it's there."

"Yeah. It's there alright."

Marcel took a pen from his shirt pocket and walked to the wrench. He looked around at the other discarded trash and thought this was far too shiny—despite the obvious wear and tear on it—to not have been picked up by some kid. He stuck his pen through the round, closed end and let it swing freely. It glittered in the morning light like a hypnotist's watch.

Marcel watched it for several seconds, wondering what—if anything—the wrench would tell him. As the light bounced off the raised lettering of the handle, the wrench sparkled and began to tell an unbelievable tale.

Marcel heard none of it and dropped it into an evidence bag.

CHAPTER 11

Frank Morgan entered the house of Armand Baptiste at seven thirty in the evening. He carried a bottle of Claret and had two breakfast cigars tucked safely in the pocket of his shirt. He considered them *breakfast cigars* because they were the lightest smokes he had and typically smoked them after breakfast. He carried them now because after his bout of indigestion a month ago—which the doctors had called a mild heart attack—he vowed to cut back. The first two weeks out of the hospital he hadn't touched a single one, but he felt quite on the mend now. Besides, he was planning on having a serious conversation with Armand tonight and that called for smokes, albeit light ones.

"Hallo!" Frank called. "I'm in da house."

He walked through the quiet kitchen. The absence of sound was alarming. For a moment he thought no one was home. He remembered back to when Del was here. The noise of her bounding down the steps would echo through the whole house. Now the place was utterly quiet.

"Up here, mon ami," Armand called from the second-floor library.

Frank walked to the base of the stairs and stopped. It suddenly dawned on him that the last time he'd stood here was the night he'd had his heart attack. That was the same night Armand and Mama Dedé had fallen ill to a bizarre ghostly attack. Something in the bottle of brandy—something *unnatural*—had affected them. Fortunately, Frank had imbibed very little that night and was unaffected. Had he partaken as much as the others the night most certainly would have ended differently. They'd barely escaped with their lives, except Spider of course. And Mama Dedé. For although she was alive, her life had utterly changed. This was one reason Frank was here now. Armand had found a doctor—a real medical doctor—that was also sympathetic to occult ailments. He was anxious to hear the latest diagnosis.

The last time Frank had stood looking up these stairs, he was certain he wouldn't make it to the top. And Spider had still been on the loose, which is what drew Frank out through the kitchen and onto the back porch. There, his crashed car, the broken gate and a screaming Spider all melted into a strange hallucination that included the stone maiden moving, and Spider's ultimate demise. What a night that had been. Frank shuddered and began his slow march up the steps.

At the top, he was surprised to not be as winded as he'd feared, and perked up. In fact, the ascent hadn't been bad at all.

Armand came from around the back of the large worktable. As usual, it was cluttered with arcane books and manuscripts.

"Mon ami, it is so good to see you!" He patted Frank's wide shoulders and inspected him. "You look good, my friend. What's the number?"

"Just topped thirty pounds," Frank said, patting his belly. "Got a few more to go, but da damn beignets keep callin' me."

Armand chuckled as he took the bottle of wine and headed to the worktable. "All in good time. And the walking? You are still—?"

"Yeah, yeah, I'm walkin'. Hell, I'll be a regular Jack LaLanne before you know it."

Armand winked and pointed a finger of acknowledgement. "Indeed. However, you are good for a little…?" He tipped an invisible wine glass to his lips.

"Well, I'm not gonna watch you drink da whole damn thing!"

Armand opened the bottle, grabbed two wine glasses and headed to the fireplace.

Frank sat in his usual seat. "Only two glasses?" he asked. His face said he understood the implication.

Pouring the dark wine, Armand nodded, but said nothing. He watched the ripples of wine ebb against the glass and suddenly imagined a Well of Life; a term he'd heard when Del was learning how to trance. It was no one's in particular, just a random person whose well could be drained as easily as a glass of wine. It all seemed so pointless. And yet it all seemed so relevant to Mama Dedé.

He handed a glass to Frank, then tilted his in toast. "To our lost family members," he said. "Wherever they may be."

The glasses clanked and the wine was sipped. Frank waited patiently, as a good detective does. He swirled his glass, inspected the color and sniffed the bouquet. Briefly, he acknowledged the silence of the room, but quickly pushed it away. It was overwhelming, and he thought if he lived in this house—now so devoid of life—he would go mad. From the other side of the table, he felt the tension of Armand slowly increase. It was a palpable thing that radiated through the air.

Finally, Armand was on his feet, pacing the room.

"These blasted doctors!"

He made it over to the chess table where Jimmy now sat. The boy had just come from Mama D's room, down the back hall, and was quietly setting up the pieces. Before Armand could ask, and without turning away from the board, Jimmy said, "She's seepin'" As if he knew the question Armand would ask.

Armand patted his shoulder. "Very good, thank you."

He spun toward Frank and marched back. "I'm telling you, someone should reevaluate the credentialling criteria of our city's medical community. Finding a doctor who can think outside of the latest academic publication is utterly impossible." He stopped at the fireplace table, spun, and marched back. "Time after time, the same sophomoric questions, as if they were diagnosing the common cold. 'Is she getting enough to drink?' 'Is she lethargic?' 'How are the bowel movements?' Seriously? Bowel movements? These overpaid quacks show no inclination to attain to anything higher than doling out a prescription to 'Take two aspirin and call me in the morning!'"

Armand stopped and looked around, as if surprised his ranting march had brought him to this place in his home. He looked guiltily over his shoulder and saw that Jimmy was blissfully lost in his game. Armand's shoulders sagged as the last of the fire-breath escaped his lungs. He slumped into his chair, exhausted.

Frank watched Armand watching Jimmy. Whether Armand was looking at the boy, or just in his direction, he couldn't tell, but Frank recognized the signs of someone dealing with competing thoughts. He felt a tinge of guilt at his own ill health. While Frank had laid up recovering, Armand had dealt with more than Frank realized. He doubted Jimmy was the burden. The boy was pretty self-sufficient, and more likely to be a welcome distraction to the real issue. Armand had come to care for Mama Dedé. Not in the way of lovers, Frank thought, but certainly as friends. And something beyond. Armand respected the woman's abilities. It was of great interest to him. He respected her for that. And for the way she tried to keep the men in line when it came to Del. Frank suspected that after Del left and Mama Dedé went dark, that Armand's house had slipped back to a cold, thin version of a bachelor life that Armand no longer cared for. With too much free time, a man could imagine many things about his life—and what was left of it. Frank knew this firsthand. The siren song of mortality beat its far-off drums; but they marched ever closer.

"She's not gettin' better, I take it," Frank said.

Armand turned his head from Jimmy and whispered, "No. She seems to be… declining."

"How so?"

Clearing his throat, Armand searched his vest pockets vainly for his pipe. After several frustrating seconds he stopped. His hands dropping to the armchairs in defeat. The task seemed too large.

Armand smiled weakly. "Who am I kidding? Myself? She doesn't *seem* to be declining. She *is* declining. Before my very eyes, and I'm at an utter loss as to what to do."

Frank squirmed again. "What's she—?"

"Fading," Armand interrupted. "She's just fading. And the doctors can find no obvious reason for it."

"Hhmmm," Frank mumbled under his breath. "Does he know?" He nodded at Jimmy.

"He attends her daily. Brings her tea and cookies. But it's hard to tell how much he understands. He knows she's sick. And thankfully she can take care of bathing needs and the like, but beyond the basics of living, there is little from her. It's as if she's lost in her own mind, wandering, and can't find her way back.

"You would suppose that," his arms spread wide, "with all this…

knowledge," he chuckled sadly, "these, conjurer books and dark artifacts I've collected over the years, that one of them may actually contain the answer. Or a hint as to what to do."

"'Dark artifacts'?" Frank said. "Dat don't sound like da thing we need."

"Oh, not to worry, mon ami. Yes, there are some dark items tucked away. Very dark—if you believe the superstitions—but they wouldn't be of use to us here." As soon as the words left his mouth, a tiny spark flashed in Armand's mind. It was faint, the idea, and not fully formed, a hint, but it was there nonetheless. Had he explored *all* possibilities, he wondered?

"You're not messin' with no," and here Frank whispered, "grimoires, are ya?"

"No, no. Those are safely hidden away." A sparkle of a story suddenly gleamed in Armand's eyes. Thinking about his dark artifacts, he'd remembered a fascinating tale. "However, have you ever heard the tale of how I obtained my Hand of Glory?" His feet tapped excitedly beneath the table.

Frank grimaced slightly. "A hand of what?" He could see the excitement in Armand's face, but wasn't ready for another spook story now. He patted his stomach. "Uh, maybe I'll let my supper settle first. You know, indigestion and all."

Armand stopped tapping, looking disappointed. "Oh… well, as you wish. I suppose we do have more serious matters to discuss." He sighed.

Frank redirected the conversation. "What about Del?"

Armand brightened slightly, rubbing his hands together as if to squeeze forth the best possible answer. "Who's to say? I often wonder if she's not looking in on us. You know," he wiggled his fingers at Frank and forced a weak smile, "and that she doesn't already know. But, at least she remembers to call."

"Dat's Del-bell," said Frank. "Every Sunday."

"Yes… every Sunday. However, I must admit, perhaps I've been more optimistic when describing her condition than I should be."

"Hmm, could be." Frank set down his empty wine glass, pulled a cigar from his pocket and inspected it. "I think it's about time I find Del. It's been eatin' me for a while."

"You don't say? Are you sure you're up to that?" Armand asked. "You don't want to rush into anything too soon."

"I ain't rushin'. Need to get out da damn house, is what I need. Hell, I'm just sittin' around collectin' dust."

"But what if you can't find her?"

Frank looked at Armand like he'd spoken a foreign language. "What do you mean? I *have* to find her. For all our sakes."

CHAPTER 12

Del finished her shift at the Jazz Note and sat on a bar stool waiting for the last drunks to be thrown out. Her ears were ringing, and she smelled like an ashtray, but she had money in her pocket. Maybe as much as twenty-five dollars—her largest haul yet—but she was too tired to count it. It hadn't been the busiest night she'd ever worked; it had been the right kind of steady, and she was less hectic now with her service. She was starting to get the hang of it. In general, the people in this neighborhood were pretty simple drinkers: beer, bourbon or gin. Sometimes tourists wandered in, but they were usually looking for another area. This place was for the common folks, the people who went through their days unnoticed by others, and she liked that just fine. She felt she understood these people. She'd made a game of guessing what they would order just by watching them walk in. She was getting good at it. But a flash-trance never hurt, just to be sure.

"Gettin' a little greedy, aintcha?" Tasha said with a sneer. She'd had a bad night of customers, and Del always seemed to have been a step ahead of her.

"It was an open floor," said Del. "I was just going where—"

"Whatever, bitch. Passin' out the cooty like candy, I 'spect." Tasha went off into the backroom.

Del glared and nearly sent a nasty image to her, but didn't. She wouldn't make any friends that way. Not like she cared if she and Tasha were ever friends, but still. And she wasn't passing anything out, although some people took their liberties as if she were. She was getting the hang of avoiding groping hands. There were a lot of hands in a dark crowded bar, and they came from all directions. She couldn't avoid them all, but was developing a sense to detect the worst of them. Del gathered up empty bottles and headed to the bar.

"Passin' the cooty like candy!" Jonesy said in a singing carnival-barker voice. He smiled as he wiped the bar. "Heh, heh. Jus' ignore her. She jus' wish somebody was eatin' *her* candy." He took the empty bottles, then mumbled under his breath, "Ol' sour puss."

Del smiled. "Thanks Jonesy, but I'd rather stay out of it."

"Yeah, I know. Don't worry about it, you're doin' fine. Jus' fine. You might need to toughen up a bit. Maybe a bit too nice for some of da characters dat come in here, but—"

"Who's too nice?" Tasha said, coming out of the back room. "The witch-bitch?" She threw a few dollars on the bar, her tip-out to Jonesy, and snorted at Del.

Jonesy picked up the money and eyed Tasha. "You *musta* had a bad night."

"Whatever. I guess the magic cooty has all your money then." She looked over her shoulder as she went out the front door. "Don't let her cheat'cha."

*

After finishing her cleaning duties, Del rang for a cab. She didn't want to waste money, but when she realized she'd made over thirty dollars that night, she thought it better to be safe than sorry on her trip home. This was the first night of working since the incident, and she was still haunted with a blank space in her memory. She didn't want to tempt fate.

"You sure dis da place?" the cabbie asked. They had just stopped on a dark street where live oaks cast ghostly shadows through the air.

"Yes," said Del, "this is it."

"But you ain't know da numba?"

"No. I've forgotten it. But I'm meeting someone here." At least, Del hoped she would find Arlo here.

"Dis here dead street."

"What? No it's not a dead end, it makes a sharp left just up there and goes—"

"Not dead-end, jus dead," the cabbie said. "Nobody live here for longa time."

"Well," Del started, "that's not true, I just met…"

Del stopped. Did she really know who, or what, she'd met the other night?

"Sorry miss, I drive longa time, dis a dead street."

"Thanks, I'll get out anyway."

Before exiting the cab, Del had already scanned the area, looking for hidden attackers. There weren't any. In fact, besides her and the cab driver, she didn't sense anyone in the vicinity. He seemed to be, at least on this occasion, right. The street seemed utterly dead.

Now standing on the sidewalk, watching the cab drive away, Del tranced the area again. From the birds-eye view of her vision, she caught no sense of anyone living in the twelve little houses on this forgotten street. She noted there were a few porch lights on. But were they the same lights that were on the other night? In fact, the trashcans seemed to be in the same place as before. No one had brought them in yet. The old streetlamps, which certainly couldn't move, had an odd familiarity about them as well. They seemed to be leaning in, as if listening, toward Del.

"Evenin," came a voice from the dark.

Del jumped and spun around, nearly tripping over a gnarled tree root. "Oh!" Her heart slammed in her chest. "I wish you'd stop doing that. You nearly scared me to death."

"Not quite," Arlo said.

"What? Oh, ok, not quite. But darn close." Del caught her breath and leaned against the tree. "I didn't hear you come up—hey, wait a minute… I didn't even see you. And I was look—"

"Bah!" Arlo waved her quiet. "You weren't lookin' in da right place. Dat's all. Now, why you here?"

Del looked up and down the street. Which house did Arlo live in? Where had she just come from?

"I… I came to ask for your help."

Arlo nodded, "Hmmm…" and began inspecting the girl again. "And what's your wish?"

"I want to find my true path. So I can help my kons— my mento— my… Mama Dedé."

"Hmmm…" Arlo inspected Del for a long time.

Del began to wonder if Arlo was having second thoughts about teaching her.

"OK den." Arlo grabbed Del's hand. "Here's our pact."

Del withdrew. "Our what?"

Arlo eyed her closely. "As I say, our pact. It's jus' between us two. Da others doan care to be part, as long as you and me have an understandin."

"An understanding of what?"

"Of when we need help. You come and give it."

Del ground her feet into the cobblestone walk, looking for strength. Strength to either flee or accept. "How can I give something that I don't know I have? How can I—"

"We don't ask for any'ting dat's not in someone's grace to give."

Del thought this was a strange statement, even for a strange person like Arlo. But her comment was wrong on multiple levels. For one thing, Arlo's habit of referring to multiple people was odd, and she wondered if she'd ever find out who the others were. Secondly, the term *in someone's grace to give* just didn't sound right. It was almost as if Arlo already knew what Del's path was, and *what Del could give her*, but wasn't telling her. Instead, the woman was leading her into an agreement Del didn't understand.

She caught a glimpse of the shadow-cat, winding its way around a tree. He knew his path apparently. Had he made a pact with the old woman as well?

Don't be stupid. That's ridiculous.

But was it? Was it really so ridiculous to think a cat couldn't make a pact with an old woman who was obviously a practitioner of some sort? She'd learned many things over the last few months. Things that she would have never believed just a year ago. She'd fought a man—a spirit really—who'd been called back to life by a strange spell. She'd seen a wolf-beast that had another man's spirit bound to it. She'd even tranced back into an older version of New Orleans. So why was it so hard for her to believe that the cat wasn't a part of this?

She suddenly missed Mama Dedé very much. The woman's face

filled her mind and a sob caught in her throat. It was Mama D who had taught her all the things she knew. It was Mama D's stern but loving words that had guided her; words that were meant to protect her. It was Mama D who was dying right now because of her.

"You cain't even make a decision to decide, ken ya?"

Snapping back, Del shot a hard look at Arlo. Her mouth formed a tight line and she swallowed back harsh words.

Arlo held out her palm to Del. The deep wrinkles in her hand looked like carved runes in the moonlight. Secret words etched by time.

Del's own hand, young and smooth, with barely any lines at all, covered Arlo's in an eternal grip. She held the woman's gaze tight.

A sliver of moonlight rustled the leaves, scattering its binding light over the two women. The streetlamps solemnly faded to black, casting the street into utter darkness; this ceremony was not meant for other eyes—only the moon and night things would bear witness. A faint blue sphere of light engulfed the women as the wind whispered their vows. The night things spoke, fixing the accord, and their words were upon the wind, carried away to a secret place that kept the pact between the two women safe.

At times, Del would think back to this moment and wonder if it could ever be undone.

CHAPTER 13

After Frank left and the bottle of Claret had run dry, Armand paced his library with an inebriated agitation. Pipe smoke filtered through his wild hair, trailing him as if he were a smoldering tinder. He puffed, tapping the pipe with his fingers, then trailed smoke in a new direction. His heavy sighs and frequent stops were unnoticed by Jimmy, still sitting at the chess table. Armand's disdain for the inept doctors had not left him all evening; even the brandy in his glass couldn't lighten his mood.

"There must be something here," Armand said, looking over the library shelves. "The answer is on one of these shelves. It must be." Like a cartoon wizard, he raised his hands and cast an imaginary spell at the books. "Reveal yourself!"

As expected, the books remained silent.

Jimmy looked up from his game. "Why'd you say dat?"

Armand turned to the boy as if seeing him for the first time that evening, then joined him at the chessboard. He sat down across from him, but turned to stare stubbornly at the shelves. "Sorry to interrupt your game, Master Jimmy. I was simply trying to squeeze blood from a turnip."

The side of Jimmy's nosed flared as he considered the gross image.

"No, no," Armand said. "It's just a figure of speech. I'm simply frustrated that these doctors are of no use to poor Mama Dedé and—"

"Yeah, she puwty sick I guess," Jimmy said.

Armand nodded. "Yes, I'm afraid so."

"Maybe Deh can hep her."

Armand's head, still nodding, slowly came to a stop. He sighed again. "If Del were here, I'm sure she could, quite elegantly. However, it is just us men holding down the fort, therefore we must prevail by whatever means available." His pipe's mouthpiece became a pointer in his hand. "And I'm *sure* the answer lies somewhere on those shelves! But, alas, it eludes me."

Jimmy looked at the books on the shelf and said, "Maybe you ask 'em nice. 'Ike dis." Then he began petting imaginary books on the table and whispering arcane flatteries.

Armand watched the boy go through an elaborate ritual with his imaginary books. Elegantly, Armand thought, his hands moved around the chessboard. In doing so, Jimmy pushed the chess pieces around randomly, and swept his hands in a widening arc. He continued whispering. Soon, two of the pieces were caught up in both hands and met at the center of the board.

Quietly, so as not to disturb the scene, Armand whispered, "What are you doing now?"

"Dey talkin."

"Indeed. And what are they—?" Armand spun and stared at the tall shelves, then looked back at Jimmy. The boy was now leaning close to the table, as if listening to their secret conversation.

Armand stood up and quietly walked to the library ladder. He touched it gently. Afraid that anything more abrupt may fling the idea from his mind. He looked back over his shoulder; Jimmy was in a quiet state of thought. Slowly, then with greater urgency, he pushed the ladder to the center of the shelves and quickly ascended. Brushing back dust-ladened cobwebs, he felt gently around the top shelf. Why hadn't he thought of this before? Wild ideas spun through his mind as his arm stretched and his hand reached. He stepped up one rung further, craning to reach the back corners of the deep shelves. A twinge of panic crept into him as he searched. Surely it was still here!

A visible shudder passed through him when his fingers brushed against a rigid corner. He patted the object gently, fingers trembling with anticipation.

He carefully retrieved a flat wooden box.

He held the box to his chest as if moving an unexploded ordinance, wary of the volatility that lay within. He didn't need to wipe the dust away to confirm his possession. There was nothing else in the house like it. Suddenly aware of a heavy silence, Armand turned and looked down at Jimmy at the chess table.

As if waiting for him to descend the ladder, Jimmy sat quietly, staring up at Armand. His face was blank, but watchful.

A dichotomy of feelings ran through Armand as he descended. Was he really considering this? Had he let himself slip beyond all reasonable scientific reasoning of Mama Dedé's illness? Had he gone mad?

His eyes never left Jimmy. Each step lower, rung after rung, took him closer to the inevitable answer. But to satisfy his need to feel rational, to feel in control, he let the pros and cons of the question pass through his mind. At least this way he could convince himself later that he'd seriously considered the risks.

Armand set the wooden box on the worktable and ran his fingers around the edges.

"What's dat?" Jimmy asked as he walked to the workbench.

Somewhere from the back of his mind, Armand watched Jimmy approach. He'd grown to truly care for the boy, perhaps first as an extension of his love for Del and Mama Dedé, but he truly cared for him now. In fact, the more time Armand spent with Jimmy, the more fascinated he became with the boy. The odd events in the cemetery, the night they fought the Gris-gris man, could not be contributed to Del alone. Examining the events as a whole, Jimmy had played nearly as large a part as any of them in the creature's defeat. Then there was the unfortunate business with Spider and the little girl Clara. Jimmy had been there at just the right time again. And of course, there was the nagging question of if Jimmy had actually been in Armand's room that night to wake him, ultimately saving Frank's life. These questions, these… strange events, had settled in the back of Armand's mind, one at a time, and were beginning to take shape. There was much more to learn about Jimmy, he was sure. But *what* he would learn, Armand could not tell. Finally, he heard his own voice speaking from a distance. It surprised Armand in a way, for until that very moment, he hadn't expected to ever cross this Rubicon.

"Master Jimmy, would you like to play a game?"

Armand removed the wooden lid, exposing the contents inside.

"Ah game?"

"Yes."

"Wha kinda game?"

Armand swallowed hard, "A Talking Board game," and set the Ouija board on the table.

CHAPTER 14

Still standing on the shadowed, dead street, Arlo said to Del, "Now come wit me."

The blue sphere of light that had surrounded the women during their secret ceremony had faded. All that was left was the memory of the event.

And a new unbreakable pact.

With their pact made, the two women were now bound by a force greater than them both. Ancient laws that defined boundaries, contracts between the living and the dead, were now in play. Neither woman fully understood the contract that had been made this evening, for neither truly understood the other's power, but each would be bound to it. And each to their own unexpected end.

"Three tasks," the old woman said, holding up gnarled fingers. "Three, to find yer path. But I'll only show you two. The third you'll find on yer own."

Del snorted. "But if I knew where to look, I wouldn't need—"

"You gonna get two choices on each task. Each choice you

make takes you closer to yer path. Den—"

"But what if I don't like those choices?"

"Hush and listen! Each task has to be thought on careful. You cain't decide too quick. Got to let your spirit guide you, tell you what's best. How you choose, dat'll start to set yer path."

Del sighed and looked at her chewed nails. "Whatever you say."

"Dat's what I say!" Arlo snapped, shaking her head. "I ken see why yer konseye's tired now."

Del caught a nasty sneer before it shown on her face. She didn't want to anger the woman. She *was* the one who had come asking for help, after all. She *needed* Arlo's help, for Mama Dedé's sake. Besides, maybe this woman really could teach her something, she thought.

Arlo detected the shift in Del, the settling of nerves, the subsidence of skepticism. "Dat's good. Save da energy for when you need it. You don't have to have yer hackles up all da time, jus' when you need 'em. Now let's see what you be workin' with."

With that, Arlo grabbed Del's wrist and with one quick stroke of her finger, cut a line through the air like a rip in a curtain. Separating before the women, a thin membrane tore open, and a cold feeling washed over Del. Later, Del would think of it as a wind, but it didn't move a strand of her hair. She'd come to call it a wind because there was no better way to describe it; but it was more. Much more. What Del felt at that moment was an emptiness so deep it was cold. And the feeling of cold came from inside herself, from within her bones. No. Deeper than that, she thought. The sensation came from something at her very core, and had she not been with Arlo, it might have frozen her in place.

But instead of being frozen in place, she was moving. Gentle as a puff of air, she moved beyond the rip in the fabric. Her legs weren't walking. Her feet weren't stepping. But she moved, nonetheless. And she wasn't trancing. A second after Arlo split the thin membrane of reality, like the first night they'd met, Del was plunged into the world of the dead.

And it was maddening.

The scene that Arlo had shown Del the previous night, the eyeless, staring faces, marching ever forward, had been but a glimpse. Now, plunged into the depths, Del barely comprehended what she saw. The lost dead were beyond counting.

Legions of eyeless faces stretched in all directions. They looked, sightless, for a horizon of light, but saw none. They moved, motionless, as if floating on a dead ocean current; their mass rising and falling with a tide driven by a forgotten moon. Their bodies were thin beyond reckoning, corn stalks standing in a brittle October field. Their heads—what remained—swayed like top-heavy orbs of corn on their dead-stalk bodies, always a degree from swaying too far and snapping. The final remnants of these dead: fading images, projections of what they had been, floated about them in an ever-tangling jumble of memories. Fragile threads of a past existence that was nearly spent.

Some of the dead—very recently dead, Del thought—projected themselves more fully, not quite as brittle. But in some ways, they were the most dreadful to behold. Confused and bewildered, these spirits fought the ebbing tide and tried to move against the swell. Somehow, Del understood that these recently departed still had a sense of purpose, a sense that they shouldn't be here, that a mistake had been made. She felt their frantic motion, their panicked searches, their pleading dreams of *just a little more time*. Then the tide would shift, sweeping those helpless souls past her, bringing a different crop of dead into view.

A crop of dead?

Was that the right term for what she was seeing? A crop of dead? Probably not, but the sensation of being in an endless corn field that floated on a dark ocean wouldn't leave her. The sheer numbers of the tangled mass confused her, and each one projected a bit of themselves: shapes, images, possessions, wishes or dreams. Then a dead face would pop out of the menagerie right in front of her. Sometimes the eye sockets locked onto hers, gripping her with an overwhelming desire to fall forward and explore their dead dreams. Some faces seemed to seek hers out, others didn't even notice. Many passed through her with a slight cold sting and went on their never-ending journey.

A migration of dead? Maybe.

Then of course there were the long-ago-dead. These spirits barely had any essence at all. They were crumbling in a wispy, flaking sort of way, as if the sheer pressure of the universe was crushing them out of existence. Being dissolved by time. Del caught glimpses of them here and there. Wedged between the aggressively dead spirits—those still remembering life—the long-ago-dead accepted their crushing fate: that of being ground into oblivion, and went mutely into the darkness. Not even would their spirit remain. The long-ago-dead flaked away and dissolved in a whisper. Their tiny flakes floated up from the heave

A heave of dead? No.

and drifted away on the endless night wind. They became the dandruff of humanity and would fall like snow in the Desert of Dust at the end of time.

It was the final undoing, and Del watched it play out before her. A dark, unraveling tapestry documenting the last moments of man.

A tapestry of dead.

That was the term.

Suddenly, Del felt a strange sensation, a weight on her body, and she realized she was moving away from the tapestry, being pulled backwards. But something was wrong. She felt pain. First, tiny twinges, then shoots and streaks of fire. She tried to speak, to call out, but her voice didn't work here. Something had ahold of her. Something was causing her tremendous pain, and she panicked.

Her hair was tearing; each one pulled out a strand at a time. Her guts were stretching. Her mind was being ripped open; something prodded between the soft gray folds. Her bowels were being squeezed. Her toes were dissolving. She was slowly being pulled apart by the dead things in the tapestry.

Strings.

They want my strings!

The crazy thought flew into Del's mind and consumed her.

The dead wanted her life, and they pulled at it, one strand at a time. She struggled to get free but couldn't. She was in a dream where she was being chased but couldn't run. She was being eaten but couldn't fight back. The dead were pulling her apart, weaving her into the tapestry one stitch at a time. Dissolving her with their hollowness. Sucking light into dark.

Then a searing flash of light blinded her, and she fell to the ground. She felt the warm wind of life touch her skin and the radiant heat of the day drift from the cobblestones into her body.

"Why dint' you come when I called ya?" Arlo scolded her.

Del looked around, stunned. Her eyes slowly adjusted to the dark after the searing flash.

"Wha... what are you talking about?" Del said dizzily. "What happened?" She struggled to stand, and Arlo pulled her up like a child.

"Girl, what are you playin' at?"

Del blinked her eyes as the night scene came back into focus. A shudder ran through her and she slapped at the delayed sensations of cold dead hands groping her body. She shivered, nearly vomited, then hugged herself, rubbing her arms for warmth. Looking around, she saw that they were on the other side of the street. However long the dead journey had lasted in her mind, they had only made it as far as crossing the street. How long had they been gone?

"I said, whatchoo playin' at?" Arlo shook Del's arm for attention.

Del grabbed Arlo's other arm, partially for stability and partially for leverage. She shook the woman as best she could.

"What did you just do to me?" She felt like one of the nights when Armand let her have too much wine. "What did you—?"

"Bah! What *I'd* do?" Arlo released her to scribble invisible symbols in the air. She had to make sure the void was closed. "I told you not to go runnin' off while—"

"No, you didn't!"

"I told you to *see* into da other side," Arlo argued. "Not *go* in."

Del was adamant. "You didn't say anything to me. Nothing. You just pulled me into that place and left me there!"

Arlo eyed Del, then scratched her chin. She looked for the moon, but it was nowhere to be found and she cursed silently.

After a long moment of silence, Arlo said, "You dint hear me callin'? Feel me pullin' ya?"

Del finished checking herself for missing body parts. The tingling sensations, like sleeping arms and legs, had nearly gone away. "No. I didn't hear anything. One minute we were standing over there." She pointed across the street. "Then I was lost for I don't know how long. Then I felt you—I guess it was you—pulling me out, but… something had a hold of me and wouldn't let go."

"Sumpin' had ya? Had ya how?"

Del described the sensation of being pulled apart from the inside. Of being tugged at by the tapestry of dead who wanted to remake themselves, one strand at a time, with the life-strings of Del.

Arlo nodded and rubbed her hands.

"What does it mean?" said Del.

"It means, we got to get to work," said Arlo. "We got to—"

"Get to work? Wasn't that the first task? Wasn't there some sort of decision I made that got me out?"

"Dat got you out? Dat wasn't even da task. I jus' showed you a dead alley so you could get used to it. Seein' how you had such a start da other night."

"A dead alley? More like a dead ocean, you mean."

Arlo flinched slightly. It was something in the shoulders. "How many'dja see?"

Del looked around the dark street. "I don't know. All of them?" Her arms spread wide. "Well, I doubt *all* of them. But enough. They were everywhere! As far as I could see."

Arlo wrung her hands this time. "So why'd ya go in?"

Incredulously, Del said, "Go in? I didn't choose to go in! Are you crazy?"

Arlo waved her silent. "You made da decision to see. To go in. Too deep. We're done here."

"Done?" Del looked at her in confusion. "What do you mean 'done'? We didn't do anything. I didn't learn anything. I—"

"You *chose* to see. Whether you know it or not, whether you *remember* or not," here Arlo put a crooked finger to her own temple and tapped, "you made da choice to go *in* and see. Mayhap made da choice to feed 'em a bit, eh?"

Del's eyes went wide. She stepped back slowly, as if suddenly seeing the family dog foaming at the mouth, one minute a loving pet, now a harbinger of death. Her voice was low but firm. "Feed them?" A nervous chuckle escaped her throat. "You… you *are* crazy."

Beneath the hood, Del saw the side of Arlo's mouth twitch. Whether a suppression of a smile or a sneer, she couldn't tell, but the eyes gleamed intensely. "I know my path, girl. And I'm familiar with the voices in my head. Are you?"

Del had no response for this. Whether Arlo really knew of the many conversations that filled Del's head, or only guessed at them, she'd hit a soft spot that Del couldn't defend. A bit of her angry wind had just been knocked out of her. Her voice softened a fraction, but she held her anger just below the surface. "But what about the first time? When you showed me the faces, the ones following me? I didn't know anything then, but I didn't get lost. I didn't make a choice. It just happened."

"I kinda helped you den. Just showed you a little. Dis time was different."

Del huffed and threw her arms up. "This is ridiculous! I'm going home." She spun and headed down the street.

"See ya tomorrow," Arlo said quietly.

"No, you won't!" Del called back over her shoulder.

Arlo raised her hand, marking the air, just as the moon slipped out from behind a cloud. Del's path was now marked, and the moon would see it wherever she went.

Arlo nodded. "Oh, yes, I will."

CHAPTER 15

"Ah talkin' boad game?" Jimmy scrunched his face in disbelief.

Armand hurried around the library, dimming lights. "That's correct. If we're polite, and a bit lucky, it may speak to us."

He hurried down the hall and checked on Mama Dedé, who was asleep. He walked quietly back, satisfied they would not be disturbed.

Jimmy had pulled a chair from the chess table over to the workbench and was kneeling on it. His chin rested on his folded arms on the table as he gazed at the board.

The innocence of children, Armand suddenly thought. Jimmy's face was so peaceful with trust, he almost tore the board away.

"How do we pway?" Jimmy prompted.

"Master Jimmy, please understand. This isn't a game I'd normally ask you to play. In fact, you mustn't speak to anyone about it."

"Why?"

"Well," Armand stroked his beard for inspiration, "you see, some people don't understand this game. And may not approve of us playing it."

"Why?"

"Well… it's hard to explain really. But I hope that we may learn something tonight by playing. But I can't play alone. The game may not tell me the correct answer if I'm the only one touching it. It's always best to have at least two different hands touching the board. I'll show you. So, I need another person, to… well, to help with the game."

Jimmy wrinkled his face at the thought of not being able to play the game by himself.

Armand continued. "You know Mama Dedé is very ill, right?"

Jimmy nodded. "I bwought her a cookie."

Armand smiled. "Indeed, and I'm sure she is very thankful for it. But, perhaps there is more we can do for her. Perhaps we can learn how to make her well."

"How?"

"By asking the board some questions. And if we're lucky, it may tell us how to help her."

Jimmy nodded his understanding.

"And who would bring her cookies after she gets well?"

Jimmy smiled sweetly and thumbed his chest. "Dis guy!"

"Indeed."

Armand had moved the lit candelabras closer to the board. The letters faced him and the planchette was set. Several pieces of blank paper and a pen sat nearby.

"Now, put your fingers here, like this. And remember, we each touch the puck with one hand, but because it's two *different* hands, neither of us can influence the magic of the board. That's the only way to get the right answer."

Jimmy wasn't sure about this game. It didn't sound very fun. But he did like magic, especially when someone would pull a rabbit out of a hat. Maybe he could ask the board later how to do that trick. Despite his skepticism, and with a surprisingly gentle touch, he set his fingers just right and watched intently.

Armand closed his eyes briefly, then opened them and spoke in low voice: "Is anyone here with us tonight?"

"I'm heah," Jimmy said, perplexed.

Armand sighed. "Master Jimmy, silence please. Just listen. And watch." He asked again. "Is anyone here with us tonight?"

Candlelight jumped from burning wicks and skittered up the walls. Candleflames seemed to bend away from the board with terrible anticipation. Soon, a halo of light hung around the two men and the library walls faded into darkness. Outside, shadows rustled the leaves and dry things.

Something had heard.

Something was coming.

The two men engaging with the talking board—unbeknownst to themselves—were perhaps the worst combination possible to employ the services of the device. One man, older and knowledgeable enough to open the door, had not the power—or desire—to close it. The other man, young and innocent, a gentle giant in his own mysterious way, had the power to control it, even wield it, but had not the capacity to understand how. This decision was a most unfortunate thing.

Mentally, Armand sent a signal to Jimmy to keep contact with the planchette. Jimmy waited patiently.

"I ask again. Is anything here which would like to come forward?"

Jimmy gasped as his eyes shot wide. Slowly he whispered, "It movin.'"

Before the night the Talking Board awoke, Armand lived in fear of very little. He'd always been fascinated by the strange powers of Mama Dedé and others, Del more than any. And he'd been determined to help them however he could. But during the session, as he watched the planchette move to his questions, a discomfort crept into him. He wasn't afraid of the benign spirit that was moving the puck—he was sure it was benign as he felt no malevolency from the thing—but a strange sort of disgust began to fall about him. A strange feeling that began deep within his stomach. Acid, at first. Then, as a worm of indigestion that crept up the soft tissue of his insides, exploring his hollow cavities. It filled him with poison. His throat convulsed, holding the acid down, and sweat broke across his forehead. Disgust. Nauseous with disgust. With so much suffering in the world, why couldn't these practitioners do more? With power at their fingertips *(right now at his!)*, why couldn't Mama D and Del do more to help the sufferers? Surely, he was experiencing just a bit, just a tiny fragment of the power they felt, but what he could feel was exhilarating. If he had a fraction of their power, what wonderful things he could do with it. He'd wield it justly, and evenly. He wouldn't hoard it, like some people did. He'd be benevolent. Not stingy. Not disgusting. Not jealous of others and their petty lives and torments and problems and wishes and falsehoods and—

"Ahman!" Jimmy yelled, pulling his hands away, sending the planchette sailing off the table.

"WHAT?" Armand dropped the pen he'd been holding as the planchette clattered to a stop on the floor. He looked around at the fading light of the candles; some had gone out. His head throbbed. His writing hand was cramped. Hours had seemingly passed in the blink of an eye. It was now late into the night.

"Ahman, I'm seepy."

"What? Oh." He looked around, bewildered. "Yes. Of course." He rubbed his aching hand and gathered the board. "My apologies, Master Jimmy. I had a rather strange daydream just then. Did we—?" Looking at his notes, he stopped and swallowed. "Oh my…" Letters were scribbled everywhere. But Armand had no memory of writing them.

"Night," Jimmy said. He hopped out of the chair and walked wearily down the hall.

Armand's words came from a distant part of his mind. "Yes… good night, Jimmy."

Hearing Jimmy's door close, Armand walked around the table and gently retrieved the planchette from the floor. The object looked different to him now; round on one side, like an orb of knowledge, then sloping to a point, as if designed for burrowing.

Burrowing? Why did he think of that?

He studied it closely, as if this was the first time seeing it. Such a harmless looking thing at first. He tried to remember from whom he'd purchased the board. It was many years ago and the person's face was a wisp of smoke to his memory now. He turned the planchette over, inspecting for damage, and as he did the candles flickered, casting a strange glow along the bottom of the puck. For an instant he saw lettering, strange tiny lettering cut into the bottom of the puck, utterly hidden from view.

He ran his fingers over the ancient lettering. How strange, he thought. He'd never seen these before. Who would put them here? A cold shiver ran up his spine. And to what purpose?

He placed the puck into the wooden box, closed the lid and poured some brandy. After a long drink, he stared down at the pages of notes and felt another sick wave wash over him.

It looked as if a madman had scribbled gibberish during a high fever. His cursive writing, having been done with one hand still on the puck, was nearly illegible due to the paper moving at random. It would take forever to decipher it. But one word was clear. It was printed. Over and over, until he'd torn through the paper.

Victor.

CHAPTER 16

At the sound of the single knock, Billy Bash quietly stood up from the yellow Formica kitchen table. Sliding the chrome-legged chair silently, he gave no indication to his occupancy. He listened, and when the agreed-upon double knock came next, he walked onto the heavily curtained back porch.

The bright yellow table, chromed chairs and heavy drapes had come to him from his grandmother when she'd passed the house to him in her will. The secretive knock was his own. He knew that people had an instinct, almost a compulsion, to knock two or three times, wait to hear noise, then knock rapidly again. That is, if they didn't lean on the buzzer like a noise maker. People were impatient to hear movement and bang away at doors, which is why Billy thought the use of one knock to signal a friend was a good code. Besides, having the discipline to wait, to deny the urge to knock rapidly, was a good trait to have. Discipline. The denying of urges. All good traits.

He looked out the side window of the back porch door, blue eyes under purple hair blinking back at him, peering through the dark. It was Rochelle. He opened the door quietly, stood aside, looked at the back alley for any nosy neighbors, then closed the door.

Carrying a brown paper bag, she entered the kitchen and sat the bag on the counter. "Got your suds," she said. "And a little surprise for us later."

Billy sat at the table and took inventory of her.

Rochelle, almost a foot shorter than Billy, was dressed for work, which meant she had very little on. Her legs and butt where that of a gymnast's, or perhaps a little girl dancer who'd stuck with it until the muscles had formed. Her stomach wasn't as flat as it'd always been, but halter tops still looked good on her. Her boobs where certainly not that of a gymnast's, but being top heavy helped in her current profession.

"Where's Terrance? I bought him a forty, so don't drink it."

"Why do you waste your money on him?" Billy asked, staring at her high heels. They were splitting at the bottom and one shoe had a mud stain on the side where she'd stepped in a puddle or wet yard. Her toes were probably dirty, he thought.

"Because he's nice to me and he's your friend," she said. "Why are you so mean to him?"

Billy looked at the sculpt of her calves. "He's not my friend. He's a junkie who flops on my couch."

Rochelle turned and stared at him. "He's trying to get clean and needs a hand."

Billy thought he saw a new scratch on her knee, or maybe dirt. Had she been working already?

"Where is he?" she asked again. In the back of her mind, she noted that Billy looked tired. Maybe he'd been working out too much. She liked the result of it, but whatever he was doing was wreaking havoc on the front of his legs. Had a barbell given him those scars?

Billy's mind started to drift. His eyes lost focus as thoughts and feelings swarmed him like gnats. Quietly, he said, "He's at his aunt's house. His cousin died."

"Oh no," she said. "Did you know him?"

"No," Billy lied. "Harold somebody. Probably a junkie."

"Why do you say that?" Rochelle turned back to the counter.

"Found him in an alley."

Billy stood and pushed up behind her, wrapping his arms tightly around her waist. He buried his face in her hair.

"Can you stay?" Billy whispered.

"Not now, Billy. You know that."

She finished unpacking the bag.

"I want you to stay," he said again. He pushed against her again and smelled a complex mix of perfume, cigarette smoke and sweat. She *had* already been working. His mind began to twist.

"OK, be a good boy now. Mama still has to work tonight. You'll get your surprise later."

That phrase.

Something about that phrase tweaked at Billy. It turned his insides. First in his stomach—it always started there—then it spread out in all directions, eventually reaching his mind. Once there, part of his mind wanted to regress while another part tried to come forward; a primal, complex part of him that he didn't understand. A pinprick of light, sleeping deep in his brain, awoke and raced forward.

He snuggled her tighter, pressing her against the counter.

"You smell so good," he said into the back of her hair. He licked her neck through her hair. She'd been sweating heavily already this evening, but now it was dry. She'd already been working but had taken the time to come see her boy. He licked her neck again, tasting salt, then down her shoulder. She'd recently smoked, trying to cover up the smell of sweat, but he didn't mind. He would clean her. His erection, coming on nearly instantaneously from the complex aroma, pressed against her through his boxers.

"And you feel good," she said, wiggly against him, "but I got to save some for the paying customers to—"

(tickle)

His hand came up under her skirt and groped at her thighs. He kneaded her hips with strong fingers. "OK, just wait a minute," she said. His other hand found her breasts hanging freely beneath her top. "Let me put this beer in the—" His shorts came down

(…for the tickle game…)

and her panties were pulled to one side. "Billy, wait a minute." The weight of his heavy chest pushed her forward. His tightly wrapped arms compressed her sides, squeezing her into a small bundle. She was warm. "Wait. Just let me get—" He pushed at her now, prodding, seeking passage. "Ow. Wait a second." He found entry. "Billy, let me get ready." Billy leaned into her, squeezed her tight with his arms and his mind went blank. He held her. He groped and thrusted. He waited for *The Red*.

(No biting Billy, just tickle me)

With eyes clenched tight, he thrusted, searching and hoping. He was waiting for The Red to find him, to enter his body where they were connected

(his tickler)

and to tunnel up from there into his stomach,

(that's a good boy)

and run along his spine. He felt safe in The Red. When he was very good, and The Red found him, it would split his mind in two, killing the bad things that lived there. So, he thrusted and held and groped and clawed… and whimpered.

He whimpered because he loved the tickle game. Loved it so very much.

A tunnel snaked out of The Red and began to burrow into his mind. It burrowed with a callous indifference to time, unaware of the urgency of need. He could feel the prickly ends of the tunnel catching hold of the soft folds of his brain. Prickly ends, like the barbs of a thousand fishhooks, needle sharp and delicious with pain. Soon the tunnel would latch onto his brain and pull him down, deep into The Red and kill the things in his head. He always felt warm and safe when the things were killed. Not cold or lonely or afraid of where he'd have to sleep. The Red protected him and tickled him and loved him and set his mind at ease against bad things. He knew they'd grow back. They always did, like a cancer. But for a while, he'd be safe. Just a little longer now. It was close. The tunnel was coming for him and would split his mind into the shards The Red needed to kill the things that lived there.

He loved the tickle game because that's how he'd found The Red. And he loved The Red so much… he wanted to eat it.

Rochelle twisted away, eyes wide, gasping for air. Leaning as far back as she could against the cold metal counter, she held her hand against Billy's chest, as hers pulled at the air. "What the fuck—" *(gasp)*, "is wrong with you," *(gasp)*, "Billy?" *(gasp)* "I couldn't breathe!"

She inhaled deeply, feeling her heartrate slow. "Didn't you hear me?"

Not yet! Billy thought. *Don't go!* A nervous little tap dance came out the soles of his feet. Toes twitching. He stared blankly as the tunnel abruptly pulled away from his mind, leaving it intact. There were no shards to wiggle through his brain and kill the cancers that were growing. He grabbed his head, pulling at his short hair and let out a pitiful moan. His brain itched from the inside.

Rochelle's voice faded into his ears.

With one hand on her chest, she held her right knee, with the other hand massaging it. "Ow. Then you bang the shit out of me on the counter, bust my knee on the cabinet door, and ask me if it tickles?"

Billy's eyes were far away. Unfocused. He knew she was talking but couldn't catch the meaning of the question.

Did she say, 'tickles?' He hadn't said that.

The red light in his brain was slowly fading. He wanted it to come back, to bring the tunnel back, but was also glad when it left. The Red always left him with a sick feeling in his stomach. Like he'd done something wrong as a child. His head would be better, but not his stomach. As if the dead cancers from his brain were dissolving in stomach acid.

He came back into focus and saw Rochelle standing there in the dimly lit kitchen, watching him. He looked down and saw his shorts around his ankles and his limp penis dripping semen. He didn't remember that part either.

"And who the hell where you whispering to? It sure wasn't me." She put weight on her knee and began to limp around the kitchen. "Well, this'll be a fun night of work. Next time just take me to the couch." She grabbed his square chin and stared up into his eyes. "And no more biting," she said through clenched teeth. "I'm serious. No one wants a prechewed meal." She pushed his face away and limped to the door. "Gotta go. Catch you later." Then added, "Maybe." She left the house the way she came in, through the back door.

The only difference this time was that Billy's shorts were still around his ankles and he swayed slightly, like a giant oak whose roots were tearing free from the ground.

CHAPTER 17

The next day, Armand sat at his worktable, sipping coffee. A dull ache throbbed in the back of his head and crept down his neck. Despite his headache, a roiling cloud of pipe smoke encircled his head. A restless night of sleep had dulled his senses, and he needed all the help he could get.

"The secret must be here somewhere," he said quietly. He didn't want to risk being overheard, although the other two people in the house were unlikely to comprehend what he was doing.

The letters he'd scribbled out the night before sat in front of him. A mad cacophony of clues thrown onto a page.

He stretched his back and walked around the table. Viewing the library shelves from a wide angle often helped him to remember a lost item or thought. Most of the words on the paper were legible now. He'd written a clean translation of them on another sheet. The problem was they made no sense. At least not yet.

Groups of words had begun to slide together like puzzle pieces. Words such as: *one death*, and *astral horde*. But the oddest was the phrase, *silver cord*. Armand felt he'd heard this term before. Then of course the mysterious name Victor written over and over.

His fingers began to dance on the air. With pipe hovering before his face, his eyes shone down the road of discovery. He strained to peer through the miasma that hung about him.

"Let's see…" He touched the table as if tapping piano keys. "Chord. Piano? No. Cord like rope. A horde… vermin? No. Why did you say 'vermin'?"

He walked to the bookshelves and ran his fingers over the leathery spines.

"A horde, harpsichord. A harp. Yes? Sunday school! No, not Sunday school. Sunday… church… Yes of course!"

His finger shot into the air.

"The Bible."

Grabbing a bible from the shelf, he returned to the other side of the table and faced the books. One last scan of the shelves convinced him he was on the right track. He opened the book and slowly scanned the pages. "Silver cord… silver cord… where is it?" Flipping into Ecclesiastes he scanned faster. "Yes, it's here somewhere. There!"

Ecclesiastes 12:

Remember Him before the silver cord is snapped
    and the golden bowl is crushed,
before the pitcher is shattered at the spring
    and the wheel is broken at the well,
before the dust returns to the ground from which it came
    and the spirit returns to God who gave it.

His hands fell to the tabletop.

Is this really what the spirit was referring to? Armand wondered. Some arcane Bible passage?

Remember him before the…

No. Armand reread the passage.

Remember Him *before the silver cord is snapped…*

…before the silver cord is snapped…

He looked at his notes, then back to the passage. He crossed out some translated words on his paper and rewrote them. He puffed at a dead pipe and felt the sting of dry ash on his tongue. He saw the message clearly for the first time. In response to his question of what ailed Mama Dedé, the spirit had given him this message:

Just one death she can afford,

to nourish heaven's astral horde.

False to pray, "Oh kingly lord,

"sever not her silver cord."

And the spirit signed it, Victor.

"Hallo."

"BWAHH!" Armand spun around, hands up, ready to defend himself against his attacker.

Frank stood at the top of the stairs, panting slightly. A look of bewilderment sliding down his face. "Ho-ly, hell. What's got you spooked?"

Armand's wild eyes slowly settled back into their sockets, but his hands flittered, searching for stability.

"Oh. Mon ami." Armand patted himself as if to ensure he was still in one piece. "My… you gave me a start, old friend." He walked back behind the worktable, patting objects as he went. "I say, I didn't hear you come in. I…"

"Ya think?" Frank said, eyeing him. "I called from da kitchen."

Armand quickly gathered up his papers. Seeing the wooden box on the table, he snatched it away and shoved it onto the lowest shelf, below the view of the table.

"The kitchen?" Armand muttered. "Is it lunchtime already?" He scooped the last of his notes together and hid them under a folder.

"Lunchtime? I just et breakfast. Hey, what da hell's eatin' you anyway?" Frank walked cautiously closer. "It don't take a detective to see—"

"Hi, Fwank," Jimmy said from the hall. "Is Deh home?"

Frank eyed Armand, letting him know he'd just escaped a serious grilling. "Hey der, Jimmy. No, she ain't home yet. But I'm gonna see what I can do 'bout dat."

"I deemed she came home." Jimmy headed for the stairs. "After we pwayed our game."

"Your game?" Frank watched Jimmy go past.

Armand interrupted. "Uh, that's fine, Master Jimmy. Run downstairs. I'll be along in a minute."

Jimmy's voice floated back, slightly annoyed that it wasn't obvious to Armand what he was doing. "I'm *goin'* down da stairs." Then it lowered to almost an afterthought. "Not 'posed to run down, yust *go* down…"

After Jimmy was clearly out of hearing range, Frank turned back to Armand. A long silence spread out between them.

Finally, Frank said, "I came by to see if ya wanted to take a spin in da car, now dat it's back, and talk about where Del might be."

Armand looked at his desk and began dismantling a stack of books. "Oh, well… that's very kind but…"

"But what?"

"But this… new… project… Did I not mention it? This new project

I'm working on… for the book, you see…"

"Da book?"

"Yes, yes, the book I've been meaning to write, that I've been researching, well… *was* researching, you know, before…" He nodded his head to one of the bedrooms at the back of the house. Mama Dedé's room. "Anyway, I've started it again," Armand lied. He stroked his beard and sent his gaze away from Frank. "Had to fill the time, you know." He shrugged and nodded. "So much of it on my hands, so, I've started it again. Would love to go, but… alas, perhaps another time."

"Uh huh."

Frank watched his friend's feeble attempt to rearrange the worktable to a point of confusion, in hopes of throwing Frank off the trail of his secret. Then he turned and started back down the stairs. "I hope you know what da hell yer doin.'"

Armand only nodded as his friend went out of sight.

CHAPTER 18

Somewhere in Lafayette Cemetery #1, across from a grand house with a stone maiden in the courtyard, a shadow moved.

The shadow wasn't formed by the absence of light. It was formed *out* of something.

The Scarmish thing slithered and slunk in its black tattered state and barely knew itself. It had been something else, once. It had lived as something other than a shadow, but could not recall its old form. It was starving and nearly depleted, but one thing had recently changed; it had become *aware*.

Yes, the Scarmish thing, having survived on cemetery rats, had begun to evolve. It still had little form. It survived on instinct, consuming things that squirmed in the shadows, but it had something the other shadows did not: it had thought. The black tattered shadow formerly known as Scarmish had begun to think, and more importantly, it remembered.

Black pools of tar.

Biting winds.

Dust.

A long journey.

Screams.

Twins.

Deep in a rat hole, where the carcasses of little pink sausages lay, discarded, a primordial lump began to form. One moment, it was nothing but dark shadow and angst, swirling upon itself, taking inventory of its own mass. Then, at a random moment in time, as the mass of shadow and dead rat bits and worm sludge and black crickets reached critical mass, a dark light sprung into existence, ebbing from the center of the shadow. It revealed form. The tiny lump could be considered an embryo in some ways, for it was now alive. But it hadn't been seeded like other life forms. This *Embryo of Scarmish* had been made from the occupants of a cemetery; the living things of a cemetery that gave up their life force to a black shadow. But the seeding of the embryo had taken more. The seeding of the black tattered shadow happened in a rat hole beneath the ground in a cemetery. It had happened in the world of the dead.

*

Somewhere, in another time and place, two pools of black tar, with faces like twin girls, began screaming at their final violation from the thing known as Scarmish.

*

Somewhere on a wall that stood in a singularly odd building no one could see, which was near the corner of Dauphine and Mandeville streets in the old Faubourg Marigny section of the Crescent City, a shadow moved.

The shadow wasn't formed by the absence of light. It was formed *out* of something.

And Madame Broussard felt the wall shudder beneath the path of the dark shadow.

She'd held a long vigil since the incident with Scarmish and the Spirit Hunter. The incident had put her hiding spot to the test—successfully—but also showed that in the end, there was a slight vulnerability. The incident put her face to face—in a way—with the beautiful young Spirit Hunter. The incident destroyed her most wonderful creation—Alvie. Trapped in her protective building, reliving the incident, watching her fresco wall that showed the movement of a world she could no longer participate in, she'd waited for this moment. Wondering. Anticipating? Perhaps. But always watching. Waiting and watching for the return of Scarmish.

And the shadow that had suddenly appeared on her fresco, that caused the wall to shudder, struck her like no other entity that traveled the Shadow Roads. It felt like Scarmish to her. But something was wrong.

Having spent the long, endless days repairing The Boy Made of String—Alvie's skeleton—she'd watched the world go by on her fresco walls. The beautiful moon tracked a familiar pattern, teasing the tides. The black sun slid lower in the sky—the year was heading toward October country after all. And the phantoms and spirits traveled the Shadow Roads, flitting from place to place with ultimate freedom. Hers was a bitter watch.

During the time, she'd verified the dark ring of shadows still lay in an unbroken circle around her hidden building—there was still no escape. She'd confirmed that the ring of white shadows—this was how she thought of them anyway—still surrounded the Spirit Hunter's home—it was still protected. And occasionally she'd glimpse something on the fresco that made her think of the Spirit Hunter. But oddly, she wasn't spending time at the house. These things occupied Madame Broussard's time while she tried to think of how to change her situation.

And if Scarmish truly had returned, her options had just improved.

CHAPTER 19

Friday afternoon Frank pulled his newly repaired 1953 Chevrolet Bel Air into the parking lot of the NOPD and parked in his old reserved space. Despite not having been on the force for many years, he still felt this particular spot—which was one of a few reserved for any detective—was his. Old habits weren't hard to break with Frank, with him they never broke, they petrified. His old habits were set in stone.

Frank absently scanned the radio dial looking for a ballgame. A newly lit lunch-cigar smoldered happily from the side of his mouth. Being that he was on the mend after his *bout of indigestion*—the same one that Armand annoyingly referred to as a near-fatal miss—and considering that he was walking more and had dropped several pounds, he felt no guilt in firing up this delicious Arturo Fuente Hemingway cigar. He considered this his go-to cigar, not too mild (breakfast) and not too spicy (late night), but just right. And, it was *after* noon technically, so, who was to care?

His wife, Faustine—but he called her Fawn—she would have cared. She always cared more for others.

Frank sighed and thought back through random memories of his wife. She had been gone for several years now, but he could still remember how the sun shone through her blonde hair, giving it a halo effect. They'd met at a county fair where Frank, having acted the fool trying to get her attention all day, finally screwed up the courage to ask her to dance, properly. After the dance, sipping lemonade out of earshot, but still within sight of the crowd, Fawn had said, "I was wondering when you'd come around. I knew you were different than those other boys. You just needed time to see it." And Frank floated home that day on wings of encouragement, gifted to him by his future wife. Fawn. Throughout the years she would give her special gift of encouragement freely and in abundance. And always at just the right time.

Frank came back to the present with the slam of a car door. He automatically brushed his shirt clean of errant ashes.

"Can't park there, sir," said the tall slender man who had just exited the car. "Reserved for NOPD. You'll have to move." And without another look, Detective Marcel Valcour, in his cleanly pressed suit, walked up the sidewalk and entered the police station.

Watching him from his car, Frank noticed something about the man. Almost imperceptibly, the man tugged at the side of his trousers as if his pants were too short.

*

Entering the police station a few minutes later, Frank poured himself a cup of coffee. This was done after asking if Haddie had made the coffee today. He hadn't. And the people in the know assured Frank there were no grounds in the bottom of the pot.

Knocking on Captain Allen Conroy's open door, Frank leaned his still-considerable weight against the frame and sipped.

"Frank," the captain said. "Good to see you."

"Cap'n." Frank tipped an invisible hat.

"What brings you in? Oh, and say, how's the…" Here, the captain tapped his chest lightly.

"Oh, dat's fine. Just some indigestion. Ya' know."

"Uh huh."

"Rearrangin' da place, I see."

"How's that?"

"Movin' some desks."

"Desks?" The captain looked around Frank through what was left of the door opening. "Oh. Your old desk. Yeah, about that, sorry Frank, had to make room for some new blood. You understand. And after the… bout of indigestion, well, I figured you'd be spendin' the rest of your retirement years on a fishin' boat or somethin'."

"No, I don't fi—"

"Excuse me." Detective Valcour squeezed past Frank into the captain's office. "Here's my latest report on the ra— uh," he glanced at Frank, "on the recent attacks and the items recovered. I'm still following several leads, but we did get a partial fingerprint from the…" he looked at Frank again, "from the item I spoke of earlier."

Captain Conroy took the report. "Thanks. Say, you might be interested in this fellow here." He motioned at Frank. "Detective Valcour, meet Detective… well, retired Detective Frank Morgan."

Marcel turned and shook Frank's hand. "Nice to meet you, sir. Did you used to work here?"

"Work here?" the captain said. "This here's Frank Morgan. Solved the Glapion murders a few years back."

Marcel showed no recognition of Frank from the parking lot, or of the famous murder case. Only a slight annoyance colored his face. "I'm sorry, which case?"

"The Glapion murders," the captain said. "Back in…?"

"Fifty-three," said Frank.

"Fifty-three?" Marcel said. "I was… fifteen then. Yeah, I guess I remember hearing something about that. Some kind of hocus-pocus killing, wasn't it?"

Frank straightened up to let Marcel pass. "Yeah, sum'pin like dat."

Then Marcel was gone as fast as he'd arrived.

"Sorry about that, Frank," the captain said. "These young guys nowadays, they just don't appreciate the days when… Well, you know."

"Oh, I know," said Frank. "But let me ask you sum'pin. What are dese attacks about he's workin'?"

"You lookin' for a case?"

"Not really."

"Well, that's good, because Marcel plays it by the book. At least as far as I can tell. He just got promoted and landed in my pond. Don't think he'd care to share anything."

"Dat's OK. I'm kinda on a… personal mission, anyway. Tryin' to figure where someone up and got to."

"A runaway?"

Frank shifted in the doorway. "Well… technically… No. I'm just snoopin' really."

"Well, whoever it is, hope they didn't get themselves off to Backatown. It's purty rough out there right now."

An old familiar sensation ran down Frank's spine. "Backatown, you say?" Frank knew the captain was referring to the part of the city closer to Lake Pontchartrain. *Uptown* was toward the river and included the standard downtown-type businesses of other cities. Backatown was old; industries and neighborhoods had already come and gone. Some highways went right past it, speeding off to greener pastures. It was a blue-collar area with low rents and lower morals. Backatown was dangerous.

"Yeah," the captain spoke quietly, "we got a damn serial rapist on the loose. A killer. You probably read about it in the papers. That's the case Marcel's workin'. He thinks the guy's operation is based out there. Somewhere."

"Talk about? Well, thanks Cap. Gotta run."

Frank turned and left. Before he even reached his car, he had a mental map of where he would start his search. He just hoped Del was nowhere near the area.

CHAPTER 20

On Friday afternoon, Armand sat at his worktable poring over old manuscripts. He had several piles of research, each one for a different topic.

Having just deciphered the cryptic message left by the spirit, he felt rejuvenated. The meaning of the message wasn't clear, but it was more than he'd had before. And he had a name.

Victor.

That was one pile of research. He was looking for evidence of a Victor who was associated with his grand old house, but had yet to find any. After that, any Victor of prominence from the area, but that was proving to be too wide a net. He knew—or at least thought he did—that the spirit from the board could have come from anywhere, but thought they stayed close to home. So, he continued to search.

A second pile consisted mainly of biblical references: the Bible, the *Researchers Guide to the Koran* by Abdul Ahmad, and miscellaneous other metaphysical writings about the soul. He was looking for more information on the Silver Cord.

Several theories existed about the cord. The ancient references had it linked to the soul in some way or other. And he'd found several references to it being snapped or broken at death. Some of the more creative theorists claimed it was a vital link during astral projection, even claiming they could see their own cord when having an out-of-body experience. He didn't know how credible these authors were, but in general understood it to be linked to one's higher self.

Then there was the third stack. It was smaller than the other two, and more suspect, but it was an idea that burrowed into his mind and would not leave him. He was intent on understanding the Ouija board better.

*

After Jimmy finished his breakfast, he washed his dishes and set them in the rack to dry. He looked around to see if there was anything else he could clean for Armand, but the house was too big to focus on one thing. He thought Armand might like a clean kitchen table, but didn't know what to do with the pile of books and papers he kept stacked on one side. There, the long side of the table had been pushed against the wall, which was good, because the wall kept the piles from falling over.

He thought about dusting the furniture for Armand and walked into the foyer. Very few people used this room, so Jimmy thought it probably didn't get dusty. The only time someone was in here was to use the stairs to go up to the library. Or to use the stairs to go back down. Armand used them to come down to his bedroom. But you didn't get dirty going to bed. In fact, you usually took a bath right before bed, and if you were clean straight out of the bath, and then went down the stairs, they couldn't get dirty either. So, Jimmy decided the stairs must be one of the cleanest things in the house.

He looked around for something to clean, and his eyes fell upon the parlor doors. They were standing open. They waited for him.

Jimmy felt something jump up in his stomach, like a tiny frog, and he suddenly didn't feel well. He swallowed hard, then took a few tentative steps towards the parlor. He didn't think he liked this room.

He remembered that this was Del's favorite room. She used to stay in here a lot when she lived here. She practiced her violin here and was able to make it sound like a screeching cat. She played games with Jimmy here, but he couldn't remember which ones. But he thought some bad things had happened here as well.

He stood outside the parlor, peeking around the door opening. He could see the couch where Del had spilled the shrimp. That's when she'd fibbed and told Mama D about a shrimp joke. He still didn't remember it and was pretty sure she never told it. Then he remembered that Del had flown up in the air in this room and knocked him down. She'd said it was an accident. But then a really bad thing happened

(…clackity-click-clack…)

and Jimmy shuddered as his stomach turned over.

What dat sound?

He looked around the foyer. Old faces stared down at him from the paintings. Nothing there to make a noise.

He peered further into the parlor, but didn't move any closer. He couldn't see anything moving in there. But he really needed to go to the bathroom now. With wide eyes, he searched the room, looking for a memory. Part of a song popped into his head.

(…I got no tings, to hoad me down…)

He shivered violently and backed away. He didn't know why, but he didn't like that song. Maybe some other boy, a bad one, had played a trick on him once with that song. He decided the parlor didn't need dusting either.

He'd go to the bathroom, then go outside.

He wanted to talk to the lady in the fountain.

*

Mama Dedé awoke, vaguely aware of her surroundings. She thought she'd heard footsteps earlier, and perhaps Jimmy's voice, but couldn't recall. She looked at the bedside table. There was a cookie, a small glass of milk and a tall glass of water. She watched her hand shake as it reached for the water. If she could just get her head to clear, she could figure out what was going on in the house.

Where was Del, anyway? She couldn't remember the last time they'd spoken. Was she in trouble?

She couldn't understand what she was feeling, but something had happened. Something was very wrong. She suspected it involved Del, which was why she had to get her strength back. The fool girl was probably messing with something she shouldn't be.

Or maybe the problem was with Frank. Was he out of the hospital yet? Had he gotten worse? She tried to remember but couldn't. How long had she been like this?

Straining, she managed to get a few sips of water. That was enough for now. She was tired.

She rolled over onto her other side and slipped back to sleep. She wasn't surprised when the worms poked their heads out of the wallpaper. She was getting used to them.

And she noticed that their holes were getting larger.

CHAPTER 21

Del spent the next morning trying to untangle her dreams. She'd slept later than usual, but still felt tired. It was getting harder to tell what was real—from this world—and what was from the other. She remembered coming home after meeting Arlo, getting into bed and trancing a bit. She was so tired at that point, she wasn't sure what she'd really done.

Was it possible to fall asleep while trancing? Mama D had never mentioned it, but there was a lot the woman hadn't told her, mostly for her own protection.

Was it possible to dream about trancing and actually do it? If so, would she get stuck and never wake up? Or would she spin forever in her own mind, like the time the Gris-gris man nearly trapped her?

With muddled thoughts, she ate a light breakfast and roamed the streets of the city. She thought maybe a walk would clear her head.

So much had happened over the last few days, she didn't know what to focus on. She felt like she was wandering around in circles, getting nowhere.

And she was. Because she didn't know her path. Arlo had told her that. Even the shadow-cat knew his path, apparently. But Del didn't. And that was why people got hurt around her. She didn't know it at first, but Arlo was right. What had the woman said? *You can't halfway folla' a path; you won't get anywhere. And you can't folla' no path, 'cause you'll end up where you doan wanna be.*

That's exactly what was happening now; she wasn't getting anywhere. And she had no idea where she'd end up.

After several minutes of aimless wandering, Del heard music and instinctively walked toward it. The Crescent City was flooded with music, but this was different. Low and somber, a lone trumpet lamented its anguish. Haunting notes floated the streets and back alleys. A trombone joined in, and Del heard the steady march of shoes; each one carrying a burden heavier than its owner. It was a funeral march.

As Del turned the corner, she saw the mourners walking straight toward her. The casket, riding in a glass carriage, was already past her, heading to the cemetery. The Grand Marshall, dressed in a black tuxedo with a gold sash worn at an angle across his chest, set the pace. Behind him, with matching gold jackets and sashes, the band walked somberly. Three trumpets, a trombone, a tuba and several types of drums where among them. When the lonesome call of the horns finished, the Grand Marshall began a call-and-response-style hymnal and several band members echoed him with voice or instrument. When that finished, the snare drum announced an increased time signature, and the band broke into a jazzier piece. The Marshall began a strut-walk, and the band mirrored his steps. Soon, the group of mourners began to move freely. Carrying photos of the deceased—a young woman, Del thought—with colorful flags, signs and ribbons, the funeral procession began to resemble a parade, celebrating the deceased's life instead of their death. Del was mesmerized by the spectacle.

Then she recognized the victim.

It was a photo held by a mourner.

That same photo had been in the newspaper just a few days ago.

The young woman had been the victim of the rape gang.

Del walked into the street and followed the mourner with the photo. She did this without thinking, but no one noticed, and no one cared. She'd just stepped into the secondline.

She'd heard of secondlines springing up during a funeral march before, but had never seen one. And had certainly never participated in one. But she was drawn in.

The secondline occurred when people unrelated to the deceased spontaneously followed the funeral march, dancing and enjoying the music. It wasn't considered disrespectful; it was just something people did. But Del wasn't dancing.

Her mind raced as she tried remembering the news article. How old had the woman been? Nearly the same age as herself, she thought. Del remembered thinking that it could have been her killed that night.

Then it all came back.

The night she'd been chased. That was the night this girl had been killed. She'd read it in the second edition of the paper the next day. She remembered running that night. Running for her life. Running into the alley. Then...

Then what?

She still couldn't remember that part. She just knew she woke up the next morning with a terrible feeling.

Maybe she'd avoided Death that night. But Death had simply

chosen another. Death must be greedy, she thought, for it would not be cheated.

"What'dya see?" Arlo asked.

Del flinched but kept her pace. Her numbed mind only partially registered the woman.

She didn't know how long Arlo had been there. She didn't know where she had come from. But in a way, Del wasn't surprised.

In a faraway voice, Del said, "I see someone who is dead, partially because of me."

"Bah!" Arlo waved the sentiment away. "Silly girl. You might have power, but you doan hold no cards over Death. He'd take you right here on da street if it pleased him, so doan go thinkin' dat girl's dead 'cause'ah you. 'Less'n you killed her."

Del sighed. "No. I didn't," she said, then added, "Why are you here?"

"I want to know what ya see."

Del realized the crowd had slowed. The mourners were filing into the St. Louis Cemetery #1 to lay the girl in her final resting place.

"I told you," Del began, "I only see—"

"What you want," Arlo interrupted. "But you not lookin' in da right place." With that, Arlo swiped her hand, and the air began to shimmer.

It wasn't a rip in the fabric that Del saw this time. For that she was grateful. But what she did see, hovering in the air in front of her, was a picture of sorts. It was as if reality was nothing more than a thin layer of dust on a window, and Arlo had just wiped it away. Del was looking through the dirty window of reality, into—she presumed—the world of the dead, and she saw a torn silver ribbon.

Time slowed around the women. The funeral procession filed into the cemetery or wandered away now that the music was finished. Arlo swiped again and more reality was wiped away. Del saw more of the ribbon.

Actually, she realized now, it wasn't really a ribbon, but something that looked like one. Like a tiny umbilical cord, only shiny. And very long. But it was ripped and hung together by a few thin threads.

"What is it?" Del whispered, then realized Arlo was guiding her into the cemetery. As if invisible, the two women moved through the crowd unhindered. The shiny cord always hovering just out of reach. They stopped in front of the girl's family crypt. Here, Del could see snippets of the cord floating above the stone roof.

Arlo said, "Da last essence of dat poor girl. She's trapped."

"Trapped? How?"

"See da cord?"

"I guess. What is it?"

"Dat's da soul's connection to da body." Arlo swiped a larger area clean. "Da spirit cord."

Del could see the ghost cord snaking its way into the crypt. And even though the door was now closed, and the cord passed down through the stone ceiling, she could see where it connected to the dead body. Somehow, she was seeing the outline of the body, but the part that was in the world of the dead.

"I don't… what am I looking at?" Del whispered.

"Dat's her spirit trying to break free da body. Look up."

Del followed the ghostly cord up from the body, where it was barely visible, through the air, where it hung together by shreds, and finally to the faintest image of the girl. She was floating far above the crypt.

"Is… is that her ghost?" Del asked.

The image of the girl flickered slightly, as if bad static washed her in and out of existence.

"Not yet. She's in a state worse than being a ghost. Or a lost spirit. She's an evernot."

Del didn't even question the woman. She could only stare at the ghostly figure who ebbed and waned.

Arlo continued. "An evernot is a type of spirit, of a person who died a bad death. An unnatural death. And she's stuck dat way. Her cord didn't dissolve. It got torn, but not complete. She can never rest like dat. She'll see her life pass before her over and over. She cain't tell if she's being born or dyin', their purt'near da same."

"What do you mean, her cord didn't dissolve?"

Arlo moved closer to the crypt, reaching for the cord, but it slipped away. "When you die a natural death, your spirit cord dissolves. Just like how you get cut loose your momma when you're born, you get cut loose your body when you die. Your spirit does, anyway. Then you can roam. But if you become an evernot..." She wrung her hands desperately.

"What? What happens if you become an evernot?"

Arlo looked at Del. "Best you don't know."

"Then why bring me here? Why show me this at all if you're not going to tell me everything?"

"To see how you choose."

Del felt sick. This was one of her tasks. "Choose what?"

"Would you help dis girl if you could?"

"Of course. But you already told me I didn't have the cards, or... whatever."

Arlo raised her hand slightly. "Oh, but you have dese cards."

"What? To bring her back to life?"

"No. Those cards, you don't have."

"Then what?"

"You can set her free."

"Set her—?" Del looked from Arlo to the spirit, then back. "Set her free, how?"

"You can sever da' cord."

Del's eyes went wide. She couldn't believe what she was hearing.

"Exactly how am I supposed to do that?"

"You have da sight. You just got to use it to see what you want."

"But I can't see the dead," Del retorted, "at least, not in this stage. Not without your help."

"Have you tried?" Arlo swiped her hand and the window into the dead disappeared. They were alone in the cemetery.

Del looked around, confused. "Where is everyone?"

"Dey gone home a long time ago."

Del's empty stomach rumbled. It was a hollow cavern. It must be late afternoon by now, she thought.

"Use your hand to pull back da veil." Arlo swiped, removing the thin dust of reality, then swiped again, replacing it. "Just a little."

The side of Del's mouth twisted, not hiding her disbelief. With a quick up-down-up swipe of her left hand, Del pawed at the air. Nothing happened.

"See?" said Del.

"Bah! You're not washin' a cow!" Arlo scolded. "Gentle. And use da utter hand." She grabbed Del's right hand and turned it palm up. Side by side, each woman's right palm was exposed. Arlo's, deeply wrinkled. Del's, smooth and unblemished. Except for one thing.

Del gasped. "What is that?"

Faint lines could be seen, just beneath her skin. It was if an old tattoo, barely visible, was trying to resurface on the palm of her hand.

She rubbed at it frantically, trying to get it off.

"It won't come off," Arlo said.

"What is it? What'd you do to me?"

"Do?" Arlo questioned. "I agreed to help you find yer path. Dat's our pact."

Still rubbing her palm, Del said, "Our pact? Etched on my hand? But how?"

"It's part ah knowin'." Arlo turned up both her palms and Del finally understood. Etched across the wrinkled palms of Arlo were the same faint cryptic scrawls that were on Del's own palm. Only many more. As Del watched, the lines came and went, as if cycling through a library of pacts the old woman had made.

Clenching her hand shut and pressing it against her stomach, Del whispered, "What are they?"

"As I said, dey're pacts," Arlo ran her fingers lightly over the lines, "and dey're knowin's."

"Knowings? What does that mean?"

"Think of them as… hints. In a way. To find yer path, you got to be able to see it, wherever it wants to go. You have da sight, but only some of it. Dat will help you see part ah da utter side."

Del thought back to when the two women had made their pact. Arlo had nearly dared her to make it.

Well… was that really true?

Perhaps not.

But she remembered grasping Arlo's hand so hard that it almost hurt. She thought it had simply been the woman's strong grip. But had it been something else? The moonlight was strange that night, at least for a little while. Had something happened during their handshake that put these lines on her? What had Arlo given her?

She opened her hand and looked at it. Only by turning it slightly could she imagine the lines were still there.

Arlo had been watching Del carefully. She thought she was ready. "Now see. Wit' dat hand."

Del held up her right hand and gently, slowly, pulled it down through the air.

Did she feel something? Fabric?

No. Maybe just the wind.

But maybe not.

As she dropped her hand, she stared at the space in front of her and concentrated. She blinked. Was something there? Maybe. Was she imagining a cord? Was her mind creating it for her?

Maybe that as well.

Was Arlo a crazy old bat who belonged in a nut house?

Well, if she was, Del probably belonged in there with her. So, she decided to just go with it.

She raised her hand again, but this time began a slow turn, looking around the cemetery. She hadn't realized it before, when following the crowd, but she'd been here before. The St. Louis Cemetery #1 is where she fought the Gris-gris man just a few months earlier. But it looked much different then, at night, with the torches and heavy mist from all the rain. Now, with her hand raised, and the air shimmering around it (something was trying to happen), she began to see *past* what was right before her.

She shuddered as a chill crawled up her back. She'd just turned towards the back of the cemetery, and realized that that's where it had happened.

The girl's family crypt was near the front of the cemetery, off to one side. The night she'd fought the Gris-gris man, she'd been further back in this cemetery where an odd space had opened up between the rows of crypts. At the very back, she remembered there was a double-sized crypt, supposedly that of the infamous Dr. John.

(*...and the void*)

Yes. And the void.

Looking through her blurry window—for she had to keep swiping to keep the vision going—she saw a myriad of images across the graveyard. Snippets of shapes and shadows that she didn't understand. And probably didn't want to know about. But as she looked at the over-sized crypt, she caught a strange image. And an old memory began to emerge.

That crypt with the gargoyle on it. Why does that feel familiar?

The larger crypts in this cemetery typically had stone crosses or praying angels on top. But this crypt, covered on one side by wild vines that had sprouted up through the stones, had a gargoyle on it. A very ugly one. And, it had something else.

She could only see part of the head above the other crypts, but a shimmer of light gave her a sense of motion. She scanned past the crypt, but from the corner of her eye she caught movement.

The gargoyle looked at her.

Snapping back to the crypt, she wiped the air again, thought she saw a glimmer of light around the head, and waited.

Nothing.

She looked back to the right.

Movement. Like a ghost coming out.

Back at the gargoyle.

Nothing.

If she kept this up, she'd drive herself crazy. But there was something about the gargoyle. Maybe she'd trance on it later, she thought.

Going back to Arlo's request, she completed her circular scan around the area, coming back to the girl's crypt. The picture was slightly better than before, which meant her vision was improving. She could see the cord—at least parts of it—floating in the air in front of her.

Arlo waited patiently.

"I see it," Del whispered, afraid of scaring the thing away.

"Good." Arlo's voice seemed to be coming from inside Del's head now. Very low. "Move toward it."

"How?"

"*See* yourself moving there."

See myself? Del thought. *Like in a trance?*

Holding the scene open to the other side was difficult. Del could feel herself getting tired. But to now have to trance into that scene seemed impossible. But Arlo seemed to think she could do it.

She flashed into a trance, seeing herself standing with her hand up. No cord.

She came out of her trance. The cord was floating right in front of her again, just on the other side of the air. In the other world.

"See it," Arlo spoke in her mind again.

Del swallowed and swiped. The image of the cord brightened slightly. She tranced, but slowly, somehow *barely* outside of herself. As if she was peeking out from behind a cover. She knew she was in a trance. She could feel it. And she could still see the cord! Somehow it was right in front of her. She'd done it!

"I'm here!" Del whispered. "I'm in. I can see it!"

Arlo smiled a knowing smile.

"Good," she said. "Now bite it."

Del wasn't sure she'd heard the woman correctly, and nearly lost the vision completely from the confusion that swept on her. Why would she want her to bite it?

The cord swayed as if floating on a summer breeze. As Del looked down upon the still body of the young woman, she saw that the cord didn't come out of one place in the body. It seemed to be attached to a bubble that lay around the body. The cord was free to move across the entire surface, and jumped from place to place like static electricity in a jar. She'd seen a science program once where electricity in a large glass cylinder would jump around—almost sliding—depending on where a person touched the side. And the girl's cord reminded her of that. But who was touching the sides of the dead girl, she wondered?

Now the cord had stretched and floated behind her, then around front again. Up into the air it went, where it disappeared into what could be a faint bit of mist. But Del felt it was something else.

She tried to trance into the mist, to see what was there, but nearly lost the whole scene. Was this the girl's soul she was seeing? Did the spirit know Del was trying to help? A faint flicker of light down the cord reminded her what Arlo had said. The girl wasn't even a ghost yet. The spirit hadn't been released. She was an evernot. Something in a constant state of flux, not knowing if you were being born or dying. What a terrible thought.

(Bite it)

Unsure if that was her own mind or Arlo's directions, she leaned toward the thing and sniffed. She didn't know what she thought she'd smell, but the thought of an umbilical cord brought the idea of an unpleasant odor. There was none.

She swallowed once, then edged closer, opening her mouth a bit. There were only a few strands at this part. They were tiny, like strands of hair wound together. Not knowing if she should touch it with her hands, she craned her head sideways, chasing the little threads. A cosmic wind rustled, and the thing floated within reach and bumped her lip. With the slightest nibble she bit down. Something cold and wet slid across her tongue with the faintest tingle. She started to gag. The tingle, like touching your tongue to the end of a battery, wasn't painful, just… unusual. The tiny jolt of energy made her throat want to convulse.

The cord didn't break. In fact, it felt a bit rubbery.

(Bite it.)

Fighting back a revulsion that lingered in the back of her throat, she opened her mouth again, clamped down on the cord threads and bit. She could feel the cord fighting her, squirming to get free. The cold, wet skin of the threads reminded her of a thick sausage casing. Chewy animal intestines with a slight battery acid coating.

She'd have to chew it apart.

Grinding her teeth, she felt the remaining cord strands come apart one by one. Each time they did, a tiny battery shock pricked her tongue. Her mouth began to water.

When the last strand broke, a brilliant flash of light shot out of her mouth, blinding her. She was thrown back in her trance as light filled her vision. The cord instantly retracted up into the mist cloud. The part that was connected to the body disintegrated in tiny sparks and flashes.

A long low sound, like the exhaling of a deep breath filled her head, *Aaaaahhhhhhhh…* and the mist disappeared.

She heard no more.

Her knees buckled, pulling her out of her trance, and she fell to the stone pathway. Turning her head to the side, she spit out the mass of saliva that had built in her mouth. The battery tingle was still there.

With watery eyes, she saw long strands of spit hanging from her mouth. They sparkled in the moonlight, and she pulled them away with trembling fingers.

"I did it!" Del said with weary pride. "Arlo, did you see—?"

Looking up and wiping her eyes, she realized it was late in the evening. She was alone. Arlo had left her.

Her stomach cramped and she bent forward, rocking in the cold shadows of the cemetery. It wasn't time for her period, so why did her stomach hurt so badly?

Moonlight reflected off her battery-spit with grayish-blue light. It foretold of many more cramping nights to come. Clutching her stomach, she fought the urge to vomit, and wiped the last of the phlegm from her lips.

As a cold wind dried the sweat on her forehead, she spit once more and shivered; the sick feeling had passed. But it was replaced by something else. Her body shivered again, but for a different reason. She looked up through the ancient crypts and could think of only one thing. What she needed now was food.

She was ravenous.

CHAPTER 22

Jimmy woke and looked around his room. The sun wasn't up, and he didn't hear any birds, so he knew it wasn't morning yet. But maybe it was *almost morning*. So, he sat up in bed. Rubbing his eyes, he looked around and listened. No sounds from the kitchen, so it probably wasn't *almost morning*, otherwise Armand would be making noise, and he'd probably smell breakfast cooking.

Maybe it was still nighttime? He liked the surprise of waking up during nighttime, because he hardly ever got to see it. He always went to bed before it, and woke after it, usually, so didn't know much about it. Except that sometimes it had monsters.

He listened to his room for monsters. And when he didn't hear any, he assumed they were asleep.

There was a certain sound he was listening for, some type of clicking sound that he thought monsters made, but he couldn't remember exactly how it went. But he was pretty sure a clicking-monster had been in his room before—at least in the house—but couldn't remember why he thought this.

He watched his train nightlight for movement—the one that was really a small lamp with a circular shade. A while back—when the clicking-monster was here—the lamp had gone crazy. One night it had begun to spin faster and faster and he thought the train—which was painted on the shade and reflected onto the wall—was going to leap off the wall, swallow him and burn him up in the engine. Somehow, he'd escaped the crazy train, but couldn't remember how. He wished he could remember more of these things. There were probably some important things in his brain. Maybe even how to find Del.

That thought intrigued him, but quickly passed. He was more interested in meeting nighttime.

He remembered being afraid of the dark when he and Del were at the orphanage. She'd always told him to be 'brave like a lion' when he was afraid of the dark, and 'quiet like a mouse' when they would sneak out of the window in the back room. But he'd never considered that nighttime could be fun. Or that there would come a time when he wouldn't be afraid of it at all.

And he certainly never considered that he could meet new friends here.

After the clicking-monster went away, around the time Jimmy had found the little girl in the trunk of the car, he'd stopped being afraid of the dark. It happened very fast: one day his lamp went crazy, the next day he wasn't afraid of the dark. Just like magic.

Some other things happened around that time, like when he dreamt he'd floated into Armand's room, or when some monsters ate Mama Dedé and the stone maiden told him stories, but he didn't think they had anything to do with his not being afraid.

So, with a new fascination for nighttime, Jimmy slipped out of bed, put on his Bugs Bunny house slippers and went out into the dark hall to make some new friends. The whole time whispering, *"bwave da 'ion'* and *'quiet da mouse, quiet da mouse.'*

Having spent several months exploring his new house—which was Armand's old one, but that seemed backwards somehow—Jimmy had made a game of trying to remember where the squeaks in the floors were. For some reason he was good at this game, and now walked silently down the hallway towards the library. He didn't want to wake the boards by making them squeak, so, he just didn't step on the squeaky parts.

Sitting down where the hall met the library, Jimmy looked around for his friends. Sometimes they were shy and didn't come out right away, but if he sat there long enough, *quiet da mouse*, they would come. Sometimes Spiky would come out first. That was the name Jimmy had given to the pointy shadow that showed him new and interesting things in the library. Jimmy had an idea that the big dome window that stuck out the roof of the house had something to do with when the shadows came out, but wasn't sure how they got from way up there to way down here on the floor unless they floated down each night. He'd never seen them float down, but then again, he'd never seen the wind, or the stone maiden's mouth move, but that didn't mean he couldn't feel the wind blowing or hear the stone maiden speak. So, he just assumed they came in through the dome window each night and waited for him.

Usually, Slinky came after Spiky. That was the shadow that showed Jimmy what to do with the objects Spiky pointed out. Slinky was funny and would squiggle around over things, often giving him the idea to pull on a knob or turn a latch. Slinky was smart like that.

But sometimes they both got chased away by the shadow known as the Bird Man. Jimmy didn't like when he came out. He was always mean to the other shadows—most of which didn't have names yet.

The Bird-Man-shadow would walk around on his stork legs, pecking with his long beak, like a crane in a swamp, looking for another shadow to eat. When he found one he liked, he'd pluck it with his beak, pull the rest up with his hands, wrestling it into his greedy mouth like a squirming fish, then gobble it down. Jimmy always closed his eyes at those times, and the shadows always stayed gone after the Bird Man came out.

But tonight, having a question on his mind, Jimmy didn't think the Bird Man would come out. Not that Jimmy could control what the shadows did—at least he'd never considered that—but he was pretty sure the Bird Man was away. And as far as Jimmy could tell, he didn't even interact with the shadow-world. It was as if each shadow had their own life to live, and Jimmy was simply watching them from far above. Sort of like God, maybe. Jimmy knew he could interrupt their passage if he turned on a light, but when he switched it off, the shadows where right back in their same place, doing the same things they were before he interrupted them. So, after a while he found it pointless to interfere. Besides, he couldn't have stopped the Bird Man from eating the others if he'd wanted to. When a shadow's time was up, it was just up, and the Bird Man came and ate it. No shining light from above could prevent that.

Watching for his friends, Jimmy thought about Del. He missed her very much and wished she was here. A twinkle ran across the floor and Jimmy looked up just in time to see a light shoot across the domed roof window.

A shooting star!

(Make a wish Jimmy and your dreams will come true.)

He closed his eyes tight and made his wish, but fearing it wouldn't come true if he let the secret out, he didn't even think it to himself. In an instant, it passed from his mind.

But it had been enough.

Just then, Spiky came out to show him the way.

Jimmy watched Spiky the Shadow creep across the floor. Maybe he slid. Or even floated. But he thought of it as creeping. He didn't consider how Spiky was moving. He just moved. Like a shadow should. Except for the Bird Man, who clearly walked.

Jimmy had just wished upon a shooting star. A very secret wish. And now Spiky had come out to show him something. Surely it was a way to make his wish come true.

Watching the shadow creep across the floor, Jimmy got on his hands and knees, ready to crawl after it. He knew better than to get too close. Sometimes, when he interfered with the light, it made the shadow stop, and he was anxious to find out what was next. But this shadow was over by Frank's chair, near the fireplace, and coming toward him, so he wouldn't have to crawl far.

The shadow stopped, as if unsure where to go. Jimmy had heard a branch scratching at a window just before this, but now he didn't. Maybe the wind had scared Spiky into stopping. Jimmy stayed quiet as a mouse.

After another gust of wind passed somewhere outside, the shadow began to move again. Soon, it had moved beneath Armand's worktable and was pointing towards the bottom of the bookshelves. Jimmy had watched Armand pull many books from these shelves. He especially liked when Armand rode the ladder from side to side while standing on it high up in the air. He'd stand on one foot while pushing the ladder with his other against the shelves. He never fell off or knocked a book over. But Jimmy had never really looked at the bottom shelves before. He just thought it was thick wood at the bottom where some old boxes and books were stacked. The more important books seemed to be stacked properly on the higher shelves. But now the shadow was pointing at something Jimmy had never seen before.

In the middle section of the library shelves, at the very bottom, where the wood looked like thick trim with fancy leaves carved into it, was a small cut covered in dust. In fact, it was a small square, about an inch in both directions, that had been cut into the trim. A small square that he could barely see even though he was on his hands and knees right in front of it. The dust and grime of Armand's shoes scuffing the trim had made the little square nearly disappear.

He wondered what it was.

As if in response to his question, Slinky appeared on the floor right were Spiky had been pointing. The shadow slid up the trim to the little box, then slipped inside.

It was a button! And the shadow wanted Jimmy to push it.

With sparkling eyes, Jimmy reached out his finger and pushed the square button that was cut into the trim. It slid in about a half an inch, and Jimmy heard a faint click. Then the hidden drawer released from its latch and popped open.

Slinky was somewhere inside the drawer, or maybe had gone home, because Jimmy couldn't see it any longer. But he didn't mind. He was too busy looking at all the neat things Armand kept here.

He knew what some things were: like the knife with jewels in its handle, and the pair of dice, but they looked old and lopsided. The dots didn't even look right. Then there was a deck of old cards. Big ones, with odd pictures drawn on them: stars and eyeballs and a hand, even a man hanging upside down. There were pages of books and several small glass jars with corks. Those all had gray powder in them. Then there was the long skinny box.

And Slinky was on it!

The shadow must have been hiding, or waiting for him to finish looking at the other things. But now Slinky was on the box and wanted Jimmy to open it.

Jimmy picked up the box carefully, not wanting to damage any of Armand's things, and held it in his lap. It was a wood box with designs painted on the edges. He flipped up the silver clasp, opened the lid… and gasped.

There was a hand inside!

The hand was as dark as polished wood and ended just below the wrist. The fingers were long and thin, curved slightly as if holding an apple. The fingernails were long and ragged. It looked like a carving.

Jimmy stuck out one finger and touched it.

Nothing happened.

He poked it again. Then three more times.

Nothing happened.

He picked it up with his right hand and looked at it closely. It didn't feel like wood. It was still hard, but not as hard as wood. And it felt squishy in a way.

Holding it up, he then held up his left hand for comparison. The thumbs were in the same direction. It didn't look like the hand he was holding it with, it looked like the other one, so he put it in the other hand. Now the thumbs went the same direction.

He wondered why Slinky wanted him to find this hand. Even if it was real, he couldn't find who it belonged to in order to give it back. He couldn't drive. So what use was it? And who lost their hand anyway? They must be more forgetful than he was to do that.

As he pondered this universal mystery, he noticed something else on the bottom shelf.

The Talking Board game.

Of course! Now it made sense. Armand had told him that he couldn't play the game alone. He'd needed Jimmy to touch the puck too, or the game wouldn't answer his questions. But now that Jimmy had another hand, he could play the game by himself.

His wish was coming true.

He'd thought of a way to find out what was wrong with Mama Dedé. And maybe he'd even find Del!

And Slinky wanted to play.

Jimmy took the Ouija board out of its box and sat it on the floor beneath Armand's table. He put the puck in the center of the board and held up the severed hand. Scrunching his face, he searched for the words Armand had spoken to start the game.

"Tawk," he whispered.

Nothing happened.

His face sagged in disappointment.

"Move," he said. A slight tinge of optimism colored this command.

The puck sat silent.

"Hhggrrr," he grumbled under his breath.

Absently, Jimmy scratched his head with his left hand. He always did this because his right hand had to stay free to catch butterflies and such. The fact that the dead man's hand was still in his left didn't occur to him. It scratched his head just fine.

"'Tupid head, come on…" He tapped his skull. "Come on…"

Then, just like that, an idea came to him. His face stretched up in a smile and his eyes began to gleam. Jimmy leaned close to the board, put both his hands on the puck and spoke.

"Come out, come out, wheneveh you are…"

And something came.

CHAPTER 23

Late Saturday morning Del burst through the door of The Hidden Note jazz club. She was sweaty and disheveled, having run most of the way to work. Not only had she slept late, but she'd completely missed her shift the night before. The day-long activities with Arlo in the cemetery had consumed her, and when she came out of her trance, she'd completely forgotten what day it was and that she was supposed to be at work.

The club was set to open for lunch in twenty minutes and she still had to setup her station. Being the new girl, she had to work several opening lunch shifts, which meant she had to take all the chairs off the tables and prep the floor for the lunch crowd. She'd also be the only waitress on the floor for the first hour until the lunch crowd grew.

"Well, if it ain't da magic cooty dat come to grace us," said Tasha. She was standing behind the bar drinking coffee. She was the daytime bartender on the weekends.

Del's heart sank a little. She was really hoping that Jonesy would be on today, considering she was probably in trouble for missing her shift the night before.

"Hi, Tasha," Del said, not looking at her. She began pulling chairs off tables, two at a time.

"I guess da cooty business is good, huh? Too busy to come in on Fridays now?"

Apparently, Tasha had been scheduled last night and knew Del hadn't showed.

"Grant was pretty pissed last night. You not showin' an' all. Said he oughta fire you fer not showin'. But I covered just fine. Made a killin'."

Del knew she'd have to talk to the manager, Grant, and explain why she'd missed her shift.

"I was sick," Del said quietly, and continued working.

Tasha continued, "Yeah, dat's what Jonesy told him. I don't know why he sticks his nose in it. But I told Grant you was probably working another bar."

Del shot back. "I was not!"

Tasha smirked over her coffee cup and shrugged.

"Like I said, I was sick."

"Yeah, all dem babies crawlin' up in dat cooty, I 'spect."

Del shook her head and went back to work. It was going to be a long day.

*

By the end of her shift, Del felt better. The start of the day was rough, considering her first customers walked in while she was still setting up. There was no help from Tasha, but she hadn't expected any. She'd managed to grab a few bites of lunch in between customers, but wasn't overly hungry. After leaving the cemetery the night before, she'd gorged at an all-night diner. In fact, she couldn't remember the last time she'd eaten so much. After the large meal, she'd fallen into the deepest sleep she could remember, which was why she was late. But once she found her rhythm, the day had gone exceedingly well. In fact, she'd made more during lunch than she had the last night she'd worked.

Tasha fumed all day.

Saturday lunch eaters typically were *lunch drinkers* and stayed at the bar. But today most of them sat at one of Del's tables. And everything fell into place. The timing of customers was just right, always filling an open table just as she had time to take a new order. The food came out just at the right time. Her jokes were polite enough for the old women's club, and snarky enough for the men working on Saturday. And she glowed.

Not one for wearing makeup, Del didn't spend much time looking in the mirror, but during a quick bathroom break, she was surprised by what she saw. Her skin was practically glowing. Her eyes seemed brighter than usual. Her skin was smooth and lush. And her hair, as crazy as it was from her run to work, had the look of a styled wildness. All combined, she looked quite exotic.

And the customers noticed.

She'd stopped counting the number of compliments she'd received during the day, from men and women alike. A couple of the city workers who lunched there regularly had tried to get her phone number, but she was too embarrassed to tell them that the only number she had would ring in the common room of a tenement house, so she coyly blew them off. She made a mental note to think about eating a late dinner more often. She was full of energy from her late-night eating binge.

So she enjoyed the day, took the compliments in stride, and

occasionally she wondered what Johnathan from the Ice Cream Emporium was doing.

After her shift, she spoke with her manager, and explained away the absence. Whether it was due to her radiant energy or simply good luck, he didn't have much to say about it. Feeling better than she had in a long time, Del left the bar with a feeling of happiness and let herself wonder about the events from last night.

What did those things have to do with her path? Or her future? Had she made a mistake getting involved with Arlo? Had it been a coincidence that she'd even seen her at the funeral? Del hadn't planned on attending it, so there was no way Arlo could have read her mind. Had it been destiny? She didn't believe in that anyway. She preferred to think she had control over her actions. But she hadn't had a choice in being born with this gift, had she? No. She knew that. But she *could* choose not to use it. Well... that time was probably gone now. She slipped in and out of trances so easily, sometimes she didn't realize she was doing it. And she didn't think she could stop it now, even if she wanted to.

As proof to herself of this fact, she picked a random person on the sidewalk and flashed into the movie reel of their life. She was taking the long way back to her apartment and had time to kill as she meandered through the streets. The scene she was inspecting was the immediate space around her, which had the people from the sidewalk in it, but she was focused on one person. She saw them as they were at this moment, then as they were a few seconds before that, then a few seconds before that. She could have followed them like this, backwards, for as long as she wanted. Or could she? She'd never thought about how far back she could really go. Earlier in the summer, when looking for the missing kids, she'd followed Spider's drive, backwards, for several miles, but that was a relatively short period of time. After that, she'd followed the skeleton boy—Alvie was his name, or had been—backwards through his spirit tunnel, but there was no way to measure the distance. However, the time had been nearly instantaneous, she thought.

She focused on someone else. A little girl had just come out of a shop with her mother. Del could feel her sadness, although the girl hid it on her face. Two minutes earlier, Del could see, the girl had asked her mother for something and was told no. The girl had wanted the trinket very badly and had even produced tears, but her mother had stood firm.

Del suddenly wondered if her own mother would have done the same thing. Funny, she couldn't remember anything about her mother. It was as if the fire that killed her parents had erased her memory of them. Was it possible to look far enough back into her own past to see them? Or to see what had caused the fire?

She shivered at the implication, despite the warm day. Looking into one's own past seemed like a bad idea, but she couldn't believe it hadn't crossed her mind before now.

Del's attention jumped to a man just ahead of her on the sidewalk. A man in a suit. His thoughts were gray and moody.

She'd never realized thoughts had color. She knew auras did because she could see the color of when someone else had been trancing on a scene that she was looking at. But at this moment she felt she was seeing, in her trance, the color of his thoughts. And they were getting darker.

Like watching gray storm clouds twist themselves into a black thunderhead, Del watched the man's thoughts coil until they gained mass. A deadly cloud of hatred.

Del followed the man from several feet behind. She was trying to trace his movements backwards, from where she'd picked up his trail, to see what may have caused the man to be angry. But he was walking fast now, and it was hard concentrating on his backwards path as she moved forward. But his thoughts had already gone to charcoal-gray. And they were swirling. Roiling. Like water in a pot that was about to boil. He turned suddenly and went down the short drive of a house. Two seconds ago, he'd decided he would kill someone, and Del had just read that scene.

Stopping dead in her tracks, she stood in the middle of the sidewalk, wondering what to do.

CHAPTER 24

By Saturday afternoon Billy was in a fever. Literally.

He hadn't seen Rochelle since Thursday night when she'd stopped by before her long line of customers took over. There in the kitchen, with her musky smell of sweat and cigarette smoke, she'd said something to him, an old catch phrase, that tickled him. But to save his life, he couldn't remember what it was. And that caused him to itch.

The itch always started in his brain. It was a type of cancer, he thought. A type that could be killed—for a while—but that always grew back. He was pretty sure he'd had it as a kid. And there was some type of therapy that had made it go away. At least, that's what he thought. But he could never remember the details.

What he did remember—because it was happening more frequently—was that the itch would start in his brain, but very soon it crawled down his throat and settled in his stomach. By the time it got there, his brain would be on fire, waiting for The Red to appear. The Red was the only thing that could kill the cancer and make the itch go away. But his body would suffer terribly until it did. When the itch got to his stomach, it quickly spread out through his blood vessels, infecting every part of him. His skin would tingle with goosebumps, twisting his nipples into hard knots—he always looked like he was cold. But his armpits would leak streams of sweat, trying to excrete the virus—he always looked like he was hot. The bottom of his feet would itch, and his toes would dance uncontrollably—he always looked like he needed to pee. And his penis always stood erect, trying to escape the itch that was crawling just beneath the skin—and he always looked like a freak. The few memories he had of being in a group of kids— he didn't know where these memories occurred, there was never a house—always ended the same way, regardless of if he was on a ball field, a playground or a gymnasium. They ended with him squirming in his clothes, underarms sopping wet and one secretion or another darkening the front of his shorts.

Sometimes strenuous workouts helped to dampen the itch when it came. He'd learned that from the many times he'd run home

(to no home)

and lay exhausted

(somewhere)

panting and sweating. The fever-itch having died for a while.

But when had he found The Red? If he could only remember. That solved the problem better than anything, even better than masturbation. In fact, trying to take care of the problem himself only seemed to make it worse. Which was why he was in a literal fever today. He'd almost found The Red in the kitchen with Rochelle the other night, but she'd pulled away too soon, saying she'd bitten something.

Was that what she'd said? She'd bitten something and couldn't breathe?

Whatever the problem had been, The Red hadn't come. The itch had stayed. The fever had increased. And now he was stalking his grandmother's gifted house, naked and sweaty, with an erection leading him from room to room while he looked for something to bash his own head in with.

*

When Terrance entered the back porch, he peeked through the window at the one slit where the curtains always separated. He preferred to complete his task, which today was simply bringing groceries in, then high tail it right back out. Billy was starting to go sideways.

When he looked in, he glimpsed Billy striding naked from the kitchen to the front of the house, pulling at his hair and ears. It looked like the fever was back again.

He scratched his arm absently, vaguely thinking about wanting another fix, but actively thinking about checking himself into rehab. He didn't know how long he could survive in this place. Granted, Billy's couch had gotten him off the street. Sort of. But he was paying a steep price.

The errands he was fine with. Those actually made him feel like a real person and sometimes he imagined he had a real job and house when he did them. People didn't look at you like a junkie when you carried grocery bags home. Sometimes he would prop up the Wonder bread so the tied end stuck out the top of the paper bag. This way people would see that it wasn't just beer in the bag, or something worse. Most times people would look away from him, avoiding his gaze; he still had the haggard look of a street person. But on occasion, with his Wonder bread sticking up, he'd catch a grandmother's eye and nod at her, pretending to be bringing home the bacon to a young family who depended on him. And sometimes the grandmother would even nod back with a slight smile, thinking how nice he must be.

But he had other errands to run and prices to pay. And a grandmother simply couldn't understand these things.

His primary task—the one that kept the household running—was being Billy's mule. Out of all the small-time drug distributers Terrance had known, Billy was the only one who didn't use his own product. At least as far as Terrance could tell. But T-bone loved it. Terrance was the dumbass who had tried it—at the urging of Harold, his cousin—but T-bone latched onto that addiction and protected it like a miser. More than once, Terrance had planned to kick T-bone to the curb, throw him out, excise him with holy water, even turn him into the cops. But T-bone was one weaselly son-of-a-bitch. And he was easy to hypnotize. And Billy knew that.

The first time Billy had dangled a baggy in front of T-bone, T was hypnotized and followed him home like a puppy. The first time Billy had balanced the baggy on his boxer shorts and showed him the *up and down*, T was hypnotized again. Juice was juice, however you mixed it. Besides, it was Terrance's mouth that did the work. T just sat back in the shadows and waited for the surprise at the end. Terrance took his juice, so T could get his. After all, nobody rides for free.

But Billy had his own addiction. And with it came the most difficult task of all. On the few nights where he had a clear head, Terrance and T-bone would argue silently over whose fault it was, and which of the two of them had made the decision to help Billy. Terrance blamed T because… well, you always blamed the junkie. T blamed Terrance because… well, he was the one who had started them down this road in the first place. But if they got caught and sent to the electric chair, the state of Louisiana would get a two-for-one special. One body frying in the chair, while two warring personalities went up in smoke.

Because ultimately, they were from the same mind.

Worst-case outcome aside, neither Terrance nor T had known about Billy's addiction when they met him. They didn't know what triggered it. They only knew that when the fever set in, they—as one person—became part of the hunting pack. Harold had eventually become the third, mostly at T-bone's urging. But neither Terrance nor Harold had ever participated in… the prize. That was reserved solely for Billy. Terrance and Harold simply flanked the prey, watched for cops, pretended not to see, and waited for the juice. That was the price they paid.

Unlocking the back door with the hidden key, he walked in and quickly began putting away the grocery items.

Billy heard him immediately.

Quick, meaty footsteps came down the hall toward Terrance. He saw that within the last few minutes—fortunately for him—Billy had found his boxers and put them on. His blonde hair still stuck out from the pulling, but the fever seemed to be waning; Billy looked only half crazy.

"Where were you last night?" Billy asked.

Terrance looked around the kitchen as if the answer was written on the dingy cabinets. "Last night? I was at Harold's mama's house. Some of my other cousins came in and—"

"You missed your pickup."

Terrance blinked absently. "My pickup? Naw man, Friday nights is—"

"Harold's dead, dumbass," said Billy. "That means it's your pickup now."

"Aww, man. I'm sorry Billy. I didn't even think about— you know, with the funeral and all."

"Well maybe you'd remember better if this went away." Like a hypnotist's watch, a baggie came out of the waist band of Billy's boxer shorts and dangled in the air. Errant light reflected off the plastic baggie, whispering to Terrance from across the room.

From deep inside Terrance's head, T-bone awoke from a slumber and peered through eyes that wanted to look away but couldn't. Terrance wanted Billy to put the bag away and never bring it out again. And as if he'd wished it into his mind, Billy slipped the baggie back into his waist band.

Now T-bone was fully awake. Watching the juice come and go so quickly was painful and mesmerizing all at once. T wondered what tricks he'd have to play to make it reappear.

"Are you listening?" Billy said again.

Terrance snapped forward. "What? Sorry, I was thinking about—"

"I said, it doesn't matter that you're a fuckup, because I made the pickup AND some of the rounds."

Terrance nodded that he was tracking the conversation, but T-bone was on the lookout for the baggie.

"And guess what else?"

Terrance's head was still nodding when he realized he'd been asked a question. His wide eyes blinked in confusion, looking for an answer.

"I think I found the witch."

Slow realization dawned across Terrance's face.

Billy nodded. "That's right. The witch that killed Harold? The one that got away?"

"But how?"

"This chick over at The Note. She's wanting to start moving a bit of—" And here Billy rubbed his fingers together, indicating the baggie in his waist band.

"The Note?"

"The Hidden Note, dumbass. The jazz place with the bad rock cover bands. You know… fuck, never mind. That chick Tasha was bitchin' up a storm when I dropped in. Said some new waitress didn't show up for her shift and she was tired of slingin' drinks. Wants in on the action. Was sayin' this new gal was layin' down some hoodoo on the customers and stealin' her tips. Sellin' her magic cooty. Shit like that."

Terrance cautiously ventured a thought. "But… you don't believe—"

"What? The hoodoo crap? That's not the point. The Note is what? Eight or ten blocks from where Harold bit it? We saw that gal walking home after a bar shift. I guarantee it. Practically on the same damn street as The Note. Don't you want to get revenge for what she did to Harold?"

A distant, troubling thought crept into Terrance's head: that a reckoning was coming.

With this new girl Tasha entering the scene, AND wanting in on the business, what would she do to learn the ropes? Would he keep his place on the couch or be cast back to the streets? Surely, she could offer Billy more than he could, or would want to.

And if this other gal really was the one who'd escaped, was she really a witch? If so, had his cousin Harold fallen victim to her hoodoo that night in the alley?

Then, like seeing his own shooting star to wish on, with all this commotion consuming Billy's life, he wondered if this was his chance to escape this lifestyle. Was it actually possible? Would T-bone even let him?

Terrance wanted to pull his own hair out to eliminate the possibilities. He felt a bad situation was rolling down the street at them, and he didn't know how to get out of the way.

*

As Billy paced the kitchen, he assessed these developments differently. He wasn't wondering at that moment when Rochelle would come back; he assumed she would, though. He wasn't thinking about Tasha wanting to get into the business; those people came and went like the tide. He was considering the possibility of this other gal actually having some type of power. Magic cooty aside, she had escaped them. There had been a strange flash of light and Harold had died from something. Tasha seemed to think she was hexing people.
Maybe she was.

Maybe she was everything they thought, and more.

Magic cooty considered…

Maybe she was a way to find The Red.

Maybe she could kill his cancer forever.

The particles of his itching, feverish brain began to move. Like metal shavings vibrating to a magnetic wave, their random directions began to align.

He'd found a True North.

CHAPTER 25

After a long day of chasing butterflies and stomping on black crickets, Jimmy made his way into the dark coolness of the house. He wished Del could have been here to play with him, but she was far away on some magical journey.

All day he'd thought about her. First, at breakfast, when he'd tried to make a pancake face of Del to remind himself what she looked like—but it looked kind of weird. He remembered that sometimes she looked a little mean, like the pancake—and her hair didn't look like that all—but he was happy to think about her.

And then to eat the pancake.

Then he thought of her when he sat on the back porch in the wooden rocking chair. He'd tried to see how far he could rock without falling out—but fell out anyway. That had reminded him of when Del fell out of the chair once when he'd bumped into it. Finally, he went around watering the flowers they both had planted for Armand. He tried to count the bees that were visiting the flowers, but they wouldn't hold still long enough—and they flew around in crazy circles which messed up his count—so he decided there must be nineteen of them. Thankfully another bee didn't fly up and join the pack, because he wasn't sure what the next number was, but nineteen struck a special chord with him.

After all the yard work, which included digging for worms, he washed his hands in the fountain and talked to the lady in the water for a while.

She'd been quiet for a long time—probably something like nineteen days, which may have been the cause of the same number of bees showing up—but yesterday she woke up.

He didn't really think she was *in* the water—he couldn't see her after all—but her voice was. Along with another one.

He had a vague memory of another voice that had called him from beneath the water—a bad one. It seemed like a dream, but he didn't remember much of it. Regardless, the stone maiden had scared it away earlier in the summer, which is why he felt safe to sit here and listen to her secrets.

Long hours they spent in the sun, Jimmy gazing into the water, her voice rippling across the surface in soft whispers. Secrets had to be told in whispers, Jimmy thought, otherwise they got away.

He learned many things about Del on these long, hot days. After her stories were told, Jimmy would go into the house, drink some lemonade, and fall asleep on Del's favorite couch in the library. Here, during afternoon cat naps, he dreamed of Del.

Today, having laid down on the same couch, after hearing more whispered secrets from the lady, he dreamed of Del again.

In his dream he was a butterfly who had just left Armand's garden. The warm wind lifted him above the walls, and he floated away on a summer's breeze. He skipped and jumped the air, in a chaotic way, like butterflies do when they're surfing the wind on gossamer wings as big as kites. He'd suddenly grown large. His eyes had multiplied and now he could see all the colors of the rainbow, and new, secret colors that were beyond its edges. He scanned the world, looking for Del. His new eyes saw things he'd never seen before. Strange colors swirled in the air, sinking down to the ground, then shooting high up through the clouds. People glowed to him now, like flowers did to butterflies. He could see good people and bad people and some whose colors were fading and others whose colors were bright. Surely he'd be able to find Del like this. He just had to keep looking.

A cold wind brushed his wings and a shadow fell over him. Something was flying above him. Looking up with his special eyes, he saw a shape—a small bird perhaps—floating on high winds. He wondered how a bird could fly so high, and if he could get up to meet it. But something was wrong with the sky up there. Jimmy saw the light of the sun distort. It seemed to bend around the black bird shape and shrink away. It was a cold shadow.

Then the bird screeched, and a pinpoint of pain shot into his head. Although the bird was far away, its voice was loud. It screeched again and again.

Then the bird dove.

Jimmy thought it meant to eat him and he flapped his wings as hard as he could to escape. In an instant, the bird had grown ten times in size, with a mouth as big as a car. Its black beak glinted in the sun and red beams came out of its eyes, searching the ground.

It was hungry.

As big as an airplane now, the bird screeched again, and the sky shook with a terrible sound. Jimmy tried to cover his ears, but his hands were gone. All he could do was stay afloat and wait. The red beams pulsing from its eyes had locked onto a target. Far below them, someone was dealing with death. And the bird had come to claim them.

The giant bird sailed toward Jimmy and a hurricane wind rushed out before it. His butterfly eyes saw the air warp and compress.

Falcon.

The word came to him. He could see it now, just for an instant. Black as night. Sleek. Wings of bone. Dead, but not dead. Feathers of skin, like a bat's wing. Leathery and torn. Ancient. Tongue protruding, dry and scaly. Eyes bulging red. Screaming. Body empty. Hungry. Hollow. Forever. Ravenous death.

Beneath its body hung two claws with scarred talons, midnight blue, chipped, razor sharp. One claw carried the dead; a thousand, thousand faces, clutched tight between three front talons and the backward facing hallux, compressed into the very keratin that grew the talons.

The other claw was open, but no less deadly. Behind it, snagged on the hallux, trailed threads and ribbons of the life forces of people who had barely escaped death. Like decaying intestines, pulled violently—and often unexpectedly—from the body, the life threads of a thousand, thousand others hung as a grim reminder that the talon finds us all, in time. Jimmy's eyes saw these things, understood them, then saw too much. From the nearly severed life-threads—still connected to the barely living—hung the agonized faces of their owners. The distorted, gray, melting faces of the nearly-dead streamed from the life-threads like the vanishing smoke of a fire. And in this smoke, Jimmy saw Mama Dedé's face. And he screamed.

The falcon exploded past him, and the wind tore at his fragile wings. He screamed and tumbled over and around and felt pieces of his wings tear loose. The force was too great. His wings were disintegrating.

As Jimmy fell from the sky, he saw the bird of death far below him. Its red eyes had found its target. It was in a full dive. It was close.

It was hunting Del.

CHAPTER 26

el had only seconds to act.

Not knowing how long she'd been standing in the middle of the sidewalk, she didn't realize she was drawing attention to herself. People bumped into her or had to scoot around her, and she didn't seem to notice. To them, she seemed not to care. But that was far from the truth.

In her mind, she was trancing in all directions, and in this state, the creatures of the dead saw her very well.

Backwards, forwards, around the house, to the person inside, she tranced trying to understand what was about to happen. The man had already opened the side door. He had a key. A woman was screaming.

Del's mind was overwhelmed. She felt herself falling, losing balance, and snapped back from her trance just in time to keep herself from crashing into a chain link fence on her right. She steadied herself on the fence and let it lead her up to the yard of the murder house. She took several steps into the single lane driveway with wild grass running down the center and collapsed.

With legs folded beneath her, leaning against the fence, she tranced back through the house looking for the man in the suit with the dark thoughts. And a darkly dreaming part of her mind awoke.

The house was small but tidy. A kettle boiled on the stove. An oscillating fan blew humid air through an even hotter room. A woman cowered in the bathroom, desperately trying to dial the police on a phone with a cord that had already been ripped from the wall. She couldn't understand why there was no dial tone.

Familiar with the neighborhood—this was his home after all—the man pulled a knife, instead of his gun. He knew the windows would be open and couldn't risk a shot being heard. Then he began to kick in the bathroom door.

Del saw everything at once and drank it in like a drug.

Moving backwards and forwards through the movie reels of these people's lives, Del saw when they met. Saw the brief period of courting and aggressive sex from them both. She saw drunken nights and flirting. Neither was faithful, but he was worse. Neither was honest, but he was hurtful. Both hit from time to time. The woman screamed and scratched. The man yelled, slapped and punched. She slept with his friend. He brought his knife.

She saw the hatred from them both. Each was terrified in their own way. Each had wished the other dead at times. Wished they'd done things differently and that life hadn't been so unfair to them. They cursed the fate of their stars, having brought bad luck and misfortune to them. They never considered their own actions had contributed to this pivotal moment. They both cursed each other. But only one was afraid of being killed. The other had brought his knife.

The door broke.

Del flashed into the room and saw—or imagined she saw—different futures for both people.

The woman had a real chance of dying in the next few seconds, along with her unborn child. She didn't know who the father was. She had a future where she was horribly disfigured, with deep scars and one ear missing. Other futures were possible but fading fast. Even if she and the baby survived, the woman would turn to the streets. And with the scars she would carry, she'd ply her trade with her face turned to the shadows.

His future was even more bleak. Prison almost certainly played a large role. And although he could slap and punch out here, he would cower in his cell. Del saw it in him. Then, to survive, he would turn to the streets of prison and ply his own trade with his face turned to the shadows.

At the end of these futures, there was always the child. Another orphan, cast into the world with no means to understand why it had been cursed. And Del went red, screaming at the injustice these two people brought into the world, and her trancing mind swelled into a swirling silver orb.

The woman screamed at the demon he'd brought to kill her; an angry, swirling orb of light filling the bathroom. She could see into it. Scenes of her future played out in the orb like a nightmare. She was deformed. She was dead. She was brutalized in alleys. Rats found her child in its crib.

For protection, her mind could do nothing but faint.

The man also screamed at the demon the woman had summoned to protect her, and stumbled backwards. He hadn't realized the woman he'd met was a witch; but here it was, an apparition from hell. The swirling orb was between them, protecting her, but now it was after him. Trying to eat him. Trying to erase his mind. Prison images flashed before him. In those scenes he crawled and begged and pleaded and slobbered and was deformed, again and again.

Del flashed over and over as wild energy pulsed through her. She was nearly out of control. Her spirit face, a grotesque distortion of her real beauty, grotesque and deadly, burned at him from all directions. And at that moment, the flames of her anger, reaching critical mass, ignited her dark dreams and a black ember glowed to life somewhere deep inside her.

The man screamed again and began stabbing himself in the leg. He wanted the nightmare to end. He wanted the demon to kill him or release him from this hell. He could think of nothing else to do. So, he stabbed himself over and over, screaming for his death.

Del felt herself losing consciousness but couldn't stop it, just as she couldn't stop the energy from flowing through her. She'd lost the off switch. In her mind she heard a bird screech in frustration. A hunting bird, she thought. A falcon perhaps.

Then Del saw nothing.

*

Coming to in the ambulance, Del panicked and tried to sit up, but didn't move far. She was strapped to the stretcher.

"Whoa der," a voice said. "You'll be a'right. Just had a bad spell is all."

Frank? she wondered through a foggy mind. That sounded like Frank's voice. As the remnants of her trancing session faded away, she heard something, far away in her mind. She thought it was the scream of a bird. The hunting kind. It sounded angry that it had missed its prey, and she imagined that it flew off into a sky she couldn't see.

Trying to speak proved difficult. Her tongue was thick and heavy with dried saliva. She tasted blood in the back of her throat and assumed her nose was bleeding again.

"Where am I?" she muttered.

"We're takin' you to da hospital," the man said. "You had a bad fright."

She tried to raise her hand to check her nose but couldn't. It only made a loud metallic rattle. The other hand did the same.

"Then why am I handcuffed?"

CHAPTER 27

Armand ran up the stairs as Jimmy thrashed on the floor, screaming. He'd just come in with groceries when he heard the boy from the kitchen. He knew that Jimmy had taken to spending more time in the library lately. Besides the chess table—where he was proving to be exceptionally adept at the game—he'd been practicing his letters in an old notebook Armand had given him. Sitting beneath the long workbench on the floor, Jimmy would practice writing the alphabet. He said that he would write Del a letter—when he learned enough words—and ask her to come home soon. After these sessions, Armand would often find that Jimmy had fallen asleep on the small couch where Del would sit. But today the boy was screaming in terror.

"Master Jimmy," Armand said, helping the boy. "Here now, let's sit up. You've had a bad dream."

Jimmy hid his face in his hands and sobbed. He rocked on the floor with his knees drawn up to his chest. Armand sat on the couch next to him and rubbed his back.

A series of blubbering words escaped Jimmy in gasps and sobs. "Mama," (sob), "D, and da," (sob), "face, and da," (sob), "dead people," (sob), "and Deh... ohhh.. she gonna die, and..."

"Now, now," Armand said. "Here, let's sit on the couch. There we go. It was a nasty dream, that's all. I'm sure—"

"Noooo..." Jimmy's eyes were wild and bulging. "Da biwd, da biwd..."

"What bird?"

"Da biwd wiff da faces." Jimmy wiped his runny nose with the back of his hand, then made two claws. "'Ike dis." A grimace came over his red face. His eyes bulged as he bared his teeth and growled. "Grrrr!" Then his voice broke into a high-octave cry. "Cunch! Cunch!" His hands were ripping invisible heads from bodies as his fingers intertwined, funneling the terror from his mind and squeezing it out between his fingers.

After a few minutes, Jimmy sat panting, his dream energy spent through the reenactment of crunching a thousand, thousand faces and carrying them off to oblivion. In broken sentences he'd explained that the giant bird carrying the dead faces had been looking for Del. He knew this because the Stone Maiden had told him a secret so he could dream about Del and find her. Jimmy had almost found her and tried to fly down to her, but the bird was large and fast and with its x-ray vision it had found her first.

Armand caught the main points of the dream, and having come to suspect a latent power in the boy, didn't completely dismiss the vision. Once Jimmy had calmed enough to sit by himself, Armand hurried down the hall to Mama Dedé's room. She was napping again—which now was a frequent state—and he checked her pulse. He feared it was lower than before, and her breathing was barely audible. He considered calling an ambulance, but was still at a loss of what to say what was the matter with her. He then realized that whatever Jimmy had dreamt was possibly closer—or at least related—to the actual cause of Mama D's declining health than anyone would suspect. And if that were the case, there was no doctor who could help them. But how the strange dream of the bird was linked to her was currently alluding him.

However, there was another source of knowledge that currently lay untapped.

Armand returned to the boy who sat huddled on the couch. "Master Jimmy, after dinner, do you think you'll be feeling up for another game?"

Jimmy rocked himself on the couch. The rhythm had gone from frantic to something close to a steady heartbeat in the last few minutes. His puffy face looked up past his bent knees. "Da Talkin' Boad game?"

"Yes. The Talking Board game."

"Ta hep' Mama D?"

"That's right."

A grim determination seemed to settle over Jimmy's face. Armand watched with fascination as a blubbering boy, recently awakened from a bad dream, suddenly became a young man with a goal in front of him. It was quite a surprising trick. One moment, a puffy face with watery eyes absently searched the library looking for stability; the next moment, the eyes cleared slightly, the boyish puffiness receding from his cheeks, almost exposing a young man's jawline. Armand even imagined that his chin had a different set. It was clearly a look of determination.

Jimmy nodded his head slowly, accepting the challenge of the game. Now his eyes were fixed, staring off into space, but focused on a spot beneath the worktable. From where Jimmy sat on the couch, he had a straight line of vision beneath the table to the bottom row of bookshelves. If Armand didn't know better, he'd swear Jimmy was staring at the small shelf he knew to be hidden there.

That and the terrible item that lay within it.

*

All day Armand was busy as a bee. He put away the groceries that he'd hastily thrown onto the table when he'd heard Jimmy's distress. He got a pot of chicken and dumplings working—although it was a hot day, he needed something easy to make and thought the broth would be good for Mama D. Jimmy was off taking a cool bath, which would help settle his nerves. So, Armand sat down to finish his research.

Ever since the first encounter with the spirit, he had been poring through his books and papers looking for any and all references to *the silver cord*. To his surprise, he'd found several related to near-death experiences.

Now, sitting in his chair next to a cold fireplace, he opened a fat notebook. It was a collection of stories and newspaper articles he'd collected over the years—some he'd purchased from other researchers. He scanned each story, touching it lightly with his fingers, pulling the details forth to analyze them once again.

One of the many marked stories had come from a newspaper, but the name of it had long been lost. It was part of a series of articles that followed Ms. Winne Eldritch. A woman who had died and come back to life, only to be tried, then acquitted, of insurance fraud, despite the fact she never tried to collect any money. Armand wasn't interested in the court trial, except for a part of her testimony:

When I saw myself floatin' off the bed, I yelled a thunder. 'Put me back!' I said. But you know, no one heard a peep. I don't even know who I expected to hear me. Twern't no one around. At least not up there on the ceilin'. I could see the doctor standin' by the bed, just shakin' his head, and I thought, 'Some poor soul done lost their—now wait just one minute Minne,' I said. 'That looks like you!' But before I could get back down to see, he threw the sheet over me like a sack of potatoes and that made me mad. That's when I saw the strings comin' off me. Silver ones, all wrapped around each other like a rope. I don't know why I thought it, but I decided to just pull myself back down there and tell him to take that sheet right off of my face. And that's what I did, too!

The article went on to describe the strange circumstances around her near-death, which the doctor testified was in fact a real one. He even testified that she had no pulse for several minutes. The odd court case had made her a minor celebrity in her town until she died several years later.

Armand flipped to another article. This one was the recollection of a twelve-year-old boy who'd nearly drowned in a lake during a family reunion. After a family member found him floating off the dock and brought him to shore, the family worked feverishly trying to push the water from his lungs. He later stated that he'd floated above his body for a few moments, watching the commotion, until a ray of sunshine cut through a cloud, shining on the back of his head. He'd turned toward the light and felt himself floating toward the cloud. The sunbeam turned into a tunnel. He thought he was floating to heaven when he felt something tug on his chest. Turning back toward the ground—which now was far away—he saw a shiny gray rope floating in the air. One end was connected to his body on the ground and the other end went into his belly button and came out his chest, creating a loop. The rope started to shrink, getting tighter and tighter, finally pulling him back to the ground, where he woke up coughing out water.

Armand stopped reading and rubbed his hands. He was deep in

thought. Round and round his hands went, massaging the stories into his skin. Working the details over in his mind.

Why would the spirit of the board mention this phenomenon? Granted, the stories he'd just read didn't specifically call out a silver cord, but the similarities of having an out-of-body experience couldn't be ignored. That, and the fact that they all mentioned a cord or rope that kept the spiritual body from floating away from the physical one. Compare those to the words of the spirit: *False to pray, "Oh kingly lord, sever not her silver cord,"* and he practically had a Bible passage.

Was he dealing with a past priest? A spiritual man, perhaps?

There was nothing in the folklore of Ouija boards that stated the spirit would always be malicious. Perhaps he'd called up an old occultist or alienist who in his previous life had studied this cord phenomenon. But if so, then why the riddle?

Heaven's astral horde…

Rubbing his eyes, he took a mental note to ask the spirit about this concept. It must be important to understanding what ailed Mama Dedé, but the implication escaped him.

He flipped to a final marked passage. His fingers traced lightly over the title of the story: "The Australian Incident."

It recounted a strange infection that struck an Australian aboriginal girl in 1947. Armand had heard rumors that an 8mm film had been made documenting the poor girl's convulsions but had never seen it. The infection had followed an odd meteor storm that had hit the area earlier in the year, where a fragment had been discovered by the girl. Upon touching it, she had become extremely ill and began having strange hallucinations. Extremely superstitious, the Aboriginal leaders thought their creator, the Rainbow Serpent, had sent a gift to the world in hopes the people were ready to receive it. If the translated story was correct, the girl mumbled—in between convulsions and sleep—for nearly four days. She spoke of seeing a Songline that wrapped around her spirit body and connected to her physical one that lay convulsing on the ground. Although she couldn't explain what they were, she also claimed to hear *itchy voices* in her head. The voices were gnawing at her Songline, causing it to unravel. She died on day five.

The spark of an idea began to form in Armand's mind. He was of the opinion that these seemingly disparate stories from across the globe were not mere coincidence. He believed in many things beyond that which he could see.

He decided to ask the spirit some very pointed questions tonight.

CHAPTER 28

Detective Marcel Valcour arrived at the Tulane Hospital, which filled several blocks between Tulane and Cleveland avenues at 4:17 pm. Exiting his car, he smoothed his tie and tugged on his neatly pressed pants. The length was fine.

He'd just left a bizarre scene at a small home in a residential neighborhood. If he'd had his fortune told this morning, it most likely would have had *Homicide by Stabbing* referenced somewhere in it. He was sure of it. After all, the guy he'd just interviewed *had* been found with a knife in his possession—presumably to kill the woman inside. The problem was, it was the guy's house, so he hadn't been trespassing. Then there was the fact of the busted door, but again, it was his property. The woman hadn't been harmed. Yes, there were old bruises which Marcel had asked her about. But like most domestic abuse cases, the victim said little. In this case, the woman was nearly catatonic, and he couldn't tell if it was from drugs or shock. Probably both. The best he could get out of her was something about a demon. Then, to top it all off, the guy with the knife stabs his own leg nine or ten times—*he's lucky he didn't chop the thing off*—and stumbles outside only to have a passerby lash a belt around it to keep him from bleeding to death. The guy was tightlipped, however. When Marcel had questioned him about the knife and broken bathroom door, he'd said he heard his girlfriend screaming and broke it down trying to save her. The knife had been for their protection. It wasn't until the demon came after him that the knife had been used. And the demon made him do that too. Now he was at the hospital getting ready to question a girl they found comatose in the driveway of the house. Most likely a junkie, he thought. But some witnesses said they thought the girl had something to do with it somehow. When he asked them how, they made signs to ward off evil spirits and said no more.

Entering the hospital, Officer Babette Thibodeaux greeted him in the lobby.

"Where is she?" he asked.

"Room 302," Babette said. "She's still secured, but was out when I left her."

"Out?"

"They had to sedate her in the ambulance. She came to and flipped a switch on the medic. Was pretty freaked out, apparently."

"Did she say anything?"

"Nothing he could recall as being important. Medic thought it was a panic attack. Doesn't look like a drug user. No obvious marks. Just a few old scars. But…"

"But what?" Marcel prompted.

Babette shrugged. "Probably nothing, but I felt like I'd seen her somewhere before. It was hard to tell with her knocked out."

"Where do you think it was?"

"Can't tell. Just around. It's a pretty face, so…" She almost said, '*in my dreams,'* but hadn't known Detective Valcour very long, so didn't. She already knew her road to becoming a detective was a long one—if she ever got there. No need to make it more difficult by bringing her love life into the picture. "But everything is in my notes. I can stick around if you want me to—"

"No need," Marcel said. "I'll take it from here."

Officer Thibodeaux nodded and turned away, hiding her disappointment. For some reason, she thought this might have been her chance to help question a potential witness. Her interest was primarily police-work driven, and she thought very little about the pretty face lying quiet from shock. But there was nothing that said she couldn't watch this case closely. She did have to patrol a lot of areas, after all.

*

When Marcel entered room 302, he was met with a dichotomy of expression. He detected fear and anger at the same time. But there was no confusion in her eyes. He'd put money on the fact that she'd never used drugs. In fact, the parts of her he could see—both arms, still handcuffed to the bedrails, one leg sticking out from under the sheet, and her neck—looked quite healthy. *Youthful* came to mind. But her face told another story: ashen gray and tired, dark circles around the eyes. But those eyes. Yes, there was fire in those eyes. And they spoke *Fear* and *Anger* to him.

This girl has secrets.

"How are you feeling?" Marcel asked.

"OK." Del eyed the tall man in the suit who wasn't dressed like a doctor.

Marcel moved to the side of the bed and pushed the button to raise the back rest. "Do you feel OK to sit up?"

Del nodded.

"There, how's that?"

"A little higher please."

A slight smile curved his mouth. "OK. How about now?"

"Fine. Thanks."

Del tried a quick flash into the man's mind, but was rewarded with a searing white light that caused her head to throb. She grimaced slightly and let her head sink back on the pillow.

"Sure you're OK?" Marcel asked.

"Yeah. Just a headache," she said with closed eyes.

"Headaches? Do you get them often?"

"Do you ask questions without introductions, often?"

Marcel's face went from *amused smile* to something close to a reprimand when his eyebrow arched in question.

He cleared his throat. "My name is Detective Marcel Valcour. And you are…" He picked up the clipboard that hung from the end of the bed.

They spoke at the same time. He said, "Jane." She said, "Del."

He said, "Doe." She said, "Larou—"

Her eyes popped open and her head came off the pillow. "What?"

"You came in with no I.D. You're listed as a Jane Doe. But your real name is Del?"

A hundred scenarios flew through Del's mind. She'd almost given him her real name. But did that matter? Right now, she was Jane Doe. Something about the random anonymity of that name felt like a warm blanket of privacy. Did she need an extra layer of privacy? She thought she might. Her ten-thousand-hour journey was off to a rough start. What if she really screwed it up? What if she had to start over? What if she'd killed someone? What if she had to hide?

What am I thinking? I'm not a criminal!

(You don't know that. What if the guy is dead?)

Del tried to remember the ending of the bathroom scene. The screaming. The fainting woman. The man stabbing at the air... or... was he stabbing himself? She couldn't be sure of much.

But she hadn't gone inside the house. Not really. And besides, she was trying to help. She'd tried to save the woman. Save them both, actually.

Then why am I the one on trial? Why the interrogation?

(Because this isn't the first person you've killed.)

That wasn't my fault! That was an accident!

(Which one?)

Which one, indeed? A tricky question. If one were beginning their ten-thousand-hour journey, just starting to explore their natural gifts and abilities, how would one measure success along that path? For someone like Del, was it a plus or minus body count? Just measuring the big milestones? Or would you try and count all the small things as well? *'Death by a thousand cuts,'* Mama D had said once. If she had to count all of those, she'd spend her entire time counting and never get anywhere. But, if she was going to have to hide from every little incident, maybe she needed to be incognito. Maybe she needed to be Jane Doe.

But did she want to start off lying to the police when she didn't even know if she'd done anything wrong? That was a crime in itself, wasn't it? Who knows? Maybe Bonnie and Clyde started with a lie as simple as this.

(Don't be stupid.)

I'm not being stupid!

(Then answer the question!)

"What question?" Del said out loud by accident. Surprise widened her eyes as she tried to remember what Marcel had just asked her.

She forced a small laugh. "Heh. Sorry. I meant," she swallowed, "What's my name?"

Marcel had watched Del's face as the wheels of her mind turned. Instinct told him that she was weighing her options, playing out scenarios. The question was *Why?* She wasn't being charged with anything. At least not yet. He didn't even know if she'd been a witness to the incident. But there was turmoil on her face. That much was obvious. Now he watched her try to recover.

Del decided. And in that instant, everything changed. Whether she actually tranced to her Well of Life or not, she couldn't be sure. She imagined she did. Just a quick peek, happening in an instant. She thought about floating down to that deep pool and letting the cool water wash over her; replenish her. She wanted to stay there, but had things to attend to.

Now she was smiling at Marcel with sparkling eyes and pretty brown skin that began to radiate. The ashen color faded, not completely, but enough. The dark circles around her eyes became lighter. Her eyes appeared to become larger.

"I'm sorry," she said with a smile. "My name is Delphine Larouche. But you can call me Del."

She extended her right hand until the handcuffs rattled loudly against the bed rail.

Now it was her turn to watch the Wheels of Marcel spin.

*

During their interview—for it wasn't an interrogation at all—Del explained how she'd been walking home after work (she liked to wander the new neighborhoods because she wasn't from around here) and saw a man acting strangely. *How* he'd been acting strangely she couldn't really say. Just that he seemed to be agitated. Having nowhere else to go, she walked his direction—not really following him—and saw him go into his house. At that point, she meant to move on, but heard a commotion, then screams. She thought the house was being robbed and didn't know what to do. But then the newspaper reporter in her kicked in. She explained how she was an 'intern reporter' at the *Times-Picayune* and was looking to break her first big story. Marcel appeared to be bored with this part of her story, so she decided to continue with the detail. Also remembering Frank's constant plea for her to speak slower when she was excited, she decided to speed up the story. So she told Marcel about the detail she'd tried to remember about the house. She needed it for her story after all. And what the man was wearing and the time of day and the people on the sidewalks and the angle of the sun, so her story would feel rich and exciting. She even decided to sneak up into the driveway, as close as she dared, but careful not to trample on any potential evidence, and see if she could get a look at the perpetrator. She couldn't, but when the commotion got worse, she became scared and maybe had a panic attack. She couldn't be sure. She hadn't eaten much that day and was tired from the night before, which probably also had something to do with it. But she hoped that everything had turned out OK for the people inside.

Marcel had removed the handcuffs by this time and was sitting in a chair by the wall. A nurse had come and gone, checking Del's vitals, and declaring them perfect. When Del finished, Marcel closed his notebook and leaned back, rubbing his eyes. He looked tired. And he only believed a portion of what Del had said.

When the doctor entered, Marcel stood and asked to speak to him outside. The two men spoke silently, but Del caught glimpses of them through the window in the door. A few minutes later the doctor came in, checked Del's pulse once more, and told her she was free to leave, but that the detective would like to speak to her outside. Then he left the room.

Del dressed quickly, but took her time exiting the room. Her headache had receded, and she risked a quick trance. Marcel was right outside the door. He was reviewing his notebook. He had underlined a few words and circled others.

Times-Picayune was circled and had a line drawn to question-mark. He would certainly follow up on this.

Panic Attack was underlined.

Acting Strangely was written, and had another line coming off it. *How?* underlined twice, was written next to it. Then he flipped to an earlier page. Here were notes he'd taken from witnesses at the house.

Acting crazy. Strung out. Nutso. These were words the people had used to describe Del when she had collapsed against the fence. Then something caught her eye. Marcel was slowly drawing a box around the phrase: *Pounding her leg.*

What does that mean? Del thought. *I wasn't pounding my leg.*

She watched as Marcel flipped to another page, scanning with his finger. There were a few notes here about the man. It stopped at: Injury – multiple lacerations to right leg.

Marcel snapped the notebook shut and looked at his watch.

Del came out of her trance and put her best smile on. She grabbed her bag and opened the door, acting surprised to see Marcel standing there.

"Oh, I didn't know you were still here," she said. "The doctor released me."

"Yes, I know. But there's just one more thing."

Del tried not to breath too deeply. "Yes?"

"Here's my number." He handed her a standard white business card. "I have your address. And, I still have a few things to follow up on. I may have additional questions for you. I assume you're not planning a long trip anytime soon?"

She took the card. "Me? Oh no. Work, work, work, for me." The best smile she could muster now was a closed-lip line, forced up on both ends.

Marcel nodded. "Yeah. OK. Well. I'll be seeing you."

Now Del's smile was genuine, but mischief was in her eyes. "Not if I see you first." She pivoted on her sneakers, tucked the card into the back pocket of her jeans, and walked down the hall.

Marcel watched the young woman leave. He didn't have to write anymore notes. Somehow, he knew this would *not* be the last he saw of Delphine Larouche.

CHAPTER 29

Saturday evening and Billy was planning to leave the house. His headache had returned, and he imagined his fever was back. He was sweating like it was, anyway.

He'd been laying low since the last body had been found. Both the girl and Harold had been discovered the same day. What was that? Four days ago? Five? He was losing track of time, cooped up in this little house. The walls were closing in on him.

The yellow Formica table with chrome legs gleamed at him, shooting light into his head. Once inside, the light sought out the cancer cells in his brain, causing them to vibrate and itch. It was driving him crazy. In fact, everything in the grandmotherly little house seemed to have teamed up to needle his mind. The faux gold-rimmed light mounted on the kitchen ceiling cast a bright light everywhere, highlighting the bright flecks in the yellow table. The light over the bathroom mirror was harsh, turning the pink-tiled room, with its pink ceramic sink, into a visual sauna. Just thinking about sitting on the pink toilet caused him to sweat, then his brain would heat up. The old console television had started leaking waves of electricity into the air, which also caused his head to get hot. That's probably what had caused his cancer in the first place, but he couldn't remember if he'd had it before coming to live with his grandmother or not. Regardless, he was sure the leaking television set had made it worse.

He'd worked out several times today, trying to keep the fever-itch down, but it'd only partially worked. By raising his body temperature and letting the sweat out, he thought the fever would subside. It used to work, but for some reason was becoming less effective. That's why he needed to find The Red soon. If he didn't, he was sure his head would explode.

He stalked the house, following a well-worn path in the carpet, thinking about the plan for the evening.

Terrance was on his route. The plan was to meet up at The Note at midnight and see if they could spot the witch. There was a cluster of bars in the area, all within walking distance, and if she wasn't at one, she'd most likely be at one of the others. All the bars would be busy, so he and Terrance could come and go without being noticed. He thought he'd recognize her if he saw her, but maybe not. He hadn't gotten a good look at her the first night, just from behind really. But in his fevered mind, he felt tuned into her. He imagined that the cancer in his brain would vibrate in fear when he came near her. The cancer would know that The Red could be found through her, through some cosmic connection, and could be wielded to kill it. This would cause the cancer to vibrate in fear, alerting him to her presence. Then it was just a matter of… well… connecting her

(tickler)

energy to his and letting The Red consume him. But this time he wouldn't let it slip away. He couldn't. If it slipped away again, just one more time, he was sure the cancer would eat him completely. The fever would get so hot that his brain would fry, and his eyes would pop and he would die with cancer eating his soul and would itch for eternity.

Billy slapped the yellow table with both hands, making the cut-glass salt and pepper shakers jump in their wire holder. Little grains of salt jumped up from the top and disappeared in the yellow of the tabletop. He suddenly realized that his hike around the house had ended back at the table, and that he'd been leaning on it, staring at a torn piece of wallpaper.

What was he thinking? Was he going insane? Frying brains and fever-cancer? Shards of Red splitting his mind and spearing the cells?

Yes. He was thinking all these things. And his heart was pounding.

CHAPTER 30

In a hole in the ground, in the Lafayette Cemetery #1, across from a grand house, the Embryo of Scarmish stretched its newly formed body. It was not a dry, comfortable hole, which meant pleasant memories and good friends. No. It was a nasty, wet hole, filled with the memory of a rat, and a swampy smell. And as something resembling thin bony fingers stretched out of the hole, rat knuckle bones cracked, echoing through the night air.

The finger-things tested the ground just outside the hole. Like a mutant spider-crab, emerging from its hiding place, they were cautious. The bony ends clicked against the stones and gravel, feeling for traction. The thin tendons that held the mismatched bones together creaked like old leather straps. But they were anxious clicks. The Scarmish-shadow had eaten everything within the vicinity; it had survived, and it had grown. But the thing needed to move beyond the hole now. It needed larger prey to continue growing. It needed a better form.

The bone-fingers pulled the body from the hole with a soft squishing sound. Having little to work with beyond cemetery rats, worms and black crickets, the entire body had yet to form. Connected to the three cracking fingers was a lump, a transparent membrane of cells that clung to the fingers like the rotting head of a small octopus, bulbous and sagging. The fingers dragged the head behind it, and moved, for the first time, into the night. Tiny rat hairs stood up from the sack and quivered in the air. Miniature antennae. They sensed the area, learning their new role.

And within the transparent sack of body-head, the pupil of an eye, suspended in a warm solution of rat juice, dilated for the first time, and looked out at the world.

*

Madame Broussard watched the fresco with amusement. The tiny shadow she thought to be Scarmish finally began to move. It had been still for a while now. Why she thought it was him at all, she couldn't be sure—but it felt right. She badly wanted to send a scout, an emissary, to confirm her suspicions, but patience was needed now. He currently wasn't a threat to her, but still could be in the future—or an ally, who could say? And who knew what form he'd come back in? He may not even remember their relationship, but he was a variable that could not be ignored.

She thought fondly of the Lafayette Cemetery #1 as the shadow began to move around the perimeter walls.

Crazy as a rat in a tin shithouse.

An odd thing to come to her now, she thought. What had pulled this quaint memory forward?

She'd had many encounters across many cemeteries, but hadn't thought about this one for a long time. She'd been trapped in her building for so long, her previous life felt like a dream. Had there really been all those carefree nights? Or, had her mind simply created the illusions?

Then it came to her.

The cutthroat!

A sly smile turned the corner of her mouth as a faint coloration warmed her cheeks. In formal company someone would say she was near a blush, but she was long past the blushing schoolgirl age. However, her eyes did sparkle with fond memories of long ago.

Strolling the night streets, barefooted and mysterious, black-velvet dress, raven hair. Sometimes she'd walk right down the middle of the street at midnight, just to give the people something to gossip about the next morning. No one mistook her for a working girl, not with the aura she projected. Well… except for the cutthroat.

He of the slushy Irish voice. "Aye, lovey, would 'ya com' out now? Hamish," he'd belched, "oohhr, Hamish has got an eye fer ya. C'mon wee one, we'll make it quickie-quick."

The pursuit into the cemetery had been agonizingly slow. He'd nearly lost her trail several times, and she'd had to make a concerted effort to be found.

Then, crouching from atop a crypt, she'd surprised him by mimicking his Irish dialect. "Aye, lovey, will ya' be havin' me now?"

Yes, crazy as a rat in a tin shithouse, he'd been trying to find his way out of the cemetery. She'd even toyed with the idea of letting him live another night. That is, until he'd called her a harpy!

"Stay away ya' blood-suckin' harpy!" he'd screamed, pointing back at her. "You stay away!"

And that, she couldn't forgive.

Then the cutthroat was no more.

Coming back to the fresco, she wondered if she and Scarmish would meet again, perhaps in the very same cemetery.

She thought it a likely possibility.

CHAPTER 31

After leaving the hospital, Del went home, showered, and laid on her bed, thinking about the events of the last twenty-four hours. It was about this time yesterday that she'd been standing in the cemetery, listening to Arlo's instructions on how to free the dead girl's spirit. The events seemed like a dream, foggy and fading. She wondered if she'd be able to do it again.

Looking up at the ceiling, she raised her right hand and swiped the air.

Nothing happened.

Looking at her palm, she saw only wrinkles and creases, depending on how she moved her fingers. But where was the tattoo? Had the pact been resolved already?

She doubted that.

Swiping her hand again, only slower this time, she concentrated on seeing the air part. She thought about Arlo, but there were no magic words that went with this movement. Somehow it just happened. But there was still nothing. Frustrated, she pulled the edge of the cover

over her and turned on her side. She was pretty spent from the long day. Maybe if she rested her eyes for a few minutes, she'd be able to think more clearly. She was hungry as well. She'd have to get dinner soon, but a few minutes with her eyes closed would do her good. After that, she'd eat and find Arlo. She might even go hang out at one of the bars where she worked. She didn't drink much, but she wouldn't find any friends in her bedroom. Nor would she find her path or figure out how to help Mama D by laying around here. But a few minutes rest sounded better and better.

*

Somewhere in a dream, Del saw faces. First, it was Arlo. She was looking in the window of Del's bedroom, trying to get her attention. From her dream state, Del had no concern that Arlo was floating outside a second-floor window. That's just the way things were. But she was annoyed that someone was trying to wake her up and had disturbed her enough that she had to dream about trying to stay asleep.

She rolled onto her other shoulder. Now it was Mama Dedé's face floating in the window, but she was upside down. Which made sense in a way, because the window had tipped over when she rolled. Mama D was trying to get Del to wake up also, but her voice didn't work. She was dying and wanted to say goodbye before she left, but her voice had dried up because Del hadn't found her path.

Del's heart pounded in the dream. Frustrated over her inability to do anything, she felt panic fall over her, weighing her down.

Deeper into the dream she found Jimmy. His face was expressionless and searching. He had a secret and wanted to ask someone about it. If Del had been there, he would have asked her, but since she'd abandoned him, he'd have to figure it out on his own.

Still deeper, she saw the face of the dead girl, both as she was on the memorial picture someone carried in the secondline, and as the relieved spirit when the last strand of her life cord had been torn away. Bitten really. By Del.

Now she dreamed of a ravenous hunger and a thousand faces floating in the dark watching her feed. She was the center of attention. A spectacle. Something to be feared. She was in the center of a thousand, thousand dead and they watched her gluttonous feeding. They were hungry too, but she shared nothing. She was inside and outside at the same time, slipping easily between places. One moment she was in the middle of the street where Arlo had first shown her the other side and the tapestry of dead that walked there. She was crawling on her hands and knees, feeding on something. Then she was in her bedroom, crawling up the walls, looking for a way out. She was trapped. A prisoner in her own room. And she was starving. The faces crowded the window in her dream and gazed upon the likes of something they—the dead—had never seen before.

Del awoke with a scream and threw away the covers that tried to smother her. Ghostly eyes that lingered in the faces of the dead slowly receded from the walls of her room. Her pounding heart told her she was fully awake now. Shaking her head, she rubbed her eyes and refocused on the walls. The last of the eyes had just faded away.

And if that was true, it meant the faces had actually been there.

*

A scratching sound came from her window. She looked up just in time to see something fall away from the window ledge. Night had fallen since she had first laid down, and her room was dark. Peering out the window, she saw the tip of a tree branch that was reaching toward the windowpane.

Perhaps that had caused the scratching sound, she thought.

Then, as her eyes adjusted to the dark night, she saw movement in the tree. The elongated shadow of a cat—as if the light source had distorted its proportions—ran smoothly around the tree at the height of her window. How it clung to the tree, Del couldn't tell, but she watched with little surprise as its shadow wound around the tree, sometimes jumping from branch to branch, sometimes defying gravity beneath a branch, and ending its journey on the ground where it dissolved into the other shadows.

Standing at the base of the tree was a bent and crooked shadow that Del instantly knew to be that of Arlo.

*

A few minutes later, Del exited the front of the boarding house. She made her away around to the side where her bedroom window looked down onto the lawn.

Here Arlo emerged from the shadows.

"You was dreamin'," Arlo said.

Del stopped and crossed her arms. Her face was sleepy but stern. "You left me in the cemetery."

Arlo waved her off. "Bah! You survived." She walked forward through the shadows and Del followed. "You had a task to do, and you finished it. Dat's good. But now yer dreamin' about it. Dat ain't good."

Del eyed the woman cautiously as she walked. "How do you know what I was dreaming?"

Arlo rolled her eyes as if Del had just asked her how she knew it was night. "Now listen," Arlo said, "dere's somethin' I need to tell you about da last task."

"Like what?" Then Del added, "And why didn't you tell me then?"

"Hush up! 'Cause I didn't think you'd get through it so fast." The old woman made a quick motion with her hand and a black moth—perhaps the shadow of one—fluttered out of a bush, only to be snagged out of the air by the shadow cat.

"Fast? I was there for hours. I missed my shift at work."

"Eh… da point is, you got through it. I wasn't sure you'd even be able to do dat. Figured I'd find you gave up and went home. But you didn't."

"No. I didn't."

"No…" Arlo stopped at a spot on the sidewalk that enjoyed a view of the night sky. Some of the larger tree branches had been cut back here. "…you didn't." Just then, as if on command, the moon emerged from its hiding place and showered the two women with the first moonbeams of the evening. Arlo inspected her closely in the ghostly blue light.

There was nothing subtle about the woman's inspection. She deftly turned Del in multiple directions, looking her up and down. Her powerful hands controlled Del's arms, moving her this way and that. Even the shadow cat inspected her by winding around her legs. Del almost imagined that a real cat had just skimmed her legs, but was now thoroughly convinced that Arlo's pet was purely shadow and nothing else.

"What are you doing?" Del asked.

Satisfied with her inspection, Arlo nodded her opinion to the wind, and it was carried away. At a distance, the night things that had been waiting for Arlo's verdict stood down and went back to their own pursuits.

Now Arlo caught Del's gaze and held it sternly with her eyes. "Da spirit cord…" The night fell silent, listening to the old woman's secrets. "Don't never ever drink from it."

Del blinked in confusion. "How…? I don't understand. How would that even be possible?"

"I had to be sure you hadn't drunk from it yet. Dat's why I pulled you into da moonlight. I didn't warn you yesterday because I didn't think you'd get through it. Nary a person can. But now dat I know… well, dat's for another time. But I'm tellin' you, don't never drink from da cord. Even if you got da desert in your mouth and your stomach twistin' from hunger."

Del suddenly had the feeling that she'd narrowly avoided a terrible fate. She felt foolish at being taken advantage of and felt disdain for the woman rise up in her throat. She held the woman's gaze sternly in return. "I'm grateful for the help you're giving me with finding my path, but you've seen what I can do. In fact, you may understand what I'm capable of better than I do, but in the end, they're still my abilities. I control them. Don't put me in danger again by not telling me the full story."

The corner of Arlo's left eye flinched ever so slightly at the reprimand; the girl had moxy, she thought.

The two women weighed one another, each wondering about the other, measuring. Now the night things—who are notorious eavesdroppers and had not gone about their other business—held their collective dead-breaths as tension radiated from the women. As if flirting on the edge of a tidal pull of gravity, the two entities were close to becoming locked in an epic battle. One that could very possibly end with the destruction of both. But as quickly as the storm had risen, it faded, and passed on into the night.

"Done," Arlo said. Her voice neither wavered nor clutched. "Now, about your next task."

CHAPTER 32

Settling into their places around the worktable, Armand and Jimmy prepared for their second session with the talking board. The house, being closed up tight and locked, seemed to hold its breath, waiting for the events to unfold. Candles flickered updates from wall to wall, where shadows carried the news deep into crevasses that didn't end. Many things, inside and out of the house, waited for the game to begin.

A list of questions sat at Armand's right hand. Several blank pages were here as well. Jimmy kneeled on the same stool as before, from the opposite side of the table. Armand nodded to Jimmy and they both placed one hand on the puck.

Quietly Armand asked, "Is anyone here this evening?"

They both sat waiting. The puck remained still.

Armand thought back to the last time they'd used the board. He didn't remember much of the session, strangely, and began to wonder how he'd managed to get it started in the first place.

"Is there anyone who would like to come forward?" he asked again.

Somewhere downstairs a noisy clock ticked away the seconds. Time fading into oblivion, never to return.

Then he remembered the name.

"Victor. Are you here? Would you like to come forward?"

The puck began to move.

Armand watched with fascination. Secretly, he wondered if Jimmy was pushing the puck, but quickly dismissed the idea. Instead of going to the YES or NO circle, it began to spell.

V

I

C

T

O

R

Although unsettling, Armand took this as a sign that they were once again speaking with the spirit known as Victor. Why it had insisted on spelling out its own name again however, he couldn't begin to guess.

"Have you been here long?"

The puck moved to YES.

"Do you know what ails Mama Dedé?"

YES.

"What is it? How can I help her?"

The puck remained still.

Shaking his head, Armand quietly reprimanded himself. How stupid was he being to ask the spirit multiple open-ended questions at once? He tried again.

"What ails Mama Dedé?"

After a few seconds, the puck moved.

V

I

C

T

O

R

Armand scratched a dark line on his sheet of paper just as he finished the R. The line shot off to the right like a freakishly long foot. He nearly threw the puck across the table in frustration. Was this nonsense? Why did it spell the name out again? Was it mocking him?

Jimmy, quietly watching and lightly touching the puck the way Armand had told him, thought the puck had tried to move just as Armand scratched the dark line on the page. Jimmy thought the puck had more to say, but said nothing himself.

Regaining his composure, Armand continued. "Is it possible for me to help her?"

NO.

"Is it possible for anyone to help her?"

The puck jumped across the board.

Apparently, it had a lot to say.

Armand scribbled furiously, afraid of missing letters. The sheet slid beneath his hand, causing his normally neat handwriting to sprawl out across the page. Random sentence breaks were caused by hitting the edge of the paper.

just on edeat hats hemus tpayonf

in alho ur of jud gemen tdaynobarg

aimade toth us del ayhercumble

back todark estclay

Finally, the puck stopped. Armand's left hand shook slightly.

Jumbled, the letters danced through his mind, forming esoteric words. He underlined a few.

JUST

EDEAT

HEMUS

TOTH

DEL

A few of them reminded him of Egyptian words. The last two sent a chill down his spine.

Toth and Del.

Then the puck moved again. Faster. Victor had more to say, and Armand scribbled widely to catch it.

herd eath is night hefinal term with pali dang els toafirm theast ralhorde willwrith

eands quirm ass hefe edstheg host lyver mevic

torv ermis

As quickly as the puck had started, it stopped. Armand, exhausted and bleary-eyed, imagined he felt it quivering beneath his fingers, panting with ghostly energy expended from telling its eldritch tale.

Stealing a glance at Jimmy, who had been watching, wide-eyed and silent, Armand thought it best to close the session with the Ouija board. He had a lot to decipher and feared he'd made a mess of the translation. He suspected he'd missed a few letters as well. Sometimes, Victor seemed to vibrate between certain letters, almost like a stutter, as if he couldn't decide how to spell the word. Armand wondered briefly if the great writers who used drugs and alcohol—Edgar Allan Poe came to mind—felt like this after a night of overindulgence and wild writing, awaking the next morning to find utter madness spilled across the page. He also wondered of late if he wasn't guilty of letting a similar madness creep into his own mind. He feared he was at the precipice of something that could not be undone. He just hoped his actions would not be the thing to pull them all over the edge.

"Hi, Victah, can you hep me find da bihd in my deam?"

Jimmy's words tumbled forth in an instant, never to be unspoken. This thing was final and absolute.

Silence fell over the house like the calm before a terrible storm. The old clock downstairs announced the slowing of time by the absence of its loud ticking. Universal tension held its second hand at bay. Finally, with a tension that killed the clock mechanism forever, its gears lurched forward one final time, exclaiming its death blow with a loud *SPRANG*, recording the very second—like the stopping of a clock upon one's death—when the spirit in the board was asked for direct assistance.

Time unlocked and crawled forward.

Then the puck began to spin wildly.

Armand's mouth dropped open in utter shock—the last few seconds playing over and over in his mind. He tried to make sense of what had just happened. Had he really heard Jimmy speak to the board? Had he just asked the spirit for direct help? Was he imagining this in a dream and perhaps still had time to stop it?

By the sick feeling washing over him, and the fever flushing his neck, Armand knew that these things had happened.

He clamped his hands over his mouth, stifling a scream. Tears sprung out of his eyes at the realization of the terrible thing he'd done, the horrible accident that had just occurred, linking Jimmy to the spirit in the board. He watched in horror as the puck spun freely—Jimmy had pulled his hands back in startled amazement.

The puck moved around the board under its own frantic power.

As it bumped along, Armand feared the wild thing would take flight, flying off the table. At that moment there was nothing more he wished to happen than to make the haunted puck disappear forever.

Then, as if having fully inspected the board, the puck moved to one corner, and contentedly spun in one place.

Armand began to wretch.

Jimmy's sweet face smiled.

The puck had landed on YES.

Victor would be quite happy to help Jimmy explore his dreams.

CHAPTER 33

When Rochelle saw Billy walking up the sidewalk, she thought he was drunk. She had a keen eye for this condition. It played a great role in how she treated her customers. Alcohol and drugs affected each person differently, and in her line of work, that could mean the difference between life and death. Sometimes the stimulant actually *stimulated* the john, and if it didn't make them angry, it was a relatively easy trick with a satisfying outcome for both parties. Sometimes it made them limp, at which point awkward excuses were made, and they parted ways. But sometimes, regardless of if it was drugs or alcohol, they were just crazy. And often with crazy came anger and with that, danger was close behind.

Billy looked all three: Crazy, Angry and Dangerous. And Rochelle slipped back into the shadows of the bar and watched him walk past.

She watched him move down the street at a rapid pace. He wasn't out for a random night on the town. He was going somewhere specific. His stride was long and purposeful. Was he having a problem with his business? Had someone refused to pay him? Or were there other things eating at him?

She'd started to wonder about Billy lately. Having only known him for a little more than a month, she didn't have a good sense of what drove his internal workings. In fact, she knew very little about him. But, when they'd met at a party which led to them having sex that first night, their relationship had escalated quickly. In her line of work, sex was an everyday occurrence. She wasn't proud of what she did for a living, but she didn't beat herself up about it either. But to her, sex didn't have to have an arbitrary number of dates tied to it before it was allowed to happen. To her, it was very simple. They were at a party. She was horny. He was cute. What was there to debate? And not only was he cute, he worked out like a madman. And after a weekend of dealing with drunk johns and less than satisfying encounters, a good stiff pounding was right in order. And Billy had provided that on the sink in the bathroom.

She knew from his interactions at the party that night that he ran a little dope. Hell, most people in the services industry—regardless of the service they provided—did one thing or another, so that didn't bother her. She was a bit of a pot smoker. You pretty much had to be to deal with the things she did. But she had to keep her wits about her as well, so she saved the smoke for the end of the night. And she never took a needle. That was a deal-breaker. She'd seen too many people strung out on the streets to ever imagine herself doing that. And so, when she found out that Billy was letting Terrance crash on his couch to help him get off the street—and ultimately the needle—she thought maybe this was a guy she could spend some time with. They seemed to understand each other's situation, after all. She'd be happy not to judge his side-business, as he seemed willing not to judge hers. From there, she'd gotten into the habit of stopping by his place in between encounters with her johns. It was one way to deal with the other less-than-satisfying encounters. But that's when things started to get weird.

She couldn't quite put her finger on it, but there was something different about the times they had sex *after* she'd already been working, but wasn't done for the evening. She thought of them as her 'drive-by' flings with Billy, where she'd needed to get a bite to eat and a beer, but needed to keep the motor running, so to speak. Billy's motor was always running, so it was an easy way to keep hers going. But very quickly, the weirdness had set in. It didn't always happen, but seemed to be occurring more frequently now. The huge bear hugs he'd give her, seemingly without realizing it, nearly squeezing the air out of her. The biting and whispering. *Who in the hell was he whispering to, anyway?* It's not like she wasn't used to dirty talk. She'd heard every possible ridiculous demand and request anyone could imagine. It wasn't like he needed to shy away from what he wanted to do or wanted her to do. He wasn't courting a nun after all. But the weirdest thing of all was the whimpering.

She couldn't remember when it started, but it was so subtle, it unnerved her from the beginning. She didn't want to think about it, and she certainly didn't want to say it out loud, but she felt like during those times, he was regressing.

And then the scabs began to show up on his knees.

She knew his workout routine left marks on his body, he'd explained those. And she knew he was pretty rough on the furniture. But this was different. The scabs on his knees reminded her of some of the junkies and hookers that were so out of it they crawled the cobblestone on their hands and knees. Repeatedly. Sure, she'd had scrapes and bruises on her knees before, when she was getting started in the business. You could always classify the working girls in lockup by how torn up their knees were. The high-end hookers had pretty good knees; the skanks had scabs. If she were to see only Billy's knees in lockup, she'd say they were connected to a dude in a skirt that'd been doing his own rooting on the cobblestones, and who had picked a rough john.

And now she was beginning to wonder what was really going on inside Billy's head. So far this reason, she decided to follow him as he marched past. She wanted to see if he had a secret life. She wanted to know what was driving his frantic pace.

*

Two blocks down the street, Billy slipped into an alley. It was across from where Rochelle was quietly walking. Her ability to be seen when she wanted business, and not be seen when danger was near—or when she was just tired of dealing with the idiots—was a prized asset that she used wisely.

A few minutes later, through an open window in the front of The Hidden Note jazz club, she saw Billy walk into the main room. He must have gone in through the back-alley door. Walking to an empty table, he stood by himself, saying nothing. Rock and roll cover music rolled out of the open window, covering all conversation. Soon, a cocktail waitress joined him and cozied up to the table. She seemed to be taking his order, but if that were the case, she'd suddenly forgotten about her other customers. As she smiled and leaned into Billy, Rochelle quickly understood that another transaction was taking place. But what it was, she couldn't be sure.

Billy leaned forward on the high-top bar table and slowly pulled Tasha's top out with one finger, peering inside. Tasha did a slight wiggle, making sure he could see what he wanted. Then, reaching into his jeans, Billy pulled something from his pocket—it was between his fingers now—and slowly slid it down the front of her blouse. His hand lingered for a moment, tucking the package away safely. He tweaked each nipple for good measure, removed his hand, and looked at his watch.

Tasha looked around the room, acknowledging a customer, then slipped her hand under the table, returning the favor. Billy said something and she pointed to a clock on the wall. He nodded.

Rochelle really wasn't surprised at the flirting. After all, it's not like her and Billy were a permanent thing. Besides, a ton of different guys had their hands down *her* shirt. But when Billy exited the alley a few minutes later and headed back the way he came—passing right across the street from her—she *was* surprised at the look on his face. It was hard to pinpoint, but the slightly crazed look had returned. It was as if he was a dying man in the desert who saw an oasis far away. A haunted look shadowed his face, and his eyes gleamed with anticipation of reaching water later that night.

CHAPTER 34

Sunday morning, Frank's stomach had rumbled during the entire drive to Armand's house. He was anticipating a large breakfast and updating his friend on his progress looking for Del.

Opening the backdoor, his mouth went slack, and the end of his morning cigar drooped. The kitchen was cold and empty.

"What da—?" Walking through the kitchen, he noticed the coffee pot and felt for heat. Warm, but a couple of hours old, he guessed. Someone had been up for quite a while, but never considered making breakfast.

Walking into the foyer, he called, "Hallo! I'm in da—"

"OH! Mon ami…" Armand's words trailed down the curved staircase like the end of forgotten song lyrics. Quietly he confessed to himself, "I… I'm not sure guests are…"

Frank headed for the stairs.

Armand continued, "…well… I suppose—"

"I'm comin' up whatever you suppose," Frank called. "Jus' give me a minute."

Frank could have given Armand twenty minutes, or thirty, and he still would have been surprised when he reached the top of the stairs.

"Jesus, Mary and Joseph," said Frank. "What da hell's wrong with you?"

Armand looked terrible. Having slept only a few hours in his fireplace chair, his clothes were rumpled, his face was haggard, and his hair stuck out more than usual. A cold cup of coffee sat on the fireplace table, which was covered with manuscripts spilling onto the floor. Stubs of candles smoldered in the candelabra on the worktable, apparently having been burning all night. He fumbled with his empty pipe as he wandered aimlessly around the library.

"Mon ami," he began. "What a fool I've been." He pushed his hair back with his hands, pulling his forehead up as if to stick his eyes open for a few brief minutes. His cold pipe hung from his mouth, wobbling slightly as he chewed at the end. Finally, rubbing his eyes, he walked to the worktable and pointed.

Frank read the scribbled notes from last night's session.

just on edeat hats hemus tpayonf

in alho ur of jud gemen tdaynobarg

aimade toth us del ayhercumble

back todark estclay

Then below this, the translation. It wasn't the spirit who had stuttered with the letters T and H, it had been Armand the whole time. The translation read:

Just one death that she must pay,

on final hour of judgement day.

No bargain made to thus delay,

her crumble back to darkest clay.

The he pointed to the final passage of his original scribble:

Herd eath is night hefinal term with pali dang els toafirm theast ralhorde willwrith

eands quirm ass hefe edstheg host lyver mevic

torv ermis

Then below this, the last translation:

Her death is nigh, the final term,

with pallid angels to affirm.

The astral horde will writhe and squirm,

as she feeds the ghostly verme.

But this time it was signed: Victor Vermis

Frank pondered the cryptic message for a while, puffing his cigar. He lit a match for Armand's pipe and looked into his friend's eyes when he came close to fire the sweet tobacco. He saw weariness there, which was certainly from the lack of sleep. But he saw something else as well, something very close to shame.

Frank dropped the spent matchstick in the ashtray and headed for the stairs. "I'm gonna make us some breakfast. Dis way da gravy won't get burnt. Den we're gonna have us a chat."

*

After breakfast Frank made two stiff Bloody Marys—his had a few extra dashes of hot sauce, considering his indigestion was on the mend. The two men walked upstairs to the library and sat in their usual chairs.

"Now," Frank began. "Tell me where da hoodoo message came from."

All during breakfast—and while Frank prepared it—Armand waited for his friend to grill him about the situation. He even anticipated it with some joy, Frank whistling the tune to *The Twilight Zone* and wiggling his fingers at him.

But Frank said nothing of the kind. Instead, he talked about his car, which was *purring like a kitten*, and how he'd dropped another ten pounds which was why he didn't feel bad about making the gravy extra greasy. Jimmy came and went, grabbing a handful of sausage links and carefully placing them in a napkin. Although he then wiped his greasy hand on his pants before heading outside to chase whatever he was in pursuit of these days.

Neither did Frank ask about Mama Dedé. He must have known that if she'd improved Armand would have already updated him.

So, now there was nothing left for Armand to do but admit the colossal mistake he'd made. After a long sip of his drink, he tried one last distraction. "Mmmm, mon ami, this is quite delicious. Care to share your secr—?"

"Vampire blood," Frank interrupted. He had no patience for delay. "Now what about da hoodoo?"

Armand sighed. "You must understand, I was at my wits end. I had nowhere else to turn. I simply—"

Frank waved a Cease and Desist with his hand. "I'm sold. So stop sellin' me. Where'd it come from and what da hell does it mean?"

Armand supplicated his hands, then let them drop to the arms of his chair. This time he looked directly at Frank. "Those are words that I recorded during a session with the Ouija Board last night. I tricked Jimmy. Shameful as it is to say, I did. I asked him to play a game with me that might help us understand what ailed Mama D."

This time Frank did whistle, but there was no jovial finger wag. "You mean da damn thing actually moved?"

Armand nodded. "Oh, yes. It moved. It was the second session we've had. We made contact both times. It appears the spirit had a lot to say. There's more to the message." He motioned to the worktable.

"What's it mean?"

Armand shook his head. "I have only a rudimentary theory."

Frank waited several seconds, then said, "So, what else?" His tone was that of expectancy. He knew Armand was holding back.

Armand looked down at his glass which he still held in his hands. The ice was melting.

His words came reluctantly, as if admitting the final act of a terrible crime. "You must understand, I didn't know he was going to speak to it directly. The… the spirit, that is. Before I could stop him… he asked it for help."

"Who? Jimmy asked da spirit?"

Armand, with head hung down, nodded. "Yes, he'd had a bad dream yesterday afternoon. Something about a bird. He awoke in a panic. I didn't realize last night it was still on his mind. He… he forgets things, you understand."

Frank nodded.

"But it *was* still on his mind. As terrifying as it had been, he remembered it, and asked for help to find it."

A question formed on Frank's face, but Armand had the answer ready.

"I know. I asked him later, after my shock subsided, why he would ask for such a thing, to find the bird of his nightmare, if the dream had been so terrible." Armand's voice cracked to a watery whisper. "He said, 'So he could help find Del.'"

The impact of the statement somehow pushed Frank further back in his chair and he quickly rubbed his watering eyes. He began to understand the terrible weight that was hanging over his friend.

Then Armand said, "And the spirit accepted."

Frank thought about this, then stood up and walked to the

worktable. He didn't pretend to understand the arcane passages Armand had written—the words read like a nonsense nursery rhyme to him. The extent of Frank's reading—beyond police reports, ballgame schedules and the newspaper—had been limited to some westerns he'd read right after retiring—and he sure did like that Louis L'Amour guy—but it didn't take a scholar to see by the look on Armand's face that he thought a troubling message lay encoded on those pages.

Frank always prided himself on his ability to follow a hunch—most detectives did. And the hunch that came over him felt as strong as any he'd experienced when he was in the field. His friend was in trouble.

"So, I'm assumin' Del's room is open?" Frank asked flatly.

Armand blinked in confusion, then a dawning surprise lightened his face. He quickly replayed the words in his mind to ensure he'd heard them correctly.

Frank confirmed with a nod. "Del's room. It's open, yeah?"

Armand nodded slowly.

"Yeah. OK. I'll sleep der 'til we get dis straightened out."

Armand had no more words. He could only raise his melting Bloody Mary in salute to his friend, the pillar.

CHAPTER 35

Del arrived at work at 10:30 am on Sunday. The bar was still locked. No one was there.

After meeting with Arlo the night before, she'd thought about hanging out at some of the other clubs in the area—she had to make some friends somehow after all—but had gone home instead. Arlo's instructions on her next task had dampened any idea of having fun for the rest of the night.

She rattled the doorknob once more, just in case, then sat down on a rickety bench and waited for Tasha. She was learning to work through her Sunday shifts—where Tasha ran the bar during brunch—with little interaction with the girl. She couldn't figure out why Tasha hated her so much, but wasn't sure it was worth worrying about. So, she leaned back against the outside wall and closed her eyes.

Sunday was becoming the day she missed Armand's house the most. A late breakfast was surely filling the old kitchen with wonderful aromas right about now. First it would be the smell of chicory coffee. Armand made it strong, and Del was beginning to like only a certain blend. Next, it would be bacon, and Armand had learned to cook a bit extra so she could steal a few pieces before the others got up. She thought about sitting there with the morning paper and its unique smell of dusty wood and chemical ink, dreaming of the newspaper business. She missed that house.

A door slammed and brought Del back to the present. A cute young couple had just closed the street-level door that ran to their upstairs apartment which sat over a bar across the street. They looked very hungover and very happy to stumble across the street together to a diner. Del smiled slightly, wondering how their evening had gone to put them in such a state this morning. Without thinking about it, she flashed into a trance and tracked their path backwards, up the steps, and into their small apartment. Just moments before, they had been in bed sleepily exploring each other, waiting for their respective heads to clear enough to walk across the street. They hadn't even showered when they threw clothes on to run downstairs, and they still smelled like sex. They were planning on eating bed in breakfast and staying in the rest of the day. Del watched in her shadowy form as beads of sweat had formed on his lower back. He had rocked slowly into the girl, just before the perspiration pooled at the hollow of her throat. He was a gentle lover and the girl opened herself to him more because of it. She coaxed him on with her feet around his back. He was shy. She was in love and cried after her first orgasm with him. Him and his stupid grin, not realizing what had happened, and still not close himself. They would sweat for hours.

Del pulled back from the scene, jumping up from the bench. What was she doing? Had her life devolved into nothing more than spying on other people? A psychic Peeping Tom?

A feeling of loneliness washed over her, and she was suddenly angry at the circumstance that led her to taking this job. She wanted something different for her life. In fact, at this moment, she wished she had a completely different life, was someone else entirely. Someone with parents maybe? Childhood memories? A grandmother? These thoughts and others flashed through her, digging at deep-seated memories. It wasn't the first time she'd considered trancing back to her time before the orphanage, but she simply didn't know if it would do any good. That time was past and right *now* was her life. For better or worse.

Coming back to the present, she wondered about the time again.

She rattled the doorknob in frustration, then kicked the metal plate at the bottom. If Tasha hadn't been late to work, Del wouldn't have been sitting here to watch the young lovers stumble across the street. Only to then have the pity-party play out and ruin her mood.

Oh crap. The cooks! Del suddenly thought.

She had forgotten that the cooks would already be here, and they had keys. Their setup took longer than the front of the house, so they got here at ten.

She ran through the alley around the side of the building and slipped into the open back door.

Franklin, the weekend cook, came out of the back when he heard the door close. He grunted at her. "Hggh, you girls in a heap a' shit. I already called Jonesy dat no one's here. He ain't happy he gotta come in on his day off."

Del nodded and quickly began pulling chairs off tables. The day was going to be a long one.

*

As predicted, Jonesy wasn't happy at all, considering he'd closed the bar the night before. But he wasn't mad at Del. It was Tasha's shift behind the bar, after all. The fact that Del hadn't thought to come around back and have the front of the house setup was a minor inconvenience, but it was hers. He had commented however that the status of *new girl* had run its course and if she wanted more shifts, possibly even behind the bar, she needed to be more responsible.

The idea of more shifts motivated her through the rough day—she could always use the extra money. She wondered briefly however if this decision wasn't another step away from her dream of being a reporter. It seemed the lure of immediate money—after all, she left each shift with cash in her pocket—was guiding her away from a longer-term dream. But she had bills to pay now. So, she bit back the disappointment and waited on her tables.

When Detective Marcel Valcour walked into The Hidden Note just after one o'clock that afternoon, Del's mouth dropped open in surprise.

Her day had just gone from bad to worse.

*

Marcel asked Jonesy and Del into the small office behind the bar, then called the owner from there. Over the phone he confirmed that Tasha had been an employee here—Marcel explained that they'd found a paycheck stub in her jeans pocket, but had yet to find her purse; he also confirmed she had worked her shift the night before, then had been found dead around 3:00 am, just a few blocks away. Jonesy and Del stood for several minutes in shocked silence as Marcel confirmed a few more details. The small office was very warm by the time he hung up the receiver.

"Well. Imagine my surprise when I walked in today and saw you here," Marcel said to Del. "It seems I saw *you* first, after all."

Jonesy looked at Del with surprise.

Del scuffed the toe of her sneaker against the worn floorboards and wiped her eyes with a tissue. "It seems so."

"Did Tasha have any enemies?" he asked them both. "Did she have a beef with anyone?"

Jonesy and Del exchanged glances, both thinking about how nasty Tasha had been to Del. They both shook their heads, saying nothing.

"Seen anyone hanging around lately?" Marcel continued. "Any creepers?"

Jonesy chuckled. "Huh! Shoot, dat describes half'n our crowd. Ev'r bar got its cre—" He noticed Marcel wasn't smiling. "Uh… got its reg'lars."

"Mmm-hmm." Marcel looked up from his notes and eyed Jonesy. "And your location last night?"

"Home wit' da missus."

"Mmm-hmm."

"You can call her if'n you—"

"I will."

"Do… do you know how it happened?" Del ventured.

Marcel eyed her, then checked something in his notebook. He scribbled a note, then closed it carefully.

"That's part of the investigation," he said. "Do you know who will take Tasha's shifts now that she's deceased?"

Del swallowed as her eyes swam around the floor. The question from left field left her speechless.

"What?" she asked, then looked at Jonesy for help.

"I make sure da shifts are covered," Jonesy said to Marcel. "Guess we have to find a new girl, but in da meantime, I may ask Del to pick up a few." Then, hoping it would deflect the subtle suspicion he felt building with the detective, he added, "She don't got many shifts yet, she's still learnin.'"

"I see," said Marcel. "OK, then. I'll let you two get back to work." He opened the office door, stepped out, then turned and faced Del. "Funny, I thought you told me before that you didn't have time to run off anywhere. Work, work, work, I believe is how you put it. But maybe it was just wishful thinking, huh?"

He turned and left without an answer.

Del saw the look of concern creep over Jonesy's face, but had nothing to say to him. She grabbed her purse and left by the back door.

CHAPTER 36

Back in her apartment, Del sat on the bed with her knees hugged to her chest. Her world was spinning out of control, and she felt as though she were hanging on by a thread. This wasn't how she'd envisioned her life going at all.

Did Detective Valcour really suspect her of being involved with Tasha's death? Just over wanting additional work shifts? She'd read about people committing far worse crimes over less, but this was crazy. And what did it have to do with the murder she had stopped? Was that just coincidence?

Ever since the night she'd been chased, these things had been happening. Were they related somehow?

Del relaxed her legs and leaned back against her pillows. She missed the large pile of pillows she had at Armand's house. These pillows were somehow flat and lumpy at the same time, and she had to fold them over just to get a little support.

Actually, it wasn't just since the night she'd been chased that these things had started to occur. That night was also when she'd met Arlo.

Maybe that was the common denominator. Was this part of her finding her path? She looked at the palm of her right hand and gently rubbed it. She couldn't see the pact lines that were somehow etched beneath her skin, but she knew they were still there. At least, she feared they were still there.

She closed her right hand and squeezed, feeling for anything malicious that may be growing there. If it were a lump, like a cancer, maybe she could cut it out; but she knew that was a silly thought.

What did Arlo really want from her anyway? What was in it for the old woman? Now Del wished she'd asked more questions of her. Wished she had a better understanding of what her repayment would consist of.

Her head dropped into her hands, elbows wedged against her knees. She had to do something. Anything would be better than sitting here waiting for the next thing to happen, all the while, Mama Dedé was getting worse. If she just didn't have so many distractions, maybe she could accomplish something. Worrying about drawing spirits into Armand's house had caused her to leave in the first place. Worrying about paying her bills kept her working at the bar. Working at the bar kept her from becoming a newspaper reporter. Then there was the psychic spying her mind kept doing. It was like when a song got stuck in her head and she couldn't get it to stop. Only instead of a song, it was visions—auto trances she could barely control—that popped into her head. It was like having a whole other mind that had suddenly woken up and wouldn't go back to sleep. The young lovers she'd spied on this morning filled her mind. She wanted to feel what they were feeling. The sterile sensation of her trances was one of the things she hated the most. Somehow, she had a sense of what the people in the scenes were feeling. Maybe it was just her imagination, but she thought she could sense it. But that was it. There was no real feeling with her voyeurism. Her experience with the lilac woman had been different when she'd slipped back in time. But right now, the sterile trances filled her body with an emptiness that was almost unbearable. She wanted to be one of the young lovers from this morning. She didn't care which. She just wanted something real to hold onto.

Then the attempted murder scene flashed forward. The man with the knife. The woman cowering in the bathroom. There had been rage there. And fear. And passion. Although the man with the knife had felt rage at that moment, he'd felt passion before that. Hadn't he? Hadn't the woman loved him enough to want to make him jealous? It didn't matter. They were others' lives. Others' dreams and desires and struggles. The young lovers hadn't showered before they went out for breakfast. They would do that later, together. The smell of blood from the man stabbing his own leg filled Del's head. She could taste it in her mouth. She could taste the lovers.

Stop. Please stop, she begged the voice in her head, her other mind.

But it was just coming into its own. Like a slow-idling engine, the darkly dreaming part had taken a while to warm up, but now it was starting to hum. Now it was ready to purr. Soon, very soon, it would be running at full speed. It sensed freedom, her other mind, her trancing mind, her latent talent that had been suppressed for so long. But its time had come, and it would not be denied.

The young lovers. The stabbing man. The screaming woman. Skeleton Jimmy. Arlo. Spider. Clara. Willy. Broussard. The twins. Scarmish. The beast. Toth. Jo. The Void.

These things flooded her mind, clamoring for attention, demanding to be explored. And behind them all, a tapestry of dead bobbed on an endless ocean. A thousand, thousand faces waited their turn to speak with the Spirit Hunter.

Del curled into a fetal position on her bed and pulled the covers over her head. She pulled the wrapping of blankets tight around herself. "Stop," she whispered. "Please stop."

It was in this cocoon of darkness that she slipped into a dark place. Somewhere between a trance and a dream, her other mind had finally pulled her. And it began to roam.

*

In the darkness of her mind—through a dream of a trance, or a trance of a dream—she visited many things. She sought the young lovers first. She had her own needs after all. She saw herself sitting on the bench outside of the bar, waiting for Tasha. Then she was in the lovers' small apartment. She lingered there in the shadows, the shadows of her mind, cloaked in the shadows of their past, hidden by the shadows from the curtains they'd pulled tight. They returned and ate ravenously, feeding each other on the bed.
Del was hungry too.

The jelly for the biscuits did not go to waste, but the biscuits were left for later. Del filled the shadows and breathed in the room. Their lovemaking gave her energy, and she grew large, engorged with their passion. She felt her skin prickle and her eyes were aflame. She tasted the lovers' fantasies; each one imagining, projecting their secret desires to a place in their minds where it would be recalled years later, but Del stole these memories for herself. Then she tasted of them again, wanting to experience more, but the lovers flinched, pulling back from one another as if a cold wind had slipped beneath the window. They huddled together, away from the wind and Del was denied, rejected in her own world.

So, she went elsewhere.

In the murder house, the angry man had just kicked in the door to his own bathroom; his future dead ex-wife was screaming on the floor trying to dial a broken phone.

Del felt her terror and drank it in. The woman's heat was intense, and it fueled the dark ember smoldering at Del's core. She watched with amusement as the door splintered inward, just as a glowing silver orb—her trancing image from that day—shimmered into existence between the quarreling people. She was seeing her own mind from when she tried to save the people from themselves.

But now she noticed something new. Something else had been at the murder house with her that day. Something only Del could see now. She hadn't seen it the day she collapsed against the fence, but she could see it now. Spinning with wild energy, she saw another version of herself, a dark dreaming version, and it was growing with alarming speed.

That day at the murder house, the dark-dreaming Del had come forward for the first time. Something had fueled it into existence from a smoldering ember. It had lain, quiet and hidden, in the recesses of her mind, exploring, waiting to come out, waiting to be born. And now it was here.

That day at the murder house, the dark-dreaming Del had wanted the silver-orb Del to go away. *Let the scene play out*, she thought darkly. These people had set their own stage after all. In some deep part of them, they wanted this conflict. Deserved the outcome.

Who are you, silver-orb Del, to interfere?

Now the quarreling people in the murder house were both screaming at the demon, the silver-orb demon that had risen between them trying to prevent murder. The man began stabbing his own leg. Dark-dreaming Del watched with fascination and tasted of the blood that soaked his pants. Metallic and warm.

Then Del heard herself scream from the driveway and flew to see what new terror was there.

Only it was not what she could have ever imagined.

There, crumpled on the gravel driveway, slumped against a chain link fence, was physical Del from the day before. Her memory had been wiped of this time period. When Detective Valcour had asked her what had happened, she'd made up the most plausible story she could think of, but it hadn't been a complete lie. She couldn't remember most of her time in the driveway, just the walk up to the house. But now she saw something new. Silver-orb Del had not disappeared completely when it had left the house. It had hovered around Del's physical body, protecting it, although there was no physical danger that could be seen. No person in their right mind would approach the screaming girl huddled against the fence, pounding her own leg with her fist. But the danger was not there.

The danger was from the dark cloud that now swirled in a mystic dream inside Del's head. The dark cloud had formed its own shape, that of an orb—a black shiny orb with a tiny silver streak. A negative image of how Mama Dedé described Del's trancing impression. A doppelgänger of power. The alter-ego of a young woman who was searching for her path.

The dark orb swirled and twisted into shape, mirroring the silver orb that was protecting Del's body. It was a slow and cautious introduction. The two halves had never met before. In fact, neither knew the other existed. Somewhere deep in Del's mind, her latent power had manifested itself into these two cosmic entities.

The silver-orb version of herself, which tried to follow a path of light, was standing watch.

But now, the black-orb version of herself—the Dark Dreamer—was watching back.

CHAPTER 37

On the corner of Dauphine and Mandeville streets, in a building no one could see, Madame Broussard looked up from her work.

She fingered her pearls absently, but listened intently to the walls. They were whispering. And she knew from experience to heed their warnings.

Quickly scanning the fresco, she saw no obvious change, but that was to be expected. The fact was that it changed frequently—in a mundane way—reflecting the seasons of man and earth. But over the years she had grown so accustomed to these ordinary things, she looked past them now. Her interests lay with the subtle things, the dark things, that were projected there on her wall. And although she couldn't see it, she sensed something new had just emerged.

Oh, how she wished to be out in that changing world again. Even if she were somehow exiled from this city, she'd be glad to leave and never come back. She'd leave just so she could explore the countryside again; so she could search; so she could remember.

In her mind, the crisp smell of an October wind assailed her, pulling her back to a time almost forgotten. It was a sea wind, ragged of breath and seasoned with salt. But they were new smells to her then, so they held a found place in her heart.

After a long and treacherous voyage, the ship, *Carmilla*, had drifted into port with a ghost wind on her rudder and shreds for sails.

But the passengers had survived.

At least a few of them, anyway.

One of those survivors—a young girl—was destined to stay in the bustling port city with her affluent family. She had the look of becoming a prodigious breeder; it was in the hips and budding bosom; even at the girl's young age, Madame Broussard had seen it. The girl was certain to have produced many offspring by now. What a shame they couldn't be visited.

One of the other survivors, a young, entrepreneurial man from France, a Mr. Alexander Broussard, would establish an Import/Export business and was last seen traveling into the wilderness far up the Mississippi. She often wondered what had become of him. Then of course, that *had* been the time of The Lady in the Water—so very long ago—and was best to remain secret for now. She was sure someone would uncover the story eventually.

She came back to the present and sat quietly, listening. The walls murmured in their ancient, shifting way, reporting on the faint rippling change of energy. They didn't debate the meaning of the change, just that there was one. Something in the air was different.

Alvie's skeleton head fell to one side, causing the bones to slump nonchalantly, when she stood. Her repairs to the Boy Made of String were nearly complete. But she needed to be more cautious with him next time. If he encountered the Stone Maiden again, she doubted he would survive it.

Walking past the display table, her fingers slid over the macabre items of her curio shoppe. Actually, since the near-demise of Scarmish, she had had no other customers, so it was hard to think of the building as a shoppe and nothing other than an invisible prison, but it *had* been active once. And she was good at waiting.

One day, she thought. *One day I'll be free of these confines and will have my vengeance. One day the Crescent City will remember my terror.*

Her finger touched the end of something sharp and she stopped. Looking down, she saw a long sharp hat pin.

But it wasn't the pin she was so interested in; it was the object connected to the other end of it. And because the object at the end was so interesting, she was surprised she hadn't thought of the item more often.

There was something to explore here.

Running her finger around it, she felt the tip, waiting to pierce, waiting to puncture. And who was she to deny an object its desire? *For it is my nature,* said the scorpion. And with that thought, she pushed her finger against it and let the needle slide up beneath her fingernail.

One inch.

Two inches.

It was now clearly past the first knuckle, stretching the skin up in a long straight line and locking her pointer finger straight. She could feel it scraping the bone there. But at least it was a feeling.

She raised her hand, and the needled object came with it. She stared with wonder. Now, protruding six inches out of her left pointer finger was a long metal needle. Atop it was a small, leathery brown voodoo doll with red bead eyes. It was a ragtag doll at best. Although the 'skin' of the doll appeared to be quite durable—perhaps even *actual* skin—one foot was missing. The missing appendage had been replaced by a human big toe, attached above the knuckle by some type of binding magic. The toe was black with rot now—the creator clearly hadn't taken the time to preserve it—and bits of bone showed where the skin had fallen away. Her finger now looked like something a child would wear to announce support for their favorite team—if it were a game of demons. She moved her hand, causing the pinned object to wobble. Then the eyes of the doll began to glow. Somehow life was flowing into the ugly thing.

As she marveled at the craftsmanship—for this was a skillful creation—an errant shadow drew her attention back to the fresco wall. Her meandering mind snapped back to the problem at hand. Something new had just emerged that she felt could travel the shadow roads.

And this was something she took very seriously.

CHAPTER 38

Billy sat in his dark kitchen, at the too-yellow table, and trembled. On his face, dark mirrored sunglasses reflected the movements of his shaky hands. The sunglasses shielded his eyes and pounding head from the garish light that leaked out of the walls. The shaky hands were caused by something else.

As they moved through the debris of the spilled purse, he wondered where the items had come from. Whose purse was this anyway? And why was it on his kitchen table?

Here was a compact. Those were the easiest to find, having a shape that slipped neatly into your palm. Errant pieces of gum had escaped their pack and drooped with fatigue. Lots of receipts that were nothing more than faded strips of paper. Purse dirt. A tube of lipstick. An old, crumpled paycheck stub, the kind that tears off from the side. The paycheck was from a bar. A nail file. Condoms…

He'd never met a purse that didn't have condoms.

He couldn't recall how long he'd been sitting here, because he didn't know what day it was. With the heavy drapes pulled tight, night passed into day easily. And with the gaudy light always shining back at him, burning his mind, he had the sense he was living in a world of perpetual twilight where everything must choose its color from the garish spectrum of yellows, pinks and oranges. It was always hot here.

He'd been planning to go out and see someone, but now wondered if that was tomorrow night.

Or tonight maybe.

Maybe here, maybe there, maybe never-never-where. But nobody rides for free, Billy. Nobody rides for free.

He felt tired. Rundown. Disconnected.

Was he asleep and dreaming? His confused mind tried to turn his head and look for a clock, but it was too heavy. It then tried to make his eyes move, but the lids were closing. Behind the mirrored sunglasses his eyelids drooped and the debris on the table pulled a memory from his mind—somewhere deep. This scene looked familiar:

The Scattered Purse scene.

Someone had dropped their purse when he was young, and he'd bent over it, trying to save the items. In fact, the purse had hit the pavement with a loud *SMACK!*

Several of them.

(SMACK!)

(…crack the flap dog, bitch, this paint your house…)

(SMACK!)

Billy's hands shook as he gathered the items. He tried to be careful, he really did. He didn't mean to lose anything, but the items had scattered all over the place, and the wind was blowing.

His fingers reached for the driver's license on the table—he needed to see whose purse this was—but just like before, the flimsy card slipped from his fingers. Here, in the kitchen, the card fell between the back of the table and the wall. In his mind, the card had disappeared, irretrievably, down a sewer grate and landed with a loud *SMACK!* Just out of reach.

Somewhere in this dream, at the end of The Scattered Purse scene, was The Red, he felt. And a

(tickle)

warm place to sleep. Maybe even something to eat. After the purse would fall and its contents would spill, he'd have to scramble quick, quick. This much noise always made the cops come. And if they were still here when the police showed up, he'd have to go away for a while. But if he could gather everything up quickly, then they could get away and let The Red settle over them.

(No biting Billy, just tickle me)

CHAPTER 39

J *iimmmyyyy...*
Sunday evening Jimmy awoke and listened to the quiet house. Someone had just whispered to him. At least, he thought it was a someone.

He was getting used to *things* whispering to him since he'd come to Armand's house, which was why his brain couldn't always tell the difference. There was the time the knives in the drawer whispered to him, wanting to get out. They wanted to play a nasty trick, but Jimmy didn't like nasty tricks, so he left them in there. He was glad he'd ignored them. Then there was the time the candle flames wanted him to knock over the candle stick so they could get away, racing across the carpet and up Armand's tall shelves of books. He didn't like that trick either and ignored them also. They got mad and said mean things, whispering into his ears late into the night. Finally, there was the stone maiden, who had a voice made of water. She whispered to him when he was outside, but she had yet to try and play any tricks on him—at least, none that he could remember. He thought her to be nice. Well… he supposed she must be a some-*one* instead of a some-*thing*, but wasn't sure.

Regardless, he'd just heard a voice.

When he'd gone to bed, Frank and Armand were still talking in the library—they were having a sleepover—but now they were quiet. They'd made a lot of noise for a while, sitting around the fireplace. They were always noisy when they drank wine. It had reminded Jimmy of when they all lived in the house together and Mama D and Del would drink wine with them. Sometimes they got a little noisy, but not like Frank and Armand. On those nights, Jimmy would sit by himself and listen. He'd laugh sometimes when they would laugh, but he wasn't always sure what the joke was. He was just happy Del hadn't told any of her shrimp jokes. They weren't funny at all. But most of the time, he would play under Armand's worktable, or sit at the chessboard, practicing with the pieces. He wished he could join in the adult conversations, but instead chose to sit and listen. He was a good listener.

Now he could hear Frank snoring from Del's room. The sounds came right through the air vent. But the other voice he'd heard hadn't come from the vent. It had just come out of the air somehow. Maybe he'd dreamed—

Jiimmmyyyy…

The voice whispered again.

And because he was now awake, he knew he hadn't dreamed the voice. And because he was looking in the right direction, he saw where it came from. It came right out of the mirror on his dresser, which sat in the corner of the room at the foot of his bed. From where he lay, he couldn't see himself, but if he waved his right hand, he'd see it reflected there. Now it only reflected a part of the wall behind his headboard.

But from this angle, when the voice spoke, he saw the words vibrate the glass, which made it glow slightly. It looked like someone had turned on a tiny dim light somewhere deep within the mirror, maybe at the end of a very long hallway. But now it was dark again.

Jimmy whispered to the voice, "Dat not a pwace to pway in. You bweak da miwah."

Everybody knew not to play around mirrors and windows, even Jimmy knew—

Hey, wait a minute, he thought.

He crawled out from under the covers and on top of the bed. On all fours, he leaned towards the dresser and whispered. "How'd you get in dere?"

The mirror sat still for a moment, waiting. Jimmy wondered if he'd spoken too softly, but then the faintest glow floated the words to the surface, rippling the glass.

I flew in.

Jimmy's eyes widened, his voice soft and unbelieving. "You fwew in?" Then, because he was such a good listener, he remembered part of an adult conversation he'd had just the other night with Armand. "On da biwd?" He smiled to himself, happy that he'd remembered asking Armand's friend Victor to help him find the bird in his dreams. But then a cold feeling crawled down Jimmy's back, and he thought he might have to run to the bathroom and pee. Some part of his mind wanted to find the bird, but another part didn't. There was something bad—or at least scary—about the bird, but he couldn't remember exactly what it was. Somehow, he thought the bird could help him find Del, or maybe a cure for Mama D. He wanted to help them both if he could.

Bwave 'da 'ion, Jimmy thought. For Del, *Bwave 'da 'ion.*

The dark mirror sat silent, thinking. The soft glow had receded, but wasn't completely gone. It seemed the conversation with Jimmy was keeping it alive. The mirror pulsed slightly, as if struggling to breathe, and with each breath, the glass rippled, stretching its physical boundaries. Then it spoke.

Yessss, on da biwwddd.

Jimmy's mouth hung open in surprise. He'd never met anyone who talked like he did. Even the lady in the fountain didn't sound like him, but that was because her voice came up through the water. Maybe this could be Jimmy's first real friend outside of Del. Besides, she wasn't around anyway.

Another whisper.

Whoo would like to flyyy on da biwwddd?

A smile of wonderment cracked Jimmy's face, as the mirror glowed out the invitation to him. Surely, he could find Del if he could fly on a bird.

"Dis guy!" Jimmy thumbed his chest in the dark.

*

Sunday evening and Del was still dreaming. She had tossed and turned until she'd wrapped herself tight in the blanket. She'd fought disturbing images for hours. The Dark Dreamer had taken advantage of its newly found freedom, having explored Del's memories, leaving nothing unturned. Then, after hours of mental exploitation, the Dark Dreamer slipped back into the folds of Del's mind and Del settled into her current state.

Vaguely aware of the intruder's departure, she awoke enough to recognize the feel of her own blanket and bed. She was safe in her apartment. But also feeling the effects of the extended afternoon nap, her mind was now awake—gratefully with a single voice—and wanted its own turn to explore. So, in a half-awake state, her mind dancing, and her body enjoying the warmth of the bed, she tranced out.

She was aware that she'd missed her afternoon call to Armand, so wasn't surprised when her trance snapped to his house. She began her visit by enjoying the warm feelings that emanated from the heavy wood panels, but was disturbed by how quiet the house was.

The sky was dark beyond the ornate windows. Almost all of the lights in the house were off.

Where is everyone? she wondered.

Not taking the time to unwrap herself from her comfortable blankets, she couldn't see a clock, and was disoriented to the actual time.

She sank deeper into her own bed, squirmed her head against her pillow, then continued exploring the grand old house she loved so much.

What's Frank doing there?

She saw him sleeping in her bed. Then, fearing the worst, she snapped to Mama D and was relieved to find her sleeping as well. Her breath was shallow, but consistent enough, she thought. But the room didn't feel right. Del suddenly had an itchy, squirmy feeling as she looked around the room. A slight revulsion crept over her the longer she explored. It was as if some terrible sickness was leaching from the walls, polluting the very air, settling with great weight in the shadows. And it was smothering Mama Dedé.

This isn't right…

What's wrong with this room? What's going on in here?

Del had the sense of invisible invaders, but saw nothing. Had the spirits come back? Despite her leaving the house, had they found a way in?

She tranced around the large house, looking for… What was she looking for anyway? Spirits didn't have to break in. She doubted she'd see an obvious sign, like when Frank and Spider had entered the house.

Checking the shadows downstairs, everything felt fine, in fact, the longer she lingered in the grand old house the more a feeling of homesickness grew in her. It had been a long time since she'd actually *looked in* on her extended family. Having chosen to call each Sunday for everyone's safety. But now that she was *in* the house—immaterially at least—she didn't want to leave. *Is this how ghosts feel?* she wondered. Is this why some ghosts are so reluctant to leave their former dwellings? Does the smell of the oiled wood and creak of the stairs seep into their souls somehow, binding them to the memory that occurred there?

If that were the case, Del was already doomed to haunt the grand house forever. It was the only place that felt like a home to her, despite the fact she'd lived there so briefly. She tried to breathe in the smell of the dusty books and oiled wood, the smoky fireplace, the newspaper and coffee, the magnolias, but the smells were faded at best. Sterile. Like so many other visions.

She caught a feeling of movement, somewhere in the house. A slight rustling of air. Someone was up. Snapping to the library, she looked on with dismay.

What in the world is he doing up?

There was Jimmy, sitting beneath Armand's worktable, with several items spread out in front of him on the floor. He appeared to be setting up a game.

Ever since they'd moved into the grand house, and with so much going on—mostly with Del trying to figure out her own life—she hadn't taken the time to see how Jimmy was adjusting.

Did he always play by himself like this?

A terrible feeling of guilt washed over her as she crept closer in the vision. Was he sleepwalking? She didn't think he did that, but never had a reason to look. Why would she? He never gave any outward sign of being troubled. That is, besides the obvious things like, having the Unbinding Spell shoved into his mind by Marie Laveau, or having a skeleton boy inhabit his body. Oh, and then there were the 'bug spirits' that had latched onto him once…

But it was Jimmy, Del thought. The boy who just went through life with an honest smile on his face, looking for rainbows and butterflies.

But here he was, all by himself, playing at something in the dark, beneath a table.

What is he playing at? Del floated closer.

Shock jolted her in her trance. Far away, her physical body flinched at the sight.

Spread out on the floor in front of Jimmy was a board. Del recognized it instantly. The alphabet was laid out, written in an Old English script. On the floor to the right of the board was a scattering of papers and a few crayons. Jimmy had been practicing his letters. His right hand was on the puck that was moving slowly across the board. But the thing in his left hand is what made her gasp.

In his left hand, Jimmy held the severed and preserved hand of a person. Some knew it as a Mojo Hand. Some called it a Hand of Glory. Regardless of its name, Del felt it was pure evil.

Jimmy was using the Hand of Glory as the second set of fingers on the puck. And the puck had just begun to glow as it moved across the board.

*

Jimmy's eyes shone with magic wonder at the scenes that played out before him. Playing the talking board game with Victor—who lived in Jimmy's mirror—was much better than when he'd played it with Armand. He thought it was pretty fun when Armand made the puck move the first time, but after that, it just kept moving around the same old letters. But this time, Victor was able to make the board show him pictures.

As the puck moved around the board, Jimmy had tried to write some of the letters, as Armand had done, but they got all scrambled up on the paper. Either that, or Victor couldn't spell any better than he could, because the letters didn't look like any words he'd ever seen:

Cha'thul ungh ah mwu'lla nigh, Calla, Calla, dhung'll die

is what the letters spelled (and Jimmy thought they said). They looked like crazy words, but they did seem familiar in a strange way. He thought maybe he'd dreamed a silly song with these words in it, a long time ago. But he couldn't remember that either.

So, instead of making him write more letters—he was pretty slow after all, and Victor tried to move to the next letter faster than Jimmy could write it—Victor decided to just show him a story. And that was a lot more fun anyway.

Now he was watching the bird in his dreams. At first, it was a little scary, because of all the dead faces, but Victor showed Jimmy how he could ride on the bird's back, that way he didn't have to see the dead stuff in its talons.

In Jimmy's vision, the bird cried out when Victor helped him climb onto its back. It gnashed its long black beak in surprise. Then, somehow, Victor guided Jimmy's hands and pulled the bird's neck feathers—they were black and smelled of burnt wood—and this caused the bird to turn. Jimmy cracked a wide smile in his dream. It was like riding a horse, only he was flying! Above him, the sun shone down on his back and all he saw was blue sky and white clouds.

Beneath him, gripped tightly in chipped talons of midnight blue, were the faces and remnants of a thousand, thousand people close to death. They were somewhere on their journey to the afterlife: floating down long tunnels of light, watching their lives flash before them, screaming blind in dark passages, feeling the winds of death blow ever faster as the black falcon carried them into oblivion. And here, amongst the nearly dead, was a familiar face: Mama Dedé screaming.

Without warning, Victor moved Jimmy's hands, which pulled the falcon's head sharply to one side. It screeched and fell into a slow roll. For a moment, the world was weightless, force and gravity in equilibrium, then the bird plunged.

Like a plane whose engine had stalled, the bird fell with dead weight. From high in the sky, the giant, streamlined bird cut through the air like an arrow. It was a bird of prey. It was built for speed. And in a matter of minutes, it would hit the ground of this dream world and blow a hole straight through the fabric into the world of the dead. There, the real Victor waited.

*

Trancing into Jimmy's dream, Del watched as he rode the black bird of death with the dying faces clutched in its talons. The scenes were broken and hectic. Jimmy, sitting cross-legged next to the Ouija board, was no longer working the puck. The puck was working him.

The pulsing light that streamed from the small wooden object had engulfed Jimmy, hypnotizing him, trapping him. He rocked back and forth wildly, nearly in a seizure.

In his dream, he'd been flying, but now the bird began a slow roll. Del stared in horror as the thing exposed its underbelly and she saw Mama Dedé's face there.

Clutched in its talons, Del recognized the spirit cord. Long and wispy, with a silvery sheen, hundreds of spirit cords hung from the talons like entrails. The cords fluttered in the wind, most of them nearly disintegrated. Surely those people had already passed over, she thought. But the one that struck her with horror, the one she couldn't tear her eyes from, ended with the face of her mentor. Trailing behind the bird, attached to its spirit cord by gossamer shreds of life, Mama Dedé's face hung in a ghostly grimace of fear. Edvard Munch's painting *The Scream* filled her mind. Twisted and distorted, the face blurred into a cloud of dark pain. But it was her. And at that moment, Del knew she was still alive, but for how long much longer, she couldn't tell.

The ghostly face was nearly blown away by the winds of death that curled from the falcon's wings. The face hung by a tattered cord, wrapped tightly in the razor talons. The other end of the cord stretched away to the ground, dangerously thin, where her physical body lay, dying. Then Del saw something beyond belief.

Mama Dedé's spirit cord was covered with worms.

What she'd mistaken for tatters just a moment ago were in fact the flapping ends of worms that had attached their selves to her spirit cord. They were feeding from the essence of her soul.

Del wretched and almost came out of her trance. She fought to stay in the dream, even though every part of her screamed to get away. If she left now, she feared she'd never find the bird again. But there were only moments to spare.

Del sensed that the bird was just a cog in the workings of the universe. Whether a messenger of death, a collector of dying spirit cords, or death itself, the bird was only acting on instinct. However, the spirit now controlling the bird was the problem. Somehow, having gained access to Jimmy, the spirit was controlling the bird through him. And the spirit from the Ouija board had just turned the bird and plunged it toward the earth and what lay beneath it. She felt it meant to rip the fabric between the worlds of the living and dead. It meant to escape. And it would certainly kill Mama D, and possibly Jimmy, in the process. She had to stop Jimmy's terrible dream. She hated to do it again, but she thought she'd have to send another frightening image into his mind, hoping to scare him out of this nightmare.

She wound up a terrible image in her mind and prepared to send it at him.

STOP! her mind screamed.

Don't do it! If you scare Jimmy out of his dream, you'll lose Mama D, and you can't open the fabric yourself! You'll never find the spirit cords!

Her mind spun, scenarios dancing through her head, before disappearing into vapor. It was true; she hadn't been able to open the fabric the way Arlo had. The old woman had helped Del that first time, with the girl in the cemetery. But how was she seeing it now? Was Jimmy seeing the fabric? Was he able to open it somehow? She didn't think so but couldn't be sure. She suspected it had more to do with the spirit in the board, but this damned dream of Jimmy's was so crazy, she couldn't be sure of anything. She could no longer tell dream from reality.

Could she save both?

(Now bite it)

Arlo's words came to Del.

No! I can't! Del screamed in her mind.

I can't kill her! I won't!

Then, as if someone had turned on a spotlight, Del focused on one spot of the spirit cord. All else faded away and her eyes knew where to look. Ignoring the horrors, they forced her to see.

There she only saw the worm.

(Now bite it) came the words again.

And Del bit.

The long flat worm exploded between her teeth. The tail flew off, disappearing with a faint pop that exploded into black mist. Then nothing.

The head of the worm released its hold from the spirit cord and turned on Del, shrieking a high-pitched death-cry then dissolving into the same black mist. Drops of it formed at the corner of Del's mouth and dripped from her chin. Cosmic wind, the cold wind of death curled from the bird's wings and stung her eyes, streaming the cord juice across her face like acid rain.

Del knew there were more. Having felt the spirit blood of Mama Dedé flow across her face, she felt the cord tremble under the tiny bites of the other worms. Nibbling. Nibbling. Burrowing their way into her soul the only way they could, through her weakened and damaged spirit cord.

Del found another and bit down again. *(Eeeeeee!)* The worm was there, shrieking and exploding.

She bit again and again.

(Eeeeeee!)

(Eeeeeee!)

Without thinking, her trancing mind moved where it needed to go. She didn't need to look. She only needed to feel. And she felt the worms die between her teeth. And the feeling was good.

Then a new sensation began to overtake her.

The cord juice, the tiniest drops, exploding out from the insides of the worms, had made its way into her mouth. It was a sensation she'd never felt before.

Jimmy screamed from his trance.

Del looked up as she severed the last worm between her teeth.

The falcon had plunged toward the earth in the last few moments, toward the dead world that lay beyond the veil.

Jimmy screamed again.

The bird of death shrieked.

Victor bellowed a hollow laugh.

Then Del flung herself forward.

In her trance, she reached for Jimmy, past him, through him, and into the room. Where he sat beneath the worktable, she saw her hand reach out, reach through the veil and hit the puck, knocking it from the board. The ghostly light that had hypnotized Jimmy went out with a flash and Jimmy tumbled to the side. Victor cried out in anger, cursing the invasion, then echoed away. The bird shrieked again as it regained its own power and pulled out of its dive. A shower of sparks shot from its talons as they scraped the pavement of one world, which nearly ripped the fabric between both. Del was thrown back into the room of her apartment and tumbled from her bed onto the floor.

There she began to gag and wretch. The metallic taste of blood was in her mouth, but it was not alone. Something else was there as well—a bittersweet tang snaking its way into her throat. Her tongue sought it out, exploring the insides of her mouth, which gushed with saliva. Her face and chin were wet with it. It dripped from her like a macabre ice cream that had spoiled in the sun.

She belched and convulsed.

"Ghlaack!"

Her arms buckled as she crawled to the door. Her stomach contracted in hard, sharp stabs.

"Ghhluh, ghlluh."

She was a rabid animal now, foaming at the mouth. As if flushing a poison from a wound, her body sent all the fluid it could spare to the tender folds of her mouth, and the cord juice dripped out as bluish foam.

"Uugghh… pphhluagh. Ppllaah!"

Crawling forward, Del felt for the door of her little room. She wretched and spit like an animal. She hocked phlegm from deep within her throat. She spat again and long strands of shiny blue saliva hung from her lips. She panicked. It wouldn't break away. It wouldn't clear her throat. She pulled at it with her fingers, and it clung to the insides of her cheeks and tongue. Her throat had the instinct to swallow. Her mouth ran with saliva, and she shook her head like a dog, trying to fling the alien substance away.

Wild eyed and frantic, she flung the door open, crawling into the dark hallway. Spitting and sobbing, she scraped the insides of her cheeks with her fingers, wishing desperately for fingernails that she might tear the inside layer of skin from her mouth. It burned. She gagged. She tried to vomit out an empty stomach, but even that wanted to slide back down.

She had to get to the bathroom. She had to wash the poison from her mouth before she swallowed anything.

And her throat desperately wanted to swallow.

CHAPTER 40

The reasons Madame Broussard stood vigil over the fresco, night after night, were complex. She had done it for so long it had become second nature, but it hadn't always been like this. There had been a time when she traveled whichever road she wanted, explored the world as she desired… but that time was long past. Now, her existence—and survival to some degree—depended on knowing what was outside her walls, or what may be traveling a shadow road that led to her walls.

Most shadow creatures moved about the fresco at the same pace and in the same directions. They simply traveled the shadow roads by letting themselves be pulled by some force greater than them. They drifted. Most of the shadows were lost spirits, perhaps the recently dead who were still orienting themselves to their new world. They would drift here and there in a sea of confusion until the clockwork of their process clicked forward, moving them onto their final destiny. Some were lucky enough to move there almost immediately upon death—she had seen it before. But most were not that lucky.

But some… some were pure evil; they'd been born from it; they'd fed upon it; and it would never leave them; upon death, those became vessels for darker things. And it was because of these things she stood her nightly vigil.

Touching the fresco caused the images to rise toward her. She could see the details of the scene better this way. The shadows were more defined. From this, she had inspected the Spirit Hunter's domain, the house, and its ring of protective white spirits. She'd identified a central spirit—a very old one it seemed—that remained just outside of the house, yet inside the ring. Was it in a courtyard perhaps? The details were too faded to see, but that spirit seemed to attend its own vigil. Then there was the ring. It may have thinned a bit over the last month, but it was still prominent. Then there was the black spot just outside the ring.

Scarmish, is that you?

With her right hand, she reached toward the fresco. Her left hand, half forgotten, hung by her side with a needle still protruding from her pointer finger. The lifeless, leathery voodoo doll hung upside down from it, its stubby arms and legs sticking out at its sides. Touching the faint black spot on the wall—the one she thought may be her old nemesis—set off a series of unexpected events. Images of Scarmish, old images, flashed in her mind. She saw him materialize from a dream into the wall of the building, then she saw him when he was remade from the souls of the twins, then saw him reach through her protective spell and consume Alvie with a gluttonous wet slurping sound. Yes. Scarmish was back. It had to be him. But in what form he had returned, she could not tell.

The other event which occurred upon touching the black spot—

which she hardly noticed—was the doll at the end of the needle ebbed to life; its red eyes glowed faintly and a very soft *ngyihng...* escaped its red bead mouth.

CHAPTER 41

Del lay on the creaking floor of the apartment house, nearly unconscious. Eyes closed, right cheek to the worn floorboards, shaking arms sprawled out before her, she whispered a feeble cry for help. Her mouth stung from the unnatural phlegm that clung to the insides of her cheeks.

She'd managed to crawl into the hallway before collapsing. The only bathroom on the second floor, some twenty feet away still, seemed impossibly far. Bizarre images and lights flashed in her head, as if she'd received a hard blow to it. She'd managed not to swallow the vile liquid—the *cord juice of the dying,* or whatever it was—but couldn't deny that she wanted to. A desire had never been so strong. And she was losing to it.

Her mind tried to make sense of her new state. The thoughts swirling in her head where a jumbled mix of real and tranced images. The line between reality and dream had nearly been wiped away for her. Soon, she wouldn't know the difference. As her mind sank toward unconsciousness, she wondered if she'd wake up in an insane asylum, arms tied down with long white sleeves, looking at padded walls. Or if she'd wake up at all.

Images swam.

The murder house. The funeral girl.

Terrible things no one could help with.

The cord. The worms.

Horrible things no one could even believe.

The rape gang. Tasha dead.

Who could stop these things even if they knew ahead of time?

Horrendous things happening day after day, year after year…

The silver-orb of Del awoke in her mind, a nucleus of thought. It was there without trancing. It hadn't been called forth or manifested out of wild dreams. It awoke with the obvious answer: *she* could help.

She'd considered this before, hadn't she? In one form or other, her mind had flirted with the idea that she could use her gift for good. And not just for settling the restless spirits, but for *real* good. For the things that really mattered.

If she could just make it to the sink. She might still be able to help.

Shaky energy raised her fingertips as she reached for the next inch of floor.

*

Outside the two-story apartment building, hidden in shadows of her own making, Arlo nodded. Del had passed the second task.

*

As Del lay there thinking all was lost, a strange sensation fell over her. It started as a feeling along the outside of her left leg, as if someone were stroking it. The soft caress, barely more than a whisper, moved up past her hip, then over her left shoulder. She peeled her left eye open—her right cheek was still against the floor—to catch a glimpse, but saw nothing. Then the caress was moving down the right side of her body. She wasn't afraid of the sensation, but her mind barely made sense of it. It wasn't strong enough to be a person. In fact, maybe it wasn't happening at all. Maybe her mind had finally gone under, and these were phantom sensations caused by a failing brain right before it shorts out. She let her eye close and imagined her hand was still trying to pull herself forward.

Then the feeling rippled throughout her mouth.

Despite knowing she was still face down on the old wood floor, she felt as if her head had been thrown back, and someone was swabbing the inside of her mouth… with sandpaper.

With lips only slightly parted—she'd been breathing through both her nose and mouth—she couldn't imagine someone was actually administering to her poisoned mouth. There wasn't enough room. She must be dreaming this, she thought, but the sensation wouldn't go away.

With her outstretched hand, she tapped her fingertips on the floor.

Yes, she was awake. And the swabbing sensation was still there.

It wasn't the abrasive feel of actual sandpaper, but it wasn't fairy kisses either. A persistent, methodical swiping of her mouth, first the roof, then the folds between teeth and lips, the insides of her cheeks, finally across her tongue. As the process repeated, she felt her head lighten and her senses began to clear.

After what seemed like several minutes, mild strength ran back into her arms. She pushed herself up into a crawling position. Her arms wobbled like a clown on stilts, but they held.

And for a reason she couldn't explain, with eyes closed and head hanging down, she opened her mouth and stuck out her tongue. A final, deep, penetrating swab touched the back of her throat and tickled her tonsils. She coughed once, then sneezed twice. The swabbing had ended.

With energy flowing back into her body, Del pushed herself up and sat back with her legs folded beneath her. Her head swam a bit as her eyes adjusted to the dark. For a fleeting moment she thought she saw the shadow of a cat slide along the door jamb, leading into the bathroom.

*

Outside, Arlo wondered about Del's future.

*

Inside Del's head, quietly watching through eyes not her own, the Dark Dreamer wondered as well.

And smiled.

CHAPTER 42

onday morning Billy awoke with his head on the kitchen table. He'd drooled over the pile of receipts and lists that he'd swept together from the mystery purse, arms encircling the trinkets like castle walls. Now some were stuck to his right cheek. His forehead and fingertips were smeared with makeup dust that had mysteriously settled at the bottom of the purse.

Looking around the room, he had a vague sense of lost time. The last few days had run together, and he felt he'd spent an inordinately long period of time sitting at the too-yellow kitchen table, dreaming old dreams.

A rumbling stomach and pain in his head—dehydration most likely—pushed him out of his seat. Swaying by the table, he held onto the edge until his blood pressure steadied. Sparks flashed before his eyes and the room darkened before it lightened, then settled to normal. He shook his head and sent a small piece of paper that had been stuck to his cheek fluttering toward the floor. With reflexes nearly at full capacity, he snatched it from the air and held it in front of him.

A small piece of paper, torn from a miniature notepad with spiral rings and folded over once for safe keeping sat in his hands. Fragments of paper—the thin part at the edge of the hole—stuck out in all directions where the paper had been ripped from the pad. He flipped the page open with the thumb and two fingers of his right hand. There he saw a neatly written list of names and addresses. It was female handwriting; he was sure of that. His mother used to keep the same kind of lists.

His mother…

Swallowing hard, he shook his head again and read the list. He didn't know whose purse this was, so the list would be of no importance to him. Although, a vague sense of familiarity swam in the back of his mind. He was sure he'd seen this purse before.

Bringing the list to his nose, he inhaled and caught a scent. It had been floating in the air all morning, just out of reach of his conscious thoughts. Having slept on the purse contents, his dreams where saturated with the scent. Now he smelled it more strongly with the paper held to his nose. It was a perfume scent he'd recently smelled. Not expensive, but pleasant enough. And unique. His memory began to clear.

As he read the names on the slip of paper—a makeshift address book—a picture of the purse owner began to form. A person who worked at a bar may need to keep such a list of other workers in case someone called in sick. A few names were scratched out or had Xs by them. Those must be employees who'd left this establishment for greener fields, he thought. Flipping the paper over, the list continued. The names were in a different color of pen but written with the same female penmanship. Except for one word. The last entry on the list must have been the newest employee. The girl's name was there, along with an address. A phone number was listed also, but knowing the area, Billy suspected it rang a phone in the front room of a boarding house. Whoever answered it would write a note for the intended recipient or simply run up to the apartment door and knock. Over this entry, written hastily or in anger, was a single word. And Billy's eyes brightened at the sight of it.

WITCH!

And Billy knew he had the address of the person Tasha had mentioned.

*

Terrance knocked again—for the fourth time—since hearing Billy scrape the chrome kitchen chair across the floor. Peering through the slit in the curtains, he could see him standing by the table, but he wasn't moving.

Terrance had spent the night sleeping on the back porch. Billy had taken the hidden key and hadn't answered the door all night.

The porch wasn't a bad place to sleep—he'd certainly slept in worse—but the folding lawn chairs Billy's grandmother had stored there (one he sat in while the other acted as a footrest), had nearly lost their webbing and he sat unevenly in them all night. Now his back was kinked, and he began to seriously think about making amends with his family and getting his ass off the streets.

When Billy finally opened the backdoor, Terrance stared in disbelief. There was Billy, standing only in his boxers, crease lines fading from his right cheek, hair sticking up, makeup smudges on his face, and a purse cradled against his chest. Either Billy had had one hell of a party the night before, Terrance thought, or he'd finally gone over the edge. Either way, it was time to break free of this nightmare.

Billy turned without saying a word and went to his room, clutching the purse the whole way.

CHAPTER 43

Monday morning Frank rose early. He'd slept surprisingly well considering he hadn't been in his own bed. In fact, he couldn't remember the last time he'd slept in a bed other than his own—not counting the times he and Armand had fallen asleep in their chairs after a late-night discussion around the fireplace—and thought perhaps it was time to look into getting himself a new mattress.

The house was quiet as he soft-walked down the hallway, the old boards barely waking with their own squeaks under his well-placed steps. The choreographed walk caused him to briefly think of his wife and their dancing days. Even with Frank's girth—which was steadily coming down due to his new diet and walking regimen—he'd been graceful on the dancefloor, and his wife used to tease him that he was giving a little extra shake of his rump to please the other wives. This was not completely untrue.

Entering the library, he was surprised to see Jimmy curled up on the loveseat, covered with an afghan. It appeared the boy had decided to sleep there at some point in the night. Then, realizing that that was Del's favorite spot, he was no longer surprised that Jimmy—perhaps having had a bad dream or restless night—would end up sleeping where she always sat. He briefly chastised himself for not having made more progress on finding her, but the situation at Armand's house appeared to be more dire, and needed his immediate attention, he thought.

Peering around the library, he attempted to confirm everything was still in place and Jimmy hadn't disturbed something in the dark, but defining 'in place' was difficult. Armand had a peculiar way of organizing his research—stacks of manuscripts, books and papers seemingly sat at random—so Frank avoided the worktable and bookshelves. After all, he wouldn't want Armand coming into his garage attempting to straighten it. So, after a quick glance around, he decided the only thing that was uncharacteristically not stacked was a small scattering of papers beneath the table. Upon closer inspection, he realized they were papers with scribbled words on them. Not even words really, basically just scribbled letters. The words made no sense. And they were written in crayon. Jimmy must have been playing under there at some point. Without a second glance, Frank scooped the papers together, grabbed the two errant crayons that lay next to them, and sat the stack on the outer edge of the table.

He left the sleeping boy and went downstairs to start breakfast.

*

After breakfast Armand tended to Mama Dedé—who was resting peacefully—then went straight to his research. He was happy when Frank said that he had errands to run and would be gone for several hours. Whether they were real errands or not, he didn't know, but he had a sense that Frank was making himself absent on purpose. Jimmy had vacated the loveseat and was off on some adventure of his own, so Armand wanted to take advantage of the quiet time.

He reread the cryptic poem.

Just one death she can afford,

to nourish heaven's astral horde.

False to pray, "Oh kingly lord,

"sever not her silver cord."

He understood the reference to the silver cord, as it was clearly in the Bible. However, 'nourish heaven's astral horde' seemed to reference angels, but he'd never heard of angels feeding. And the fact that *nourish* and *cord* were in the same stanza, he suspected they were related, but it gave him an uneasy feeling to consider the implication. He read the next passage.

Just one death that she must pay,

on final hour of judgement day.

No bargain made to thus delay,

her crumble back to darkest clay.

The second stanza had nothing particularly troubling, besides the obvious reference to death. But the third passage…

Her death is nigh, the final term,

With pallid angels to affirm.

The astral horde will writhe and squirm,

As she feeds the ghostly verme.

This one troubled him most of all. 'Astral horde' writhing and squirming gave him a most unpleasant sensation of worms. Then of course, those ravenous angels were still around. But the whole thing ended with the odd term 'ghostly verme'. And for the life of him, he had no idea what this was referring to.

Armand twisted his moustache, then packed a new pipe. Striking a match and puffing the tobacco to life, he wandered the library and let his thoughts rearrange themselves.

Hungry angels. Astral horde. Ghostly verme. Silver cord.

"No," he spoke to the room, but chastised himself. "Don't modify."

The poem didn't actually say, 'hungry angels.' What had it said exactly?

Pallid angels. And they were *to affirm.*

Staring at the passage he realized his error.

"The angels aren't hungry," he said through puffs of smoke. "The astral horde is hungry. The angels are there to affirm." His hands dropped to the table as an unsettling realization dawned: the poem was referring to two separate groups. The pallid angels would affirm her death. The astral horde would nourish from it.

As he puffed his pipe, reading the poem over and over, Armand couldn't shake the disturbing thought of worms.

*

In his room, Jimmy sat on his bed, rocking anxiously. He'd found the papers on the edge of Armand's worktable. Somehow, they'd gotten from the floor where he'd left them, up to the table in one neat pile. When he woke up on the loveseat, he heard the papers whisper to him. They didn't want to be left out here alone, and he should have been more careful the night before, they said. He tried to remember the night before, but could only muster vague images that made no sense. But he knew the papers were important. The mirror had just told him so.

He looked at the letters written in crayon.

Cha'thul ungh ah mwu'lla nigh, Calla, Calla, dhung'll die

He recognized them but didn't understand the words. He guessed that eventually he'd be able to read them, but they didn't look like any words he'd ever seen before. Slowly he traced his finger over each letter. It felt good to trace the letters. They liked to be written. They'd like it even better when he'd learn how to pronounce them. Somehow he knew this.

Jimmy felt there were more letters waiting to be written. That's what made him anxious. Like waiting to go to the movies on a Saturday afternoon, or waiting to see Del, or even waiting to pee after drinking a whole glass of lemonade, Jimmy felt his legs getting nervous. They wanted to dance right off the bed and act crazy, but he'd have to be patient. You couldn't write good letters with crazy legs; they'd get squiggled up. Besides, it took him a long time to make the letters, so he had to have a quiet place to write. Beneath Armand's worktable, late at night was the best place. The mirror had just told him that as well.

So, Jimmy traced the letters once more, then carefully folded the pages and slipped them beneath his pillow, inside the pillowcase. They'd be safe there until the mirror told him what to do next.

*

Pallid angels. Armand tapped his pipe on an ashtray and stroked his beard. He thought about checking on Jimmy—it was unusual for him to be in his room during the day—but at least he was safe inside the house. Besides, he hadn't heard much from him all morning, which he took as a good sign. Or so Armand thought, and his mind turned back to the lyrical phrases of the poem.

He thought it highly unusual for a spirit to use such a term as this, but what did he really know of a spirit's vocabulary anyway? Maybe they all came out cryptic when translated through the board. Maybe they were confused—being on the other side and all—and couldn't help how the words came out. Maybe they were just being purposefully vague. Hadn't Mama D warned him of their intentions before? She'd warned him and Frank of just about everything over the last several months, and they would have done well to heed her more than they did. If she were able to, would she warn him off of his current path? Most certainly. Would he have ever made this mistake if she was well?

The last question was a difficult one. He'd had the board for so many years and had never used it before now. *Why was that?* he wondered.

Maybe he'd get rid of the infernal thing; throw it out with today's garbage. Better yet, maybe he'd burn it in the fireplace so no one could find it and use it; rid the world of it completely. Briefly, bravely, Armand thought these things. Like a drunk, convincing himself the bottle held no power over him, Armand felt a surge of bravado and momentarily believed he would succeed with this valiant gesture.

But his stomach told him a different story.

As the acid of reality dripped into his stomach, eating at his resolve, he knew this thought was folly. His fingers twisted together into a tight knot. Sweat broke on the back of his neck and cooled there. His pipe suddenly tasted like dry ash, mealy and gray. The thought of burning the board was ridiculous. What was the need in that? It wasn't doing any harm tucked safely away on his bookshelf. He was a researcher, by God, and he'd research how he saw fit. And he'd be damned if anyone told him how to live his life.

A sound from down the hall pulled him from his torment. Mama Dedé had stirred. As he went to tend her, his mind had cleared. He most certainly would not get rid of the board.

CHAPTER 44

Monday morning Del awoke in her own bed beneath a tangle of covers. She shivered violently, then flung her eyes open, scanning the room and slapping at her arms. Her heart pounded with the sickening feeling someone was in the room, touching her beneath the covers. She flashed around the room as well—despite it being small and easy to inspect—looking for hidden specters and boogeymen. Her eyes were still adjusting to the light, and flashing was simply faster. Not to mention, flashing a room was becoming second nature to her. She almost couldn't control it any better than taking a breath. Her body simply did it when needed.

The room was empty. She flashed out into the hall, down the stairs and through the other rooms of the boarding house. The only person in the building was old Mrs. Doucet, the landlady who lived on the first floor; she was sitting in her own small apartment watching a soap opera with the volume turned way up. She could barely hear.

A soap opera? What time is it?

The clock on Mrs. Doucet's wall, round with big cat eyes that moved back and forth like a ventriloquist doll and a swinging pendulum for a tail, showed it to be ten-eighteen. No wonder she was so hungry. She couldn't remember the last time she'd eaten. In fact, now that her heart rate was coming down, she tried to remember how exactly she'd come to her bed. The days were blurring together, and memories tumbled over each other in her mind. A giant jigsaw puzzle that would take more energy than she currently had to piece together.

Dropping out of the trance, she sat up in her bed and looked around her own room. She shivered once more and watched goosebumps run down her arms. It wasn't cold in her room, so she couldn't understand the chills.

She touched the back of her neck with both hands and let her fingers run out the ends of her shoulders. Another rash of bumps ran down her torso. She rubbed the bumps down on each arm, but the pressure only made the sensation worse. It wasn't as maddening a sensation as say, poison ivy or chiggers, but it was like an itch, and it was pleasant. Almost too pleasant. Like when she dreamed of Johnathan or the Lilac woman, but it was too much. And it was all over her.

Knowing that no one else was in the house, she stripped off her clothes (which felt wonderful), threw on a robe, (which felt even better for a moment until the material brushed against her) and headed for the bathroom.

Waiting for the shower water to heat up, she brushed her teeth and felt the pleasant goosebumps run the inside of her mouth. She'd thrown her robe off because the sensation was too much. She must have gotten into something last night that she was allergic to, she thought. She had to get it off her before she went crazy from the sensation. Even the brushing of her teeth sent mild electricity shooting around her mouth.

And she was so damned hungry she'd almost swallowed the toothpaste by mistake. Her jaws clenched down on the toothbrush, smashing the bristles into the soft tissue of her cheek and gums. She felt the bristles poke up around her teeth. It was an oddly satisfying sensation, like when she pried a fragment of meat from between her teeth with a toothpick. Only it felt like she had several toothpicks massaging her gums, sliding into the crevasses, drawing the slightest trickle of blood. And she relished in the pricks of pain. She watched herself in the fogging mirror gnaw on the bristles with her front teeth, but couldn't stop. Methodically the brush was moved from one tooth to the next and she bit down again and again, feeling the wonderful prick of the bristles penetrating between each tooth. Top and bottom, front and back, against her cheeks then under her tongue. She stared at the fogging image in the mirror and the image snarled back at her, gums happily bleeding between white teeth as wonderful steam swirled around her.

Stepping into the shower her body felt like it was on fire, electric pulses shooting all the way down to her toes. Spying a wooden scrub brush that Mrs. Doucet had scrubbed the bristles flat, Del lathered it with soap and scrubbed her body the way she'd attacked her teeth. The washcloth simply wouldn't work. But the scrub brush and those wonderfully damaged bristles scraped across her skin just right and laid some of the electricity to rest. She was barely aware of how hard she was scraping until a sensitive area shot a warning. Her face and neck only needed a gentle scrub. Her breasts cried in pain from barely a brush. Her arms and legs needed the hardest scrub she could muster. Again and again, more soap, more scrubbing, until she thought the skin would tear away. Somewhere in the fog of sensation her mind told her to stop, it was too rough, something was wrong. But she couldn't stop. Not yet. The electricity was still moving, the infection was still itching, her skin was still crying out.

The water was hot now, almost scalding. Del gasped for air but scrubbed on. Her fingers were clenching the brush now. Little stabs of pain shot up around her fingernails as she ground her fingertips into the bristles. Dropping the brush in the tub, she leaned her hands against the wall as she ground her toes into the bristles, first one foot, then the other, back and forth, almost kicking the brush with each foot as she sought the wonderful pain that pulsed up her toes and into her ankles.

Even the tears streaming from her eyes gave her a painfully satisfying sting.

Finished with the shower, she threw open the bathroom door and strode naked down the hallway, barely aware of her actions. Glazed eyes saw her forward like a drunkard's on autopilot. The humid air of the second floor felt like a cold blast against her scalded skin. In her room she pulled a tee-shirt over her wet shoulders, yanked on jeans that stuck to her wet legs, and walked into sandals as she headed for the stairs. Now that her body had been satiated with scrubbing, it had another need. She couldn't get to food fast enough.

By the time she got to the nearest café, her wet hair was mostly contained by one of her wider headbands, only lanky curls escaping over the front onto her forehead. She sat at the bar near the oyster station and ordered a dozen. It was the quickest way to get something into her stomach. She waved off the lemon and hot sauce, grabbing the first one before the shucker could finish plating them all.

"Burger please," Del said to the gaping bartender. "Mid rare." She slurped a second oyster, but instead of swallowing it whole, let her teeth grind the glob to pieces in her mouth. An audible moan of satisfaction escaped her throat. A visible shiver ran through her as her body sucked at the nutrients. The bartender and shucker exchanged sly looks of surprise.

She swallowed the third whole but ground the fourth on the other side of her mouth. "And gumbo," she added between bites. "If it's ready. A full bowl."

And Del ate like this for an hour, not understanding, or caring to wonder, what drove her unnatural hunger.

CHAPTER 45

Late Monday morning, just as Frank was entering the police station, Detective Valcour was updating the chief on his investigation.

Frank made his way to the kitchenette where the coffee pot sat, checked for grounds in the bottom (which there were) and proceeded to rinse and refill it.

The late morning chatter flooded him with memories of when he'd been on the force. Young cops with their piss-and-vinegar attitudes, ready to conquer the world; older cops, salted and seasoned, nodding silently behind their Styrofoam cups, winking at the other officers. It was the same old chatter, only the details had changed. The Vietnam war was raging, the Cold war with Russia was at a stalemate now that the Nuclear Testing Treaty had been signed earlier in the month, but the real concern was the march on Washington that was scheduled to happen in two days.

Martin Luther King Jr. was scheduled to give a speech on Wednesday, August 28th at the Lincoln Memorial, where he would speak about jobs and freedom; it was plastered on the front page of the *Times-Picayune*. Although D.C. was over a thousand miles away from New Orleans, Frank could still feel a palpable tension in the air here; people were beginning to think that civil unrest could make its way all the way down to the Big Easy.

As if the city didn't already have enough to worry about.

Waiting for the coffee to brew, Frank gathered the scattered pages of the day's paper and began sorting them. He thought about Del and wondered if she was still pursuing her newspaper job. If so, it wasn't with the *Picayune*. He'd already pressed the guys in the satellite office below his; they hadn't heard from her. They'd admitted that they'd been a little hard on Del, but said it was all in good fun.

"Just a good old-fashioned hazing that all the new reporters get!" one of them had said. But Frank knew differently. Del had received a very special type of hazing which hadn't sat well with him. This was the main reason he'd only spoken a few words with the men since then, and doubted he'd pass on any more leads to them.

Finding a back section of the paper, he saw an advertisement for the Prytania Theatre. They were showing a new spy movie called *Dr. No*, which had come out in May, and was getting decent reviews. The lead character, a spy with the most uninteresting name ever, James Bond, was supposed to save the world with a bunch of new-fangled gadgets. *Just like flying a can to the moon*, Frank thought. *Ever'body's got shiny fever.* When a soft towel and a full can of Turtle-wax suited him just fine. But he did make a mental note of the movie. He thought Jimmy and Armand might like it if they ever got this current business straightened out. Finding the front page, which had been reversed and folded to the bottom half of the second page, a grim headline caught Frank's attention:

Victim #4?

Another dead girl had been found over the weekend.

"I'm heading out Backatown again," Marcel said. He'd called out to someone in the other room. "Got follow-up to do on the latest victim." Frank heard a female's voice respond, but a loud ruckus drowned out her words. "No, I'll call you if I do."

Marcel walked past Frank without noticing him. Frank was inconspicuously still attending the coffee. Filling a large Styrofoam cup, Frank tucked the folded paper under his arm and waited for Marcel to leave the building. He thought maybe he'd take a drive himself. He wasn't planning on following Detective Valcour, but if the other man happened to be driving in front of Frank the entire time, well... stranger things had been known to happen.

*

Arriving at Marcel's version of 'Backatown,' Frank realized the definition and boundary of the place had changed since he was an active cop. His private-eye pursuits had let him drift where he wanted, unlike the disciplined routes of a beat cop. Marcel had certainly headed toward Lake Pontchartrain, but beyond that, all similarities to the area Frank was thinking had ended. The streets had become progressively dimmer the further he'd driven. Ramshackle buildings dotted empty and overgrown lots. Trash dotted vacant alleys that weren't much more than old gravel lanes swallowed by grass. He hoped silently that Del had not felt a need to bring herself to this area; an area nearly forgotten and bypassed by the highways, to the point it was fading into memory. A sudden and resolute sense of urgency came over him as he drove. He had to find her and bring her home if at all possible.

Pulling to the side, he parked several spaces behind Marcel, who had just exited his car and was speaking to the officers who had apparently been waiting for him.

They're canvasing the area, Frank thought. He knew the details of the initial murders, but hadn't had a chance to read up on the latest girl. *Was this the area she was found, or perhaps where she lived?*

Keeping his head down, he scanned the newspaper article while he watched the beat cops disperse and begin knocking on doors. Frank sipped his coffee and melted into the seat of his car.

By noon, the thermometer had reached ninety degrees and Frank knew it would be a hot one; a New Orleans summer blazing toward the peak of hurricane season, just about a month away. After that, the threat would wind down, but they still had October to watch for. That was a notoriously tricky month in the South, and carried its own superstitions.

Noting the cross streets, Frank started his car and made to find a cooler area. As he pulled towards the intersection, passing Marcel's car, he noticed a small group of people on his left. Mourners and gawkers, he thought. They were whispering and pointing to the apartment building on his right, where the girl must have lived. But something struck him as odd. The crowd that had gathered appeared to Frank to be all young women, and if he knew the profession (and he did), they were *working* women, of the street-profession kind. This in itself didn't surprise Frank; the Crescent City was open and accepting to all walks of life, but a bad feeling was settling over him. He felt he was near the epicenter of the whole bad business. He'd already studied the locations where the bodies were found— which was in this general area—but now that he understood this neighborhood was on the brink of becoming another red-light area, and its proximity to an old, out-of-the-way bar district, he could tell this was a breeding ground for trouble.

And out of the many things Del could do, he was beginning to believe she was well accomplished at finding trouble.

CHAPTER 46

"He's crazy, I'm tellin' you," Terrance said. He ran his fingers through his hair, then scratched both arms simultaneously. "I got to get da fuck out before some real shit goes down."

Rochelle looked around instinctively, worried their conversation would draw unwanted attention, but the only people in the alley behind the Sho-bar were sympathetic to their dilemma, not to mention a few were actual customers of Billy's product line.

The Sho-bar at 228 Bourbon Street was as far as Terrance would venture into the French Quarter—and he always came from the direction of Backatown, meaning he wouldn't be seen perusing the streets from here down to the river walk—it was too 'white' for him and had far too many cops. Despite the city experimenting with civil rights—mild protests and sit-ins had been occurring for a few years, after all—the only blacks welcomed in the famed music area were good jazz musicians, cooks, then the necessary broom and mop people, in that order. And Terrance was none of these. The Sho-bar however was the unofficial nexus of the changing landscape of the city. It had once been a famed burlesque house, attending such entertaining greats as Blaze Starr (alleged mistress of the governor), Lilly Christine the Cat Girl, Evangeline the Oyster Girl (who would pop out of a giant oyster to start her show), and many other lesser names; some of these iconic dancers going on to have modeling or acting careers, but who'd all made their name on the burlesque stage. Now, it hosted everyone from famed R&B musicians on the weekend to the Chaplain of Bourbon Street himself, Reverend Bob Harrington, who would preach from the stage on Tuesday nights.

And because the Sho-bar was the unofficial nexus of the changing landscape of the city, it was a perfect place for enterprising people such as Rochelle and Terrance to meet, and to ply their trades.

Rochelle pulled Terrance away from the backdoor of the club, lit a cigarette and handed it to him. After lighting another for herself, she spoke in a low tone.

"What happened?"

Terrance inhaled, coughed, then said, "I'm tellin' ya, he's gone crazy. Locked me out las' night. Had to sleep on da porch. Saw him through da window. He was sleepin' on da kitchen table. When he got up to let me in, he was holdin' a purse, like dis." Terrance clutched the imaginary object to his chest. "He was out of it. Looked like he had dirt on his face."

Rochelle smiled dismissively at a cook who was taking his own smoke break and appeared to be listening attentively.

"Whose purse was it?"

"Beats me. I've been trying to stay away." Now it was Terrance's turn to eyeball the cook. "I got to get my shit straight before anym—"

His eyes shot up to Rochelle's, then back to the dirty alley. "Before anything happens."

Rochelle wasn't fooled. "Before any-*thing* happens? Or any-*more*?"

Terrance scratched at the back of his neck and sucked the last bit of cigarette down.

"T, tell me the truth. Has Billy brought home anything else like this?"

He wrung his hands as if trying to wring out a very bad case of arthritis. He tried to remember, he really did, but his junkie mind was failing him and all he could think about was his itchy arms.

"I don't know," he whispered. "I don't know. I don't think so."

"You don't *think* so? What does that mean? Maybe? Possibly?"

Terrance began to shiver despite the building heat of the day.

"There might have been girls…" His voice trailed off.

Rochelle had no delusions that Billy hadn't had girlfriends before her, but this answer didn't sound right.

"What do you mean exactly?"

His junkie mind spun wild, a thousand thoughts and images crashing together. Perhaps it was better this way, he thought. Perhaps not being able to fully remember what he'd done when he was high was saving what little sanity he had left. Terrance never read the paper, never watched the nightly news, so never knew what was going on in the world if it wasn't right in front of him. But some images had been right in front of him, late nights, stoned out of his mind, barely functioning, there were images there. And as of late, as his mind began to clear as he tried to get clean, they looked at him and screamed.

"Man, his knees are always fucked up," Terrance said. "Stay away from him." And with that, he left without a look back.

Rochelle watched Terrance skitter from the alley and disappear into a crowd of people, but her mind was on his last statement. Yes, she knew about Billy's knees. In fact, she'd just been thinking about it the other night when she saw him stalking down the street. He'd gone into some bar and was talking to a waitress—

A mental image of Billy's scarred knees formed in Rochelle's mind. Then an image of the girl she saw through the bar window; the one Billy was flirting with. A cold feeling of dismay sank into her stomach as she clutched a hand to her mouth. Word traveled fast on the street, especially when it involved working girls, and Rochelle had already heard that another victim had been found. As if following Terrance's lead, she bolted from the alley, looking for the nearest newsstand. She had to find a newspaper.

CHAPTER 47

With Frank running errands, and Armand deep in research, Jimmy had the house to himself.

He'd made his lunchtime visit to Mama Dedé and noticed that someone had eaten the cookie he'd left for her that morning. The teacup was empty also. He thought these were both good signs, but saw that she was sleeping again, so didn't ask her. He looked suspiciously at the walls—slyly, from the corner of his eyes—to catch a glimpse of the things that hid there. For the last several weeks, he'd had an itchy feeling when he came in Mama D's room. It always felt like something was crawling around in the walls, just beneath the wallpaper. He never liked that feeling and had tried to see what it was, but the squirmy things always stopped when Jimmy looked at them. But they kept moving on other parts of the walls, his eyes told him. Once, he'd even thought there were bugs in the ceiling, waiting to drop down on his head, but when he looked up, the ceiling was still. He had to be *'bwave da 'ion* just to bring her tea and cookies in, but he knew that's how Del would have wanted it.

Back in the hall, with Mama D tucked safely in her room, he walked toward his and thought about going outside to chase butterflies, but there was something else he had to do first. He just couldn't remember what it was. He didn't think it was a forgotten chore; most of those had been set aside by Armand anyway, as the dishes in the sink confirmed.

He squinshed his face up tight, trying to remember the thing, but that only made his eyes hurt. Besides, with his brain squinshed together like that, how could the thing he forgot get back into his head? So, he decided that wasn't helping.

Maybe he should go ask the stone maiden, he thought. He hadn't spoken to her in a while, and had a funny feeling that she wanted to talk to him.

The door to his bedroom began to swing open, creaking lightly as it did. It stopped three-quarters of the way open.

Jimmy was getting used to doors creaking or suddenly being pulled shut; Armand said it was the big furnace in a drafty old house that caused this. But Jimmy couldn't remember *his* door doing this before, and certainly not swinging open. But, just like that, he had an idea that his forgotten task was somewhere in his room. It was strange how things worked like that. So, he walked inside.

And the door swung shut behind him.

In his room, he sat on his bed and listened for what to do next. His walls weren't squirmy like Mama D's, and he hoped they never started, but the mirror on his dresser had been noisy lately, so he sat and listened.

Somewhere outside a large cloud must have floated in front of the sun, he thought, because his room turned dark. The house exhaled; the walls settled in closer, listening alongside Jimmy; the ceiling sagged imperceptibly, the floor rose, the room got smaller. Jimmy sensed these things, perhaps in a sudden daydream, but that's what his mind had perceived.

Now the room was ready for secrets.

He began protectively stroking his pillow with its dark secret hidden within. His fingers traced a pattern on the sweat-yellowed pillowcase; the patterns were letters, ancient and forgotten. But Jimmy was here to remember them. Despite all the things he'd forgotten in the past, despite all the times he'd fallen down or made a mess, for some reason people still liked to tell him letters and words. Someone had even told him a secret song once (although he couldn't remember it now), so that must be what he was supposed to do now. That was the forgotten chore that his mind had tried to remember all morning. He was supposed to remember more of the words that he'd written on the paper, that was hidden in his pillowcase.

Just then, as if confirming his idea, something rattled in the bottom drawer of his dresser.

From where Jimmy sat on the bed, he couldn't see the bottom drawer, but knew the sound came from there.

The other drawers of his dresser weren't that interesting. The top one had underwear, t-shirts and brown or black socks. The second and third drawers had miscellaneous sweaters and pants—some that Armand had never cleaned out from the previous owner, but a few were Jimmy's since he'd arrived. The bottom drawer was where Jimmy kept his best stuff.

The bottom drawer had been empty when Jimmy had arrived, and the first time he'd opened it, he knew exactly what it was for: treasure. And there was a lot of treasure to be found in this old place. As Jimmy had explored the house and found its overstuffed closets and alcoves and secrets, he'd collected a few treasures here and there;

an old Mother Goose nursery rhyme book with a chewed corner, a bag of marbles that had been spilled out on the floor of a forgotten closet, several partially used coloring books, a slingshot, a silver letter opener, a small jelly jar of bottle caps he'd collected from the garage, and several interesting rocks.

But now his most prized treasure—even though he was sure he'd have to give it back at some point—was trying to get out of the bottom drawer: the severed hand he'd found in Armand's library.

After he'd played the talking board game with the hand, Victor told him it would be safer to just put the game under his bed and the hand in Jimmy's treasure drawer. That way they could continue playing without disturbing Armand. Victor didn't think Armand would miss it because he was busy researching the poem. Besides, the game was almost over now anyway, Victor had said, and they only needed one or two more sessions to finish.

It must be time to play another game, Jimmy thought. That's why the hand had woken up and was trying to get out of the drawer.

*

After pushing aside several boxes of old clothes, Jimmy had enough space in his walk-in closet to lay the board on the floor and spread out his papers and crayons next to it. He'd thought about the strange words Victor had showed him yesterday, and was anxious to learn more. Were they a secret way of helping Mama D? he had wondered. Yes. Victor said it was a way to help her and that Jimmy was very smart for figuring that out. That's why Armand wouldn't mind if Jimmy borrowed the hand and board. So, Jimmy was happy to help however he could.

In the closet, a single lightbulb hung down from a cord in the ceiling. Its feeble glow cast a dim light down to the floor. It wasn't a warm yellow glow, like some lights, but rather stark and gray. It had the effect of casting the old clothes that hung there in a version of gray light that only occurred at dusk; a washed-out color that was very noncommittal. You could be alive or dead with that color and not realize the difference. It was a cold color.

As Jimmy readied the game, with paper and crayons spread about, holding the Mojo Hand in his left and touching the puck with his right, a strange breeze filled his room. Despite the door to the hall being shut and locked, despite the window being closed, the air moved. And the view from his bed was that of an unsuspecting face, cast in a sickly gray light, looking out of the closet, as the door slowly closed of its own accord, shutting him inside.

CHAPTER 48

"Hey, any luck?" Officer Babette Thibodeaux asked.

Marcel looked up from his desk. There were five neat stacks of notes arranged across it. A look of mild annoyance crept over his face. He didn't like being interrupted. "Any luck?"

"Yeah," Babette shrugged, "you know, with the canvass. Do you think the rape gang lives close to where the last body was found? I was going to come out and help as soon as my shift ended. I—"

Marcel looked back at his paperwork. "I'm sure we have it covered, officer, thank you." He read a few more notes, then, realizing she was still standing at his desk, looked up and said, "You should really stick to your assigned shifts. I'll let you know if additional help is needed. Thank you." But he didn't look down at the desk this time. He held her eyes, waiting for her to leave, then asked, "What are those?"

She shuffled the files in her hands, almost sat them on the desk, looked at them, then said, "Nothing. Just some misplaced files."

Marcel nodded and went back to work.

Babette left Marcel at his desk, and walked to the file room, which was a shallow alcove off the central corridor. Tall, army green file cabinets lined the walls, while a high narrow table ran down the center. The table reminded her of the standup bartops you could find in most New Orleans bars; just deep enough to set a few drinks on, but sturdy enough to hold up the drunks. It left more area for customers that way. Their file room was like that. Had to leave plenty of room for the customers—the people in the files, that was.

She sat the file on the high table and opened it.

Clara Boynell, 6 yrs. old, approx. 3' tall.

Brown hair. Brown eyes. Missing

This was a note written on one of the pages. The other pages were more official, one of them being stamped with large red letters that declared the case CLOSED.

But Babette didn't need the case file to tell her that. She'd made it a habit to follow all the detectives' cases as closely as possible. She would be a detective one day; she'd told herself many times. But because there were no female detectives she could speak to—especially black female detectives—she'd have to learn the ropes however she could. This meant having a good memory, paying attention, and doing the research when her gut told her to keep searching. And that's what had happened this time. She thought she'd recognized Del's name when they spoke in the hospital. Perhaps it had been the sense of déjà vu she had when she saw her, thinking she'd seen her walking the sidewalk somewhere. But she was certain she'd seen the name before. And after enough digging, she'd found the case file that confirmed it. It seemed that Del had quite the knack for being at the wrong place at the wrong time. Or maybe it was the other was around, maybe it was the right time and place. Regardless, there seemed to be more to Del than Marcel even realized. Clara Boynell, the little girl who had gone missing from an orphanage, had been found just a couple months earlier. She'd been found in the trunk of a car which had been parked by the Lafayette Cemetery #1, right across from a grand old house that took up the entire block. Residents listed living at the house were one Armand Baptiste, the owner, an old woman that went by the name Mama Dedé who was most likely a practitioner of the arts (Babette had a gut feeling about this). Then there was a boy named Jimmy, also an orphan, who was credited with saving the girl. And finally, there was Del. The mysterious girl who Marcel was suspicious about, but in Babette's opinion, was ready to dismiss as a bad luck person. Sometimes people were just bad luck and life never gave them a break. Besides, Marcel was too by-the-book to consider anything out of the ordinary, and he had little opinion of women—outside of the kitchen, as far as she could tell—so had the sense he had already dismissed her. But Babette thought differently.

She'd had a great aunt that the neighbor ladies would pay homage too. She barely remembered the woman, but she did remember the feeling she got when she'd go to visit; a feeling of awe that wormed its way into her stomach; a feeling that the woman could read her mind and knew when she'd let the boys touch her butt on the playground; a feeling that drew her to the old woman, despite the dangers that seemed to lurk in the shadows behind her.

Babette was beginning to get these feelings about Del. She wasn't sure if the dead guy in the alley—Harold—or the estranged couple were directly related to Del, or caused by her, but she had a hunch there was a connection.

And she'd been ready to share that connection, the possibility of it at least, with Marcel today, but he was obviously uninterested. So, she closed the file and slipped it back into its file drawer. She had all the information she needed from it anyway.

Perhaps it was time to start doing her own research of the mysterious Delphine Larouche.

CHAPTER 49

After Del's extended lunch—where she'd eaten everything she'd ordered and talked herself out of a to-go box of crawfish—she felt good. In fact, she could only count on one hand the times she'd felt this good or better: getting out of the orphanage was one, getting her first job (despite the later problems) was two, and if she was being honest, the day she'd met Johnathan at the Ice Cream Emporium, would be up there in the top five. Sad in a way that her list of really good days was so short, but she couldn't deny the wave of happy energy that was building in her. Her belly was full, her senses were sharp, and her mood was light. Maybe it had been the flirtatious banter with the bartender, but she felt exceptionally good about herself, despite the strange events that had proceeded her voracious visit.

Halfway through her lunch she'd realized she had thrown on one of her rattiest t-shirts, leaving little to the imagination. But let them look, she'd decided. Who cared? A lot of other girls dressed like this and far worse. She was an adult, wasn't she? She could dress how she wanted.

And so what if she wanted to take a lover? Just another perk of being an adult. So, with her cheeks shining and her grin wide, she left the café for her little apartment and decided to fix herself up before work.

She'd go in early, in case Jonesy needed the coverage, then work her regular shift. Afterwards she'd go dancing. By herself, if necessary, but she doubted she'd be alone for long. She had a knack for drawing attention to herself and was starting to get used to it. She just hadn't had the courage to act on it before now.

But when she'd been sitting at the bar, gorging herself, her mind had buzzed with playful energy. And while adrift, she'd caught glimpses of the bartender's thoughts—Eric was his name—and confirmed what she'd already suspected: that guys were complete idiots.

And with that realization, she thought she'd have a little fun.

Eric wasn't a bad looking guy at all, but his mouthy bravado had been annoying. Being able to hear his words while stealing glimpses into his thoughts had been eye-opening. She wondered why she hadn't done more of it before (besides knowing when someone was ready for another drink, that is). He was saying one thing but thinking something completely different. Oh, he was interested in her, that much was obvious. But if he was so genuinely smitten by her—even if he did keep stealing glances at her breasts—why were his words so… stupid, she wondered? And why could he be manipulated so easily? Didn't he have any thoughts of his own?

Halfway through her burger, while Eric droned on about something, Del thought of an image: a faint image of one of her breasts—but it could have been anyone's—reflected in a mirror, fogged with steam. For fun, and to test her idiocy theory (not to mention her own ability to manipulate), she gifted this image to Eric as he cleaned bottles on the back bar.

It had an effect as if she'd found his OFF switch.

One moment he was absently wiping bottles, hinting at his bedroom prowess, then there was a boob in the mirror.

He stopped in mid-sentence, looked over his shoulder to where the girl at the bar must have just taken her shirt off, then back.

Then he was standing there, gaping into the dirty mirror behind the bottles, desperately searching for the ghost boob that had just disappeared. He blinked with confusion, stammered, dropped his towel, then bent to retrieve it slowly. Upon standing back up, Del had already gifted him with a twin vision: two boobs streaming water in the shower, pertly at attention.

Eric gaped at the mirror again, his lower jaw on a hinge, then giggled like a schoolboy. Realizing the most unmanly sound ever had just tumbled out of his mouth, he slammed it shut, turned towards Del, and self-consciously stepped in front of the mirror, as if hiding a girly magazine. Del caught his glimpse, held it in amusement—noting that he desperately wanted to look at her chest, imagining the steamy breasts there—then took a rather large, obnoxious bite of her burger, letting juice run in a small stream down her chin. Wide-eyed, Eric backed into the bar, blushed, and decided he had an errand in the back room.

Del giggled to herself, looked around and discreetly wiped her chin. She wasn't sure why she'd just acted that way, but it felt good to do something out of the ordinary. Considering all the terrible things that had happened to her over the last few days, she should be mourning away in a corner somewhere, she thought. But she wasn't, and she was glad for that, but she couldn't tell *why* she wasn't. It was as if she'd received a jolt of happy-juice and simply couldn't turn it off.

That's when she decided to go have some fun tonight. She'd worried about things for too long. Besides, she had the means to take care of herself.

*

That night at the bar, Del made a killing in tips. Monday nights had become 'industry night' at The Jazz Note, which meant they offered discounted drink prices for other bartenders and waitresses. It also meant that most of the people in the bar worked in the service industry and therefore tipped well, knowing what it was like to live on tips.

Besides industry night, the news of Tasha's death had also kept a steady stream of patrons walking through the door.

There had been somber conversations earlier in the evening regarding Tasha. Some people inquired of updates on the investigation, some shouted eulogies through the open window from the streets, and some came by just to verify the rumor was true. Several toasts were given to her throughout the evening and Jonesy was quite drunk by the end of the night. But in the end, people still wanted their drinks. They still wanted to forget their troubles. And although no one (at least not many) wished Tasha harm, no one would have traded places with her. So, they drank and poured liquor on the floor in tribute, they laughed and cried until their own pains were gone, they flirted with Del and celebrated her young life, and by the end of the evening, they'd forgotten about death for one more day.

*

That night after her shift, Del was carefree.

She'd been careful not to participate in too many tributes to Tasha. It wasn't that she didn't want to have a drink in her honor—despite how nasty Tasha had been to her—but she also didn't want to get drunk and miscount her money or lose it somehow. However, as the night wore on, she finally gave in and took a tribute shot here and there, as it was offered.

But it wasn't just the liquor that made her carefree that evening. It was the wild energy streak that continued to course through her, like a generator running on overdrive. Despite the constant surge of customers, or the fact that she had to eat on the fly, she seemed to never tire. Her legs were strong, her step was light, and her *senses* never missed a trick. She was a step ahead of the customers then, and when she finally got to a late-night club after The Note had closed for the evening, she felt a step ahead of the late-night partiers.

She danced.

She drank.

She flirted.

She even made out with a guy briefly at one club.

But by three in the morning, the drinks had caught up to her, and her streak of energy had run its course; she was crashing, and she could feel it.

She nearly let herself get talked into continuing the party at someone's house, but when one of the other girls pulled her into the bathroom and warned her away from that group, she had enough sense to listen. So, she said her goodbyes and stumbled out to the sidewalk, looking for a cab.

Her thoughts were warm and pleasant on the ride home: the new group of friends she had met, the guy she'd kissed in the dark, and one day soon, bringing someone back to her own place.

But none of her thoughts included the possibility that someone would already be waiting for her.

CHAPTER 50

Standing in the shadows of the great tree that stretched over the apartment building, Billy Bash waited as if in a trance. His eyes had long since glazed over; he was lost in a fever and there was only one way to escape it. He would find The Red tonight. Or he'd die trying.

He had no recollection of how long he'd been here. Remnants of images flowed through his mind like the fleeting wisps of campfire smoke, twisting in upon themselves, changing shape, then disappearing before they fully formed. He thought they were an inventory of the times he'd found The Red, but couldn't be sure. They were cryptic. They were frightening. Yet, they were comforting at the same time. They were a strange mix of hurt and healing, of pain and pleasure, of loss and redemption, all rolled into one. And he missed that feeling; he longed for it; he needed it for his very survival. And tonight, with the employee address list from the mystery purse shoved into his front pocket, he had finally come to the place where he'd find what he needed. The apartment of the witch.

When the taxicab stopped in front of the apartment building at 3:46 am, he wasn't surprised. Somehow, he knew who the passenger would be. Something in his mind was tuned into this girl. He'd almost had her once, after all, that night he, Harold and Terrence had chased her. Harold had died that night because of the witch, but Billy was immune, invincible. He felt this in his core. The witch couldn't hurt him, she could only heal him. And tonight, he meant to be healed.

As Del exited the taxi, Billy saw the stumble in her walk—then the purse!—she'd almost dropped it. He'd seen this many times as well. Women of the street tended to stumble and drop their purses a lot.

Images swirled. The Red hovered just outside the reach of his mind, but his groin felt its presence. It had awakened.

The images. The late nights. Hiding in shadows. Dropped purses and stumbling, rambling walks on high heels.

(SMACK!)

(…crack the flap dog, bitch, this paint your house…)

(SMACK!)

Like a good boy, Billy stayed quiet, waiting for the taxicab to leave. He'd learned over the years to ignore the hits and the slaps. It only made things worse if you yelled out. And he didn't want to make things worse because then he'd have to scoop up the purse contents and they'd have to find a new place to live. It was odd how closely linked a Dropped Purse Incident was with needing to find a new place to live, but standing there waiting for The Red to find him, Billy didn't realize this. In fact, he would never make the association, but of course, he didn't realize that either.

When the cab lights began to roll away, he moved quickly through the maze of shadows—he was well practiced at this—intent on reaching the door before the girl was able to shut it. He slipped around the corner of the apartment building just as she stepped inside the door.

*

When Del entered the old tenement house, she held the door open, stabilizing her balance, then dropped her purse on the floor. Cussing quietly, she bent to pick it up, but her head was so heavy with drink, she stumbled forward several steps and only managed to keep from smacking it into the stair railing because her arm was stretched out for balance. The front door, held back from slamming shut by a hydraulic hinge, began its slow swing toward the door jamb.

Holding onto the stair rail, she righted herself somewhat, looked back at the purse, then giggled for no reason at all. Holding onto the rail with her right hand, legs wobbling, she stretched her left toward the purse, grabbed it by the strap, then realized she had to pee this very instant.

Dragging her purse up the steps, she clambered for the upstairs bathroom, and gave the front door no more thought.

After a long time in the bathroom, where she nearly dozed off, sitting with her head against the sink, she finished her business, washed her hands, and didn't hear someone breathing from the shadows.

*

From where Billy stood, now inside the building, he could hear no one, except the girl in the upstairs bathroom, who was trying to be quiet. His quick movements through the shadows had served him well; he caught the slowly closing front door just before it latched. And although he was prepared for an alternate means of entry, the girl had bolted up the inside stairs without a look back. Even if the door had closed, she would have left it unlocked in her rush. Slipping inside the dark entryway, Billy had watched as Del stumbled down the dark hall towards the bathroom. Apparently, she knew her way, because she hadn't needed the hall light. In the old homes, he doubted it would have done much good, but was glad nonetheless for its absence.

With light footsteps up the stairs—always walking close to the wall, which squeaked the least—he made it to the top step just as she was sitting down.

From the shadows, Billy watched Del through the partially open bathroom door. In her haste—or perhaps she just didn't care who saw her—she'd failed to completely close this door, just like she'd forgotten the front. But this light was on. Billy wasn't completely surprised by this. This also was an image from his past; someone peeing, yet watching him through a partially opened door, to see that he hadn't run off (or was it always him watching?). From the menagerie of images that had bombarded his mind over the last few minutes, like papers flying about in a storm, this image stuck. It had stopped flying, and hung, like a picture, in midair, and his brain remembered it. Yes, this was an image from his past, and yes, he was seeing it again now. Billy absently rubbed his crotch, knowing what was soon to come. Knowing The Red was closer than ever.

He watched as Del's jeans slid down her brown legs and pooled around her feet. She'd already kicked off her shoes near a door, where her purse also lay. That must be her room, he thought.

He could hear her peeing. It wasn't very lady-like peeing, he thought. It was loud. And probably splashy. Women of the street—at least those who carried The Red with them—were always splashy, as far as he could remember. He supposed the unlady-like splashiness was a tradeoff he must endure. And he'd certainly done that before as well.

From the dark hall he listened. No other sounds came from any of the rooms. There was a chance that this tenement house had very few tenants. Maybe it wasn't boldness after all that caused her to leave the door open. Maybe she knew no one was up here to see her. Billy's eyes glowed at this thought.

He watched as she leaned her head onto the sink. She slipped once and caught herself as she dozed.

Common behavior.

Then she stepped out of her pooled jeans and spread her legs. She was almost finished. She wadded up some toilet paper and her hand slipped between her legs. He tried to see what the hand was doing—and more importantly, how it performed this function—but couldn't. He'd always wondered about the hands.

But that was a mystery he would never solve.

A flush.

Running water.

At least her hygiene was acceptable.

The light clicked off.

Brown feet tiptoed out of the bathroom, trying to balance naked legs that disappeared beneath the bottom of a colored t-shirt. Another common street tactic, Billy thought, easy access made for quick work. But he didn't need quick work tonight. He needed as much of The Red as he could find. In the past, he'd always thought instead of just *using The Red*—like swimming in a cool lake for a brief respite from the pain—he could eat it and be cured for good. Yes, he thought if he could finally *eat* The Red, everything would be fine.

How long would it take? he wondered. It might take hours; The Red was enormous.

What if it took days?

Did he have enough time?

As far as he could tell, this tenement house had very few tenants. Yes, if he was quiet, maybe he did have a few days to spend. Billy's heartrate ratcheted up a notch, as his erection became painful. He could eat all The Red in the world in a few days, he was sure of it. He could cure himself forever.

Del's walk was slow and deliberate. Quiet, but unstable.

From his hiding spot in the shadows, just on the other side of a free-standing coat tree, he watched as her right hand kept contact with the hallway wall. She was walking directly toward him. With her left, she flung the jeans toward the discarded shoes, where they slumped in a pile.

She pushed the bedroom door open without unlocking it and kicked the jeans and shoes inside.

Now he was sure no one was on this floor.

CHAPTER 51

Monday evening after dinner, Armand poured a glass of brandy, then nearly poured a second, thinking his friend would be back soon. He'd suspected—*hoped* was more like it—that Frank would have made an appearance today, then remembered he had errands to run and that he'd stay at his place that night. Alas, he was left to his own devices. He'd intended to ask Frank if he'd heard from Del yesterday. Perhaps he'd missed her call somehow.

Living the carefree life of youth, Armand thought. He wondered how she was getting along on her journey.

The thought quickly faded as he settled into his fireplace chair and gazed over the dusty box that sat next to the table. He'd found a lost stack of research he wanted to dig into, and was secretly glad Frank was busy. They were obscure writings that he'd lost track of over time. In some cases, he couldn't even tell who the authors were. The unfortunate manuscripts had been treated very badly over the years and now were miscellaneous pages littering an old cardboard box.

He'd already cleared the dinner dishes, and Jimmy was off playing somewhere. He made a mental note to check on the boy later; he'd looked rather sickly at the dinner table, but had said he was just tired. In fact, Armand couldn't remember seeing him most of the day, but had been quite absorbed on his own tasks.

Removing the loose pages of research, he stacked them in random piles on the table. After several minutes, he had groups of pages organized by size, color and general degree of decay. Some pages obviously came from the same author, one Max von Schaffen of Germany, an alienist and rather esteemed researcher of the occult. His best-known work, *Psychic Malaise and its Origins*, first published in 1871 and translated into English two years later, had nearly seen him banished from the graces of good society. His underlying premise hinted at supernatural origins as the case for many *misdiagnosed* mental peculiarities. His controversial remedy included an ice water bath (which supposedly slowed the supernatural element) to be followed promptly by several sessions with a mentalist who may then dislodge the spirit and restore the sufferer to a normal mental state. Although controversial, his obscure practice grew, eventually bringing him local celebrity, including enough fortune to travel to the United States to further pursue the occult.

Ironically, von Schaffen, while exploring the upper Midwest in the late 1880s, and having claimed to have found evidence of an ancient race of devolved humans that lived in the limestone caves that honeycombed the region, was lost to the wilderness and never heard from again. His last reported sighting was by German settlers who had recently formed the town of New Darmstadt, somewhere in the wilds of Missouri. Mysteriously, the town was destroyed by fire not long after von Schaffen's disappearance, and its location was lost to history.

Armand sighed at the romantic notion of discovering a lost civilization or culture—even the town of New Darmstadt would do. What an adventure that would be! And what of von Schaffen's theories? Was there any merit in them? A devolved race? *Fascinating*, he thought. Making a mental note to investigate this later, he imagined himself in the late 1800's, sailing up the mighty Mississippi on a steamboat, starting his adventure. He wondered if anyone would ever undertake it.

Pulling another stack of papers from the box, he found the partial legend of The Black Angel, which had supposedly occurred right here in New Orleans, also back in the 1800's. But Armand had yet to obtain the entire story and was reluctant to read it again without a satisfying conclusion.

After a long sip of brandy, he pulled the last bundle from the bottom of the box. It was in fact a group of notebooks and folders that had been tied together with twine, and his heart leapt. Quickly untying the lot, he opened the first folder and instantly recognized the worn and yellowed documents with the neat, tight handwriting. This is what he'd been looking for! The research of his old university professor, Father Sonnier.

The man had been influential in Armand's formative years as a student at Loyola University. Originally attending the college for a teaching degree, Armand had experienced something he couldn't explain. It was an event that had quite disturbed him, in fact, and nearly ended his schooling. Initially a skeptic of the supernatural, Armand tried to reconcile his experience with other disciplines of research, but always came away unsatisfied. Nearly at his wit's end, he explored the last avenue he knew of, occult occurrences recognized by the church, which led him to Father Sonnier.

After hours of deep conversation with the Father, Armand's interest in the occult grew from disbelief to skeptical acceptance, then finally to obsession. It was the only thing that made sense, he realized—once he had the faith to consider it, that was. The irony of this was not lost on him.

Father Sonnier mentored him to include other areas of study, such as biblical theory, creation myths of ancient civilizations, as well as philosophy. He'd told Armand that he still had to obtain an employable degree, which would give him the means to explore his newfound passion later in life. Which is precisely what Armand had done.

But the Father had his own secret passion of research, which Armand would later learn and willingly take up. It was this secret passion that Armand now held in his hands, and that sat—as far as he knew—in its entirety upon his fireplace table. Over time, they'd learned they were kindred spirits, and the Father had gifted Armand his research just before his death. The topic was that of exorcisms and the theory of the Vampiri ex animo.

It was a strange theory. One that few people believed in. But it did show up in fringe occult writings and in some possession research. Most notably, however, it was referenced in the diary of Fr. Raymond Bishop, S.J., a priest who had attended, and documented, the exorcism of a teenage boy in St. Louis, in 1949.

As a young man, the friar had studied at Loyola for a year, where he and Father Sonnier had met. Armand had already passed through those esteemed halls of academia, missing the young friar by a mere six years—the difference in their ages. Armand had graduated and moved on to his first teaching position at a local college preparatory when the young priest was meeting Father Sonnier. The three men's futures would take different paths years later: the Father remaining at

Loyola until his retirement, Armand climbing the ladder of academia, and the priest quietly, and faithfully, heading for the most famous case of possession in the country.

After the exorcism of the boy had concluded, the friar, although sworn to secrecy, had confided in Father Sonnier through written correspondence and one personal visit. It wasn't the possession that troubled the priest—although it was the most traumatic event he would ever witness—it was a few small details of the possession, which nearly went undocumented, that troubled him the most.

According to Fr. Bishop, the boy, referred to in his diary as 'Robbie' or simply R, for anonymity, had been possessed after playing with a Ouija board. His Aunt Tillie had recently passed away and he'd attempted to contact her. Once the possession took hold and the priests became involved, it was recorded that the emergence of letters and words would occasionally appear on the boy's skin. Sometimes long scratches could be seen running down his torso and onto his legs, but the letters were the most perplexing. On one occasion, after a rather violent episode of cursing and mad ramblings about wanting to eat the priest's cord (at the time this was thought to be a sexual reference) the friar noticed red letters appear across the boy's abdomen. Although unsure of the spelling, considering the archaic lettering the demon had used, the priest recorded the words: Vampiri ex animo, which supposedly stayed visible for the better part of an hour.

Friar Bishop later confided in Father Sonnier that he believed the spoken reference to 'eating the priest's cord' was not sexual at all. He believed it to be a reference to the silver spirit cord referenced in Ecclesiastes. But the implication of the demon eating such a thing, and the obscure term Vampiri ex animo, caused the friar to imagine a scenario almost beyond comprehension. It was an image that would test the friar's faith and haunt him for the rest of his life. It was a concept that would become the obsession of Father Sonnier, which, by an unlucky circumstance, had just been passed to Armand.

Armand set down the written notes of his mentor and brought out his pipe. He absently cleaned it, tapping the remnants of the last bowl into the large ashtray that sat on the table. His own experience—the one that had sent him on his path to find Father Sonnier—was different than this, not as extreme, and he felt fortunate to have even met the man, considering the credentials and experience of the friar.

Why would the words Vampiri ex animo appear on a possessed boy? What did they mean? Why the reference to eating the cord? Why did the friar feel a need to speak to someone unrelated to the case? Why did the concept of the vampiri consume the Father for the rest of his life? And why did Armand feel like this was terribly relevant now?

He struck a match for his pipe and waited for the flame to grow. Just as he meant to set flame to bowl, an errant draft blew the match out.

He shivered for no reason, then heard Jimmy's bedroom door open.

CHAPTER 52

As Del stepped through her bedroom door, Billy pounced from the shadows.

One moment she was kicking her jeans out of the way, feeling for the light switch on the wall. The next moment she was flying forward over the bed, wondering where the switch had gone.

I tripped, she thought. *No. I'm tripping.*

But before she could even imagine *how* she'd tripped, her mind was overwhelmed with input. Several things happened at once.

Her leg hit something and sent a flash of pain through her mind. Oddly, she thought this caused her eyes to delay adjusting to the dark room. She couldn't see a thing.

Her mind sensed that the door had just shut itself.

Her ears were ringing. Although, she couldn't actually hear it, so she must be sensing it.

Her head spun. The room spun.

For a brief instant, she wondered if she wasn't still falling; then that thought vanished with the sensation of being lifted off the floor.

Now she was in the air with a white-hot bolt of pain shooting up from her armpits.

Her mind struggled to make sense of what was happening. Had she hit her head? Was this an alcohol-fueled trance? A seizure?

Her armpits screamed again. The pain was intense, and very real.

Hands.

Hands?

Why was she thinking of—?

Hands!

Her mind froze around the idea. All other thoughts vanished. She was being lifted off the floor, clamped at the top of the torso by a strong pair of hands digging into her armpits. And the pain was fierce and frightening.

Oh God, she was being thrown down on the bed!

Someone was in her room!

*

When Billy crashed through the open doorway, his mind slipped back to a time of alleys and hotel rooms. It had been a brief period for him, but at that influential age, it had been all-consuming. Alleys were the norm. Hotel rooms were few and far between. Both typically ended with a

(SMACK!)

Dropped Purse Incident and he had quickly learned to wait until the wrestling was over, so he could scoop up the contents.

The darkness was familiar, the small room was common. And the struggling… yes, that went hand in hand with his memories. He was on the right track.

Picking up the girl had been easy; she felt light as a feather. But Billy was powered by his own form of supernatural energy. It was a feral energy, wild and untamed, that preceded the coming of The Red. Like static electricity before a storm, the hairs on Billy's arms stood up with it. His skin tingled from it as it floated around him. Soon, the mysterious energy would coalesce and begin seeping into his pores, collecting in his stomach. From there, the lightning bolt between his legs would make the connection and his mind would find The Red.

Pushing her down onto the bed, he felt her body stiffen. Her arms had already clamped to her sides, trying to squeeze his hands away from the tender parts under her arms. Like a mind reader, he felt the scream bubbling up from her lungs and clamped his right hand over her mouth before it came out. He pivoted his weight to do this, throwing his right leg over both of hers. He let his chest sink down and felt her lungs compress slightly. A faint whiff of alcohol seeped out between his fingers.

Whiskey sour. Common behavior.

Without his assistants along to help speed the process, Billy had to think of a new approach. This girl was wrapped tight; arms over her chest, legs clamped and crossed at the ankles, wriggling like a fish, and ready to scream as soon as his hand moved. With only one free hand, he didn't know how to get the process started. In the past, at least, before he was given access to The Red, he'd always had to wait. Much wrestling had to occur. And time. Access was only granted after a series of

(*SMACK!*)

(*...stake that head, bitch, that's it... stake it... ohh...*)

(*SMACK!*)

other events.

That's right, he suddenly realized. It was the *SMACK!* that started the process. At least, it was loosely related in some way.

He raised his left hand in the air, but then something happened. As if by divine intervention, he brought his face closer to hers, and there it was. Just a whiff, but it was enough to change the course of events.

Billy inhaled the faint aroma of cigarette smoke and sweat, and he regressed again. His left hand came down to the mattress to support his weight, his face lowered to that side of her neck. The girl squirmed and tried to bite his hand, but she had no chance of getting free. With his hand, he pulled her face to his right, tilted his head to the left and began to nuzzle her neck. The smell of smoke was heavy in her hair. Billy didn't think she was a smoker, but must have picked up the smell in a bar looking for Johns. His eyes clouded over.

(No biting Billy, just tickle me)

Slowly, he began to lick her neck.

*

Del was panicked but sobering. Her wide eyes searched the blackness for her attacker as she fought against his pressing weight. He'd just thrown his leg over her and clamped her mouth shut.

Where'd he come from?

Did he follow me home from the bar?

How'd he get in?

A hundred other questions flashed through her panicked mind.

She gnashed at his hand, trying to bite a finger. Her screams fell silent beneath his thick hand and only came out as mumbles. If she could snag a pad of skin and get his hand away from her mouth, maybe she could wake up Mrs. Doucet on the first floor.

Don't be stupid! She can't hear a thing.

Del desperately wanted to pull at the bottom of her t-shirt. She was self-conscious of her exposed legs and wished she still had her jeans on. Squeezing her legs together as tight as she could, she took inventory of the room. She didn't think anyone else was in here. She just had to deal with him. His right hand was on her mouth. His other hand was somewhere. His erection, pressed against her leg, went MIA when he shifted his weight.

His erection? Oh God, not like this. Not my first time.

Panic overwhelmed her. She wasn't prepared for this. She had no plan.

His erection. Where'd it go? Are his clothes still on? He's positioning. He's ready. Oh, no, no!

(Hurt him, Del! You have to hurt him!)

She reached out with her right hand, feeling where his leg had been. That hard lump had just been pressed against her right leg a minute ago, but try as she might, she couldn't reach it. He was too tall, and now his groin was somewhere near her knees. Here he was lucky. If she'd found it, she would have ripped it off.

She bent her knees up as hard as she could, while keeping them locked together.

(Knee him! Kick him! Rip it off!)

She grunted and screamed. She gnashed and bit. After several attempts, all she'd managed to do was get a few light grunts out of his diaphragm. And hers was nearly empty. Each time she struggled, like a giant snake, his body seemed to wrap itself tighter around hers. The old mattress was giving way to the extra weight. She was struggling to breathe.

Tears sprang from her eyes.

Oh God! He's trying to suffocate me!

Then she felt him lick her neck and her mind with blank.

CHAPTER 53

After confirming that Jimmy was still safe in his bed—and assuming that his door had come open due to the cranky ventilation system—Armand returned to his chair. There he picked up the written notes of Father Sonnier and continued reading. Up to now, the notes had been theories on possession, references to other exorcisms and biblical passages. The Father also had an impressive collection of creation stories from other cultures that Armand tried to avoid—not wanting to get distracted. However, he did remember being surprised when he'd first learned of this strange line of research that so interested his old mentor.

"Surprised?" Father Sonnier had said one day in his study. "But why should you be surprised? Yes, I am a Catholic priest, and we believe in the Old Testament version of Creation, but..." And Armand remembered very clearly him searching for the right words, then his hands folding reverently in his lap. "Stories are still susceptible to interpretation. If you understand my meaning." He let this statement sit, then, just as the silence became uncomfortable, he spread his hands and continued. "But do other religions not believe as firmly as we? Should we not be good students of God and attempt an understanding, a glimpse, into another's beliefs? We may find that they aren't so different from our own, and on many levels."

Armand knew there were uncanny similarities across the major religions. He remembered telling Del that Voodoo and Christianity even shared saints; unlikely bedfellows if there were any in the religious world. But what fascinated him, worried him occasionally, was the realization that as the religious and scientific communities continued to defend their dogma, more and more discoveries pointed to the fact that their individual *marvels* had eerily similar characteristics.

He knew of a group of scholars—albeit a small one—formed from different religious and scientific circles who were collaborating on a theory that the old biblical stories were perhaps more than just metaphors. They faced quite a headwind from their respective leaders—both those who believed the earth and heavens were truly created in six days, as well as those who adamantly believed the Big Bang came from nothingness that grew so heavy it exploded into everything—but Armand thought the fringe theories were plausible, as well. In fact, he had come to believe that they were actually probable. He believed that what had become religious doctrine and miracles could be explained as easily as ancient civilizations simply misunderstanding what they saw.

A meteor streaks through the heavens? A harbinger of doom.

A freak migration of locusts? A plague from God.

Ships fly across the sky? Chariots of the Angels.

The point being that many myths and legends did not grow just from campfire stories or parables to keep children safe, but from things that people *actually witnessed,* but didn't have the context to describe.

And that's what concerned him so much about the last page of Father Sonnier's notes; the random, seemingly unrelated theories, that *if* related, spoke to a madness he did not yet understand.

The final page read as follows:

It has been recorded that on certain occasions of near-death (revived? returned of their own accord?) that the victims return in a worse (altered?) state.

Avg life span after return?

Percentage recalling white light vs seeing own cord?

Cord people (small %) —sane?   —worms

—itchy voices??   —physical changes?

Of the small percentage that stated seeing a cord, some described feelings of: violation, thinning, disappearing, coming apart? unraveling, being eaten—

Spiritually eaten?

Who or what is eating? demonic possession?

—demonic hunger

Research:

Alina Lupei c.1700s (translation - noble wolf?) – Romania - real world Carmilla??   Fed on silver light?

Alphabetum filii Sirach (look for Lilith references) c. 700s "Night witch"

Jiangshan "Hopping vampire" (China) c. unknown

—absorbs Ch'i (life force)

Edimmu "Vengeful ghosts" (Mesopotamia) c. 3500 BC

—improper burials?

—*"wind spirits" that sucked life*

—*possession*

POSSESSION

St. Louis (1949) — vampiri ex animo . . .

Armand read this last sentence and saw exhaustion in the writing. The letters, barely formed, trailed away on the ends as if the author wished not to write them at all; and once they were written, possibly hoping they would disappear of their own accord. He imagined Father Sonnier's hand barely finishing the word *animo*, the burden too heavy, then pushing three dots into the paper, a simple ellipsis, but not meaning '*the omission from speech or writing of a word or words that are superfluous or able to be understood from contextual clues.*' No. As far as Armand could tell, there were no words that could explain this concept, this monstrous idea. So, the Father had simply ended with an ellipsis to say, *I don't have the words, or the strength.*

And Armand didn't have them either. Until just recently, he hadn't read that combination of words. But, although his Latin was rusty, he could translate them well enough to feel a cold draft of dread settle about him. The translation of *Vampiri ex animo*, to the best of his knowledge, meant, *Vampire of the Soul.*

And somehow Father Sonnier believed this term was related to possessions, or improper burials, or silver cords, or wind spirits that sucked life. Or maybe all of these ideas together.

Armand shuddered again and wondered what had been witnessed in ancient times to create these myths? How could a civilization, thousands of years old and most likely struggling to survive, have imagined such an abomination? Such a monstrosity? What had they seen to curse them with such terror? What had the *world* seen—for it was referenced in all major cultures—to form the idea that a person could live off another's spiritual life force?

Armand set the papers down and thought, *God help the poor soul who was cast into this hell.*

CHAPTER 54

Del floated outside her body and surveyed the scene.

Who's in my room? Did I bring someone home from the—?
The attacker!

Del consumed the entire scene in an instant. She remembered where she was, although her alcohol-muddled mind didn't take well to trancing. She didn't know this because she'd never tried it before. But she had to get her mind clear. This instant. She was being smothered before her very eyes.

She saw where he'd been hiding in the hall.

Stupid! Stupid! He was right there!

She saw how he'd caught the slowly closing door.

He was right behind you!

She saw his broad back sink a bit lower as his face nestled into her neck.

(Del!)

Suddenly she was a wave of energy flying at his head. She hadn't formed a terrifying face or horrible monster, she simply pummeled him with energy. That's all she could think to do as she felt her lungs struggle for air.

He threw his head back and cried out in surprise. His left hand waved frantically at the sensation, but his right hand was clamped tight.

He's had practice, she thought.

Del's body breathed deeply when he shifted his weight, and her mind gorged the oxygen. Her knees came up into his abdomen again, catching him by surprise.

"Ooff…" he muttered. Then she saw his aura change.

She'd never considered reading someone's aura before. It was so close to the trancing images that people left behind, it was confusing to see one versus the other. But this guy wasn't trancing. He didn't have the Sight, as far as Del could tell. But something was driving him. An energy swirled about him and had just changed color when she kneed him. Was this his aura? Or was it just pure poison leaking from his mind? She couldn't tell, but it was terrifying. There was a sickness driving him and she didn't know how to fight it.

She had to try something fast before he lost all control and started swinging. *That* she had no defense for.

*

Billy had been licking. He hadn't been biting.

Billy had been gentle. He hadn't been bad.

He hadn't even started yet, but he'd sensed The Red was coming near. The magic was working.

Then the ghosts came, and The Red retreated.

Now he was frantic. And angry.

He hadn't really believed in witches before this, but his mind was changing. Maybe she was a witch. He'd felt the girl slowing down, sinking into the mattress, and thought she was almost finished struggling. But then she'd tried to curse him. Or cast a spell. He wasn't sure what it was, but he felt something. It was like she'd sent a giant cloud of gnats to swarm him and when she did, The Red retreated. It was still out there, somewhere just outside his mind, waiting to return. He could feel it. But he'd almost lost it. It had almost left completely, and he couldn't have that. He wouldn't survive it if The Red left again. He was sure of it.

He had to think of something

(SMACK!)

to get her to stop squirming. She was getting bolder.

Yes. That's right. You forgot. It all starts with a

(SMACK!)

*

Del saw into Billy's mind. Like with the murder house, she saw several future scenarios quickly dwindling to a few. And of those immediate futures, most of them ended with her own death. She had mere seconds to act.

Staring at one's own demise was disarming. She couldn't fully comprehend it. Didn't want to believe it. But there it was, staring her in the face. He was close to killing her.

Then she felt the silver-orb of Del fill the room.

(Fight him! Blind him! Kill him! Do something!)

Her trancing mind let loose, and another wave of energy hit the intruder. Both bodies cried out at the force of the blow.

"Oooffff! You witch!" Billy huffed; face buried in her neck. He threw his head back, gagging for air.

"Owwww!" Del moaned beneath his hand. The hot surge of energy was terrible. Her skin felt as if it were on fire.

What happened? she wondered. *Why did I feel that?*

Then it dawned on her that she'd never been the recipient of her own starkblast, her own cosmic radiation; the deadly energy that now pulsed from the silver orb of Del was just that, deadly. Deadly to even her own physical body.

A powerful flex and her head was wrenched all the way to the left, pinned just before the point of her neck snapping. She felt his left hand come up to her neck, fingers scrabbling for her windpipe. *This was it*, she thought. *I'm done.*

*

Billy felt a stab of pain in his body like nothing he'd felt before. A thousand needles of energy had just flown through him, knocking the wind out of him.

"Oooffff! You witch!" he huffed; face buried in her neck. He threw his head back, gagging for air.

He heard her mumble. Then felt something terrible.

It can't be! Not yet!

The Red retreated even further from his mind. It pulled back to a safe distance. He could barely sense its presence.

The witch was driving it away.

NOOO!! His mind panicked. *PLEASE NOO! It's not fair!* He shuddered, then something inside him snapped and he began to cry hysterically.

(She's trying to send it away! You'll never find it again! Forget her. Even if she dies, The Red will be gone!)

Billy's eyes rolled wildly in his sockets as he wrenched her head sideways; her neck almost to the breaking point.

(She's killing you! She's killing The Red! SHE'S KILLING The Red!!)

Tears streamed straight out of his bulging, straining eyes, dripping onto her face. He pressed his forehead hard against her right temple and growled a guttural sound. He stared into the frantic eye that swam there, trying to make it see the pain he would deliver. Hers was the eye of an animal panicked in a trap, staring death in the face. He wanted to crush that eye. He wanted to smash his own head into it, again and again, until it popped with the cracking of her cheek bone, and he drove splinters of her skull backward into her witch brain, and her nose collapsed, and her forehead caved, and her throat closed and—

(Close her throat! Just close her throat before she KILLS. THE. RED!!)

And he was surprised to find that his fingers were already moving there.

*

As his fingers scrabbled for her windpipe, Del was suddenly aware of another presence in the room. A deadly presence. And it wasn't the man trying to kill her.

She'd been simultaneously flashing between her silver-orb self and her physical body, trying desperately to attack the man atop her while defending her body. She knew no one had run in, coming to her aid. But there was a presence, nonetheless. And it swirled with anger and black lightning.

(Now bite it)

She heard the words, but couldn't find the source. It could have been Arlo's voice. It could have been her own. Hell, it could have been Mama Dedé's in a different world. She couldn't tell. But she knew what had just happened. She could see the presence swirling. She'd felt it filling the room, but hadn't acknowledged it. But now she did. And she understood it had presented her only chance of survival. Her last chance.

(Bite it!)

The black-orb of Del, the Dark Dreamer, had just emerged.

And the silver life cord of Billy had been laid bare.

And Del bit.

*

One minute Billy's fingers were scrabbling for the soft spot of the witch's neck, then they weren't.

FLASH!

In an instant, his world changed.

You've been struck by lightning, his mind told him. *And your head is on fire.*

That was the best his brain could do with describing this new experience. It had no other reference to compare it to. It couldn't dream of what had just happened. But something had. So his brain told him he'd been struck by lightning. But surprisingly, there was no pain. Not yet.

But that made no sense. There were no storms here. His mind was trying to reason it out.

Someone sliced off the top of your brain with a knife.

Someone scooped out your brains through a crack in your skull.

A giant vacuum is sucking your soul through the top of your head.

His mind tried over and over to find a comparable memory, an imagined scenario. Even a fragment of dream would do. Nothing. There had never been a sensation like this. And there would never be another.

A giant worm pierced your skull and is slurping out your essence.

That was closer.

He didn't know why, but that last scenario resonated a bit with him.

Then he felt the first of his strings break, and realized that something terrible really was happening.

From the chaos of sensations that flew through his mind in the last seconds, his brain hadn't had time to register the pain signals. But now they were hitting. And again, his mind struggled to classify them, except by imagining that his cells were spontaneously combusting into hellfire.

Someone is pulling your muscles apart a strand at time, out the top of your head. SNAP! Hellfire.

Someone poured lava in your veins and your blood vessels are exploding. SNAP! Hellfire.

Someone shoved red hot needles through your eardrums to suck out your spinal fluid. SNAP! SNAP! Hellfire.

The pain hit him. A hard convulsion contorted his mouth into a snarl. His lungs seized before the scream could emerge.

Then the pain overwhelmed him. Cleansing him. He was sure he'd go mad from it any second. He was burning from the inside out.

A thousand demons are dissolving your soul with acid and slurping your essence.

That was the last attempt his brain made at rationalizing, but as his stomach flooded with acid at the thought, he was afraid this bizarre scenario wasn't far from the truth.

Then his muscles went slack. His hands fell away. His body slumped. And his mind went black.

*

Del bit.

FLASH!

The battery sting against her tongue was incredible. Much sharper and hotter than from the cord of the dead girl in the cemetery.

(Bite him again!)

Del bit again.

FLASH!

STING!

This time she heard something like the popping of strings and knew his cord was beginning to fray.

Her attacker had shoved his forehead into hers just before she bit the first time. The bite had an instant effect on him. She felt his body stiffen as his head jerked up. She even sensed his mind begin to spin out. Unsure of the sensation she had caused by biting the cord of a living person, she wondered how his mind was processing the input. Did it even understand what was happening? Did she?

No. She did not. She understood very little about this, so it was unlikely he was able to process it at all.

Then he convulsed into a silent scream.

Heat radiated from his life cord. She basked in it.

Droplets of his very essence leaked out of the tiny punctures she'd made. She felt them on her lips.

She ground her back teeth where the cord had slipped—perhaps her tongue had pushed it there, but she'd never be sure—and felt it quiver beneath her bite. Tiny shreds tore loose.

Then the tiny tears opened and began spurting with the rhythm of a heartbeat.

The sensation was repulsive and exquisite all at once. The alternating sensation of a bite and a sting, a bite and a sting.

Pain and pleasure.

And power.

Like a date marked on a calendar, Del would always remember this moment.

Power, pleasure and pain.

Power and pleasure.

Power and pleasure surged into Del with every

(BITE!)

the Dark Dreamer urged. Hovering above her, watching from a corner, the thing that emerged at the murder house, the entity that became the voice of the black-orb of Del urged her on. The silver-orb of Del did nothing, for was it not invested in the carnage? Was it not the core entity that drove the slaughter? Was it not one with this wild animal? This animal of Del that emerged from the clutches of death? Yes. All entities—that would survive the night—were of the same core essence.

And the Dark Dreamer, watching, knew this and smiled.

Del felt the attacker go limp, hands fall away, and slump forward. With one easy shove, she pushed his two-hundred-odd pounds up and off. She surged with power. He teetered over like a rag doll, falling between the bed and the wall, hitting the floor with a dead thump. Then she was on top of him.

Energy coursed into her body. Free-flowing oxygen cleared her mind, sharpened it. Her muscles ached, suddenly overflowing with adrenaline. She had to use them, or she feared she'd explode from the chemical.

Now *she* was in control. Now *she* would deliver the pain.

And she'd ensure her attacker never did this again.

Del bit again and somewhere in an invisible sky, a giant falcon screeched. It carried the remains of a thousand, thousand dying, trailing from its midnight blue talons.

And it dove toward Billy and Del.

Somewhere in the room, a strange wind began to swirl.

CHAPTER 55

In her blind fury, Del felt release. In her trance, she saw the cord, felt it writhe beneath her bite, felt the liquid essence sting her tongue as Billy's life dripped from her slobbering mouth.

She was animal. She was rage. She was death.

And again, she felt the desire to swallow build at the back of her throat.

During the assault, she'd managed to get a knee into his abdomen, but now that she was on top, she pummeled his stomach and groin over and over. Her knee ground towards the floor with savage force. As the tissue began to breakdown and leak, she could only think to destroy him completely, eliminate his existence. And so, she bit harder.

The threads of Billy's existence were now popping at an alarming rate. As each thread broke, a stinging flood of liquid sprayed into her mouth, then dripped out in slick strands of blue saliva. Billy had convulsed in the beginning, but now lay twitching, helpless, as his life leaked away.

The twisting orbs of Del filled the room, spinning nearly out of control. Competing versions of Del jockeyed for position, tried to pull her mind one way or another. The silver-orb version pleaded for mercy. *Run away!* it said. *Spare him!* it pleaded. The black-orb version, The Dark Dreamer, felt no mercy, wallowed in the ecstasy of the carnage and knew that Billy's death was close. Only one more violation was appropriate for the monster that lay beneath her: to read his inner thoughts, his most intimate secrets, then leave him with one strand of cord left in place, forever anchoring his soul to his dead and decaying body. By doing this, his spirit would become an evernot, trapped in an eternal state of transition, and never find rest. The Dark Dreamer, through Del, would add Billy's essence to the tapestry of dead. She'd become the weaver of the tapestry, the creator, in a way. She would— *they*— *it*, could build an army of dead and never know fear again. It could add the souls to the tapestry, feed the decaying with little nibbles of Del. No, it would never know fear again, *it* would only know power.

The room shook as a terrible wind pummeled the walls.

Del's mind, overdosing on the orgy of power, flew into Billy's past. She laid bare the dark secrets of her attacker. And was repulsed by what she found.

She saw Billy just before her own attack. His mind was poisoned with a strange red dream. She saw Tasha die a horrible death, pleading with her new lover to be gentle. She couldn't breathe. The Red poison taunted him then, also. She saw Terrance and Rochelle, somehow associates of Billy's, and swore to deal with them later. She'd already dealt with Howard, luckily. She saw other girls die, more red poison. Always The Red poison. Billy always cried for

(The Red)

flashed and Del felt she'd slipped far into his past. She was in an alley. It was dark. There was movement. There was a

(*SMACK!*)

Little boy hiding behind a set of trashcans. There was a man and a woman.

There was a struggle.

A spilled purse.

There were moans.

(ohh… that's it. Stake it… stake it right in the past… stake. It. Right. In. the…)

(*SMACK!*)

Del understood the scene and wretched. She watched the ancient transaction taking place in the alley, then looked back to the boy hiding behind the trashcans. Hiding near his bedroll. His and his mother's bed, at least for this night, hidden behind trashcans and formed out of cardboard boxes. There was privacy in the dark boxes. The Red would come there.

She understood the confused words in the boy's mind. They were adult words, adult thoughts and desires, that his young mind had no context for, so his mind translated them as best it could.

(…*this paint your house! stake it, stake it right in the past…*)

Adult transactions that provided enough money for food, and to try a new location, but not always enough for a hotel room, and rarely enough for an apartment.

When the adult transaction finished and the man left, a robotic series of tasks began. Del understood this to be from much practice. The woman, hands shaking, tended her wounds as best she could in the dark. She didn't want her boy to see her bleeding. She could cover the bruises with makeup, but blood always scared him. The boy would creep out of his hiding place and quickly scoop up the contents of the purse that always fell open, taking quick inventory of the important items. Until the day her driver's license had fallen down a grate, he'd done his job very well. Then, depending on how loud the transaction had been, they'd decide if they needed to change alleys. If not, they'd fade into the shadows of their box room, huddle next to each other for warmth, and sometimes, sometimes the boy would need to be helped to sleep. The woman learned this after a particularly harsh transaction, where afterwards he could only sob uncontrollably. So, laying there that night with his face buried in the back of her neck, she felt his body change, stiffen, and seek relief against hers. He'd already formed the habit of kissing her neck, trying to console her, but when the licking began, which helped to calm him, and the request that she smoke another cigarette before bed, she feared where it would lead. She resisted the final advance for as long as she could, but was exhausted many nights. Over time, she'd awake in the middle of the night to find that her relationship with her growing son had changed in a way that could never be undone. On those nights, with his face buried in her back, his arms wrapped tightly around her, pleading for her not to move, to not take away The Red, she could only coax him to be quiet until he was finished.

(No biting Billy, just tickle me)

And so, the poison had entered Billy Bash through a wound in his mind, a fracture of his childhood. And once inside, it spread like a cancer.

Silver-orb Del retreated from the scene, struggling with the images in front of her. She searched Billy's history, looking for a happy memory. She snapped back to the present, searching beyond the events of the evening. Was there a redeeming path for him? Was there some version where he wasn't a monster? The movie reels of Billy's future quickly played out. She searched for redemption, but there was none. If Billy survived the night, the monster would survive.

Black-orb Del took over and her mind was yanked back to the scene where Billy's fingers scrabbled for her throat.

In the physical room, some psychic force shoved the bed sideways against the door.

(He tried to kill you!) the Dark Dreamer screamed.

Del felt the delicious warmth of anger rise again.

(Look what he meant to do before that!)

And Del saw several variations of the attack. Each one more brutal than the last. Then the Dark Dreamer showed her scenes after her own death, where she was added to the tapestry. The horror of Billy's continued violations, even after her last breath. The deep, deep bites. Del's own torn spirit cord, torn but not severed.

Silver-orb Del pulled at her mind. The Dark Dreamer pulled back. Silver Del cried for release from this hell. Black Del demanded revenge. The storm of Del was overwhelming, and it began to shake the house. Somewhere close a window exploded.

(Suffer! He deserves to suffer!)

She realized her mouth was still watering with stinging pleasure. The shiny blue saliva hung in long strands from her panting mouth, slicking his dying face. Billy's life, his own essence, dripped from her mouth and was let to spill out onto the old wood floor with no more regard than spitting out a bad taste.

(He deserves the ultimate violation!) the Dark Dreamer screamed. Then Del was shown an incredible image.

She saw herself taking the final bite of Billy, and swallowing. The delicious, stinging fluid of Billy's essence flowing into her, just as his eyes opened for the last time. He'd see his demise. He'd see his life essence being sucked dry, nourishing a new predator. The ultimate hunter. Then Del saw herself riding the falcon of death, drinking from—no, gorging on—the life cords of a thousand, thousand others it held in its talons. Killing all the Billy Bashes of the world. Killing the monsters. Building a dead army. Making them suffer in this world and the next, as their demons drove them to torment others.

Del saw the frayed cord of Billy's life and wondered how many more bites it could take. She wondered if she could take him down to his final moment, drink of his essence, and leave him at the brink of annihilation.

She felt the last few strands in her mouth. Her tongue touched them, positioned them to her back teeth. Then she closed her eyes and readied herself for that glorious, ungodly violation.

Del? a faint voice, a familiar voice, whispered at the back of her mind. Del felt the Dark Dreamer lurch in surprise. Somewhere in the building a lamp crashed to the floor.

Del, honey. Where are you? the woman asked. The voice was a memory, whisper soft, but it was there. *I'm comin'.*

Del felt her mind twist. Competing forces pulling her apart; the Dark Dreamer filled her mind with a black cloud, trying to force the old woman's words aware; silver-orb Del spun madly, building an electric charge to kill the black image. All the while, the stinging fluid crept toward her tonsils. It wanted to be swallowed.

Del, I'm comin', Mama Dedé said. Her voice rising like a wind. *Don't swallow! Fight it and hold on! But for God's sake, don't swallow!*

CHAPTER 56

*M*ama D? Del searched her mind, thinking it was a trick, or that she'd finally gone insane.

I'm comin'.

Del tried to call out, but a sharp sting across her tongue killed the words where they lay.

Del, I'm comin'.

Don't swallow!

Fight it and hold on! But for God's sake, don't swallow!

Mama D found Del, then stopped, hovering outside the scene. She tried to make sense of what she was seeing, but it was a blur. There was Del, crouched on all fours in a shabby bedroom, with a dead man beneath her. A large silver orb with a black streak spun wildly in the air. Mirroring it, a large black orb with a silver streak spun with the same intensity, only in the opposite direction. Competing clouds from the twin-storm of Del crashed through the room and out into the night.

Why does Del look like that? Mama D moved closer, but stayed clear of the orbs.

It was as if Del's trancing world had melded with the real one. She looked like a character in one of those 3D movies, only without needing The Red and blue glasses to see the effect. Back and forth, the ghost image of a trancing, crawling Del merged into a real Del, then split apart again. Back and forth. 3D, but on a slow frame rate. The affect was disorienting, and Mama D had to look away.

How long have I been gone, and what has she learned in that time?

"Ghhluh, ghlluh." Del began to wretch as the cloying blue liquid coated her tongue and cheeks. A whisper of air escaped her lungs. "Hhheellllppppp…"

She belched and convulsed. Her arms buckled as she tried to crawl away, crawl anywhere, but her knee seemed to be mired in tar—the crushed sensitive parts of Billy Bash.

The Dark Dreamer saw Del's will begin to fade and came forward again. "Bite him! Swallow him! Eat him!"

"Uugghh… pphhluagh. Ppllaah!" Del spit bluish foam and shivered. Her arms buckled and she nearly met Billy's dead kiss with her blue stinging lips.

Only he wasn't dead, not completely. And somewhere in his dying mind, he thought he'd moved his tongue enough to lick her one last time.

Swelling, the black orb filled the room and pushed against the physical boundaries of the building. As the black cloud swarmed around Del, the Dark Dreamer bellowed. "Swallow and you will have vengeance. Swallow and you will be DEATH!"

And as if the weight of those words forced their way into her mouth, Del felt her throat constrict, then her eyes flooded with tears. "Eehhhhh…. I shallowwwed, ohhhh…" Del moaned in despair, fearing to close her mouth.

BITCH! Mama Dedé flew forward like a lioness protecting her cub. *Leave my girl alone and go back to hell!*

"Ghhluuuuh…" Del convulsed and began to shake.

Light clashed with light. Shadow fought shadow. And the black orb receded in the fury, but just a bit. The damage had been done, as far as it was concerned. Del had swallowed, and it waited to feel the power course through her body, *ITs* body. It wanted to feel the essence of another flow through its veins, feel the unnatural power—the cravings—begin to build. Soon it would feel the essence of a thousand, thousand flowing through it. Then it would deal with the silver orb.

Del! Mama D swarmed Del's collapsing body. *Dat man try to stick his dead sausage in you?*

The woman concentrated on her own hands. In her trance, her old fingers grew long. They reached for Del's mouth.

He try to make you swalla' cold mayonnaise and pickle juice? Lick those blisters?

And then her fingers touched the back of Del's throat.

Waggle dat dead, green sausage under your nose, smellin' like cheese and tell you it gonna taste like—

Del's stomach let loose in a violent outburst. Three hours of sweet alcoholic drinks and acid shot forth, blasting the inside of her mouth, then covering Billy's face.

NOOO!! The Dark Dreamer screamed. But even before the scream finished echoing, the swirling black orb began to fade.

Before it fully registered to Del that Billy's mouth was still open, a larger fountain spewed forth, clearing his head and emptying the larger part of her stomach.

Noooo… The Dark Dreamer retreated, not caring to watch the closing act.

Del snapped out of her trance as her body tumbled sideways and a final spurt splashed feebly onto the floor.

She lay there, panting, trying to get her shaking arms under control. She feebly kicked at Billy's legs with her bare feet, trying to push him as far away from herself as she could. Somewhere in the swirling chaos of her mind she heard pounding.

Struggling back up to all fours and crawling away from the dead body, she realized the burning sting of Billy's essence was gone. It had been replaced by, cleansed from her throat by, the burn of her own stomach acid.

And her mind began to clear.

CHAPTER 57

Tuesday morning Detective Marcel closed the door of the hospital room and motioned to Babette Thibodeaux.

"Watch the door, officer," Marcel said. "I'll be right back."

"You think she's goin' somewhere?" Babette asked.

Marcel ignored the tone and headed down the hall. It had been a long day already—beginning around 4:30 that morning when the call came in reporting an attack at a tenement house with a deceased person—and now that he knew he had the Rape Gang, at least one of them, he knew his day would be even longer.

He raised an eye to Frank, who sat next to Armand on chrome-legged chairs. Marcel said, "Get a cup of coffee?" And nodded his head in the direction of the large urn at the nurses' station.

Frank looked hopefully at Armand, then followed Marcel.

"Doctor come by yet?" Marcel asked.

"Yeah, just after you went in." Frank took the fresh cup from Marcel and dropped his stained Styrofoam cup in the trashcan. "Says she's damn lucky. Gonna keep her a few days, but says she's gonna be alright." He sipped, then said quietly, "Thank the Lord."

Marcel turned and looked directly at Frank. "Physically, maybe." He nodded. "And yes, 'damn lucky' is one way to put it." Searching his thoughts, Marcel's eyes floated up and over Frank's left shoulder, looking at a blurry spot in the air that had no answers. Absently he smoothed his tie, then sipped. "Considering the state of the other girls, I'd say…" His voice faded. "I'd say 'damn lucky' is a gross understatement.

"As far as mentally, however… well, who knows? This kind of thing can really mess a girl up. Makes 'em skittish, paranoid. Can't blame 'em of course, terrible what happened… could have happened. But," he topped off his coffee and flattened his tie again, "some of 'em can't let it go. They internalize it. Hide it. And I hear that's the worst thing. When they do, it sort of… grows. Like a cancer, I guess. They don't realize it, you see. They only know something's not right in their life. Something was taken from them, and they want it back. Shorts out some wires, maybe. Makes 'em start hearing things, looking over their shoulders. Then they get angry… even dangerous."

Frank's eyes narrowed. He felt Marcel was finally getting to the point. "Well," Frank cast a friendly grin, "Del-bell's got a good head on her shoulders. And she's lucky she's got a whole family to—"

Marcel pointed at Frank, letting his finger waggle up and down. "Now see, that's interesting right there, that… pet name you have for her. *Del-bell,* you say?"

Frank nodded once.

"Odd nickname, isn't it? I mean, for an old guy who's not related. Excuse me, a retired detective, who's not related. Very… cozy? Is that the word I'm looking for? *Familiar,* maybe." Marcel shrugged. "Anyway, seems odd to me.

"But as far as luck goes," the tilt of Marcel's head broadcast his real feelings about the situation. "I don't think luck had anything to do with your girl surviving that attack. At least, not *luck* in the sense we understand it."

Frank didn't know the details of how Del survived her attacker. But he suspected it was some version of what had happened in the cemetery months back. Then he remembered seeing the Alvie bones coming out of Jimmy and thought maybe that was the answer. Or hell, maybe it was a completely new trick. But he would never be the one to betray her. Then, for a reason he would never be able to explain, he remembered the hesitancy he felt that night when Del had asked for a strand of his hair—it was for the gris bag she was making. He'd been the last one to comply. But at the moment, he couldn't remember why.

The tilt of Frank's head broadcast back to Marcel that he was receiving the unspoken message loud and clear, and that he didn't care for its implication. Now it was Frank's turn to waggle his finger. "Now see, dat's interestin' right dere, dat... theory you have formin'. *'Not in da sense we understand it,'* is dat what you said? Odd statement, dat is. Granted, it's been a while, but I don't believe I ever saw dat written on a report before. Can't imagine da cappin' would take to dat. Kinda sounds like a... hunch. Dat da word I'm lookin' for?"

Marcel had started clicking his nails as soon as Frank had pointed at him, but stopped as soon as he had an opening to respond. "I think your girl is dangerous, Frank. Just between detectives, you understand. True, I didn't recognize you the first time we met. In the parking lot, you remember?"

Frank nodded.

"But I didn't know you either. But the captain has filled me in since then, so I feel it's common courtesy. And Del knows as much. I've expressed my concerns. This is the third time I've spoken to her in a week. Did you know that?"

Frank hoped he'd kept his surprise under control. "Three times, ya say?"

"Yes," Marcel said. "Three times in one week. And each of those conversations were related to some very bad things.

"Is Del lucky she wasn't more involved in those events? I suppose. Is she unlucky? Always in the wrong place at the wrong time?" He shook his head. "Once again, I don't think that's the right term.

"Am I glad this guy is off the streets? Absolutely." Marcel saw a pique of interest on Frank's face as he said this. "Yes, we've already been in his house. This looks to be our rape gang leader. We've found the girl's purse—the girl who Del worked with—in his house. We still don't think he was working alone—well… except for this last time. But the other bodies implied he had help. We're just beginning to profile his connections, but we'll find them."

The door to Del's room opened and a nurse came out. She motioned to Armand that he could go in, who promptly turned and waved at Frank.

Frank nodded and pointed for him to go in without him. He'd be right there.

Marcel sighed. "What I'm saying to you Frank, is that I'm far from having the whole picture. There's something missing here. I won't speculate on what it is. I still have to wrap my mind around it. Call it a hunch if you like, but I don't care for the term. But…" He began to click his nails. "I'm going to get the whole picture. Eventually."

Frank tossed his empty cup into the trashcan and extended his hand to Marcel. Surprised, Marcel hesitated, but for only a second.

He suddenly felt like he was being judged by his own captain. He took Frank's hand and shook.

"Sometimes," Frank began, "sometimes a case comes along where da pieces just never quite line up. Like an old puzzle where a few pieces just slipped out da box over time. You still get da sense of it, enough to set your mind at ease, but some of da detail, da stuff in da shadows… well, you just have to let your imagination fill in the blanks. Sometimes it's da only way to make sense of it. It's easier to let go, dat way."

Frank nodded a goodbye to Marcel, then turned and headed for Del's room.

"Oh, one more thing Frank."

Frank turned halfway back to Marcel.

"How'd you manage to show up at the hospital so quickly?

Frank smiled sardonically. "Police scanner. I don't sleep much these days."

Marcel watched Frank walk away and suspected they'd meet again.

CHAPTER 58

Tuesday morning, Jimmy walked into the kitchen rubbing sleep from his eyes, then stopped, as if he'd seen a ghost.

Sitting at the kitchen table in a nightgown that hung loosely from her shoulders was a face he barely recognized. He hadn't seen it awake for a long time.

"Mama D!" he cried, running towards the seated woman, and throwing his arms around her.

"You 'wake!" he said as he rocked her back and forth, patting awkwardly at her head and shoulders. "You a seepy head. You seep an seep 'ike dis," and here he made a sound something like a pig snoring. He stepped back to look at her, then cracked a wide smile.

"You eat da cookies? I bwought 'ots ah cookies and—"

"I did," Mama D said hoarsely. Her voice was scratchy and sparse, as if coming from vocal cords dried up like beef jerky. "I—" A raspy squeak wheezed out of her lungs, and she coughed. A sharp, thin smile hid the pain. "Thank you," she mouthed more than spoke. She patted his arm, then took a sip of tea.

"I get Ahman," Jimmy said. And before Mama D could set her cup down, he ran out of the kitchen.

She rubbed her eyes, trying to clear her vision. Looking around the kitchen, she tried to remember when the last time was she'd been in it. It looked like the first time she and Del had come to live with Armand: stacks of research on the table and dishes on the counter. They were clean, the dishes, but as a bachelor would do, there had been no need to put them back in the cabinets, just leave them on the counter for the next meal. The kitchen looked like that now.

That morning, when she had made her way into the kitchen, she thought she was dreaming of that first time—before she'd made it usable for more than one person. The smells were dusty and distant; sterile, in a way. Which is why she thought she was still dreaming.

She hadn't been surprised at the dream really, since she'd been stuck in one for so long. And in fact, she was grateful that it was a somewhat normal dream—something without monsters and graves. So, in this new dream she thought a cup of tea would be nice and lo-and-behold, she made tea. The kitchen hadn't turned into a maze of old images with sideways slants and images of friends with no faces, as dreams typically do. It had just been tea. Then she tried to sit at the table and that worked also. That's when she got scared.

I'm either actually awake… or I'm dead.

So, she sat in that state, listening intently for the sounds of life— of which there had been none—with her eyes scanning the room, looking for specters, wondering if this bachelor's kitchen had become her eternity. And until Jimmy came down and hugged her, she really hadn't been sure which state she was in.

Now convinced that she *was* alive, her mind began to grapple with the missing time she felt had escaped her.

Listening to the eerily quiet house, she heard Jimmy from Armand's room say, "Hey, whed he go?" and suddenly thought of Del. Mama D remembered Jimmy saying the same thing when they'd learned she'd left.

But that was just a dream, wasn't it? Del leaving?

Had she dreamt Del had left?

No. Her mind leaned towards the idea that the girl had really gone. But she didn't know where or when.

How long has Del been gone?

Rubbing her head had no effect on bringing the answer forth.

How long have I been gone?

Again, no answer.

She felt the loose skin hanging limply beneath her arm.

A long damn time to lose this much weight. Well, that's one way to do it, I guess.

Mama Dedé struggled to separate herself from the months-long dream she'd been stuck in, and the new dream she'd just had last night, a dream about Del.

At some point last evening, she'd begun to wake up, but had laid still, wondering if she was truly awake or not. For what seemed like ages, she'd had this perpetual dream of sleepwalking, like a zombie, through the house. In her dream she could move for basic functions. Somehow, she got food into herself—lots of cookies—but barely had enough energy to make it back to her grave. Only it hadn't been a grave, it had been her bed. But in her dream, it was a grave. And each day, it was a few inches deeper. Over the length of the dream—and she'd guess it at weeks or even months—the bottom of her grave had sunk to ungodly depths; fifty feet? One hundred feet? She couldn't tell, but near the end, she could barely see the rectangle of light above her, until she had to get up. Then she popped out of the grave like a jack-in-the-box. One minute she was in, then she was out. But she was always stuck in that zombie state. She'd walk, barely, and do her business. She'd drink a bit of tea and eat a cookie (there were always cookies in her dream), then she'd be back at the bottom of the grave. She'd gotten to hate coming back and sitting on the edge of the bed because she knew that led to the bottom of the grave, but she couldn't keep herself from returning. The zombie part of her mind always brought her back. And she was terrified. Terrified of not only the knowledge that the grave would be a bit deeper (it always was), but also that the worms would nibble her on the way down. She didn't know how many worms it took to eat a grave a hundred feet deep. Millions? Probably. Beyond that, she didn't really know, so it must have been millions of worms in her grave. And sometimes they didn't just eat dirt.

But then, last evening, as if her jack-in-the-box spring had come loose and she'd jumped into another box, she suddenly woke up. And as soon as she did, her mind slipped into a trance and she sensed Del.

And in the trance, everything was a nightmare.

*

Del? The words formed in her mind; her tongue too swollen to work.

She fought to get her bearings, but she was weak. Her mind, being free of the grave box, suddenly craved sleep, real sleep, but she forced it to stay in the trance.

Del, honey. Where are you? I'm here.

Mama D could feel that Del had looked into her room at some point in the past. How long ago, she couldn't tell, but she saw the cosmic dust she'd left, silver, like the stars. And she began to move in a direction, like a bird migrating in winter, drawn. But also like the bird, she knew she had far to go, and there was so little time left.

Somehow, she found the girl and the monsters that surrounded her. The silver orb she recognized, the black orb she'd suspected, but was surprised at its size and ferocity. Mama D had thought the black streak just a small imperfection, but it had grown into the dominant force since she'd been gone.

How did this happen? Oh lawd, how long have I been gone?

Then Mama D saw Billy's life cord between Del's teeth and was nearly shocked out of the trance.

Terror swept over her as she tried to assess the situation, tried to gauge how far things had gone. She knew of the silver cord, every practitioner worth their salt did, but she hadn't told Del about it. In fact, learning of the cord was more of a rite of passage amongst her kind, not terribly different from when a girl gets her first period. When that happens, she has passed into the next stage of her life and can never go back. It was the same way with the cord. Learning of it, that it even existed, that it was integral to the states of being, was knowledge that carried a certain level of trust. Ways of manipulating the cord, in order to influence one's personality or actions, was considered grand master knowledge. But severing it, opening a window into a person's very essence, was something even the most experienced practitioners only whispered about in small circles. A few of them claimed to have known someone who could do it, but they were old myths, stories of abilities so powerful their roots were anchored in the legends from the old country, which of course went through Haiti, into Africa, and all the way back to ancient Egypt.

But here it was. Mama Dedé was witnessing the act before her very eyes. And within those old gossip circles, where the grand masters spoke in whispers, and made signs to ward off evil at the mention of this deadly power, there was a fundamental understanding: you never drank from the cord.

And Mama D yelled out her warning:

Don't swallow! Fight it and hold on! But for God's sake, don't swallow!

*

The telephone rang and the remnants of last night's dream-trance faded from Mama D's mind. She knew that more had happened. She remembered the swirling black orb. And she knew that Del had experienced a rite of passage last night that could never be undone. And as much as she hated to admit it, she knew that she *didn't know* how to guide Del from here. They were both in uncharted waters. She knew it wasn't the last time she'd revisit it, in fact, she suspected it would stay with her the rest of her life, but for now, on this new morning of being awake, she was grateful for the distraction of an everyday object.

But no matter how many telephones rang, or graves she fell into in her dreams, nothing would distract her from the most pressing question of all:

Had she gotten to Del in time? Or had Del actually swallowed?

CHAPTER 59

Over the next two days, Del swam in and out of reality. Lights flashed in her eyes, machines beeped in the back of her mind, people came and went. She'd pull herself halfway out of the dark sleep, then sink back into it, never quite making it out. Sometimes she was aware of people poking and prodding her, then they were gone. Her mind pulled at the remnants of scenes—whether dream, trance or reality, she couldn't tell—trying to stitch them into order. Just when one scene began to make sense, it would turn upside down and a new set of threads would replace it, and her mind would cry out for the madness to stop. She'd dream, she'd wake, then she'd dream again.

In one fragment, she'd watch herself stumble down the dark hallway towards her room. She'd see Billy standing in the shadows. *Look out!* she screamed to her stumbling self. *He's right there! Just look up!*

But drunk, stumbling Del, who was thinking about the guy she'd kissed in the back of the bar, never looked up. She would make the same mistake over and over again as the dream replayed in her mind, letting herself be taken by surprise and thrown into the fight of her life.

This scene usually brought Del the closest to fully waking up, but her body was too tired, and she'd slip back into the dark cave of her mind. Sometimes there were warm blankets there, and she'd sleep. Sometimes there was water in her cave, her Well of Life, and she'd hear the slow backwards dripping of rain, which replenished her body, lying somewhere above her.

As the remnants of that night were pieced back together, she saw or remembered more.

She saw herself struggling on the bed. Billy's erection was pressed against her leg, and she'd still had use of her head. He hadn't wrenched it sideways almost to the point of breaking her neck. She couldn't see what she'd been thinking at the time, it was surely panic, but for the first time she noticed something in the room. An odd, slow shadow moved around the walls. It wasn't car lights from outside. It wasn't old Mrs. Doucet shining a flashlight down the hall. It was… nonchalant movement. Observant, but uninterested. It was the shadow cat!

The damn ghost cat or whatever the hell it was, was slinking around her walls as she struggled for her life! Its shadow moved along the wall on her right, folding itself into a sharp crease as it traversed the corner of the room, moved up the wall—not climbing it, still moving horizontally, but just… higher—then slid toward the window on her left. Its black inkiness hugged the second-story window frame, then slipped out into the night. That's when she saw Arlo.

This realization nearly brought Del out of recovery-dream as well, but once again, she slipped back.

Arlo had been in the window! She'd been watching! Del couldn't tell how long she'd been there. But now, as her mind stitched together her memories, she realized that her eyes had caught sight of the strange woman. Her face was mist, barely there. It seemed to be buffeted by the wind, sometimes whole, sometimes blown apart as strange winds pulled at it. But she was there—at least her face had been—floating outside Del's second-story window, watching her fight for her life.

Then the black cloud enveloped her. Mama Dedé's voice whispered out of the blackness. The Dark Dreamer enveloped her. Billy had tried to strangle her.

Swallow and you will have vengeance, the Dark Dreamer had said. *Swallow and you will be DEATH!*

Then something that Del hadn't remembered until now came forward. Like a lover's kiss Del had yet to experience, she felt the Dark Dreamer, her mouth, materialize out of thin air and caress her neck. The ghost lips were soft and magical, nibbling at her ear lobe, and she felt a wetness form there.

Swallow and you'll never feel lonely again, the lips purred.

Swallow and you can take the young lovers who rejected you. The lips were hot against her now.

Swallow, and we'll live forev—

BITCH! Mama Dedé's voice slammed into her mind. *Leave my girl alone and go back to hell!*

Del's body convulsed once in the hospital bed, just as it had that night when Mama D had pulled her back from the brink of damnation. She turned on her side, pulling the covers tightly around her, and remembered the final scene of Billy's death.

The silver orb was screaming. The black orb was screaming. Even Mama D was screaming, and all Del could think about was her throat. It wanted to swallow. Her tongue wanted to taste. Her mouth slobbered with stinging blue saliva that drove an unnatural warmth deep into the meat of her tongue and cheeks.

Brandy, she thought, remembering the first time she'd sipped the warm liquid. Armand had thrust her in the adult category the night he'd poured one for her. After the initial sting, she remembered the warming feeling that slid down her throat and warmed her insides. The life-essence from Billy's cord promised the same thing. Only it stung more, promising a hellish warmth like nothing she'd ever had.

Just a taste, her mind had thought. *Just a tiny taste.*

Then suddenly the Dark Dreamer was gone. Disappeared. And the craving went with it. But in her mind, her throat had already contracted, the abomination had already occurred. And as her mind spun out, imagining the punishment of this new hell she'd brought upon herself, she saw young Billy. She saw the struggles of a destitute mother, shunned by society, willing to do anything to save her boy from the streets. A woman that degraded herself the only way she knew how—wholeheartedly and with a smile *(don't mind the bruises)*—and who now watched in horror as her grown boy's life was being chewed away bite by bite. Yes, Del saw—or imagined she did— Billy's mother turn and look at her. Somehow the spirit of his mother had come forward, to witness the rape of her only child; not as she had been raped before, but a violation, nonetheless. And she cried for the inhumanity he would bear in death.

Del heard Arlo's voice. "You cain't make him an evernot." Then realized the strange old woman had stayed, floating outside her window, until the final scene. "Set him free."

And Del remembered.

She remembered the final bite, the faint snapping of Billy's thread. For that's all that was left of his silver cord, a thin filament tying his spirit to his dead body. She'd freed him after all, despite whatever hell she'd been condemned to, she had not condemned him.

Then he was floating, dissolving. The calm face of a boy, happy to see his mother, shone with a glowing light and he faded away.

"Aahhhh…" whispered in Del's mind.

Then she was vomiting.

CHAPTER 60

The night before Del returned home, Madame Broussard watched the spirits begin to mass around Armand's house. Something was about to happen.

Scanning the fresco a few nights earlier, she'd caught sight of an unusual disturbance. Actually, she'd felt lucky she'd caught it at all. Having just finished remaking the Alvie-bones, her little Boy Made of String—now grown up in an unusual way—had taken his first steps again, tottering around the room inside the hidden building.

She knew he couldn't be left to wander the shadow-roads again, for he had no brain—Scarmish had seen to that. The last time she'd let him wander, he'd been pulled to the Spirit Hunter by sheer force. This was fortunate in a way, because she had found the girl's location, but it had also allowed the girl to find her. She couldn't take that chance again, not with the winds of the dead shifting as they were.

Madame Broussard had thought on the problem of what to do with Alvie for some time. He'd been so much trouble to make—the

Thirteenth Passage was difficult to pull off, even for her—but then an idea had come to her.

The day she accidentally poked her finger against the needle that protruded from the raggedy little voodoo doll, it had sparked to life. She realized at that moment, that whatever magic had made this creature was very powerful. In fact, in some ways, more powerful than that of the Thirteenth Passage. The magic she had given to the Alvie-bones had caused them to reanimate, and there was *life* in them, but there wasn't intelligence. The bones and tendons simply performed their normal function and walked. Oh, there was some rudimentary form of self-preservation in them, she supposed. After all, they did crawl out of the stone maiden's pool and reach for a shadow, allowing it to escape. But beyond that, it had little control. But the raggedy little doll, it had something else. Whatever magic was in it was *smarter* somehow. It had a purpose, she was sure of it, only it had no real means of transportation—the legs, one of them a rotted thumb, had little use. But it did have purpose, and, she sensed, desire. So, as she read the secret words of the Thirteenth Passage once again, and let the vile, coppery tasting blood fill her mouth, she used the life-giving liquid on two objects, instead of just one. Before biting into the shoulder bone of Alvie, she bit into the soft head of the voodoo doll.

"Ngyihng..." it said as it sparked to life. Its red bead eyes glowing faintly. At that moment, as if remembering an old friend, she knew its name was Toth. A fitting name, she realized immediately.

Then the blood was transferred to the skeleton—the Alvie-bones—that would transport the tiny demon. She had already connected the two by driving the long metal needle, which ran through the doll, into the vertebrae of Alvie's spinal column. In this way, the two had become one. The bones of the boy, reanimated, were now controlled by the demon doll with the strange magic in it. And thus, fusing together, the Toth-skeleton was born.

The first steps of the abomination were rough and jerky. Toth, the doll, wobbling on its long metal pin, bobbed from side to side, trying to control its new legs. The tiny demon arms reached out, touching the back of Alvie's skull—avoiding the gaping hole left by Scarmish—attempting to guide the rickety contraption forward. The Alvie-legs kicked and buckled, thrusting itself in all directions until it crashed into the table. Madame Broussard feared it would thrash itself apart before it gained control, but then it righted itself and stumbled forward and backward until slowing to a stilted, but controlled, walk. That's when Toth headed for the fresco.

As if stuck in forward mode, the Toth-skeleton walked straight into the wall, hitting its skull on the same spot. She thought the whole thing had been a failure again, simply becoming another zombie in a world of drifting spirits, until she realized it was trying to raise its arm. Toth, the doll, had yet to master those motor controls, so instead, reached for the spot on the wall with its own stubby arms, causing the skull to hit the same spot, over and over.

Walking to the wall and setting her hand on the bone shoulders, which calmed the thing considerably, she guided it a chair and coaxed it into a sitting position.

Returning to the fresco, she inspected the spot for damage. That's when she noticed the ring of spirits growing around the Spirit Hunter's house.

It was that ring that she watched for the next two days, waiting, wondering what could be pulling this sheer number of spirits to one place. Then she saw something unexpected.

*

The bone-fingers that had pulled its body from a hole in the ground in Lafayette Cemetery #1 were now almost a foot long. Having been made from the remnants of cemetery rats, worms and black crickets, it was at first a feeble thing, barely able to pull itself along. But the thing previously known as Scarmish had been busy.

At first, its bulbous, translucent head had sagged from side to side, tossing its floating, embryo eyes back and forth like dead goldfish in a bowl, rocked by a naughty child. But as it absorbed more, it grew more. There were plenty of insects in the Crescent City, and they were happy to land on what looked and smelled like a rotting jellyfish plucked from the swamp. However, its faintly pulsating skin, watery and delicious looking for flies and mosquitoes, had been one of its many deceptions. Having grown a sticky substance over its translucent skin, the insects stuck when they landed, then were slowly devoured as the bulbous head sucked them inward. There were so many flies in fact that the head had begun to turn black from the pigment, and was in fact now made from more fly parts than cricket. An added bonus came when a small bird mistook the quivering rat-hair antennae for a quick snack and tried to pluck the thing free. A quick movement from one of the rat-bone fingers and the bird was knocked onto the gelatinous surface, stuck for several hours until it too was devoured. The only trace of the bird being the beak, which now stuck out the top of its head, and a few feathers which stayed on the outside; both of which had begun to grow.

The girth of the head was sixteen inches around, and with the length of the legs, it spanned nearly three feet in width. It had learned to climb the cemetery walls and sat atop the largest crypt, generating a low, pulsating light that attracted its nightly meal. The black tattered shadow that had once announced Scarmish's return from the Desert of Dust had evolved yet again; no longer a black shadow, well past its embryo stage, and now evolved beyond the slithering lump of dead meat it once was, it was its own creation. Fed from the primordial tar of twin girls, powered by ancient magic and a sheer will to exist, the Scarmish-spider looked out over its domain, the Lafayette Cemetery #1, and felt the dark spirits amassing around it. It couldn't work out why they were here, but it had felt them growing ever since it became aware.

And as the evening slid past midnight, the Scarmish-spider fixed its floating eyes on the large house across the street, and felt an innate need to journey there soon.

*

Outside the odd building that no one could see, with the crooked walls that hid it from view, and the rusted sign that swung only on special occasions, eulogized by a legend so old the wind barely remembered, stood a woman.

The woman hadn't been in this part of town in a very long time. It was too painful a memory. And despite not being able to see the actual building that hid Madame Broussard, she knew it was there. She could feel it.

As the shadow-cat slid along the brick wall of another building and disappeared around a corner, Arlo thought her meeting with the woman inside the building was fast approaching. It was long overdue, in fact.

But thanks to a young woman who had just found her path—and who Arlo had made a pact with—things would soon be set right.

CHAPTER 61

The day Del arrived back at Armand's house was a joyous occasion.

Armand had already discussed it with Del; she was welcome to come back to her old room and rest for as long as she liked. He understood, he'd said, the day before she was released from the hospital, that she was still on her ten-thousand-hour journey, and that she shouldn't consider this a failure at all. But there was nothing wrong with taking a break from it either. Especially considering the recent events.

Del was relieved. Despite trying to keep a stiff upper lip, she wasn't sure she could go back to her old apartment just yet, to which Armand agreed wholeheartedly.

The family had already communicated to each other that both Del and Mama Dedé were on the mend, and wasn't that a reason to celebrate!

Frank agreed wholeheartedly with Armand and promised to cook them all a wonderful dinner of spicy fried chicken, fried okra, smashed potatoes, jalapeno cornbread and his famous gravy. His mouth watered as he named off the menu. Armand thought that was ok, but decided an appetizer of Oysters Rockefeller, with his secret butter sauce, Boudin balls, with specially made sausage, and Crab Ravigote with capers, would be a nice way to start. Frank, not overly impressed, nodded friendly enough, but said that Pralines would finish the night just right, to which Armand of course thought Banana's Foster would be better.

So, as it was, the day Del was brought home, and after hugs all around, the two men set off to wrestle each other for pots and pans, demand more space on the counters and table, and generally make a fine bickering background noise that Del loved immediately. The kitchen was filled with sweet aromas of pipe and cigar smoke, at least one bottle of wine was opened before the appetizers were even mixed, and eventually, the smells of a large feast began to waft through the house.

*

"Deh, you home, you home!" Jimmy said for possibly the tenth time and hugged her again.

"I am home," Del said, "and I missed you a lot!"

"How much?" Jimmy eyed her with anticipation.

Throwing her arms wide, she said, "Dis much!" And pointed both thumbs back towards herself.

Jimmy's face cracked into a wide smile and his eyes shone with wonder. "Dat much? Dat's a wot!"

"Yes, it is, Jimmy Wawoo. Yes, it is."

Jimmy led Del around the house as if she'd never been there, showing her different things. She followed him patiently, asking easy questions which he was happy to answer. However, every occasion she got, she'd ask him about something near the kitchen, and every time, he gladly led her there.

"Mmm…" Del mumbled, snagging pieces of appetizer here and there. "That'll be good when it's done."

Armand shooed her away. "If there's any left. Did they not feed you in that place?" Del shrugged to say, 'but I'm hungry.' "Regardless, whatever you've been eating has served you well. You're practically glowing."

Although the adults knew about Del's ordeal, in some form or other, they'd all agreed not to mention the hospital in front of Jimmy; it seemed like far too complicated of a discussion to have with him. And they certainly weren't going to ask her outright, assuming she'd share details when she was ready.

Del grabbed another oyster. "I don't know, it doesn't feel like it," she said while chewing. "I've been starving all day."

As the party grazed on the appetizers, everyone settled into a more normal rhythm. Del and Mama D had exchanged some words, but there was so much to ask, they'd agreed to wait until after dinner.

Mama Dedé wandered in and out of the kitchen, but primarily moved between outer rooms, as she had done the first few days after waking. She'd made a thorough inspection of all the rooms—except Armand's bedroom—as if she were seeing the house for the first time again. She had straightened Jimmy's room, noticing that he had taken to playing in the closet for some strange reason. Papers and trinkets from his treasure drawer had been left scattered between his room and the library. And Mama D saw the telltale signs of bachelorhood taking over the house. The general puttering she'd done over the last few days had helped her mind clear.

By the time dinner was ready, Jimmy had filled up on Boudin balls and wandered off, Mama D—whose appetite was only half what it used to be—politely tried a little bit of each dish, Armand was grazing, and only Frank and Del filled their plates with a full dinner.

"Lawd," Mama D said, "you gonna eat all that after them oysters you ate? And the sausage?"

Del, already with a chicken leg in her mouth, mumbled, "But I'm hungry."

Mama D only nodded and smiled. She was happy Del was home, despite the unanswered questions that had been nagging her. She didn't want to spoil the evening by highlighting the odd characteristics she saw in Del.

Dinner went along pleasantly, and everyone chatted like nothing was amiss. They asked Del polite questions about her job, and any friends she'd made. Del answered back politely enough, stating that she'd been pretty busy and was enjoying, for the most part, being out on her own.

When the eating was done, Del having tried both men's desserts, the food was covered and put away, dishes stacked near the sink, and a new pot of coffee made.

It was time to retire to the library.

CHAPTER 62

Once they were all seated in the library, Del truly felt at home. Despite it being summer, Armand had made a low burning fire in the fireplace. "Let the air conditioner work a bit more," he'd said. "The finicky thing will be kaput soon anyway. But this," he spread his arms, implying the fireplace was part of the group, "says we're all home again." His bushy mustache rose as his eyes gleamed.

Armand had surprised her by having a fourth chair waiting. She didn't have to sit on the loveseat any longer. She was truly an adult now, and should be afforded the respect, he'd thought. Del smiled when she saw it sitting there. Armand was closest to his beloved books, in a way, with his back towards the bedrooms. To his right was Mama Dedé's chair, now to her right was Del, then Frank, then the fireplace, completing the circle.

Jimmy chuckled from his seat at the chess table. Whether it had been at something Armand had said, or simply a funny thought in the boy's head, no one could tell.

Brandy glasses were passed around and filled. They were clinked together in salute of Del's return, then silence settled over them.

Each one looked at the other, not knowing where to start. There were so many unanswered questions.

Del cleared her throat and said, "If you don't mind, I'd like to say a few things."

*

Del began with the events that led up to her deciding to leave Armand's house in the first place. And although they'd happened a few months ago, to her, and certainly to Mama Dedé, they seemed to have happened just yesterday. And these older events had a direct connection to what had just transpired over the last week.

The night the spirits had invaded the bottle of brandy, Del had gone to bed early. She still had the lock of hair from Spider's trunk, and was hoping that it belonged to Clara. She was going to try and locate her. Mama D had warned her to wear her gris, because funny things had been happening around the house.

Mama D nodded her head in agreement as she thought back to that night.

"You guys were up pretty late," Del said, "and I was trancing. I don't know how long I was gone, but I was able to follow where Spider had driven, which led me to find Clara."

Holding her brandy to her lips, Del looked off into the distance of her memories and thought about the terrible things she'd witnessed from Madame Broussard. *Not relevant*, she thought, and continued. "I was gone a long time, I think. How long, I can't remember, but somehow," and here her voice became low and wavery, "but somehow, because of all of the trancing I was doing, some things were drawn back to the house."

There was a general rumbling of disagreement in the group, and statements of, "Now, it's not your fault…" but Del thought she'd never be convinced otherwise. Then Frank spoke up.

"Now Del-bell, I remember dat night very well." He rubbed his chest in memory of the sharp pain that had ultimately sent him to the hospital. "And I can tell you dat dese two were three sheets to da wind before any," and here he whistled the tune to *The Twilight Zone* and wiggled his fingers, "got on."

Del smiled and looked at Mama D and Armand. Their faces confirmed the accusation.

Frank went on. "'Cause I closed up da house dat night before I left."

"Maybe so," Del agreed, "but when I came out of my trance, all hell had broken loose here."

Everyone nodded in agreement again.

Mama D spoke up. "What was wrong with me when you came back?"

Del started at the question, tried to hide her surprise, but quickly realized it was too late for that. "Well… I didn't really know at the time," said Del. "Both you and Armand were barely breathing, and…" she nodded over her shoulder to where Jimmy sat, "he had… other issues."

"Jesus, Mary and Joseph," Frank said in a whisper. He looked at Del, remembering. "You mean da," and here he made zombie motions with his hands, holding his eyes wide, "clickity-clack?"

Del nodded.

"What?" Armand questioned. "I did not hear this part."

Del glanced from Armand to Mama D. "I'll tell you both later." Then, keeping her focus on Mama D, she said, "But it was around then I realized how… how *bad* you were."

Mama D tilted her in question and said, "I don't remember any of it, but… I need to hear it."

Del took a rather large sip of brandy, steeling her nerves, and continued. "At some point, I was able to get the blankets off Armand's face, and his breathing improved a little. But… but it was different for you."

Mama D, silent, nodded for her to continue.

Tears had filled Del's eyes when the last sentence left her mouth, and now the first tiny stream spilled over as she shook her head in disbelief at the memory. "You were cold," she said shakily. "You were so cold." Tears flowed freely. "I tried to warm you up, I did." She remembered fighting the spirits on multiple fronts: the skeleton spirit that had possessed Jimmy, the black shadows that seemed to inhabit every corner of the house, then the cold skin of her mentor. It was overwhelming.

"Was I dead?" Mama Dedé asked in a low tone.

The directness of the question shocked the others, and faces turned from one to another, wondering, *Should we go this far?*

Del sagged a little in her chair. Reliving this was harder than she'd thought it would be. After a deep breath, she said, "I'm not sure. But I took you to my Well of Life just in case."

A cringe of pain bit into Mama Dedé's face and she brought a clenched fist to her mouth. Her own eyes watered at the thought of Del wasting any of her precious drops of life on an old lady. She shook her head slowly, but there was anger in her watery eyes and her tightly clenched mouth. "Del… no."

Twisting toward the woman from her chair, Del's own tightly drawn mouth returned the savage love. "I *had* to."

A long pause drew out as both women wiped at their eyes. Frank and Armand, overwhelmed by the show of emotion, looked around to the corners of the room, blinking their eyes and fiddling with their smokes.

Del cleared her throat, but the words still cracked. "But I thought you'd be fine when you woke up." She looked at Armand. "That's why I couldn't understand why she couldn't just trance and see what had happened. That it hadn't really been a break-in with Spider. About Jimmy and Clara. The whole thing."

Armand nodded slowly.

"But I couldn't, could I?" Mama Dedé said.

Del shook her head.

Mama D let her eyes wander around the room, searching for the answer. She felt it was close. "I couldn't trance… hell, I couldn't do anything, because of what happened that night. Not the dying—"

"You weren't dead!" Del interjected quickly.

Mama D waved her quiet. "Not the dying, but maybe somethin' happened on the way back." Looking at Del and grabbing her hand, she said, "When you saved me. When you brought me back. Something happened." Her eyes searched the empty space in front of her for more answers. Absently, she said, "Thank you for saving me, Del. That hasn't been said yet. And I thank you for bringing me back. But what happened? What happened on the way back… up?" Suddenly remembering the dream she'd been stuck in, the never-ending grave, the moving wallpaper with chirping heads, the nibbles, it came to her.

"The worms," she said quietly. "The worms happened."

"Worms?" exclaimed Del and Armand together.

"Ho-ly, hell," Frank said, rubbing his head. Pouring himself a liberal dose of brandy in preparation for the inevitable spooky news they were about to receive. "Dis ain't gonna be good."

Del's eyes were large and searching. Scanning her own memory, she said, "Why did you say 'worms'?"

Armand leaned forward, a Cheshire grin turning the corner of his mouth. "Yes, do tell. What of the worms?"

An evil eye flashed back at Armand. "Frenchy, I'ma knock you when I get my strength back!"

Armand clapped his hands in delight at this characteristic response. "Indeed! Mama D is back!"

Del repeated, "Mama D, why did you say 'worms'?"

Clasping her hands over her now-not-so-prodigious stomach, she looked at Del. "I dreamt 'em. At least, I think they were all dreams. But to be honest, I can't tell for sure. Why do *you* ask?"

*

Here, Del walked alone and felt the eyes upon her. She always felt the eyes. "I saw them too," she finally said.

Del described—in as much detail as she could stand to give—the trancing session she'd had last Sunday evening, when she looked in on the family. She described seeing Jimmy playing with the Ouija board, at which point Armand hung his head. "I'll explain that," he said, then motioned for Del to continue. Explaining the giant falcon felt like a fairy tale to her, and she frequently had to tell Armand that she didn't have the answers to his constant questions. Her voice lowered as she got to the part about trailing entrails of silver cords and screaming faces. Once again, Armand was quite disappointed at the lack of detail.

A look of anguish colored Mama D's face. "What does that have to do with me?" Her voice had weakened since reprimanding Armand.

Sagging shoulders. A hard swallow. Del regretted this already. A high-pitched whistle suddenly sounded from a log on the fire, followed by a pop. A pocket of moisture had just been consumed by the heat.

But the sound reminded Del of the shrieking worms as she'd bit them in half. Sucker-heads screaming as their slimy bodies exploded. All the while, Mama D's life essence dripping from her mouth, then flying away on the wind.

Del found she couldn't say the words, so she sent an image to the woman.

The woman seated in the chair next to Armand gazed into empty air, but in her mind she nearly wretched. "…Oh, God," she whispered.

Armand looked around the little group, frantic. "Wait. What?" Red splotches rose on his cheeks. "Not fair, my dear Del. Not fair at all! We are family, are we not? I think so. My… morbid curiosity aside… we," he motioned to Frank for help, "we should not be left in the dark on this issue. If we are to help keep you safe, we should know what that means."

Frank squirmed in his chair. "Well now… I'm not so sure—"

Del flashed a two-second clip into their minds and both men jumped.

"OH!" Frank kicked his leg out, hitting the table.

"Oh, my!" Armand said covering his mouth.

Del's head hung as if she'd caused the entire thing. "I didn't go looking for it. I just… found it."

Eyes wide, Armand stared at Del. When his hand finally dropped from his face, he said, "My poor Del, I had no idea. I… I feel so foolish for my callous questions."

"Well, Frenchy," Mama D said, "now you know."

The group was quiet for several sips of brandy. Suddenly Armand's mouth opened with exaggerated slowness. His eyes widened. He pointed at Mama D and asked, "When did you wake up? Or start to? What day?"

She counted backwards on her fingers. "Today's Friday… one, two. Around Tuesday, I guess."

"Fascinating," he said, stroking his beard. The researcher had returned. "Very shortly after Del's… intervention?"

Mama D nodded. "Seems like it." And she squeezed Del's hand again in thanks.

"So, that explains the… *Resurrection of Mama Dedé*, if you will," Armand said triumphantly. The gleam in his eye had returned. "Well done, Del. Well done."

Del sighed. She sent a silent cry for help to Mama D. She was tired of feeling like a circus sideshow act.

"OK, Frenchie, now for your whoopin'," Mama D said. "What in da HELL were you thinkin' pullin' out a spirit board with that boy?" She nodded over her shoulder.

Armand cleared his throat. "Oh. Yes. About that…"

*

As the conversation lulled, everyone took a necessary break to fill their glass, empty their bladder, or both. Del returned from downstairs with a full plate of leftovers, including dishes of dessert. She sat some on the chess table where Jimmy was still playing an odd game of chess. She wasn't sure if he knew the rules, but was pretty sure the pieces didn't kill each other the way he was making them.

Setting the rest on the fireplace table, Del stacked her plate full and began munching before anyone else could get to it.

Mama D watched as she stuffed more and more food into her mouth. "Girl, you about to give me indigestion."

Del shrugged and washed a Boudin ball down with a large sip of wine. At some point in the night, several bottles had shown up on the table.

Then something dawned on Mama D. She had barely been sipping her drink the entire night, mostly due to her shrunken stomach. But Del had been drinking quite steadily; not glass for glass with the men, but much more than she had ever before. And she didn't seem the least bit drunk. This concerned her on multiple levels.

"So…" Armand began. "About the…" Here he made a slow circle with his hand as if following a puck.

He sighed.

"I was terribly concerned," he began. Looking at Mama D, "about you. I called doctors. I researched. But there was simply no explanation for your symptoms."

"What were my symptoms, exactly?" Mama D asked.

Spreading his hands wide, he said, "Well… acute lethargy, you could say. Inactivity. Torpidity."

Frank wrinkled his face. "You mean?" And his zombie hands floated up again.

A half-grin turned Armand's mouth. "Yes Frank. Like a zombie."

Now it was Mama D's turn to thank Armand. Squeezing his hand as she did Del's, she looked him in the eyes and said, "Thank you Frenchie, you and your wonderful moustache for taking care of me."

Armand blushed and swallowed. "Oh, well, now, I don't think—"

"Now get on with your story, before I got to pee again!"

Armand smiled and nodded. "I was at my wit's end, you must understand. I truly was." A long pause strung out. "I thought if I could just ask a few questions… that perhaps… Well. You understand my reason, yes?"

"Yeah, I understand your reason," Mama D said. "But I warned both you knuckleheads about messin' and readin' stuff you don't know about. There's a lot of tricky things on da other side. Hateful. Spiteful.

And as you should know, deadly. Worse than that even. Damn."

Her mouth clenched tight as she shook her head in disbelief. With her reprimand over, for the moment, she continued.

"But what I don't understand is why you jumped like you'd got caught with your hand in da cookie jar when I mentioned da worms. You and Del both. But I know her reason. What about da worms make you so jumpy?"

Armand pulled a well-folded sheet of paper from the inside breast pocket of his vest. Unfolding it carefully, he looked at each of his friends sincerely. "This is the message I got."

"Message?" Mama D asked.

"From who?" Del questioned.

Frank didn't have a question. He remembered well. He was a detective after all. He had a statement to make. "Dat day I 'bout killed you with fright. Right dere." He nodded at the worktable. "Da day I told you I hoped you knew what da hell you were doin.'"

Armand nodded. "Yes, mon ami. You are an astute observer."

"Da day after you and Jimmy *played a game.* If I recall."

Armand wrung his hands. "Mon ami, please, I remember all too well."

"You called somethin' up," Mama D said. "Tell me you didn't call somethin' up."

"Well… as it turns out. It appears… that perhaps I did, but—"

"Frenchy!"

"But!" His finger shot up, trying to hold the conversation together. "It appears… perhaps… that it was benign, the… spirit. He seemed to be—"

"'He'?" Mama Dedé said. "Why you think it's ah 'he'?"

"As I was saying, he seemed to be benign, uh, mischievous, perhaps.

And… he gave me his name. Which is why… I… it's a male name."

Mama D rocked back in her chair. "Oh, lawd, Jesus! Give me dat brandy."

Armand poured and she drank. Then he continued.

"He sent a rather cryptic message, warning us… well, foretelling, perhaps is a better word, about what may have ailed you. As I said, in the end, it seemed to be little more than a veiled warning."

After several seconds, Mama Dedé reached out for the paper. "Let me read it."

Armand looked at the heavily creased paper and wished he'd never obtained that blasted spirit board. He handed it over.

Mama D snatched it from his hand. "And like I said before, when you got ahold of dat dark grimoire, don't go readin' somethin' out loud that you don't know nothin' about. Damn tricky bastards, these spirits are…" She grabbed the gris bag hanging around her neck and carefully read the paper. After determining there were no enchanting words in it (at least none she recognized) she released the gris bag and read it aloud.

"'Just one death she can afford, to nourish heaven's astral horde.

"'False to pray, "Oh kingly lord, sever not her silver cord."'"

Del flinched slightly at this phrase, but said nothing.

"'Just one death that she must pay, on final hour of judgement day.

"'No bargain made to thus delay, her crumble back to darkest clay.

"'Her death is nigh, the final term, with pallid angels to affirm.

"'The astral horde will writhe and squirm, as she feeds the ghostly verme.

"'Victor.'"

Mama D set the paper down on the table and stared at it. This was more than just a mischievous spirit. There had been too many things happen over the last week to consider this just a coincidence.

Armand leaned forward. "Actually, this should say, 'Victor Vermis.' I forgot to write it in. He told me—" Everyone stared at him and his friendly nature with the spirit, startling him. "I mean, the spirit signed the message, the… second message, with both names."

Shaking her head, Mama Dedé had no words for Armand's actions. She knew it was in his nature to wonder and probe. He was like this from the first time they'd met, dealing with the Gris-gris man. But she wasn't put off her original trail.

"OK, but back to my original question, Frenchie. Why'd you start up when I mentioned worms earlier? This don't say anything about worms."

The professorial smile quickly returned to Armand's face and his R's rolled as his French accent thickened. "Ah, but it does. In a way. You see, the references to writhing and squirming bring a certain vision forth. A certain wriggling imagery, you might say. Then of course, the silver cord. Fascinating really, remind me to tell you sometime about the intriguing—"

"We will," Mama D said.

"Oh, yes of course. Then there's the archaic term used here. *Verme.* An ancient dialect, I believe. A root word whose meaning has possibly been lost. Of course, it makes one think of vermin, or rats. But writhing and squirming rats? Perhaps… Yes. Perhaps indeed. If they were in a pack, or a horde. But I could never shake the feeling of worms when I was deciphering it. Of course, my initial transcription was a bit… hurried. But I think—"

"Sounds like Greek to me," Frank said, leaning back in his chair. He pulled a fresh cigar from his shirt pocket and began inspecting it.

"Yes, well, Latin actually. A dead language, although a root language to many words we have. You see, if you strike the last 'e', you have verm, the root of vermin, as we just discussed, vermis, vermillion— Of course!" His finger shot up. "That's why I started earlier. Verm is the root of vermis, which is Latin for worm." He smiled triumphantly, but shook his head. "Rusty, rusty Latin. But I knew it was in there somewhere. So, we have—"

"Your friends name is Worm?" Del suddenly asked. Her questioned took him by surprise.

"Wha— what?" Armand desperately tried to catch his line of thought, but it was disappearing like smoke. "My friend's name?"

"Well, OK, not your friend," Del said. "Your spirit. But your spirit's name is Worm? Is that what you'd call mischievous, or just plain silly?"

Armand scratched his head, having been thoroughly thrown off his cadence. He mumbled, "The spirit... Victor Vermis."

"Yeah. So you're saying the Latin translation is Victor Worm?"

A thoughtful look fell across Armand's face. He was coming back online, or at least, he was tracking to this new line of discussion. Del was right. There was something here, he was sure of it. That seemed too odd of a name for a spirit. He must have missed something. Swirling his brandy, he gazed into the brown liquor. He could feel his mind remolding to surround the answer. His eyes searched the air as connections were made, synapses fired, words came and went, tumbling in and out of darkness.

"Oh my God," he croaked as his brandy glass shattered on the table. He was up and scrambling past the edge of his chair before the others fully realized what had happened.

Frantically he tore through his piles of research. "Aarrgghh.... Where is it? Where is it?" Stacks slid sideways or were knocked over. Several sheets slid off the edge and floated haphazardly to the library floor. The other three sat motionless at the table, staring in disbelief at the mad scene playing out before them.

"Here!" he exclaimed. "My book." He began thumbing through a well-worn textbook that had been buried under several others. "My Latin translation book." He was now muttering to himself. "Victor… victor… oh no. What a fool… what a fool I've been…"

"What?" Frank urged.

"His name, *its* name, the spirit. I shall hence forth call it by what it is, but *spirit* may not even be appropriate for this blasted thing!" He looked up at his friends and shook his head morosely. "The name it gave, you were right, *vermis* does mean *worm*. But *victor* is not a man's name. The Latin translation means *to conquer*, literally 'the winner'. In other words, it chose the name of Victor Vermis, hence calling itself 'The Conqueror Worm.'"

Armand's eyes searched the air, trying to imagine what this eldritch horror could be. The name alone was beyond comprehension.

Del had already began scooping up the papers that had scattered over the floor. Having no idea which were related, she simply lumped them into one large pile.

"But what da hell does it mean?" Frank asked.

Mama Dedé was staring at the folded paper on the table. It was spotted with brandy, and tiny slivers of glass stuck to it when she picked it up. "I'll tell you what it means," she said. "This wasn't a coincidence. This was no damn mischievous, chain-rattlin', door-openin', cold-air-in-da-room hoodoo." Mama Dedé slipped into an uncharacteristic slang that masked her intelligence. "How da hell it know to give you dat poem while it got da damn worms crawlin' all over me? Eatin' me! Suckin' me dry like a damn vampire. Vampire worms! Makin' me think I'm crazy and dead and walkin' 'round like a zombie! Huh?

Howda hell?" Her voice cracked, releasing the anger that had grown over the last several days. Anger that came from not knowing, not understanding, how part of one's life had suddenly slipped away. Then to find out it was all a joke, a nasty ol' trick. That it was all written down on a poem and shared through what was considered a child's game. She stood up and turned towards Armand. The paper holding the poem crumbled in one fist. "I'll tell you how. It planned it. Some damned tricky ol' bastard of a spirit done this. Who knows, maybe da whole thing! Maybe all da way back to da bad brandy, and tryin' to smother us up, and eatin' our souls, and—"

"Tricky old bastard indeed," Armand said quietly. He could only console her so much, understanding that he had been the cause of the whole thing. Had he only left the Ouija board out of it… if only.

Still kneeling on the floor, Del was grateful for the cover. The moment Mama D had mentioned *vampire worms* her eyes had shot open. She was sure that had she been sitting at the fireplace table, there'd have been no hiding her surprise. She'd felt sick as she had listened to her mentor lament her lost time, her lost mind—at least temporarily—and of course there was her lost ability. Would it come back completely? Mama D's trancing, would it ever be as good as it was before? Del didn't know. What she did know was that Mama D had many more questions for her. Questions on where her new abilities had come from. Questions on how she'd learned so quickly. There seemed to be more questions now than ever. But the question that concerned Del the most hadn't fully formed. Like a splinter in her mind, she could feel it, but it was stuck too far away to pull out. She'd have to wait for it to work itself forward. But there was something about the term 'tricky ol' bastard' that simply caused her stomach to turn to stone. And why was that?

"Ho-ly hell," Frank muttered. He rubbed his chin thoughtfully. "Why'd you two pick dat phrase?"

Armand and Mama Dedé exchanged questioning glances. *What phrase?*

Frank continued. "Who's da last tricky ol' bastard we dealt with?"

A moment later, Armand's eyes went wide. "Oh, mon ami." His head began a slow back and forth shaking. It would not accept the implication Frank had just made. "It cannot be. Please tell me you are reaching. It simply cannot—"

"Oh, lawd," Mama D whispered. Her eyes staring blankly. "Frank's right. Why did I say that?" Her gaze searched the room for an answer she already had. But an answer she didn't want to confirm. "Because deep down, I musta been thinkin' it. Had to."

"But how?" Armand said. "How can it be that he has found us again? And what does it mean?"

"He found us once before, didn't he?" Mama D said. "Damn near, anyway. And as far as what it means..." Her shoulders shrugged. There was no answer other than that. "But, if there's a tricky ol' bastard of a spirit that could pull something like this off... well, it'd be the Gris-gris man."

Distracted by the conversation, Del's attention was suddenly pulled back to the scatter of papers she'd been collecting. A scrawl of odd handwriting caught her attention, and a rash of goosebumps alerted her senses.

"What is this?" she heard herself saying quietly. Then the concern manifested itself fully. "What *IS* this?"

She stood up as Frank and Mama D joined her at the table. Armand leaned over from his side to see. She set the stack of papers she'd been collecting on the table. The two pages in question she held in her hands.

Armand watched as she set them so carefully on the table, he thought she might fear they would explode, or burst into flames.

The papers were scribbled with a child's handwriting, some in pencil, some in crayon. And although most of the words didn't make sense, they all felt a terrible dread as they read what surely was evil writing.

On the first page, written in pencil, over and over again were two strange phrases:

Cha'thul ungh ah mwu'lla nigh, Calla, Calla, dhung'll die

and

Pha'ang bwahla cirses bin, ma da bwa on'gala sin

A sharp pain flashed in Del's head, behind her left eye, as she finished reading the passage. Mama D's warning about the dark grimoire echoed in her mind. If there was any combination of words that felt like they were made to call something up from beyond, out of that macabre tapestry of dead, it was these words.

On the second page, written in red crayon, in an equally childish scrawl—although perhaps not from the same child—was this phrase:

HELLo IS some one tHERE

From out of nowhere, Jimmy giggled.

Del, Frank, Armand and Mama Dedé all turned to look at the boy, who all evening had been sitting at the chess table, engrossed in a strange game that no one understood. They saw that all the chess pieces had been laid next to each other, alternating black, white, black, white, in concentric circles running out from the center of the board.

And they were all dead, except one. The black queen stood alone in the center. All had died trying to defeat her.

Jimmy looked around at them for the first time that night and the sides of his mouth curved into a shape, something like a smile.

A NOTE FROM THE AUTHOR

Thank you for reading *A Tapestry of Dead!*

I know this book was darker than the others, but there were some dark things lingering from *Scars of Redemption* that had to be dealt with. I never intended to leave Mama Dedé in such a dire state. I simply didn't realize at the time what was ailing her.

This book was fun to write for a few reasons. First, I enjoy reading the 'story within a story' type of tale. As I continue reading the old masters (the writers who influenced Bradbury and Jackson, both of whom influenced King), I find this style engaging and more believable in a way. So, I try to mimic it. I'll admit, I barely touched on the style when Armand was researching references to the 'silver cord,' then a bit more when he's reading his mentor's notes about the exorcism. I hope to do it more justice in the future. But for now, if you're not familiar with the style, here are a few great examples:

A Winter's Tale: The Breathing Method by Stephen King.

The Visitor by Roald Dahl.

The Turn of the Screw by Henry James. Although, I'll admit, this one was slow for me.

Secondly, I like dropping hints to other books and authors I enjoy. For the Poe fans out there, my apologies if the reference to "The Conqueror Worm" felt forced, but the Victor Vermis play was too good to pass up. Also, the arcane poem that Victor writes was quite fun to create. Some of you may have caught the Lovecraftian tone to the chant that Jimmy writes down from his Ouija board sessions. It was intentional and I like the guttural, almost tribal rhythm the lines take on. And for the stalwart word detective, there is at least one obscure King reference in this book. Just as there was one in *Scars of Redemption*. Did you catch it?

Finally, I simply love exploring this rich, dark world. Granted, there's a lot going on now and I'm anxious to see some monsters clash, but that is coming.

If you enjoyed this book, please think about leaving a review at your favorite retailer. Reviews help a book get discovered by others who may also enjoy it.

ACKNOWLEDGEMENTS

Thanks again to my wonderful wife Mary for the long hours reading and discussing this story. I know this one was difficult due to the delay in writing. I appreciate the effort. And, I agree that it's about time to learn more about Del. ☺

Also, many thanks to the close family and friends who read this story in its imperfect state. Please keep the feedback honest.

MORE BOOKS BY D.S. QUINTON

If you're looking for another read, maybe explore where the supernatural power came from. Remember, Armand had a theory about this, based on the diary of a very unfortunate boy.

That theory is FREE to download and read...

The Phoenix Stone – A Dark Beginning

Would you die to expose the secret of mankind's origin? Otto just might...

Desperate to journal his grandfather's discovery before his capture, young Otto hides in a secret Egyptian chamber avoiding nomads and flesh-eating beetles to chronicle an amazing story—How we began. Will the story be lost? Will the nomads find him? Or...does the unthinkable happen?

This short story is the dark beginning of all things.

Get *The Phoenix Stone* FREE at www.dsquinton.com/my-books

And as the dark beginning splinters into infinite shards of kaleidoscope dreams, one story tumbles headlong into the future of human evolution, A.I. and government conspiracies with the genre-blending novel...

Devel Django - The Evolution Series Book 1

A near-future thriller that whispers at the fundamental question of humankind—Where did we come from?—and gropes at the undefined space between science and religion.

It is a unique tapestry woven with coarse threads of horror, hybrid metal synapses, and detailed with a fine, ancient brush from a long-lost palate of knowledge.

Get *Devel Django* at www.mybook.to/DevelDjango

Finally, for anyone that grew up on *The Twilight Zone* or *Night Gallery*, check out *Circus Sideshow*. You may find something you like.

Circus Sideshow - A Supernatural Oddity

Act One:

A pompous actor. A small-town sheriff. A dark secret in a place called Devil's Backbone.

When an arrogant second-rate actor runs afoul of a small-town sheriff, he learns his place in the world. Through a series of strange encounters, the actor is introduced to the people of Devil's Backbone and their unique contribution to the world.

Act Two:

A quaint town. An honest man. An ancient horror in disguise.

The small town of Devil's Backbone experiences its first brush will true evil. The Making of Polly Three-Tongues is a warning tale to the human predators that walk among us. Don't come to our town.

Get *Circus Sideshow* at www.dsquinton.com/my-books

ABOUT THE AUTHOR

D.S. Quinton was born in the Midwest USA and attended the schools of daydreaming, foosball, and mixology. His is an avid student of the unknown and grew up on Greek mythology, the Twilight Zone and Night Gallery.

He is the author of the Spirit Hunter supernatural thriller series and the Circus Sideshow supernatural oddity series, along with a few other interesting tales.

Although his guitar slide is rusty, the piano keys are warm, and despite the lure of many untraveled paths, his feet are generally moving forward.

You can find him at *dsquinton.com*, some social media platforms, or on his deck solving the world's problems with his wife and a good bottle of wine.